THE EXCEPTIONS

Also by David Cristofano

The Girl She Used to Be

The

EXCEPTIONS

DAVID CRISTOFANO

NEW YORK BOSTON

This book is a work of fiction. Names, characters, places, and incidents are the product of the author's imagination or are used fictitiously. Any resemblance to actual events, locales, or persons, living or dead, is coincidental.

Grand Central Publishing
Hachette Book Group
237 Park Avenue
New York, NY 10017

www.HachetteBookGroup.com

Printed in the United States of America

RRD-C

First Edition: August 2012
10 9 8 7 6 5 4 3 2 1

Grand Central Publishing is a division of Hachette Book Group, Inc.
The Grand Central Publishing name and logo is a trademark of Hachette Book Group, Inc.

Library of Congress Cataloging-in-Publication Data
Cristofano, David.
The exceptions / David Cristofano.—1st ed.
p. cm.
ISBN 978-0-446-56735-0
I. Title.
PS3603.R578E93 2012
813'.6—dc23 2011047666

For Francis Cristofano
1928–2010

THE EXCEPTIONS

Hope is definitely not the same thing as optimism. It is not the conviction that something will turn out well, but the certainty that something makes sense, regardless of how it turns out.

—Václav Havel, from *Disturbing the Peace*

A CHI DAI IL DITO
SI PRENDE ANCHE
IL BRACCIO

(GIVE THEM A FINGER
AND THEY'LL TAKE AN ARM)

ONE

When violence arrives, it rarely knocks. It seldom taps you on the shoulder, suggests you get ready. It creates change with the most capable tools in the toolbox: confusion, humiliation, destruction. And its survivors are lucky to have coughed out a raspy *I never saw it coming.*

I learned this in my earliest days, like all great family traditions. Some mothers hand down a culinary talent, some fathers pass a skill to a son or daughter, the familial reverence for the Holy Bible or a football team. But I grew up in a Sicilian household steeped in the practice of influence over the lives of others. We are the Bovaros, one of the oldest and most respected families in organized crime, and the tradition passed down to me with faith and accuracy was violence. I first witnessed it at age eight, first delivered it at age twelve. In our world, violence is the fulcrum. It keeps everything in—or out—of balance.

Perhaps no one has learned that lesson as well as James Fratello—known in our family as Jimmy "the Rat." What Jimmy's specific crimes against our family were I was never completely sure, though his coming and going—really, the going—kick-started events that altered the trajectory of my life. Jimmy was known as the Rat long before it turned out he really was one, named so for the stringy remains of oily hair that clung to the back of his meaty head. Whatever images of mafiosos your mind conjures from the movies, Jimmy would have been summed up like this: He wasn't the strong one, the smart one, or the one with the good lines; he was nobody's favorite; he was expendable, the one who might take a bullet and you wouldn't waste the energy to shrug.

I was ten years old when my father gave the Rat what became a fabled slicing. Glad to say I never saw the result of my father's brutality that day. I was hanging around, bored out of my mind—a difficult age to be Mafia-bred; too old to be innocent, too young to understand what's really happening around you. I eventually strolled downstairs to see if I could catch a glimpse of what it was my dad did for a living, which at the time I misunderstood to be the manager of various restaurants. I stayed out of sight, watching the two of them chat in the kitchen long enough to realize nothing interesting was going on anywhere around them, around me. My father and Jimmy talked quietly, shared a few jokes. I yawned as I quietly made my way outside to the sidewalk.

All I can say is this: Jimmy never saw it coming.

Had I been inside or still within viewing distance of that kitchen, my life would have been cemented; the only way I could've survived the horror of witnessing premeditated murder by my father's hand would've been to herald it, embrace it as my own, to become a player in the same league. Instead I was outside kicking stones into the sewer, watching some yokel from Jersey parallel park his Oldsmobile, back and forth and back and forth. Here I was ten years old and I knew enough to want to yell, "You gotta turn the wheel! Turn your freakin' wheel!"

The guy spent close to three minutes inching his Cutlass closer to the curb, finished a good foot and a half shy of avoiding a citation. Then the suburban family slowly emerged. First the tall blond mother who would've had my adolescent brothers cracking crude jokes, then the father wearing an unseasonable wool raincoat and Yankees cap. But you can erase all of these images from your mind; that's what I did as soon as I saw the little girl who wiggled out from the passenger side of the car. She was a few years younger than me, but I would never forget her. It was the first time a girl caught my attention, and she did so by staring up at the buildings with genuine admiration, inhaled the dirty air like a freshly lit cigar. A little Mary Tyler Moore, she was. A cascade of blond curls danced around her neck as she spun in circles on the sidewalk, her arms flailing about. She wore a short dress popular with the teenage girls in our neighborhood at the time and shoes that were black and shiny.

I still cannot understand what captivated me; she was just a little girl and I a little boy. But I became aware of myself—fearful that she might sense my noticing her—so I slid between a pair of Chevys on Mulberry Street and hunched down, continued spying on her from a safe distance.

Her old man stretched as though he'd driven straight through from Boston or Philly, threw his arm around his wife and planted one on her. The little girl seemed to adore this, giggled as though it embarrassed her but stared like it was her favorite scene in a film. They all chatted briefly about the restaurant—my father's—then attempted to open the door.

It was 7:12 a.m. on Sunday morning. The restaurant was closed; Mass was coming soon.

Here is the first truly regrettable moment of my life: I stood back up and made steps their way in an effort to tell them the place was closed—but as I caught another glimpse of the girl, my feet faltered. Had I completed this mission, spoken a half dozen words, the story would have ended here, complete with a built-in happy ending.

Instead it went like this:

I slid back between the cars, rested myself on the hood of a Camaro, and watched them tug on that door with enough determination to loosen the hinges. Then came the conversation that suggested they might find somewhere else to go—a tough bill to fill on a Sunday morning in New York's Little Italy. Instead, the father slipped down the narrow alley adjacent to the eatery and headed toward the kitchen, waving them his way; mom and daughter followed.

That's the last I saw of them for about forty-five seconds.

I sat staring at the rear of their Oldsmobile, wondering what brought these folks in from Jersey, pretending to convert their license plate into a vanity tag. My brothers and I would fancy that the rich and famous were riding covertly through lower Manhattan disguised and hidden in average cars, slipping out of hotels and restaurants with no one being the wiser. It became a regular competition between us.

783-JCM
John Cougar Mellencamp, 783 concerts performed.
025-SRL
Sugar Ray Leonard, 25 wins by KO.
1037-EVH
Eddie Van Halen, 1,037 fully consumed bottles of Jack Daniel's.

I focused on that Olds with all my might but the combination of letters and numbers left me struggling: FNP-18X. Plates from New Jersey routinely stumped us, as the state had just started replacing the last digit with a letter on all their tags. I sat on the verge of progress—Florence Nightingale? Fig Newton?—when the screams startled me back to awareness. Down the alley came the three of them, the mother hobbling in front of the father, the little girl tossed over his shoulder like a sack of flour, the females screaming, the man a shade whiter than when he ventured down that alley, cap now missing. I remember thinking that people squeamish at the sight of rats shouldn't go down alleys in New York.

If the mother had been trying to loosen the hinges on that restaurant door, she was now attempting to completely rip off the door of the Olds with her bare hands. Dear old dad tossed the girl in the backseat like old luggage, then fumbled with his ring of keys to find the one that fit the ignition, all while staring down that alley of trash and shadows. He slammed the door, started the car, gunned the accelerator. And I guess the guy had it in him; it may have taken him forty-seven back-and-forths to parallel park his bomb, but it took him *one* to get out. Then the squeal of the wheels, the fishtailing, the coughing exhaust, the fade.

That must have been one gigantic rodent.

A minute or so later, my uncle Sal came strolling out. The guy was all salt and pepper: his hair, his freckled skin, his personality. Sal lit up a Camel, casually drifted my way, and blasted me one in the shoulder, messed up my hair. He blew a cloud of smoke in my general direction. "You stay out of the restaurant, kid, eh?"

I stared at him, but he understood I was saying *sure*. "Rat in the kitchen again?"

He took a drag long enough that he burned through a half inch of cigarette, two minutes' worth of nicotine. He looked up and down the street looking for something, for the absence of something, exhaled slowly in both directions. Then, walking away from me, toward the restaurant, he muttered, "Yeah, big fat friggin' rat."

I walked down the block to the corner store and got a Pepsi out of a near-historic vending machine resting alone on the sidewalk. This was my neighborhood, my town. Manhattan and Brooklyn combined into one beautiful myriad of possibilities. So many of the establishments my father and our family ran were in Little Italy, but home was a three-mile trek across the Brooklyn Bridge. The borders of my life existed on this side of the world, bounded by the Hudson, the East, the BQE. Everything was here: our home, our church, our livelihood. My entire family lived within these lines, every cousin, aunt, and uncle, each as thick and rich as their Italian accents. There was no reason to leave, and it never really occurred to us to try. The fact that people came in—from Jersey, Connecticut, upstate—made perfect sense. This was not merely the center of our world; it was the center of everything. New York remains the center still. I sipped that soda as I surveyed all that was around me. It was not unusual to get a nod from owners sweeping sidewalks or a *Hey, Johnny* from the folks we treated with respect. Everyone knew who I was—John Bovaro—and they always gave me space. I took my time; I had no motivation to hurry.

But when I finally returned to Vincent's, things had changed, though not as dramatically as you might imagine. Out front: three cops, one patrol car, two bystanders who wished they knew more. One of the cops I'd seen before, a kid whose folks were from Palermo and had commanded him to become a cop and ditch the life of a hoodlum. He rewarded them with partial obedience: a cop whose allegiance was to the Bovaro clan. The other two officers looked annoyed and eager, respectively. I approached slowly and Allegiant gave me a sly nod. I rolled a kink out of my shoulder. Who knows why the shakedown was occurring. It happened with regularity and never amounted to anything.

As for the bystanders, these were the Kerrigans. A husband-and-wife team, both Irish, determined to take down not only the Bovaros, but sixteen other major crime families in New York, including but not limited to the Italians, the Greeks, the Russians, and the Irish, with whom they had some not so distant relatives. When anything went down in our neighborhood, the cops were provided one common response when they started banging on doors looking for information: *I didn't see a thing; I didn't hear a thing; I don't know nothin'*. No one ever wanted to get involved. Unless the cops tagged the Kerrigans. They had an answer for every friggin' question that was ever asked, except their success rate was around

15 percent. The cops always took a statement, though they knew it would pan out to more paperwork than product.

This morning, however, was quite different. Why? Because I arrived at the wrong time. I knew nothing about what had happened in the kitchen at Vincent's—in fact, it would be days before I found out the truth and only because I read vivid headlines in the *Times*. So what could I possibly offer the cops? What value could a little kid standing on a city sidewalk offer regarding a crime that happened a building away?

Eager caught Allegiant's glance and slowly headed my way. Annoyed rolled his eyes.

It was clear to everyone—except Eager—that whatever was going on was merely a matter of procedure. In today's standards, it would be one drug dealer killing another, a matter of filling out the right forms back at the precinct, giving the coroner a heads-up, placing a check mark in the right box on the marker board outside the captain's office. But Eager didn't care, he came over and asked me questions anyway, a kid he had just watched walk down the street from a decided distance.

"And what did *you* see?" Eager asked.

I stared at him, understanding the inherent hatred my family had for cops. "I don't know what you're talking about."

"Didn't hear anything? Didn't see anyone rush out of Vincent's? Nothing strange or unusual?"

Were I twelve or thirteen at the time, I would have shut down like a prison at lights-out. But I was ten. And the girl. And the panicked parents. And the screams. And the girl. And the gunning of the engine. And the frantic escape down Mulberry. And the dust cloud.

And the little girl.

I gave him a shrug/swallow combo. "Saw a family run down the alley a while back." I tugged at my shirt a little bit. "They okay?"

Eager took a step closer. "How's that?"

"I saw a man and woman and little girl come running down that alley."

"When?"

"About an hour ago."

Allegiant started making his way toward the discussion. Now he and Annoyed looked like fraternal twins.

Eager threw up his hand as if to stop the two of them from getting an inch closer, and stop they did. He knelt before me, which made me the taller one.

With a throaty whisper, he said, "Now, this is important. What can you tell me about them?"

"Are they okay?"

"What did they look like?"

"I don't know. Plain. The girl was pretty, had blond curls, danced on the sidewalk."

"What did the man look like?"

"Plain," I said. "Did anything happen to them?"

"I need you to tell me everything you know about them." He hesitated, then, "I need to make sure they're safe and sound."

That bastard. He used my obvious anxiety for the family, for the little girl, against me, manipulated the innocence of a kid to garner a pat on the back. I haven't felt the same about cops since.

I let out a nervous sigh and started rubbing my temples. "Um, they were from New Jersey."

He inched closer, his shoes making a scraping sound against the cement. "How do you know this?"

"Their license tags."

Annoyed took a step in our direction, but Eager still had his hand up. As for Allegiant, he couldn't have gotten back into Vincent's faster if someone had loaded him into a shotgun and fired, though by his swagger he made it appear like his purpose was procedural.

Eager swallowed like he'd been salivating. "Do you remember the license plates?"

Fig Newton. Florence Nightingale.

"FN... uh, FN something. Started with FN. Had an eight in it."

Eager started scribbling on a notepad.

From the corner of my eye I could see a herd of Sicilians running in my direction. At that moment, the vertigo kicked in.

From a distance I heard, "Questioning a minor without his parents' presence or permission?"

It turns out that means nothing, but it disabled me. A wall of olive skin was coming to rescue me—*from causing irreparable damage.*

Eager leaned in and asked quickly, like I might take a bullet and he had one last shot to get the goods, "What kind of car was it?"

The Italians were closing in.

The little girl was fading out.

The words dribbled from my voice as though they were my last. "Olds. Silver. Cutlass Sierra."

What occurred next is much like what a defensive tackle must feel like when he recovers a fumbled ball: bodies coming from every direction, along with a clear understanding that the best you can do is fall on the ball and take the turnover; leave the touchdown for the offense. The only difference here is that Eager did not get leveled, but merely surrounded.

The discussion was over.

The men shepherded me back into Vincent's, never sent a harsh word my way. They spoke to one another in Italian about how I was the one that was wronged in this ordeal. Their deference and protection of me were pure, things I never doubted—though for the first time I failed to comprehend the justification. My father came to me and put his hand behind my neck, turned his mouth into a consoling half-smile as though I'd failed a test for which I'd spent my life preparing. "Let's get you something to eat, Johnny," he said, then kissed me on the head. I curled into his safe hands like a sleepy baby.

The cops took pictures, swabbed drying puddles and stains, did a lot of head-scratching. People gossiped in the streets, in the stores, on the front steps of brownstones.

I didn't see a thing.

I didn't hear a thing.

I don't know nothin'.

At 10:35 a.m. on that same Sunday, Eager performed a query on New Jersey's Department of Transportation vehicle registration database.

Number of Oldsmobiles registered in the state of NJ:
2,323

Number of Oldsmobiles registered in the state of NJ, model: Cutlass Sierra:
675

Number of Oldsmobiles registered in the state of NJ, model: Cutlass Sierra, color: silver: *177*

Number of Oldsmobiles registered in the state of NJ, model: Cutlass Sierra, color: silver, registered tags possessing characters F, N, 8:
1

At 11:08 a.m., Allegiant performed the exact same query.

What followed was little more than a simple race: two sets of men attempting to acquire the same bounty.

At eight minutes past noon, a large black vehicle with tinted windows pulled into the driveway of a modest Cape Cod in Montclair Township, New Jersey. The vehicle was not a police car. Out stepped three large men, firearms safely tucked beneath their clothes, determination in their strides.

The house held the McCartney family: Arthur, a chemist; Lydia, a stay-at-home mother; and a little blond kindergartner by the name of Melody Grace. It would be fair to say the McCartneys never really knew what hit them. Once these men were allowed into their house, they would not be leaving until they got exactly what they wanted. These men understood the power of fear, were masters at the art of manipulation.

Fifteen minutes later, a black Lincoln, brimming with Bovaros and made men—the *capodecinas*, or capos as they were called—slowed as it pulled in front of the same house in Montclair. A light mist rose from the hood of the car already parked in the driveway, a small puddle of moisture below the tailpipe. They were too late—mere minutes. They had no other option but to drive away.

By three o'clock, another vehicle was summoned to the Cape Cod, a dark Suburban with bulletproof windows. It remained in the street while two men guarded it from the outside. Thirty minutes later, Arthur and Lydia walked the forty paces from the front door of their home, adorned in bulletproof vests, flanked by two men commanded to preserve their lives. Behind them was little Melody Grace, crying as she was carried by the third man, weighed down by a Kevlar wrap draped over her tiny body, watching her home fade with every step.

The McCartneys never returned to Montclair.

To New Jersey.

To the Northeast.

TWO

There were two reasons to kill the McCartneys: to keep them from testifying or to punish them for having testified. Either way, *bleak*.

Meanwhile, the Justice Department started working its sloppy sleight of hand, a magician with only one trick in its repertoire: the disappearing act.

Federal Witness Protection.

This suburban family had witnessed less than fifteen seconds of criminal activity, and once the Department of Justice was done getting theirs, the McCartneys would be thrown out in the wild to fend for themselves, protected by the illusion of contrived existences. Five years earlier, Louie Salvone had tried giving my dad up in a plea bargain, gave the feds four crates of documentation, and they still couldn't nail Pop for a single thing.

Things didn't turn out very well for Louie. All I can say is this: shiv.

In Salvone's case, he had it coming. He could have done his six months and come out a stronger man in the organization as a result. But by that time Louie's desire to party had matured into a pretty serious coke habit, and the combined thought of going a half year without a fix—not to mention the nightmare of going through withdrawal in prison—had him looking for the fastest way out.

The McCartneys, on the other hand, were guilty of nothing more than wanting a plate of eggs, some orange juice, and a pair of cappuccinos. You can't even say it was an error in judgment; they were simply customers, and frankly the kind any restaurateur would want in his establishment. Going down the alley might have been a bit much, but what father wouldn't go knock on a few doors for his child?

A little over a year later, I started to hear more and more about taking care of the McCartneys. On our retainer were not one but two of New York's most powerful law firms. The bigger of the two, the firm with the most connections and people on the take, crafted a gorgeous defense for my father. The Justice Department wasn't foolish; they had the McCartneys deposed to what they'd witnessed mere minutes after they were thrown into Witness Protection, produced enough videotape to single-handedly turn a profit for TDK. But Pop's legal team somehow managed to get anything this innocent family said in the videos thrown out on some technicality I never fully understood, which had little impact on how airtight the government's case was; the witnesses would simply be able to retell it live in court—and Pop's legal team knew it. What it gave the Bovaros, you see, was time.

Time to eliminate the witnesses.

I was getting older, had just turned twelve, and as my usefulness surged, so did the significance of conversations I might be privy to, or at a minimum overhear. Couple that with my oldest brother, Peter, basking in the glory of knowing and hearing more than the rest of us and desperate to prove it, and the image of the future started taking shape, its brightness and vibrancy hinging on finding the McCartneys. Without them, the Justice Department would have to return to Louie Salvone's ineffective documentation of how the Bovaros ran numbers back before I was born, a business line our family all but exited once most states in the Union had sanctioned lotteries. I grew a lot during that period—physically, of course, I started to resemble the rugged structure of my older brothers, Peter and Gino, eighteen and fourteen, respectively—but psychologically, too. Prior to then, I thought my dad was in the restaurant business, and he was, sort of. He owned many—as a means to launder money and shuffle stolen goods out the back. But I soon came to realize that we were special. *Mafia* special. The terms my father's family and associates started using in my presence began sounding more significant. Guys were getting *whacked*, deadbeats were getting *roughed up*, troublemakers were *having their balls handed to them* and occasionally *shoved down their throats.* In my younger days, where my uncle Sal told me to stay out of Vin's kitchen to forestall the horror of my father's brutality, now he'd ask me to grab a mop and do my share.

I was, however, *only* twelve, demonstrated by my assumption that the only targets were the senior McCartneys. But once I heard my father speak of the plan to eliminate all three of them at once, I experienced the very first instance of disrespect for the way my family conducted its business. Why would anyone want to off a child? A child that was probably still learning how to read? Wouldn't it be easy enough to confuse or scare the kid on the stand?

But here's the term I heard over and over in our house like a frigging mantra: *no loose ends.*

I mentally ran through the roster of men in my father's organization, trying to find the sociopath who might be able to level the barrel at a little girl and pull the trigger. Only one contender came to mind: Paulie Marcone, a nut job who found heartfelt enjoyment in assaulting and killing for any loosely justifiable reason. The problem with Paulie was how odd things would haunt him and cause him to break down. The guy could eat steak pizzaiola every day of the week but couldn't fathom eating a hunk of veal. He couldn't bear to see a suffering animal or a crying kid or an old lady struggling to get her groceries to the top floor of her brownstone. Beat him backing into a parking spot on Court Street, though, and you'll drive home one-handed. This strange, largely unseen sensitive side made him useless in conducting the last hit.

Ultimately, no one materialized—because no one had to; the feds managed to keep the McCartneys well hidden. We had a few people in Justice, mostly lower-level clerks working off gambling debts, who'd occasionally cough up nothing more than advanced notice on what judge we might draw for a particular case or how many boxes of evidence were sitting in a warehouse in Jersey. But getting information on the Federal Witness Protection Program is precisely as difficult as you might imagine. For starters, the program is run out of the U.S. Marshals Service, and the entry points to that system are fragmented; having contacts at Justice wasn't enough. At the time, we didn't have direct insiders with the FBI, either—but if we had, they'd have been useless, too. We needed a source at the Marshals Service simply to figure out where to begin.

The entire thing seemed to go away for about a month—*for me*; tension in our family mounted as the McCartneys disappeared into an oblivion of safety. It should be noted that the one thing the Bovaros have done well since the moment our elders stepped off the boat is the one thing that saved my father from a life in prison. Those things we deal in on a daily basis—money laundering, carting, fixing, bookmaking, loan sharking—are the incidental things that occur as a result of the one integral component. The district attorneys call it fear; we call it influence. Possessing power over others is the most instinctive human concept; you either want it or are willing to succumb to it.

That said, my father's influence cut a wide swath across this great land, a terribly unfortunate truth for the McCartneys. While the feds did an impressive job of keeping them hidden, they could do little to stop those who served my father. A mere five weeks into their relocation, the little McCartney girl accidentally outed her entire family to her first grade class by using her birth name. Within hours the little Arkansas town was abuzz with what had happened, which eventually spilled its way to a bar where a drunken loser looking to make good on an extended debt in our organization hoped he might turn the information into a clean slate. The feds hurried the McCartneys along, but not before the information got back to New York, not before Arthur, Lydia, and Melody were being followed by men in our crew.

My life began a transformation in that moment. The little girl was to be hunted, killed, buried, her existence whittled down to a memory for her extended family that would grow fainter by the year. The flame of innocence that had been flickering for years in my family would soon be extinguished and redemption would be impossible—and most troubling, I seemed to be the only one who cared. Granted, most guys who took a beating (or worse) from a Bovaro had earned it, and even as a kid I learned to be okay with that. But knowing that this poor little girl would be running her whole life because of me became more than I could bear.

For the next eighteen months, through the countless motions to delay the trial, both the Bovaros and the McCartneys lived out a series of near misses. My uncles were on the trail of the McCartneys repeatedly, with a few opportunities for elimination that ended in empty-handed returns. Other times, the McCartneys inexplicably slipped right out from under us, as though we were right behind them—when we weren't.

Every trip, every time someone was sent to rub them out, I went sleepless. I lost weight. When I didn't actually become ill, I feigned it and resigned myself to my bedroom. I spent some time throwing up and more time fighting back tears and a burgeoning anger. Shamefully, the elder McCartneys weren't my concern, rarely crossed my mind; the little girl would come into my room and haunt me like the ghost she had yet to become.

I'd overhear the conversations and loose planning of how and who would terminate the family. They would run through a generic itinerary like a grocery list. The mother. The father. The plans to evade the feds. And the girl. One conversation in particular stuck with me, a discussion between my father and an associate whose voice I couldn't quite place.

Then they started speaking in Italian, which usually meant they wanted to talk confidentially. The only people in my family who could really get a full grasp of a conversation spoken in full Italian, complete with Sicilian dialect, would be the grown-ups. By then, though, I was well on my way to acquiring broken Italian—learned mostly through discussions like these—that I carry with me to this day, and I was able to understand enough of the language to translate the following exchange while they ate at the small table in our kitchen:

"This is our last shot, *amico*," my father said softly. *Amico* means friend, and everyone was *amico*—could have been a son, an associate, or someone about to serve him a gelato or take a bullet.

"We know how to find them, Tony. We're going to take care of it, eh?" said Amico.

"Need to be." Or something like that.

"You know what this means for our family. For me."

"I know, 'Tone."

Then some gibberish about the puttanesca.

"We can't take them out on the courthouse steps." I'm not even sure which one of them said this. The point was they seemed more determined than ever. The point was they seemed more desperate than ever. The point was...the McCartneys did not stand a chance.

They were the Smiths this time, and it turned out Melody's name was Karen. I know that all the Karens who've dwelled on this planet were at one time little girls, but the name sounded so mature to me. Karen Smith sounded like a lady running for elected office or the owner of a local business. I overheard the aliases of her parents, too, but I've long forgotten them; they were, after all, the second set in a lengthy series. And the fact that they received this series of identities exposes a truth: The Smiths survived. Long after the fact, I was informed that no one had a clear shot. I wondered if maybe even the most villainous guy on the job looked down at little Melody and knew there was no way to end her life, that some glow of purity and promise shielded her and weakened those men of madness and steel, that maybe she crystallized everything that was wrong in the way we led our lives.

But probably...they just couldn't get the shot.

Then the trial came. Arthur and Lydia testified. And it didn't matter. Six days after jury selection, an unplanned gathering materialized in our house where celebrating occurred as though we had just won the case. Wine flowed. My mother and her sister produced enough food for an Italian wedding. The house smelled of garlic and basil and braised meats and browning cheeses. Lawyers of all ethnicities and faiths filled our living room, embraced and rejoiced. The trigger of this merriment: An astounding precedent dating back to 1903 on how one is led to the acquisition of evidence, expected to be thrown out of court—laughed out, actually—caught a judge with an open mind. Arguments were well delivered from the prosecution, but remember we had the best defense money could buy (or whatever); these were not stupid men and women defending my father. I remember watching the banter, the outrage by the prosecutors, the quiet confidence of my father's legal team, the verbal sparring between them and the judge narrowing their responses. From my uneducated perspective both sides sounded well thought out and convincing. The judge let the attorneys battle until all of a sudden, on the final swipe from my father's attorney the prosecutor came up dry. He'd run out, cornered. And then the ultimate admission of defeat: He looked at the judge, flipped out his hands, and said, "Your Honor, please." The way he appeared to be whining and begging at the same time was a sure sign there would be a veritable carnival in the Bovaro household.

Let's say you coach the New York Giants. You've had five losing seasons and you've got millions of New Yorkers and New Jerseyans breathing down your neck for not just a playoff bid, but a Super Bowl title. You just nailed a powerhouse of a running back from the University of Florida for three years at twenty million. This kid is going to take you all the way. The only problem is the kid breaks his leg during the season opener and will be lucky to walk after a year of therapy. All you can do is let him sit on the bench and pay out his contract. Everyone feels bad for the kid. Everyone smiles at the kid and gives the kid pats on the back every now and again. You think the kid is a great guy, but now you're heading into your sixth losing season and the truth is you just wish the kid would sort of go away. Because let's be honest... what you really need is another powerhouse running back.

I can't imagine how the conversation must have gone with the McCartneys, their having been hurried into the courtroom under the heaviest of protection, testifying under a layer of Kevlar, then rushed back out of the courtroom to a secluded safe house. The brief feeling of relief and accomplishment they must have had. And the complete sense of loss and despair as they were told the last few years were for nothing.

And now, starting right now, *run*.

THREE

Crime is like a cult. If introduced early and with determined rhythm, it morphs into a way of life with rules one accepts and lives by without question; it becomes the only way to conduct one's existence. That Sunday at Vincent's served as my first inkling that the Bovaro lifestyle was not right, and that I had to escape a cult I happened to love because the damage was far too great, not just for me or my family but for the business owners we protected and the people we employed. But violence is a difficult drug to surrender. When used appropriately, it captures the essence of everything, cuts to the core of any dispute, finds and delivers truth. There is a tangible beauty in violence. People are typically not willing to embrace it, but sometimes you must appreciate violence for what it is. Reduce it to its simplest form and see. It starts with rescuing a fair maiden by killing a spider; she gets such peace and satisfaction in its death. Graduate to the bully who gets the tables turned, his life altered to where he might never again hold his head high. Show me a pedophile and I'll show you a hundred people who'd pay a week's wages to see him fall prey to crimes exponentially more vicious as his own. Every movie with a villain—how unsatisfied we are unless the comeuppance is delivered. God Himself displayed the most impressive and stunning displays of violence and vengeance on record; consult the Old Testament. But in order for violence to work, it requires one component: passion. You need to be behind it or your ambivalence will lead to inaction. You have to *want it.*

This concept came shining in Technicolor shortly before I turned twenty-one, when I was handed my first assignment. I was no stranger to trouble, though I labored to avoid it more than my siblings, particularly Peter, who seemed to seek it out and languished in its absence. But I was now an older Bovaro, and my place in the organization required a greater contribution. The McCartneys had not dropped off the radar, but they weren't nearly the biggest blip on the screen; Arthur and Lydia had become useless to the Justice Department, nothing more than a taxpayer expense. Where a few years ago every single person in our organization was aching to be the one to gun them down and care was taken to devise the most cunning plan, now the McCartneys were simply running from themselves, from their own resident fear that we were on their trail every step of the way.

But remember the mantra: *no loose ends.*

The McCartneys became a topic of conversation in our house the way most folks discuss cleaning out the gutters or getting an annual exam, an unavoidable task that can be repeatedly delayed. My father was no longer troubled by their potential testimony once his attorneys verified that everything the McCartneys witnessed could never again be allowed into a courtroom; the concern now was showing the world (mostly our peers and those under our influence) what happens when you cross a Bovaro.

The first time I truly appreciated my oldest brother, Peter: One winter afternoon he and I were shooting baskets against a rusty backboard and netless rim in what was arguably a rougher section of our neighborhood near Cobble Hill in Brooklyn, before the renaissance got a foothold. We were halfway through a game of one-on-one when three kids started moving down the sidewalk in our direction. I knew there would be trouble for no other reason than all three were looking right at us. They were sizing us up. By the time these kids made their way around the chain-link fence and onto our lonely court, words were exchanged between the leader of my two-person gang (Peter) and the leader of what appeared to be three big Russian kids. I don't remember the interchange, though it certainly would have been inane. Of the five of us, I was the smallest, and while looking at my brother and listening to him berate the leader of the other gang for being, essentially, *not like us*, a fist connected with my eye, knocked me to the ground, then out. A few seconds later, my head limp on the cold sidewalk, I opened my good eye and watched through a haze as Peter wiped out the entire group. Two were already on the ground, crawling in opposite directions, though clearly their collective destinations were *away*. Peter seemed to be taking his time kicking number three, the mouthy leader, while the kid begged him to stop. As the sirens approached, Peter gently scooped me up and we dashed down a nearby alley, our worn Spalding resting at the feet of the big Russian.

The first time I truly despised my oldest brother, Peter: a few days before my twenty-first birthday. On a journey to Yankee Stadium in our blackened-out Suburban, my father, my siblings—Peter, Gino, and younger brother Jimmy, the kid fated to have been named after a guy whose blood can still be spotted in the grout between the tiles of Vincent's kitchen floor—and I chatted about what I should be getting for my upcoming birthday.

Gino, my older brother by two years and possessing the most practical personality in the family, offered up the tried and true. "How 'bout a convertible—or better yet, you always liked mine. Take it and I'll get a new one. Got my eye—"

"Nah," Jimmy interrupted, "what Johnny wants is Connie Cappelletti."

"Pass," I said. "I don't consider syphilis much of a present."

"Jimmy just wanted you to have a gift that'll keep on giving," Gino said.

"Isn't Connie, like, thirteen?"

"Seventeen," Jimmy said, "going on twenty-five."

"The only thing Connie's going on is penicillin."

Gino threaded his fingers together, cracked four knuckles at once. "This world needs guys like you, Jimmy, otherwise skanks like Connie Cappelletti would live lonely lives."

My father drove with a half-smile on his face, which to the unknowing eye might appear as fleeting contentment; I recognized it as a look of concentrated thought. Peter, riding shotgun, just stared out his window. Not a word.

So there you have it, the offerings of my family as directed by their individual long-term interests in keeping the Bovaro dynasty in a flourishing state: Gino thrived in the materialism and Jimmy in the increased availability of female attention and companionship. My father offered his standard fare of aloofness and disinterest; unless reputation could be incorporated into the picture, his mind was elsewhere. Peter's silence was more confusing, though. His particular interest would have only rested in one place: power. And sure enough, it was on his mind; he was perfecting the spin.

As we sat at a red light, the gentle vibration of the engine the only sign of life, my father continued his unfocused gaze out the window.

Then, with his eyes still out and away, Peter said quietly, "Pistola."

Pop finally snapped out of it. "Eh, Pete?"

Still speaking to the window, he said, "Pistola for my little brother."

The entire cab of the Suburban went quiet, and here's why: There could be absolutely nothing significant about giving me a gun as a birthday present. We had them tucked away in our house the way most people store ballpoint pens. If you opened a drawer to get a pack of matches, you'd probably have to move a .22 out of the way to get to it. Our world is one where guns are, far and wide, disposable. After a hit they're usually left at the scene, clean of fingerprints and serial numbers—anything that might trace them to a buyer or shooter—because it's the safest place for them to be. Once a gun's been used to take someone down, the last place it should be is *on you.* "Maybe," he said, "we give Johnny his manhood this year." He glanced at Pop like he might get a congratulatory chuckle out of him, but Pop merely focused on getting us to 161st Street.

Peter had helped me to become a man in many significant ways: my first cigarette, to which I developed a fervent addiction; my first taste of hard liquor at age eleven; the way to take someone out at the knees; a comprehensive inventory of profanity that may have sounded weirdly amusing coming from a seven-year-old boy but stinks like sulfur from an adult; countless ways to use girls and misuse masculinity.

And now, the crown jewel: Peter intended on introducing me to the value of killing.

Gino turned to me, broke the silence. "Wouldn't you rather have a Mustang?"

I stared at the headrest that blocked the back of Peter's head. "Your point, Pete?"

He turned in his seat and offered his answer to my father. "Johnny's old enough now to clean up his own messes, yeah?" Then to me, "Our family's been embarrassed long enough."

These were the first years where Peter made it clear that he viewed himself as the coming replacement for my father, the heir to the empire, the chosen one to lead the Bovaro organization into a new generation. The decision to take a life—anyone's life—was never made lightly in our house. It served some specific purpose: righting a wrong, teaching a lesson, balancing the scales. Like farm kids who learn to butcher pigs as a regular responsibility, so were the bloody duties of our home; the gore is never questioned.

But the embarrassment comment was pointed to the McCartneys, crafted specifically for me, for there was one final item in the list of things Peter taught me in the pursuit of becoming a real man: the power of humiliation.

So where did my interests rest within the Bovaro power structure? Perhaps the answer shines brightest in what I really did want for my twenty-first: my mother's food, my family's congregation, and a time of celebration—didn't even have to be about me. I wanted everyone to be there. The cousins and aunts and uncles, the associates, the nut jobs. Guys like Tommy Fingers and Paulie Marcone who could rip out your liver and fry it up with peppers and onions, but they understood the value of family. When I was eight, Paulie spent four straight hours one summer night teaching me how to play poker, how to gauge the table, how to bluff. No matter how many times I got it wrong, the guy never lost his cool, would just smile and slap my back and say, "Let's try it again, Johnny." It might be best explained as a matter of culture, but to exist around these men and women is a warm thing. Tommy Fingers, a near-illiterate man of girth and fury, used to spend most mornings making breakfast for whoever would break bread with him, a culinary artist of notable capability in any other setting. All you'd have to do is casually say to yourself, "Man, I'm hungry," and the next thing you know Tommy is sliding a steaming bowl of pasta fagioli in front of you—unless he's out muscling some guy into submission. (Tommy got his nickname from his calling card, what we routinely called a *souvenir*, something to act as a permanent reminder of our power and the related event; Tommy's was the snapping of the middle finger of whoever he assailed.) I wanted Tommy to celebrate with me, put his thick arm around me and talk food. I wanted Paulie to argue with anyone who would listen about what Steinbrenner was doing to the Yankees. I wanted Peter to be my older brother and my dad to be my father and my mother to be my mother, just for one day. I wanted a room full of laughter, glasses filled with beer and wine, and the simple excuse to eat to the point of discomfort.

The silence that continued in the Suburban hinted at one of two things: Peter's suggestion was either being considered or completely ignored. We circled the block before entering the Gerard Avenue lot. Disregarding the valet, my father snaked our monster into a tight spot in a lot where the lines were readjusted year after year into slighter spaces. All four doors opened and slammed into the Benzes on either side of us, then Pop chucked the keys in the general vicinity of the nearest valet, over the hoods of two rows of cars, and the valet dove for them like he'd been tossed a handful of diamonds; no return ticket was handed our way, never was.

I remember thinking that day was going to be great—the Yankees were playing the Orioles, after all—but I'd become jammed up, leveled by the reminder that I was a Bovaro and that that meant something the way it meant something to be a Kennedy, a Rockefeller, a Du Pont; the expected legacy is expected for a reason, and fulfillment a near requirement.

Peter set me up, the bastard. There would be no way to avoid accepting the task. To back down would be weak, to let—continue to let—others clean up my childhood embarrassment and not feel some sort of anger over what happened. The McCartneys had dared to testify against my father, and for that reason I should have been incensed myself, insulted to the point that retribution served as the only natural course. But I knew as my family did—they were the ones to educate me—that the fear we perpetrated upon the masses was only bolstered by the stories told by the feds to encourage, to *frighten*, people into testifying.

I had to take whatever assignment they asked of me, lest I become the standout. The loser. I had one hope only: that my father would ignore the entire suggestion, that his pride and reputation regarding a matter of many years prior was rightly no longer an insult, that he would never consider asking his almost twenty-one-year-old son to empty a clip into the bodies of innocent people.

My father's decision had been concealed right up to our entrance of the cheer-filled stadium. He put his arm around me, tightened it around my shoulder as we walked together toward our seats, Bovaro men, and said to me gently, "Don't worry, we'll get you the car, too."

The first time you hold a gun is like the first time you hold an infant. You're not sure what to do with it. You watch the people around you for some signal that you're holding it correctly. You bounce it a little and comment on its weight. You're amazed at how beautiful the thing is. You prefer it to remain in a state of deep sleep. And ultimately, you wonder what it would be like to have one of your own.

No one ever gets a gun and thinks, *I wonder what it would be like to kill someone.* Unless you're a hunter, most balanced people never want to discharge a firearm in the direction of another living thing, including everyone in my family—even Peter, who'd prefer a fisticuffs over a gun battle any day of the week. On the scale of weapons, the gun is the weakest form of power. After all, how did my father take care of Jimmy "the Rat"? A knife to the man's gut, a gesture that read not only to Jimmy but to his peers, *This was personal, and I was not afraid to take his life with my own hands.* When people compare the Mafia to drug gangs, I'm baffled. In the early twentieth century, our types may have killed with great disregard, but when was the last time someone from the Mafia drove into a neighborhood and unloaded a half dozen automatic weapons into the side of a building, killing countless people? We are surgeons picking the particular cancer running through a system and carving it out, disposing of it, allowing life to resume like the disease had never even taken hold.

My first gun had strings. It had a purpose. They could have loaded the thing with just six bullets—two for each McCartney. All that remained was to find the targets.

It never occurred to me, as I'd previously searched the list of psycho killers in our family, running fully through the roster of men in my father's organization for the sociopath who might be able to level the barrel at a young girl and pull the trigger, that the spinning dial would slow, tick gently in my direction, and come to rest at my name. I was the selected nut job.

FOUR

Years after my father's elimination of Jimmy "the Rat," he was still riding the wave of reputation from that hit. And I suppose he managed to go out with quite a bang: The Rat was the last time my father ever took someone out, ever needed to. That hit contained all the components necessary to propel fear and notoriety: It was grisly; it was a power play; it was sloppy—a mess everywhere—yet no one took the fall. It spoke to our community of an authority and immunity reserved for few others. To set another example would not be necessary; my father's minions would now do the dirtiest work and take the biggest risks. Regardless of the end result, I always suspected that the McCartneys haunted him—not as ghosts like they did with me, but as reminders that we are not gods but merely participants in a world under His command. And I don't think my father was ever able to shake the warning.

During those years, though, something else changed: the landscape of influence. Through my young life, the most valuable tool we had was the distribution of force and fear. But an evolution was occurring, and it wasn't long before information became increasingly valuable. Some of our highest-volume debtors, mostly bottom-dwellers, were transformed into agents of utility. Guys working clerk jobs in the city with access to databases we could've never imagined suddenly captured our attention—and so did the status of their debts. One of our most consistent losers at betting pro football, Randall Gardner, managed to sustain his day job developing a system for the federal government. In lieu of paying back a debt, he gave Peter and Pop access to a particular database whereby they could see the FBI's general plans, budgets, and priorities—information that was more interesting than valuable. Our access to this fascinating system lasted a mere twenty-two hours before our login was revoked, but the taste gave Peter a lust for information. To his credit, he began to marginally shift the power of our family to a slightly cleaner though equally illegal level of influence; we started playing more Monopoly and less Sorry.

I managed to keep my Beretta in secluded silence, hoping it would serve as nothing more than a defense weapon. Though I suppose it might be obvious where Peter's longing for information took us, our family, and ultimately me.

By the time the football season was cresting the playoffs, Randall Gardner was betting his house—almost literally—on the Philadelphia Eagles to beat the Dallas Cowboys and cover the spread. Philadelphia didn't show up for that game, and by halftime it was clear there was no hope Randall could save his house—or his marriage or the ability to see his kids again. Soon the Bovaros would be arriving at an odd hour with a pair of Louisville Sluggers if he didn't fork over the five figures owed to us by the end of the week.

But Peter performed his magic on old Randall, working the guy's Rolodex like an insurance salesman looking for potential leads. *Make a list of ten people who could help you out, Randall.* Three of the four built-in advantages to dealing with addicts are: (1) They have no pride remaining; (2) They tend to automatically leverage themselves; (3) They will work everyone they know for help. And Randall needed a lot of help. By that time, he served as a computer programmer in the information technology department at a small federal contractor that developed systems for the Department of Justice. Earlier that year, he had attended a conference in Washington, DC, where he met two other programmers he casually befriended. They exchanged numbers as a means of expanding their circle of potential job opportunities.

So when Peter approached Randall and gave him an opportunity to wipe away his entire debt—the proverbial second chance—Randall wept like a girl, said he would do anything.

Anything.

We never knew how Randall manipulated his friends from Washington, never came to understand if the information materialized through charm or force or threat, for therein lies the true benefit of the minion. We never cared if the information was acquired through hacking or social engineering or stealing someone's briefcase, for therein lies the true benefit of the hopeless spirit with a need to supply a demanding addiction, the at-any-cost means of completing a mission.

Suddenly we had the exact address of the McCartneys, their latest aliases, everything.

My first gun had strings. It had a purpose.

Randall Gardner became one of our greatest assets. As for the fourth built-in advantage of addicts: (4) No matter how many times you wipe the slate clean, you can count on this: They'll be back in debt to you even sooner than before. No more than two weeks later, the Redskins cost Randall another five figures. Mr. Gardner gave us more collected data over the years than the *Farmers' Almanac* and *Encyclopaedia Britannica* combined, and Pop made sure we fed the man's compulsion for gambling like a stray cat, doled out a fresh can of tuna and a saucer of warm milk with assured regularity. Randall always arrived on our doorstep looking for more, along with a cache of information in return.

I didn't go to the McCartneys' on my own. The hits were planned, and part of those plans included my older cousin by five years, Ettore Vido, an overstrung, highly skilled marksman who'd recently proven his talent to my father, who consequently found him endearing. Ettore—Hector, if translated—spoke infrequently, as though he'd recently arrived from Catania. He possessed a peculiar personality trait of being interested in absolutely nothing at all—no sports, no music, no television. He had not a single hobby. He didn't have a favorite food, favorite car, favorite movie. He didn't prefer blondes over brunettes, voluptuous over skinny. On the other hand, ask him to scrape the serial numbers off a collection of guns or clean the kitchen and he would silently oblige. As for the overstrung part: If you did anything to keep him from finishing an assigned task—say, dropping a glob of marinara on his clean kitchen floor—he would come apart at the seams, occasionally to the point of requiring restraint. All I can say is this: *robot.* And here, on our trip to find the McCartneys in Mineral Point, Wisconsin, he served as an automaton to make sure the assignment of taking out the McCartneys would be brought to a clean, comfortable close.

He accompanied me for one reason only: mission completion.

The late-winter, fifteen-hour drive out with Ettore was memorable only because it was not memorable at all. We did speak a few times:

ME: "Need a couple bucks for the toll."
ETTORE: "'Kay."

An hour later.

ME: "Want your order supersized?"
ETTORE: "'Kay."

Three hours later.

ME: "I gotta hit the head."
ETTORE: "Right."

It wasn't until we got a room at a roadside motel a few miles southeast of Mineral Point that he finally talked about the plan.

We sat on opposing double beds, shades drawn, one sixty-watt bulb lighting the room from ten feet away. As I studied my virgin Beretta, slowly unscrewing and rescrewing the silencer, Ettore put on a pair of gloves and began piling his reserve of weapons on the table between our beds, cleaning one at a time. He pulled them from everywhere—ankle holster, belt holster, two from his duffel bag. When the cleaning was complete, he went through the ritual of putting each in its respective holster, then quickly yanking it out and pointing it at some object across the room. The guy was a caricature of himself. Then again, rituals tend to give strength to disciplines, and Ettore was a proven killer. This wasn't even his hit; the guns accompanied him on this trip for no other purpose than to act as a collection of steel security blankets. My Beretta? I tossed it on the pillow next to me and turned on the television.

"This is happening," Ettore said to me.

I glanced at him, pursed my lips and nodded a little, then turned back to the TV. There was no way this was happening. Under other circumstances anxiety would have wrapped its hand around me and delivered a squeeze tight enough to crumble me like a saltine. The act of your first premeditated murder comes hard to anyone not belly deep in drugs or sociopathy, mobster or not. But my excuse was far easier; the most talented assassins ever to have been affiliated with the Bovaro crew previously failed at whacking the McCartneys. Ettore and I were hardly a step up. I figured we'd look for the McCartneys for a few days, then return home as an expected disappointment.

Turns out, though, Ettore and I were not on the same page.

"This is happening," he repeated.

"I know." I proceeded with the ritual of opening a new pack of Marlboros, shaking one loose, placing the filtered end against my dry lips, lighting it.

"You ready?"

I tried to determine what he was really asking, blew smoke over to his side. "Of course."

"Don't get comfortable."

I shook my head at the television. "There's nothing comfortable about this, Ettore."

"There should be nothing uncomfortable about this, Johnny."

I took a long drag as I watched a Budweiser commercial—young men and women laughing on a California beach, playfully flirting, falling into foamy waves, sunning on a strip of sand and rock. Somewhere, far away from Mineral Point, Wisconsin, people were doing innocent things.

Ettore came to my side, reached over and grabbed my Beretta, tightened the silencer, added it to his stack of firearms, next in line for a cleaning.

"This is happening," one final time.

I glanced his way. "I know." This time, just a little, I believed it.

We were assassins, but not the kind that would do the type of damage where no one suspected we were there; wasn't the point that people *knew* we were there, that retribution lit this fuse? If military-trained executioners might be compared to a diamond-tipped saw, slicing a perfect divide into someone's lifeline, Ettore and I were like a chain saw, cutting a half-inch swath through anything we touched, wood chunks and sawdust flying everywhere. Best wear your goggles around us.

The following morning we dropped our key on the front desk of the motel along with a wad of cash to cover the room. We loaded the car with our firepower and set on our way. The objective: I was to eliminate an entire family, drop the gun, drive straight back to New York.

As the clock passed ten on that Saturday morning, Ettore snaked us over the gentle hills, toward the historic section of Mineral Point, avoiding Highway 151 just to the west. From the moment we left the motel, everything seemed surreal. The sky was weighted with fast-moving gray clouds destined to unload a reserve of rain on us at any second. We passed roads with names like Cheese Country Recreation Trail and Merry Christmas Lane. We waited our turn at an intersection in the oldest section of the city, atop the crest of a hill, where the stores were sheltered by trees and wrought-iron lamps were still alight on that cloudy morning. Two families walked hand in hand down the steep hill as they viewed the windows of art galleries and pottery shops and answered questions from their children. It seemed wrong to disrupt this part of the world. In my turf back home everyone sort of *has it coming.* In Mineral Point, people moved out of the way for one another, nodded at strangers, and perused shops like Papa Pat's Farmhouse Recipes and Leaping Lizards. Blood should never be spilled here.

We drove the four miles from the center of the small village to the McCartney residence on the north side, past the welding supply shop and the liquor store, past the Dairy Queen and the fairgrounds, past the open fields, and finally through the farm-rich outskirts. As we drew nearer, I noticed a few manufacturing buildings, one of which seemed likely to act as the temporary employer of the disguised Arthur McCartney.

Ettore made a series of left and rights—no doubt memorized the map to their house with great precision—and brought us to the edge of a bland street, devoid of trees and sidewalks and, in general, love. This was a flat field that someone had decided would make a good place for five carbon-copy homes, lined up like soldiers, facing and backing a distinct nothingness, a six-year-old's crayon depiction of rural life.

"That it?" I asked, nodding toward a gray rambler tucked at the bottom of a courtless dead end, to which I never received an answer. I've been told the look and life of a house is a reflection of its residents. If that's true, this house reflected death and disinterest. What landscaping remained alive had overgrown the pieces that had long since perished. The paint on the shutters had chipped and begun to drop in hunks down onto the gnarled bushes below. On the two concrete steps leading to a broken screen door sat three planters holding the stiff skeletons of deceased flowers. This house said on behalf of its residents: What's the point?

We waited from a secluded distance for an hour, not a word spoken, and the longer we waited the more at ease I became. Who was to say they were even home? I could feel the victory of failure upon us!

I jumped in my seat when the old wooden garage door of the rambler started to yawn, each framed section jerking as the opener tugged on it with all its might. Ettore sat up, leaned forward a little, and an icy smile came over his face that will never leave my memory, a look that suggested he'd visualized the series of moves leading us to checkmate.

A rush of adrenaline pumped through me as we watched their Subaru creep out from the shelter of the garage, obscuring them from view. I hadn't seen these people since I stole glimpses of them on the New York sidewalk that day as a child. They existed in my mind the way they were then, ageless and blameless and healthy. But I could no longer allow my imagination to have that latitude; after all, here we were.

We followed them to the A&P. And the gray clouds opened.

I watched them from a sheltered point of view a baseball's-throw distance away at the far end of the grocery store parking lot. It seemed I was always watching them exit automobiles, the closest thing to time travel I might ever experience. But this time, as they emerged from the Subaru, they looked weathered and worn. The father crawled out first and looked around like he was expecting the bullet already fated for his temple, trying to determine from which direction it would come. Rubbing his neck with one hand and coughing into the other, he walked to the passenger side and opened the door for his wife; she, too, looked around as if trying to locate a friend in a large crowd. They were both emaciated, the father having aged two decades in one's time, the mother thin with clothes hanging off her frame like hand-me-downs from a larger sibling and wrinkles identifiable from our veiled location forty yards away. Arthur scoped the parking lot and through the rain it seemed he lingered on our car. Could he have identified the New York plates from that distance, things might have turned out differently.

Then Melody surfaced from the backseat—and I stopped breathing. Up to that moment, she'd remained a kindergartner in my mind, an everlasting image of all the innocence we'd so cruelly removed.

Unless you've got a buddy who serves as an expert at age progression photography at the National Center for Missing and Exploited Children, there is no way to anticipate the look a child will get when she transcends adolescence, and even if I'd had the skill, I could not have imagined how Melody matured. We were closer in age now—the four-year gap meaning less than it did long ago—and now I viewed her the way a college senior might view a freshman. She wore her chestnut hair short and tucked behind her ears, her skin an unhealthy white. Though she stood as tall as you would expect of a seventeen-year-old, I might've confused her for an older girl. And her size and shape suggested she could regularly raid her mother's wardrobe. She pushed up the sleeves of a loose blue sweater, put her hands in the pockets of her jeans, stared at the ground, head hanging. I was just as mesmerized as all those years ago, fueled by the same curious interest, but now also with an obsession to understand the effect—the aftereffect—of what the world had done to this family, to this little girl.

Melody stared without aim, let the rain fall on her with no concern. She appeared as a girl with absolutely nothing to look forward to, a candidate for justifiable depression.

Ettore said, "When they come out."

I could not take my eyes off of Melody. I'd never seen the spirit removed from someone the way it had been pulled from her, and I'd seen some guys really take an emotional beating that surely would have resulted in hopelessness. Gone were the swirling dances and the curious glances at the sky, along with her parents' flirty kisses. She stood in the lot of the A&P, her face tipped down as though transfixed by the movement of a caterpillar. The look of dread and defeat on their individual faces spoke of permanent damage.

The cold rain intensified, hammered down on the roof of our car, went from dimes to nickels. Beyond the moving windshield wipers and through the wet window of the grocery store, we watched Arthur and Lydia lumber off in one direction and Melody sit down on a bench at the front of the store and stare out over the parking lot, her body twisted in our direction. She put her arm across the back of the bench, rested her chin over her forearm the way a dog rests its head on a paw.

The pain of watching them became so unbearable that I thought for a moment they might actually be better off dead. I thought that hardening my heart in the genuine Bovaro manner was the safest direction to turn my life. A hit is easier to understand when accompanied by an excuse of permissibility. They deserved it.

They had it coming.

After rubbing my eyes, I returned my gaze to the storefront. Melody had disappeared, no longer behind the window.

Then came the waiting. Ettore and I sat like a pair of mannequins, stiff and forward-facing, wearing black leather jackets and thin leather gloves and mismatching baseball caps, twins in all but our thoughts. Neither of us could comprehend what was about to unfold.

Ettore stared at the door, chewing a double-size wad of Juicy Fruit.

The rain intensified, forced us to kick the wipers into a faster rhythm.

At that moment, in the silence between us, a clarity of my existence dropped upon me, weighed me down, and the pressure pushed all the air from my lungs. How had I become the exact thing I didn't understand—and hated most—in all my father did?

I had become one of the minions.

Should I throw this entire operation, Ettore would stool it right back to Pop; then the disappointment, the shaking of the head, the comment to someone out of my earshot: "How could my own flesh and blood do this to me?" To which I would never get to counter with the question: "How could my own flesh and blood have asked me to do this?"

Everything about the A&P fit the scene; what was about to happen really should have occurred no other place. People stopped loving this store long ago. The nearly empty parking lot exposed the cracks and rain-filled potholes in the pavement. Rain cascaded off the roofline where a hunk of gutter drooped like the jowls of an aging face, and the wide front window had lost its seal long ago, the inside of the double pane patterned with irregular swirls of dust and grime. This store possessed nothing in common with the new Kroger we had passed on the way from the south, with its parking lot full of BMWs and Eddie Bauer sweaters and double incomes. Melody and I were in the same image, a hopeless snapshot of history. If a building could cry, this one would not be sobbing, but shedding a tear with its final whimper. The A&P was about to die. And now so were its customers.

Ettore kept his dim eyes on the door of the grocery, chewing in time with the wipers, his heart likely pumping a cool sixty beats per minute. He looked like he was doing nothing more stressful than waiting in line to buy the *Times*.

Want to know what the detailed plan was? *Kill them.* Walk up to them and take them out one at a time, drop them like mail sacks, then jog back to the car. From there, Ettore would drive us back to New York. Just once you'd think our approach to taking down a building would be wiring it carefully with explosives, clearing the area, imploding the structure into a nice hill of rubble; instead, we had one solution only: Come in with a wrecking ball and start making big holes.

Then, through the streaky windshield, I saw the elder McCartneys shuffle from the store, both with a pair of plastic grocery bags in each hand.

At that very second I wanted so badly to revel in evil, wanted to be enraged at the actions of these people, wanted to want them to pay for troubling my father and family, and to taste the strong bitterness of revenge. To become a legend, to honor my father, to become feared and respected among those around me.

Instead . . . nothing.

Arthur struggled with the trunk, yanking on the patch of

horizontal surface above the license plate. He put his bags down on the wet parking lot. Lydia shrugged her shoulders in some attempt to shelter herself from the strengthening rain. Melody remained out of sight.

I held my Beretta in my hand loosely, and were I not wearing gloves, a thin layer of sweat would've coated its stubbly grip. I gently tightened the silencer against the barrel of the gun.

The parking lot remained empty but for a smattering of vehicles, and the rain acted as a secondary shield of reasonable doubt for any potential witnesses. I pulled my baseball cap down over my forehead, flipped up the collar of my jacket.

Arthur yanked up twice, then the trunk opened—and that was it, the final piece in place for the perfect hit, the trunk lid offering one final defense against unexpected onlookers and a mild sound deflector. I reached for the door handle and tugged it with all the strength of a toddler.

Ettore turned my way. He knew as well as I did that this was the moment. All the years of hunting, all the attempts to eliminate the McCartneys, all the anguish of the past coupled with all that lay ahead if we failed now, came down to me opening the door of our Impala. I took a deep breath and let it out heavily enough to fog the window of my door. I tried, hoped, even—most despicable—prayed I could take life that day. Alas, the spirit didn't move me. Despite Ettore's repeated attempts at the power of positive thinking, bad news was coming his way: This was *not* happening.

MR. ROBOTO: "Take 'em."
ME: "I can't get the shot."

"Hell you mean? Get out of the friggin' car!"
Then, more honestly, "I can't take the shot."
"Get out of the friggin' car!"

"Where's the girl? We can't—"

Ettore quickly tightened his gloves, grabbed the gun from my incapable hands, opened his door so quickly it slammed back into his side as he bolted. That moment, as my cousin departed my side and without fear navigated around the few cars between us and the McCartneys, my breathing became short and clipped, adrenaline now in flood. The wipers could not wipe away the rain fast enough for me.

Ettore moved up to Arthur from the side of the Subaru, Beretta at his side, out of clear vision from Lydia. Arthur stood back at full height, slammed the trunk down, and as Ettore stood before him, Arthur smiled a little at the stranger—until the barrel of the gun was leveled at his head.

Arthur did not try to run. He did not try to duck. He did not cover his chest or face.

He took two steps to his right to move in front of his wife, to shield her one more second from death. He raised a shaking crooked finger and pleaded, "Okay... wait..."

And with the pop of a muted firecracker, Arthur tumbled face-down on the pavement, his wife left with a red mist across her forehead. Lydia winced and stumbled back as though a car had just driven through a puddle and splashed her. Her eyes gone soft, head trembling like taken by a sudden onset of Parkinson's, she did something that haunts me to this day: With quivering hands, she reached up and pulled the top flaps of her coat together and nervously buttoned them, as though she knew death was upon her, so that once she'd fallen to the ground she would not appear immodest. Lydia slowly went to her knees—she did not collapse—as though preparing for prayer.

Near gasping, I opened my car door and slowly entered the wet air.

Lydia leaned forward near her husband's lifeless body, faced her killer, closed her eyes, her hands still clinging to the top of her coat, just kept whispering, "Okay... okay..."

Before squeezing the trigger, Ettore shot a glance my way, brimming with evil, one that could only have been read as *Do you see what I am doing? This is how it's done.*

Another muted firecracker and Lydia slowly tipped over like a melting snowman.

Ettore dropped one more bullet into each of them, carefully stepped around the bodies before him, began his visual search for the last remaining target. But as I watched his motion, I feared I might have been a true Bovaro after all, that the genetic disposition toward violence might have been buried deep in the twist of chromosomes that made me who I am, for instead of being sickened and further weakened at what just happened, a surge of hatred and rage filled me—not toward the McCartneys, mind you, but wrath was well on its way.

My lungs filled with ease.

When Melody came to the front of the store, approaching the foggy glass, I saw her the same second my cousin did. He held his forearm as he leveled his sight on her.

This is when I left our car's side and yelled louder than I knew my voice could go.

"Ettore Vido!"

He dropped the Beretta to his side and looked at me like the next bullet was for me. I walked in his direction in a manner that suggested that bullet would be the only thing that could stop me. He glanced back at the window, measuring the possibility of taking her out before our escape out of town.

"Ettore Vido!"

Melody moved to the window, cupped her hands around the glass to focus her view of the parking lot, unable to see her dead parents below the ledge of the sill. With her perfect position, she could have been eliminated with a slingshot, never mind a weapon as accurate as a Beretta. My cousin took one last look her way, raised his arm quickly, and aimed it in the general direction of Melody.

"Ettore! Vido!"

Then Melody slipped out of sight.

My cousin turned to me and held the gun in my direction, quickly walking my way and cursing his missed opportunity—but mostly me—with every step, his profanity merely foreshadowing what would become a brutal storm upon my existence.

He held that gun steady, aimed right at my head, but I stood my ground. When he got within a few feet, his cursing now laced in spit that splashed my face, he swung the Beretta down on the side of my head and I immediately fell to the ground. Just as I was figuring out what had happened, the Beretta made its way to my skull again. And again. I touched my face, looked down at my palm covered in the blood from my head, running from a gash across my temple that I would wear the rest of my life.

Ettore grabbed me by the arm, lifted me up, then smashed me again, this time with his glove-covered fist. I tried to regain my composure—despite the pain, I remained enraged—but I could not get my footing. When I finally staggered to my feet, Ettore grabbed me by the back of my jacket and shoved me into the front seat of our Impala.

As bodies began to cautiously slink out from the store, we sped from the parking lot and disappeared toward Route 151, down a series of back roads until we were within a half mile of the highway. Ettore drove off the road into a field, mud splattering the windows, and spun the car around so it was facing the street again.

He got out and looked at the Beretta with confusion—not sure why it was still in his hand. The robot did not follow his programmed instructions. He walked through the field, the cursing returned, my name embedded within each sentence.

I kicked my door open and crawled out, blood in my mouth and eyes, the world spinning beneath my feet. Of all the habits I spent my later life trying to reject—the smoking, the acid tongue, the careless drinking—I could never surrender the anger and rage and propensity to destroy by intimate physical means. There is no necessity for nicotine, for vulgarities, for inebriation. Unfortunately, though, violence is a necessary thing.

The pressure was crescendoing now, making its quick conversion to wrath. It was not due to some sense of shame that I was unable to follow my father's instructions, not from Ettore's desperate need to displace me and elevate his place in my family, not from his sheer nerve to pistol-whip me, to point the barrel of a gun in my direction. This moment clarified all that mattered to me, what would come to be the focus of my life. Ettore should never have made an attempt on Melody's life, should never have been willing to eliminate that kind of innocence.

I walked to the rear of the Impala, opened the trunk, slid all the bags and boxes aside, and pulled out the tire iron. I slowly limped my way to my cousin, who stood facing the open expanse of land, raising his fist to some greater power that had failed him.

I trudged through the muddy field, my shoes filling with brown muck and slowing me even more. I approached Ettore, tightened my grip on the tire iron, and watched him writhe in the anguish of inefficacy.

In agony, I managed to mumble, "Turn around."

I gave him the time he needed to understand what was coming, to know what I was about to deliver, that I would be changing the way he looked, the way he walked, and the way he would swallow for the rest of his life, that all of this was brought about by my hands.

"Johnny!" he yelled.

It should be noted he never pronounced my name the same way again; it forever sounded like this: "*Shonny.*"

I swung against his face with all my strength, leveled him. If it might be possible to propel the soul out of a human being by sheer force, I came close to doing it here. His body twisted in nearly a full circle, a drunken ballerina, falling into the mud facedown. I left him gurgling there for a moment, then reached down, grabbed him, and flipped him over.

"Get up."

Both hands to his face, he shouted, "*Shonny!*"

"Up."

And when he finally stumbled to his feet, I swung again and cracked his right knee. Ettore was brought into this world bow-legged, but he would spend the rest of his life knock-kneed.

I let Ettore scream it out for a minute, then stumbled over him, knelt on his chest, grabbed the tire iron by both ends and pushed the center down over his neck. The look in his eyes was pleading, for he could carry none of the grace the McCartneys did when mercy showed them no sign of arrival. His choking and gagging could only be interpreted as some form of begging.

I leaned over him, and as the rain and my blood and my spit dripped onto his mud-covered face, I said, "Yeah, this is happening."

Ettore whimpered.

Then I unleashed. "Now listen to me. You never go near the girl. For the rest of your life you never go near her. You don't think about her. You don't even mention her name. Don't ever use the word *melody* again, *capice*? You like a song? Call it a tune or jingle, 'cause if I hear you say her name, I will destroy you, you understand me? And don't think what you witnessed back at the grocery was my inability to kill, 'cause you ever go near Melody I'll blow a hole in your chest big enough to thread with this tire iron."

Ettore made a feeble attempt to raise me off of him, like he was trying to bench-press an engine block. I pushed down on the tire iron and he coughed up a dark mixture of fluids.

And here is where I may have become a true Bovaro, for I played the card: "You're a loser, Ettore. You're nothing in this family. I'm Tony Bovaro's son, and we both know all I have to do is mention what you did to me today and they'll end you. What you fail to realize is that I outrank you, and I always will. You matter as much as that Beretta. Even your mother had to have known what a loser you'd be, couldn't even name you after a saint." Then with one last final push: "So, here's how it's going down. I didn't touch you and you didn't touch me. This never happened. When we get back to New York, you don't mention the girl. You can take all the credit for the killings and be the hero. As for our wounds, I don't care what you say, but that's it, you understand? Not another word about the girl. I find out she so much as gets a hangnail, I'm coming after *you* and I'm bringing something better than a tire iron."

I pulled the steel bar from his neck, stood up, cast a gray shadow over him.

"Not another word about the girl."

Ettore sputtered for some time after that, sprawled back in the mud like an abandoned scarecrow. Then, finally, "Okay... okay, Shonny."

To say there was a celebration upon our return would be incorrect. After all the stress and lost sleep the McCartneys caused my father, you might imagine ticker tape would have fallen from the sky, that our wounds might have been concealed by an avalanche of confetti, but that was never the way it went, even when it came to taking out the McCartneys. When Ettore and I walked into the kitchen of my parents' recently purchased English Tudor across the Hudson in

Tenafly, New Jersey, my father was leaning on the counter, wiping dry the remnants of a small bowl of red sauce with a slice of bread. The first he'd seen or heard of us since we departed, he looked up, stared at the clots and bruises on our faces, Ettore's odd stance.

"Hell happened?" he said.

Ettore cleared his throat, tried not to look at me. "C'ran over-ush in loh ash wuhwuh leafin'." *A car ran over us in the lot as we were leaving.*

Pop approached us, looked at me first. "You okay?"

"We'll survive. Right, Ettore?"

My father touched my cheek gently, looked at the scrapes and swollen flesh. His face sagged into a pout, was the closest I'd ever seen him come to expressing regret. But the years had depleted him, and the distance between regret and revenge had shortened. His expression soon turned into Bovaro anger, a burst of required retribution.

"Not the guy's fault. We took care of it," I said, then, changing the subject, "Ettore's a hard worker. Mom and Dad are out of the picture."

Pop took a step back and nodded, passed a subtle grin of approval. "The girl?"

Ettore looked down.

I answered, "I learned everything I could ever need to know from my cousin. The girl is mine. Don't worry, Pop. I'll take care of her. That right, Ettore?"

My dad moved to my cousin, put his hand behind his neck. "This was clean?" Ettore nodded. Pop smiled, reached around and hugged my cousin, whispered something in Italian, likely a verbal commendation. And as my father tightened his embrace, I could see Ettore's hands shake in agony, hear his staccato breathing.

Ettore ended up being celebrated for his kills, marginally elevated in our family and crew, famed for doing what no one else could achieve. He had eliminated the more important of the witnesses—what juror would truly rely on what someone witnessed as a six-year-old from over a decade earlier?—and provided proof of how impervious the Bovaros were to prosecution. And from that honored moment, he became Shimmy Vido, aptly nicknamed for the way his lame leg would wiggle from side to side with every step, remembered for his acts of heroism with a life of disrespect and indifference:

"Go send Jimmy and Shimmy down there to talk to him."

"Hey, Sh-Sh-Shimmy! What's sh-sh-shaking?"

"Throw me a beer, you friggin' gimp."

As for me, I made it clear across my father's organization that Melody was in my sights, that I would make good on taking her out, that her eventual elimination would be my absolution. That *no one else was to touch her.* But it must be understood that my absolution did not rest in her elimination, but in her insulation. If there existed any hope for my redemption, it had to be in becoming her shield.

She was all mine to take care of. All mine.

FIVE

By the time I reached my twenty-fourth birthday, it was undisputed: I became the family member no Bovaro really understood. Most families have one member who bucks the norm.

I became the rebel.

As my brothers contributed more and more to my family's burgeoning organization, I managed to keep myself involved at an arm's length. Though I might not have always been part of the decision making, I certainly remained a participant in the conversations. In our crew, we didn't exactly find a conference room and follow an agenda; conclusions are drawn and plans derived over a plate of veal or eggplant. And I certainly continued to do my share of the household chores; as the months came and went, so did the extortive measures, the cleansing of ill-gotten gains.

Unfortunately, my criminal mind was elsewhere.

I had one regret from that fateful event in Mineral Point, and that was not having gone back to look for Melody, to find out what happened to her. An impossibility, for sure—only the most foolish criminals let curiosity prod them to return to the scene of their crime—but the films my brain played of what happened after Ettore and I raced from that little town became worse and worse over time.

You can only fantasize about something for so long before you begin devising the plan to make it real, regardless of the audacity, regardless of the consequence. Wondering what happened to Melody nearly consumed me. I left her worse off, you see, parentless and with only one way to struggle through her remaining days on earth: the government, an organization apparently ill-equipped to keep its addicted employees from being leveraged into providing sensitive data to people like . . . me. I imagined her everywhere—the Northwest, southern Texas, rusting Ohio and Michigan villages—and the fact that I could not verify even the most insignificant detail wore me down. Though worst of all, I became obsessed with wondering what became of her, wanting to know she was okay. I could have gone directly to Randall Gardner and demand he hand over whatever he could find on where Melody had been transported, but what would've been the point? At that time everyone *wanted* me to find Melody, to finish what Ettore and I had started.

I'd begun taking an active role in some of my father's restaurants, the end of our business that left the least bitter flavor in my mouth. While these establishments were being used to launder almost all of the money running through the organization, everything else about them was legit. I loved the chefs and the kitchen camaraderie; the way the entire operation ran like a well-timed engine—the bar, the hostesses, the cooks, the servers—everything coming together like a tornado forming out of turbulent air; the way my clothes smelled of garlic and basil and fry oil at the end of each day. Unlike my brothers, who were more involved in the other operations—say, carting or gambling efforts. They suffered through the onslaught of liars, threats, beatings. And trash.

And so I attended a second-rate cooking school in lower Manhattan, a now defunct institution later converted into a pair of bars and an art gallery. My goal was twofold: (1) to enhance my ability to provide new culinary offerings; and (2) to occupy every available resource in my brain, to squelch the rising compulsion to locate Melody.

Not much came of the culinary aspect. Nearly all of my classmates were there escaping some other oppressive thing: pressure from the do-something-with-your-life parent, drug addiction, unbearable loneliness. The result was a class of underperformers and distracted twenty- and thirtysomethings. As it turned out, I knew more about some cooking techniques than my instructors, and couldn't help correcting them, including a fifteen-minute debate on the proper way to sauté garlic and onions. In the end, it gave me the opportunity to experiment out of my depth (learning how to make a brick roux) and to learn a few new things (the patience required to make a brick roux). A few months into class, a flirtation came my way, a sweet auburn-headed girl with a face of freckles set in celestial patterns and a voice as rich and soothing as Karen Carpenter's. Coming in from Staten Island, she showed no visible response when I told her my full name, and that alone allowed me to open up to her. We inadvertently became class partners, worked our labs together, and developed an unspoken language of how to best work the kitchen, understanding what each other needed next, when to get out of each other's way, when either of us needed coaching or help starting over; we became *in sync* in ways some married couples are never blessed to know. We began a casual intimate relationship that lasted a while. A season, maybe. The girl was stunning, a source of envy to any man I introduced her to, particularly my brothers, who noted the aspects of her face and body and recorded them to mental scorecards.

Having partnered in class, we shortly partnered in everything else after that. We shared the laughter and the personal interest and the physical intimacy that typically serve as requirements for moving toward a greater commitment. But the never-discussed distance between us was exactly as wide as my failures. And as our bodies would be wrapped together in my loft above one of my father's restaurants, I would almost always drift, my eyes turning unfocused and hazy. She would gently rub her fingers over the scars on my body, never asking for the stories that would explain them.

And then the last night: Our bodies had just relaxed, a thin layer of cooling sweat between us, and her soft fingers gently traced the scar on my forehead, the one provided by Ettore. I stared out the window into the blur of streetlights. She stopped stroking my temple, froze for a few seconds before her body went completely limp.

I could sense her staring at me. "Where are you?" she said.

How could I explain? I was in the Northwest, southern Texas, rusting Ohio and Michigan villages.

Then: "Is there someone else?"

I let out a quiet sigh before eventually answering. "Not the way you're thinking."

The end of the semester meant my less occupied mind had no excuse to remain in New York; the fantasy would be actualized.

The mere suggestion of locating Melody—under the guise of her elimination—was welcomed by all. At this point, my father wanted everything finished on the McCartney docket, and he was becoming impatient with my insistence on doing it myself. The trip to see Randall was imminent. He'd just become a senior database administrator with Justice, which meant he could access almost any records he chose without a trace—on the *back end*, as he called it—one of a very few trusted technologists who could see data without officially entering into the system as a general user. Randall knew the value of his currency had improved, and he tried once—*once*—to raise the stakes with us, to suggest he and anyone from our crew might be peers, that our relationship should be valued mutually. This notion was quickly corrected by way of a visit to Randall's home by me and Peter, during which Peter slammed Randall's face down onto his computer keyboard so many times that once Randall fell back into his office chair, the Y, G, and M keys were stuck to his forehead. Our relationship, going forward, was fully understood.

And regardless of the level of his current debt, even if he had been paid in full he would have done as we asked. We *owned* him at that point. We had become bullies who treated him with a neutral spirit as long as he always forked over his lunch money without dispute.

The lunch money he gave us that early summer day: Shelly Jones, Lawrenceburg, Kentucky.

SIX

The drive was far more enjoyable without my psycho cousin. Being alone with my thoughts outranked being alone with Ettore. The journey was taken in the promised reward from my father for my attempts on the McCartneys: a late-model black Ford Mustang convertible, a car representing something I constantly wanted to forget. It did, however, *move.* Once I'd escaped New York and suffered through the overburdened New Jersey, Pennsylvania, and Maryland highways, entering West Virginia couldn't have felt more welcome if the state had opened its lonely arms and pulled me to its chest. Interstate 79, which cuts a swath through the center of the state like a giant comma, might be the most abandoned road you can travel, the road cresting and descending countless mountaintops, where the speed limit was seventy miles per hour and where my speed was limited only by what the car felt comfortable delivering. The Mustang never complained.

Even if I'd not seen the WELCOME TO KENTUCKY sign as I crossed the line, I would have known I'd arrived. Traveling west out of Huntington, West Virginia, on Interstate 64, you can sense the change in the environment, as though those who settled Kentucky looked over their shoulders and casually said to the east, "You can keep all of that." Kentucky fields really *are* green, smooth and curved like the terrain of a woman's body, blemished only by horses of random size and color. This land of horse racing and whiskey gave me the sense that people here were healthy and happy—happy supplying the raw materials for the addictions my family kept alive and well in those beneath us. And as I made my way westward, I became increasingly pleased that Melody would be able to reside here for whatever amount of time was allowed.

I'd left New York at six in the morning on that Saturday in late June. By the time I was nearing Lawrenceburg, it was only five-thirty that afternoon. The anticipation of seeing Melody deepened in my chest as each mile drew closer, a sensation I didn't understand then, like retrieving a long-missed lover from the airport. I knew I could essentially hide in plain sight around her. She would have no idea who I was, what I looked like, what car I might drive, no sense that any threat was present. I had no nagging duty to truly eliminate her—just the pretend one serving as my purpose for being there—and no nagging partner trying to manage the operation.

When I finally arrived in Lawrenceburg, it seemed clear the government had actually figured a way to deposit Melody directly into the Middle of Nowhere. If there was a welcome sign on the edge of town, I'd missed it. Even the courthouse failed to have the word Lawrenceburg on it, merely the county name. What a perfect place to dump her—in a town with no identity of its own. And as I drifted through the maze of humble streets, Justice's strategy of relocating witnesses came together as though I'd solved a clever mystery before its end: Every town was the same. If you could take a giant iron and flatten the hills of Mineral Point, you would have Lawrenceburg, Kentucky. There was little to distinguish these villages other than the natural topography of the land; their interiors were almost identical.

I unintentionally slowed as I drove closer to Melody's address, holding the directions in one hand and alternately steering and downshifting with the other. I wound down a side street of fresh gravel that left a cloud of white smoke in my trail, the only cloud drifting toward an empty sky. Then, with a drop of the directions to the floor of the car, there I was, at my final destination.

Randall Gardner was a dead man.

The building residing at the address he gave me—901 New Frankfort Road—was an aged redbrick building with the words GREENFIELD ELEMENTARY etched into a concrete cornice, green mold outlining the shaded letters, and a fungus-stained roof. I parked my car tightly between two enormous pickup trucks, lit a cigarette, filled my lungs, and cracked the window to let the smoke escape. At first glance the building still appeared to be an elementary school, right down to the basketball courts off to its side and the American flag flying in front. It wasn't until I watched an older lady carry a full laundry basket back toward the double doors of the main entrance that I realized this place was something other than it appeared. I watched a few minutes more as two other people came and went, concluded the school had been converted into apartments or condos. That being the case, what Randall had failed to give me was an apartment number. Still dead. The place was undeniably depressing, though, residents living in a school, as though having been forced to relive childhood embarrassments and shortcomings, serving a life sentence of detention.

So what choice did I have? I sat and waited and hoped I'd know what Melody might look like now. My glimpses of her had always been fleeting, mere seconds or minutes each time. In my mind, I had burned an indelible image, an amalgam of little bits and pieces I managed to capture over my distant views, no more accurate than a rendering drawn by a sketch artist. But it wouldn't have taken much to throw me—shorter or longer hair, an extra twenty-five pounds, an excessive tan—and she'd walk right by me, nothing more than the strangers we should have been to each other.

The few people who did come and go were all elderly, and I

thought perhaps this place was some form of a residence for seniors, a small-town version of a retirement community for the forgotten, the local elders who arrived at the end of their childless lives. You didn't have to go any farther than the parking lot to sense that this facility was used to tuck people away until they passed on, a building full of temporary compartments for inconvenient people.

I suppose this place was perfect for Melody.

But when the young woman opened the door and slowly walked out, I knew the picture in my mind was more accurate than I could have imagined. Even from my distance of a hundred feet or so, there was no doubt that I had just found Melody Grace McCartney, no matter what name showed on her mail at this address.

I immediately snuffed my smoke and closed my window.

She walked far enough from the doorway to stand in the evening sun, and it illuminated the latest color of her hair—bright blond—which had been styled into a cut much shorter than when I last saw her. She wore a short sundress that could've been confused for a camisole, and as she stood in the sun, she tugged down on the edge of the dress, trying to pull it lower, as though the purpose of the outfit was more important than her comfort in wearing it. She looked at her sandals for a second, then sort of glanced up at the sky in a curious way. She straightened her posture and slowly smoothed out her sundress with the palm of her hand and I could see her chest rise with a deep breath. I slithered down in my seat as I watched. And as she let out that breath, it appeared she exhaled all of her intentions along with it; her shoulders deflated just like her lungs. She looked over her shoulder at the front door of the school with an it's-not-too-late reticence.

Whatever held her back eventually set her free. She made her way to a Honda Civic parked three spots behind me, tugging on the hem of her dress the entire walk. I slid even farther down, as far as possible while still maintaining sight of her car in my side-view mirror.

I let her pull out of her parking place and drive some distance before starting my car and casually catching up, keeping a few cars between us.

We ended up driving for a decent duration. She made her way to Route 62 and started heading east, tracing the journey I'd just completed, in reverse. The last thing I wanted was more time cramped in the cab of my Mustang, but sitting and waiting for her return didn't really make sense; my need was to make sure she was okay, and watching her walk in and out of her apartment wouldn't fill the requirement. I needed to see her *live.*

After twenty minutes or so, I began praying her destination was Versailles, but the town served as nothing more than a place to change directions, shifting from Route 62 to Route 60, pointing us both in the direction of Lexington.

You would think after all the years of casually watching federal agents staked out on our perimeters, I might have picked up some minor techniques for tailing someone, but I proved to be a lousy student. I found it quite a challenge to keep Melody's car in view while remaining far enough behind that I wasn't in waving distance every time she looked in her rearview mirror. Worse, I hadn't planned well: I was down to a single cigarette and not a drop of fluid to quench my burgeoning thirst.

And then came another unexpected turn. On the outskirts of Versailles, Melody pulled into a Chevron station, parked in front of one of the pumps in the middle of three aisles. Once we were on the road, here was something I'd not considered: stopping. I drifted into the parking lot of the neighboring Arby's and watched her get out of her car and walk into the convenience store of the gas station—except it was more of a nervous jog. Though the air that day was very warm and moist, she moved at a pace more reserved for days with wind chills.

I sat in my car, tapping my fingers on the steering wheel and staring at her Civic. A strange pull came upon me and I felt a gulp in my throat I could not swallow down. Before I could make sense of my actions, I threw the car in gear and slowly made my way to the Chevron, slithered around the lines of gas pumps until I'd positioned myself the perfect angle and distance from Melody's car. I got out and played with my gas cap a little—the most I could really do since I'd filled my tank outside Lawrenceburg just before finding Melody's address. I fiddled with the pump for a moment before the knot in my stomach and the lump in my throat returned and the drug of adrenaline began flooding my veins again. I watched the door of the convenience store, and without understanding the implication of my amateurish bravado, I was getting closer to it with every step.

I opened the door, hit sideways by a stench of stale coffee and onions, greeted with a nod from the clerk behind the counter, a scrawny guy who sported a thinning mullet and so many earrings across his face that it looked as though he'd been blasted with buckshot. He and I were alone in the store; Melody had vanished.

I quickly looked over my shoulder to make sure her Civic remained at the pump, then started walking around the store trying to figure out what to do with all the adrenaline, when it crystallized: I looked toward the pumps again, checking for any vehicle that seemed vaguely official, that maybe she *had* spotted me in her rearview, that she'd been supplied year after year with a cache of photos of our family and crew along with the statement *If you see any of these guys then page us*, that she called the feds on her cell, that they told her, *Keep driving*, that this was the reason she drove so far, that they would be waiting at the Chevron in Versailles. *When you get to the station, Melody,* run *inside and we will be waiting for you.*

As I assembled these thoughts—and the respective dread—I went to the refrigerated section and pulled out a massive bottle of water and walked around as though the biker mags and lottery tickets were really what had drawn me to this place.

I took my water to the counter and asked Mullet if he'd seen a girl come in.

"Girl?" Mullet's muted response came with a glance to a small television below the counter where I could hear a crowd cheering. "Reds suck."

"Not a girl. A young woman." I nodded to the case behind him. "Four packs of Marlboros, quickly."

Mullet mumbled as he placed the packs on the counter next to my water. "Woman?"

I started eyeing the store. "Where's the back door?"

That snapped Mullet to attention. "Come again?"

My first thought was, *That was how they got her out.* My second thought was, *That is how I'm getting out, too.*

Mullet continued, "Why do you need to know where the back—"

"Listen, bumpkin, did a girl just come in here and magically disappear? Is it really possible, as the sole operator of this store, that you managed to miss a customer both arriving and departing?"

"I don't think I saw—I don't really know—"

"*I don't I don't I don't.* Listen, you friggin' hick, I'm only gonna ask you once more: Did you—"

My rant was squelched out by a piercing screech of hinges, then a quick slam of a door from an overly tightened spring. I looked up, and straight over Mullet's head in the dim reflection of the window behind the counter I watched Melody step out of the restroom.

I stared at her image in the glass, said to Mullet with quiet anger, "How 'bout now. You see her now?"

She paused in front of the Hostess display, picked up a package of orange cupcakes and studied it as though looking for an expiration date. I always wondered who ate those things. My senses sharpened; I became so aware.

I could hear the gentle crinkling of the cellophane as she turned over each package.

I could see the shape of her face change as she licked her teeth.

I could feel the sweat arrive in my palms.

Mullet struggled to glance at the television out of the corner of his eye like a seventh-grader cheating off a neighbor's test. I snapped my fingers a few times and whispered, "What do I owe you?"

As Mullet punched the keys on the register, Melody meandered toward the counter, glancing at various food products on her way. Mullet tossed a number my direction and I missed it. I couldn't take my eyes off the reflection in the glass. Melody reached into a plastic barrel filled with ice and sodas and pulled out a Diet Coke, shook a small cube off the top of the can, and ran the cold residue between her fingers until it was dry.

I tried again. "What do I owe you?"

Mullet leaned forward and curled his hook-filled lip. "I'm only gonna tell you once more."

I think he did tell me again. Who knows; my attention was elsewhere.

Melody slid right behind me and the front of air she shoved my way was laced with sweet flowers. It came and went within two or three seconds.

Then Mullet: "How about a third time, partner. Easier if I write it down?"

I slowly reached behind me and lifted my wallet from my jeans, so near to Melody that I could have opened my hand with the fantasy that she would put hers in mine; it was the closest I'd ever been to her in my life. At that moment, I didn't try to comprehend why the thought of holding her hand went through my head, but it was distinct and undeniable.

I pulled out some bills and tossed them to Mullet. As he gave me my change, he smiled and said, "Thank you, sir, for your kind patronage of our country convenience store and gas station!"

I walked from the store head down, facing away from Melody,

and returned to my car. I tossed the smokes and water on the passenger seat and slid down on the driver's side as I spied her through the window of the store, handing over her orange cupcakes, watching her smile as she had casual conversation with Mullet. I made sure, too, that Mullet wasn't pointing in my direction, with a *that guy was looking for you* demeanor. I watched her walk out and the urgency in her pace was gone. She drifted lightly, the hem of her dress bouncing in time with each step.

When Melody returned to the pumps, she swiped her card into the reader and began filling her tank. Remember the threshold, the next step? It came upon me here:

I took a huge swig of water and exited my car and began to top off my already full tank. I stood at the end of the Mustang, this time in clear view of Melody, making sure I did not stare at her directly. Once she set the lock on the pump handle, she crossed her arms and closed her eyes as a warm breeze blew over her. After she let out a sigh, her eyes began to drift around the station. She glanced at the couple arguing over a map in a late-model Lincoln. She stared a moment at the farmer boy standing beside his father's muddy pickup. She watched the door of the convenience store, as if expecting a close friend or relative to emerge at any second.

Then, with a slow turn, she faced me. Her eyes landed directly on my face, and no amount of strength, courage, or common sense could prevent the magnetic pull that forced me to twist my face and body so that we were staring directly at each other. Eye to eye. I could feel the corners of my mouth twist into a weak smile as we looked at each other.

And then: nothing.

Melody did not respond to my smile. She didn't even respond to the fact that there was some stimulus in her field of view. Her eyes drifted on to the next person, an overweight businessman struggling to keep his tie from getting dirty as he filled his front tire with air. I meant nothing to her, just a patron of a gas station. There was no outward opinion of my appearance or who I might be, no implication that I was any more worth talking to than the farmer boy or the overweight businessman. There was definitely no love at first sight. I was nothing. Nobody. A stranger.

If only she knew.

Stocked with nicotine and water, I tailed her twenty-five minutes to what was thankfully her final destination: the city center of Lexington. We settled in a parking garage in the downtown area adjacent to the convention center, a part of town that appeared renovated and expanded over the last two decades, based on the designs of the buildings. It looked like any city's financial center—like all the ones I'd passed on the way from New York, really—but with its integrated parks and walkways, the design came across as part of a grander plan as opposed to a reaction to growth and sprawl.

If I'd found tracking Melody in my car a challenge (I'd nearly lost her at two different lights), it was almost impossible to stay concealed once we were on foot. She parked on the third floor of the garage, and I halfway up the fourth. I slipped a pack of smokes in my jeans, put on my sunglasses and a stained Yankees cap unearthed from under the passenger seat, closed the door of my car by pushing my weight against it to soften the sound. As she walked down the eastern glass-encased stairwell, I raced to the western and watched her from a distance of a few hundred feet, mirrored her pace as she went down each flight. We arrived on the sidewalk of Broadway Road at the exact same time.

She immediately turned and walked toward the town center with apparent intent. My hope was that she was meeting a friend, a date, a lover—anything to indicate that a glimmer of happiness might be on her horizon. The point of my entire journey, of the tailing and tracking and watching, was to see if the damage I had created in her life was on the wane, somehow being replaced with joy or contentment, that healthy relationships had developed in her life. What I witnessed once I starting walking in the shadow of her paces that day was not only the opposite of my hope for her, but it might have been the worst-case scenario.

Melody had not gone to Lexington to shop. She did not navigate the office buildings to meet with her accountant or lawyer or dentist. She did not visit a bar or restaurant or coffeehouse, go to see her favorite band or watch a movie. Yet she walked the streets with a specific destination in mind, a target I did not first understand even while making the journey alongside her. Her pace did not slow until we reached Lexington Park in the center of town, a triangle defined by Main, Vine, and Broadway, a scale version of Central Park, trees and trails watched over by skyscrapers. At one far edge, an enormous fountain in the style of water running down bleachers curved around the perimeter for more than a hundred feet, a work of urban art that would've been equally as admired in Manhattan. Adolescent kids played in the fountain behind signs that read PLEASE DO NOT PLAY IN THE FOUNTAIN. Couples held hands and walked slowly, joggers zipped around walkers, bikers zipped around joggers. University of Kentucky students paraded through with clothing indicating their respective fraternities and sororities. And it was here, at this large gathering place, that Melody came to a stop.

She looked around in a manner that less suggested she was looking for someone than that she was looking for the right spot. I sheltered myself a safe distance off and to the side, away from the fountain and under the shade of three towering maples. As I lit a cigarette, Melody moved closer to the fountain, approached a bench built directly in the path of the park.

Here's where things went awry: Melody sat down carefully,

crossed her legs tightly, then gently pulled *up* on the edge of her sundress. She sort of studied herself, ran her hand down the length of her leg, then leaned forward a little, allowing the front of her dress to lower and open slightly. She'd become the opposite of the woman standing on the steps of her apartment building. I considered this might be an attempt to look sexy for someone specific, except the look on her face was clearly one of not looking for anyone at all, of trying too hard to appear casual and disinterested. When I'm waiting for someone, my eyes are either constantly searching the landscape or checking my cell; Melody, with sunglasses on, simply tipped her head back and let the late-day sun bake her face as countless men and women passed her by.

In my continued effort to understand what was happening, I began to drift. The way she sat captured me, the way she'd crossed her legs, how her high-heeled sandals fit the curves of her feet, how she would run her finger in small circles around her knee—I lost a cigarette's worth of time. The thin straps of her dress barely held it to her body, making it easy to imagine her in a piece of lingerie; her sundress was little more.

I lit another cigarette with the smoldering end of the near-dead one in my mouth, snuffed the stub with the heel of my shoe. Melody sat in the hot sun for fifteen minutes, never looking for anyone, never checking a cell, never even looking down other than to readjust her dress to a more suggestive manner.

Not long after that, though, her demeanor changed and, in the process, exposed her purpose. As the people of Lexington continued to pass her by, she started *watching* them pass her by. I sat in my safety zone, unable to take my eyes off of her—for a multitude of reasons now—and this is when it struck me: *I was the only one looking.*

She would make note of a guy or group of guys coming her way and act nonchalant, but as they passed her without even a single glance, she'd watch them fade out of her view. After a half hour of being invisible to these collegiate and urban Kentuckians, she began to slouch her shoulders with each missed opportunity. Every day of my life I walk by people and never notice a single thing about them; New York is an abyss of anonymity and we're trained to ignore. How many people have I passed whose only hope is that someone, anyone, would fill this simple yearning: *Please notice me.* For Melody it had slowly built into a scream, so loud I couldn't understand why no one would come to her rescue.

I'd always been a moderate smoker, but by that time I was on my fifth successive cigarette; no amount of nicotine could alleviate my rising anxiety. I cursed as each passing guy would walk right by, or glance weakly and not return his eyes to her, as though she wasn't worth a second look. Because she *was*. What were they missing? Every yuppie doofus, every frat bastard who ignored her brought a deeper drag to my smoke. Watching her became so painful that I could barely contain myself, finally acknowledging why my eyes were moist: Melody was breaking my heart.

No matter what the government had turned her into, whoever they wanted her to be, she was still just a girl longing for attention. I could see it as plain as the sun on her skin. Based on my age, I did a quick calculation and realized she was probably just shy of twenty-one, and with that realization, I saw a glimpse of her future: In a matter of months, the parks would turn into bars, where she would surely catch the eye of some loser looking to fulfill his fleeting need, and where, for a few moments in an evening, Melody, too, would feel wanted, and the feeling would last until she returned home alone to a house with only one place setting, one bath towel, one toothbrush. The sadness would seep into her lonely life and she would find a desperate longing to connect again, alcohol softening her sadness and allowing her to open up to a lower level of loser. I was not going to let it happen.

I was going to save her before it was too late.

I was going to end it all, blow my cover. What was the point of all my worrying about her happiness and safety if I could not ensure its existence? Someone was going to notice her the way she deserved to be, and it would be me. Regardless of what she might think of me as a man, whether I was her type or not, I would send her home that day with the notion that someone found beauty in her. And as I rose to my feet and snuffed my cigarette, my services were no longer required, for this is when *they* arrived.

Three white guys who'd been smoking and laughing near the fountain's edge wandered in Melody's direction and eventually passed her. From my distance they appeared nondescript and average, neither yuppies nor frat boys, just a trio of unshaven twenty-somethings with lanky bodies and baggy clothes, their only oddity how overdressed they were on that hot Kentucky day, the tallest one wearing a sweat jacket with the hood up; had they continued on their way, I would have categorized them as nothing more than locals.

But the one in the sweat jacket finally gave Melody what she so longed for: a double take. Then she gave him what he was looking for: a response. He slowed and bobbed on his feet a little, then casually walked backward. I watched as he said something to her and she smiled a little. As his friends continued walking away, the guy said something else and Melody nodded and said something back. They chatted for no more than fifteen seconds before Melody sent up an involuntary red flag: She reached down to the top of her sundress and pulled it back up to cover the gap that exposed her chest, then a quick pull down on the bottom of her dress to cover her legs. The guy continued talking, smiling a little more as he spoke, then Melody looked down at the ground and uncrossed her legs, pressed her knees together tightly.

I closed my eyes, shook my head. Not this guy, I thought. Why'd it have to be this guy?

I reached for my cigarettes and started to pull one out when the most nightmarish scene began to unfold: The other two guys turned around to find their friend lingering with the girl, then started heading back in his direction.

As Melody stood, Sweat Jacket slid in front of her, blocking my view of her face, and as I ran into the grass to reposition my angle, the other two guys were now at their buddy's side and the four of them were in a circle. The noises of the park—the flow of water from the enormous fountain, kids playing and shrilling, booming music coming from some distant point—masked what was unfolding before the public. Even from my distance they just looked like friends chatting. But when Sweat Jacket started nudging his friends, and his friends responded with inflated laughter, and Melody reacted by bowing her head and shaking it slowly, I knew things were progressing. I grew up around people who could smell vulnerability and preyed upon it for nothing more than entertainment. That's what these guys were, future wards of the state.

I flicked my unlit cigarette into the grass, mumbled every profane word I'd ever learned as I slid closer to the scene, still out of range of their conversation. But watching their interaction, there could be no doubt as to what was happening. And as parents walked by with their kids, they stepped up their pace and pulled their children to their sides, a few frat boys looked over until one of Sweat Jacket's buddies stared at them, stepped once in their direction to indicate they should mind their own business, and compliance was delivered in the form of indifference. Turns out no matter where you go in this world everyone is the same.

I didn't see a thing.

I didn't hear a thing.

I don't know nothin'.

Then Sweat Jacket reached out and touched Melody's shoulder and she jerked away like the tips of his fingers were aflame. She stepped to the left and one of the other guys leaned in, forcing her back toward their apparent leader, and for a few seconds she nervously bounced between the three of them like a human hacky sack.

When Sweat Jacket grabbed her elbow, she yanked it away and managed to slip out and abandon them at a good clip. I walked in parallel with her a hundred or more feet away and kept my eyes on the guys. *Let her go,* I thought. *Do not follow her.* With Melody now twenty or so feet in front of them, Sweat Jacket cracked a joke for his buddies that I could not hear, grabbed his crotch in an exaggerated manner, and then the three of them were right on her tail.

I followed Melody, and as we made our way back to Broadway, I knew exactly where Melody was heading: the parking garage. She would look over her shoulder every five seconds to see if they were still close behind, and having grown up in a neighborhood with a class order determined by bullies, I knew this manner of showing her fear would keep them interested. And then the final turning point: Melody slipped across a six-lane intersection next to the garage before the light changed; the guys didn't make it in time, had no choice but to let the traffic pass. This is where I would have expected them to move on, to yell some lewd comments in her direction, wave her off, and return to their wasted world.

But they waited the light out.

As I ran across the street a half block away, dodging cars in every lane, I voiced vulgarities I had no idea were in my vocabulary. I knew Melody's exact destination, almost right to the specific parking space; all I had to do was break our triangle apart and cut off the hoodlums before they could get to her.

I reached the western stairwell and ran up the steps so fast that I fell into the door and the sound as it flew open reverberated throughout the garage like a gunshot. Melody emerged from the eastern stairwell, moving as quickly as she could in her sandals, aimed right for her car. I let her get out of sight, then sprinted for the stairwell she'd just exited. I opened the door, slid to the left and closed the door gently, watched Melody through a small square window, catching my breath as quietly as possible. I was certain she was going to make it, that the timing of all of this would work, until the heel of her left sandal gave way; she lost her footing but not her momentum, and tumbled across the concrete floor like she was sliding into home.

And there she stayed for too many seconds, an uncomfortable gap in time before she slowly turned to her side and grabbed her ankle. My instinct, as foolish as it would have been, was to run out and help her, but even in the frenzy of that moment I knew the help she really needed had to be applied elsewhere.

Below I could hear the trio ascending the stairs.

Had she not taken the spill, she would have slipped away; her lead was simply running out.

The losers were one flight below, laughing and verbally offering their crude intentions for this innocent girl.

I took off my sunglasses and crammed them in the pocket of my jeans, turned my baseball cap backward.

Melody, now crying, pulled herself to her feet, tried to resume running, but nearly fell to the ground again.

The losers came into view at the landing one half flight below. Sweat Jacket had his hood pulled tightly around his head, adjusted himself through his jeans.

Melody could barely walk, bracing herself on the trunks and hoods of the cars she passed. She did not have her keys out, and she was too far from her car. Melody was not going to make it.

And as the three hoodlums stepped up to the top of the flight, stood a mere two feet behind me, Sweat Jacket put his hand on my shoulder, gave me a weak shove, and said, “Look out.”

I sighed, turned from the door to face the men, knocked Sweat Jacket’s hand from my shoulder and simply stated, “I’m afraid this is where your journey ends.”

I spent my life assessing tough guys, who could be beaten and who couldn't. Respectively, the three guys facing me in the garage stairwell were amateurs, juvenile delinquents in the bodies of adults. My ultimate reaction to the hoodlums was driven partly by adrenaline, but not at all by bravado. Imagine three toddlers coming your way in an attempt to wreak havoc. How concerned would you really be?

Sweat Jacket, clearly the leader, as demonstrated by his constant position at the front and center of the other two, stood about three inches taller than me and six taller than his buddies, morons who giggled and laughed at anything Sweat Jacket said or did. Each of them appeared to be emaciated, thinner versions of their once healthier selves, their skin hanging on them like garments from a heavier season of their lives. They hesitated in front of me only to catch their collective breath.

So, if bravado played no role in my reaction and adrenaline a minimal one, what drove my response to these men? The answer is embedded in the snapshots that flooded my mind, the images of what might have happened if I were not there that day, what Sweat Jacket would have done to Melody, and what his hangers-on would have emulated shortly thereafter, the way they would've torn her apart in a vile and violent way, how she would learn the lesson that nothing and no one in this life can be trusted and how there is not much worth living for, how they would have reinforced the notion that she was nobody, echoing what the federal government had already imprinted in her young mind: She was nothing more than an object to be used and discarded. Regardless of how I managed to be there at the right time, how I managed to eliminate this destructive and potentially deadly event from Melody's life, understand that I am not a hero. I am not a guardian angel, for no angel could do what I am capable of, for what I ended up doing in that stairwell. The simple answer to that question is this: My reaction to those three men was based on a torrent of unabated hatred and rage.

Sweat Jacket tried—failed—to shove me to the side, decided yelling at me might get the reaction he desired. "Fugoutamaway!"

"No," I said, "and I'm telling you now this is probably going to turn out badly for the three of you."

"Dude, don't mess with me!"

One of Sweat Jacket's buddies—can't remember which one—added a warning inside a chuckle: "Serious, dude, you don't wanna mess with Willie."

"Oh, the mess is unavoidable. The challenge for me will be beating you to the point where I don't actually kill you."

Willie smirked, tried to move me to the side again with no success. Remember: toddler. He bobbed his head a few times like a prizefighter, looked more like a chicken. "Let me help you figure something out," he said. "It's three-on-one."

"No, it's not," I said. "It's one-on-one. You think these idiots are gonna help you? They only hang out with you to continue their access to meth and get your assistance writing bad checks at Wal-Mart. I'm gonna put you down, Willie, and they're going to stand here and watch. Maybe cry a little."

Willie squinted as though genuinely confused as to what was happening, then leaned in. "Dude, I don't know where you think you are, but—"

"What the—why is everyone calling me dude? Am I wearing a frigging cowboy hat? Listen, you redneck mother—" The door behind us swung open and into the stairwell walked a young father carrying a little girl in his arms. He slid by nervously, eyeing each of us as he maintained a two-foot buffer, had to scrape the wall to get around. "And that's why the Reds don't have a prayer, man. I could have called that in spring training. Seriously, their entire roster is full of guys batting in the high two hundreds. I'm telling you, the Cubs are who you should be watching. They got a few surprises coming this year, and I'm not the only one saying that."

Willie seemed to pick up on what I was doing, though not bright enough to contribute. His buddies looked completely bewildered.

From the corner of my eye, I glanced out the little square window, could see Melody fumbling with her keys. She pressed the button to unlock her car, the taillights flashed in response.

Right as the door at the bottom of the stairwell closed with a bang, I balled up a fistful of Willie's jacket and smashed him into the concrete wall next to the windows overlooking the street. He started pawing my forearms.

"Dude!" he yelled.

I got in his face and whispered, "I promise I will try not to kill you. *Try* not to kill you."

"What's your problem, man?"

I tightened the ball of material, shoved it up under his chin. The idiots stood back a little, rocked in circular patterns like Weebles. "Where were you heading? Where were you going with that open fly, stud?"

Willie considered my question, moved his scrunched-up chin and lips without a word, hesitant to form a true answer. We stared into each other's eyes and I could not find a shred of humanity in the void of his expression. The frigging *malocchio*! Ultimately, the answer drifted from his lips, an answer of full disclosure but laced with not a hint of confession.

"Bitch was mine."

And so it went.

I pressed my forearm against his neck and punched his gut with my left hand. As Willie bent over breathless, I yanked back the hood of his sweat jacket, revealing a long ponytail that I wound around my fist, used it to twist his entire body around, then smashed his head against the wall over and over and over until a pasty bloodstain stuck to the painted cinder blocks.

I could hear the engine of Melody's little Civic race as she over-accelerated, the screech of her car as she took the corner near our stairwell at an unsafe speed, the tires making a noise that might have been their attempt at asking for mercy. I glanced out the square window again just as Melody's car drifted from my view, descending the garage, heading directly for the safe streets of Lexington.

I turned to the idiots, Willie's ponytail still in my fist, his head hanging from my hand like a briefcase, his body writhing in my grip as though I were holding a cat by its tail. "What do you say, guys—three-on-one?" One of them stood dumbfounded, the other hopped from foot to foot like he needed to take a leak. "Your fearless leader needs your help."

Willie tried to grab my leg, lame swipes through the open air like a drunk trying to grip a lamppost for support, kept mumbling something that sounded like *double cheeseburger.*

The idiot who couldn't stop moving said, "C'mon, Willie, fight back!"

I laughed so hard my left knee buckled a little, could barely keep from bending over in hysteria. I tightened Willie's ponytail in my hand and twisted his bloodied, cross-eyed face to mine. "What do you say, Willie, want to go another round?" Then I slammed his head into the glass wall overlooking the streets of the city from three floors high. "C'mon, Willie, fight!" I said. *Slam* again. "You can do it, Willie!" *Slam.* "Go, Willie, go!" *Slam. Slam. Slam.*

I released him and his body fell limp and crooked to the cement floor; the only thing missing was a chalk outline.

I stared at the idiots for a few seconds before saying, "So, what did we learn today?"

All I can say is this: dust cloud.

And as Willie's troops abandoned him on the battlefield, I yelled, "Hey, take your trash with you!" I grabbed Willie by his jacket and jeans and tossed his body down the half flight of steps toward the second floor. I considered leaving him with a souvenir, but really didn't care enough about him to make the point.

I could hear the two of them running and tumbling down the steps, then the crash of the door at the bottom of the stairwell. I looked out the window and watched them fly out to the street, scatter in different directions like a pair of roaches.

I opened the door to the garage and gently pulled it closed behind me, no loud bang this time. I casually headed toward my car like I was nothing more than a visitor to the city's center, could still smell the rubber from Melody's frenzied departure, eyed the fresh tire marks she left on the cement, walked them like a tightrope.

By the time I reached the Mustang, pain arrived in all the places that would later require some form of attention, the worst of the bunch a near ripped-off fingernail from the middle finger of my right hand, no doubt still twisted in the fibers of Willie's jacket, along with some of my blood and all of my DNA. I had long since become immune to worrying about the outcome of these violent outbursts, for the Bovaros only acted out on the bottom-dwellers, the drug addicts and criminals—certainly Willie fit the bill; he'd never surrender any truths about that day, especially his attempted rape. Throughout my childhood I had watched guys stumble to their feet, beaten and bruised, only to resist assistance from police, oppressed by some parole violation or outstanding warrant. Willie was going nowhere. Not that day, not ever.

I cascaded down the ramps of the parking garage and drove

out to Broadway, headed directly for Melody's apartment. I pulled into the lot for her building and spotted her Civic parked on the edge. I crept up alongside it and turned my engine off, rolled down my windows. I could hear the engine of her car still ticking as it cooled.

The only thing I could be sure of was that she made it home. I had no assurance that she made it home *safe*. I watched the door of her building, then her car, then the door again. I reclined my seat a little, lit a cigarette, and took a drag that lasted five seconds, closed my eyes and held the smoke in my lungs even longer, felt the rush of the nicotine as the warmth drifted from my chest out to my limbs and my head, into my blood. I blew the smoke out my window and waited.

And waited.

I left three times that evening—once to get a bag of burgers from McDonald's and twice to use the restroom—and each time I returned I parked in a more secluded location, always staying within a clear view of her car and the front door of her apartment, utilizing my recently learned method of triangulation.

I'd venture a guess that during the period of time I surveilled the scene from that distant corner of the parking lot, every single resident of her apartment building came and went—everyone but Melody. I was determined to stay until I saw her again, until she came out from her shelter, until I could be sure she was even marginally okay, that whatever fear or trauma caused by Willie and his *cafoni* had disintegrated or passed. I rolled back my moonroof and a gust of crisp Kentucky air swirled around the interior, a mixture of cut grass and smoldering Kingston charcoal. I stared up at the heavens, dotted with a number of stars never seen in a New York sky. As the clock ticked forward and fewer and fewer people came and went from her building, I waited.

And waited.

The morning came through my windows damp and loud; nests of birds in the branches of the white oaks overhead shrieked with chicks begging for food, a thin layer of dew covered everything: my dash, my windows, the knob of my stick. I flipped my wrist over and glanced at my watch: 7:23. Once I'd finished wiping my eyes, I surveyed the lot and all the cars remained, including Melody's, which had not budged since she returned from Lexington, the front wheels still turned outward and away from the curb as though she had pulled into the spot with great haste.

As noon approached, the air dried and the sun shone through a cloudless sky. That type of easy summer day comes only a few times a year, the kind that instills a certain guilt if you don't find a way to enjoy it, yet there was no sign that Melody might surface, that she might enter the world again in her little sundress, show the only way more beauty could be added to such a perfect day. I hoped for that. But by the time 12:30 arrived, only four cars remained across the entire parking lot; one was Melody's, one was mine, and the other two were unlikely to move: a relic of a pickup that had special license plates designating it as a farm truck, and a banged-up minivan with a flat rear tire.

Almost everyone had returned home by seven that night. The sun had faded away slowly, as did the residents of Melody's apartment building.

I'd spent the day making myself sick on fast food, nicotine, and caffeine, getting cramped and sore in the cab of my Mustang. Unshowered and unshaven for a few days, I was having a hard time being near myself. I'd begun longing for my humble apartment, where I could sprawl across the width of my king-size bed, take a shower so hot it would sting my skin, whip up a plate of peppers and eggs before I launched into my day. Though despite the discomforts of this journey, the aching in my trapezoids from lifting Willie off the ground, the scab around the torn nail of my middle finger that looked to be heading for an infection, the constant return to public restrooms that caused glances of increasing concern to be cast my way, I had no choice but to wait for Melody to surface, to know she was somehow surviving.

That night turned cold, draped itself over me like a wet washcloth on the head of a fevered child. The fluctuation in temperatures drove me crazy, had me balancing the windows and the heat and the air-conditioning throughout my residency in the car. You might think the boredom, though, was what really did me in. I diluted it with the likes of regional newspapers and magazines acquired as an excuse to use the restrooms of local convenience stores, with half of the library of music CDs in my glove compartment, with no less than six baseball games delivered via AM radio, with slowly eaten meals and lengthy prayers. The dullness and tedium did exist, overruled by the anxiety of what was happening behind the door of Melody's apartment. Boredom performs terrible acts upon the imagination: It expands the realm of possibility to its furthest limits, the best- and worst-case scenarios. And I ran through them all with Melody, from casual disinterest about what had happened in Lexington to a resulting case of severe depression to a downright panic toward any future interaction with humanity. I imagined too many times her hiding under the covers, blinds drawn, shaking.

I could never be sure until I saw her.

If I'd brought trouble to Lexington two days earlier, by Monday morning I officially *looked* like trouble. I'd been living out of my car for just over forty-eight hours, and in that parking lot for thirty-six of it. My bathroom existed at an Exxon, my comb was my right hand, my toothbrush my finger. A five o'clock shadow was well on its way to becoming a beard, and my stomach, when not hurting, was audible.

The sun crested at five-thirty that morning and I crept out of my car to stretch and move my body in the motions of my childhood: the swing of a bat, the shot of a basketball, the sweep of a hockey stick. Once I'd finished my limbering, I slipped back in my car to procure more coffee, doughnuts, cigarettes, and a local newspaper, returned and parked a distance from Melody's Civic just as the apartment dwellers with work schedules started to materialize and face the day.

One resident, an attractive woman I would have pegged in her late fifties, came out in a short business dress, wearing makeup and heels that suggested she resented the unstoppable progression of her age—though what stuck with me was that I'd seen her twice already prior to that morning, that I'd been in residency at this apartment building for so long that I was beginning to assemble an accurate catalog of its inhabitants.

In the gap between the emergence of the workers and retirees, I flipped through the *Lexington Herald-Leader*, central Kentucky's local news source. I turned to the crime section, surprised at the level of wrongdoing that occurs in Lexington; Willie and his buddies would eventually find a place they could call home. In the prior twenty-four hours, there'd been two murders in Bourbon County, two arsons in the city of Lexington that suggested they were serial acts, and in Whitley County over fifty guns were stolen from an evidence room at the courthouse. The Bovaro crew had, as an organization, a presence in many cities across the United

States, though nothing in Kentucky as far as I knew. I made a mental note to suggest it to my father; we'd fit in better than I might have guessed. The remainder of the crime appeared petty; where I grew up much of it would not be worth investigating, never mind mentioning. I read each and every crime report, and as my eyes zigzagged from article to article, there was one story missing.

Willie's.

I'm certain that whoever found him in that stairwell called the police, and he was quickly transported to a nearby hospital, where the nurses pulled back his hood and removed his jacket to reveal bruises and dried blood that suggested a drug deal gone bad.

DOCTOR: "Can you tell me what happened?"

WILLIE: "I fell."

With that, their collective interest in his story would dissipate, they would clean him up, mend the cuts and emerging bruises, send him off with a prescription for a drug that would turn into a profitable venture and allow him to return to his drug of choice.

And when the police officer started his way to ask a few questions, Willie would slip out of the room, out to the street, and back to his crappy life.

The *Lexington Herald-Leader* got it right: This story was not newsworthy.

As I closed the paper to refold it and open a new section, Melody appeared in the doorway of her building. I quickly unfolded it again, used it as my cloaking device, only my eyes and forehead exposed to the scene. At the sight of her, my heart pounded not faster but harder. I could feel my pulse in my stomach and throat, tried to swallow it back down more than once, the increase in the depth of my breathing causing the paper to undulate before me.

The powerful onset of emotion pushed out the sense of reason I'd seemed to have built up over the prior two days.

She walked to her car at a healthy pace, a purse over one shoulder and a large leather bag over the other, slowing only when the leather bag would slip off and she'd have to pause to hoist it back up. She wore slacks of a forgettable color and a white tank top with a light blue sweater covering all but the straps of her top, and each time the leather bag dropped, it would tug both the sweater and the straps down to expose her bare shoulder. I memorized her rhythm of reassembling: the strap, the sweater, the bag. If you put Willie or Mullet in a lineup, I'd be hard pressed to pick them out, but if you asked me to recreate her motions from that morning, I'd do so with near-perfect accuracy. As I watched her pace, her movements, I remained baffled. The way she looked—recovered—was the one look I was not expecting. In fact, I'd convinced myself she wouldn't surface at all. Her back-to-my-regular-schedule demeanor suggested she'd been through related disappointments before and become desensitized to them, though her eyes had a redness that implied tears had been wiped away not much earlier, and the bags beneath them suggested lousy sleep.

She balanced her purse and bag, reached in the pocket of her slacks, and pulled out her keys. Her headlights flickered, then she walked around to the back door on the driver's side and put both items in the backseat. As the back door closed, she paused at the window. At first I thought she was staring at something in her car, until she brushed her cheek lightly and I realized she was looking at her reflection in the glass.

I viewed her from my car, my head turned oddly, newspaper drifting lower and lower as I became absorbed. Melody stood up straight and did something that, in a most unexpected way, modified my personality. As she looked at her reflection, even though her hair was very short, she tucked her hair behind her ears. Her movement was slow and gentle, an act performed with the tips of the middle fingers of both hands, the motions occurring simultaneously, and from my distance it looked as though she were trying to trace the delicate shape of her ears. I immediately replayed it in my head two or three times. I wanted to watch her do it again, live. How odd it is the way a man's mind is randomly shaped toward preference; it's impossible to predict the triggers. My brother Jimmy, for example, would never admit it but he's a people-watcher with a real preference for young women. His obsession manifests itself in the movement of a girl's legs as she crosses them, in the sound as the skin of one leg rubs against the other, and the slower and more seductively it occurs, the more likely he will turn to me and say, "Man, I love it when a woman does that." But his statement is hardly true; he really means that some woman he knew at some time in his life did that *thing*, it flipped some irreversible switch in his head, and he spent the rest of his days trying to find another woman who could replicate the motion that left this permanent predilection in his mind and desire in his heart. Every guy has them buried somewhere, things that had little business entering the realm of sensuality—the crossing of your legs, the chewing on the end of a pen while you think, the way your hand rushes to your chest with a hearty laugh, how you close your eyes when you whisper in a friend's ear, the motions that compose the act of putting your hair in a ponytail or the way your hair gently falls to your face when you pull the band back out—somewhere a man is mad for it. As for me, for many years to follow, when I would see a girl tuck her hair behind her ears in nothing more than a vaguely similar manner, that delicate trace of the ears, I would think, *She's really cute*, and never understand exactly why.

The paper had dropped all the way to my lap.

Melody started her car and after a few seconds she pulled out of her space, made her way down the gravel road. Her car became enveloped in a white burst of limestone dust, the loud crunching as she drove over the rocks overpowering the birds and distant machinery, and as the powdery air disappeared, so had Melody.

I turned the ignition of the Mustang; that was as far as I got.

For all the hours I had spent idle in the parking lot outside Melody's apartment building, you'd think I would've found any excuse to move on, but I remained in that spot for too long, paper dropped in my lap, newsprint-stained fingers on the steering wheel at ten and two, head-cocked and blurry-eyed and openmouthed like a catatonic fool.

I had some sense that I should follow her, but *common* sense trumped it, helped me to realize that there was little point in further visiting and staking out various parking lots of rural Kentucky. The only windows of her existence that I could see through, the insignificant glimpses of her life between starting points and destinations, offered nothing but a rising tide of questions that always remained unanswered, with the ultimate question, the point of it all, never being heard: Is she okay?

Yet I could not surrender the obsession. I would never be at peace until I knew.

I called home, spoke briefly with Peter, even briefer with my father. I never found her, I said. Sat outside her place for two days, I said. Never surfaced, I said.

I'd try again soon, I said.

And as I made my way to the east, following the now familiar path toward Lexington, I began the reconciliation of the past two days.

Around the time I'd driven deep into the eastern Kentucky countryside, I finally conceded that this journey had done nothing for my paranoia except elevate it, that Melody was not okay, that she was always at risk. If I'd come out to bring rest to my conscience, to somehow convince myself that despite all her years of misery she was turning out all right, I was heading home more jammed up than when I left. Who would be watching out for her? The feds would not be in the dirty stairwells of the parking garages, they would not be in the parks, the bars, the impending dark corners of her life.

That trip only made things worse. Before, I was worried Melody was not safe, not happy; now I was certain of it.

As the Mustang renavigated the mountains of West Virginia, I spliced together the scene at the gas station where I nearly bumped into Melody and the scene in the park where she so obviously longed for a lingering eye. How it bothered me the way she wanted someone to notice her.

And as I merged those two scenes, a realization came across my mind with such power that I inadvertently pulled my foot from the accelerator and the jerking forward of the car startled me: *I* noticed her.

She made eye contact with me at the gas pumps, and I smiled at her. I gave her what she seemed so desperate for at the park. The truth is I would have noticed her anyway, that she would have stood out from any other woman. I would have given her what she wanted. She was that special.

But she had looked beyond me, like a glass of wine held to the light, trying to make sense of characteristics within the object, not the object itself. Her eyes had landed on mine—connected, without a *connection*—but after assessing me, she decided to move on to the next stimulus in her field of vision.

She wanted attention that day, just not from me.

Through the hills and valleys of southeastern Pennsylvania, I tried to resolve myself to the life I was destined to lead, the one waiting for me at the end of that journey, waiting with anger and forgiveness like an abandoned spouse, to embrace the life I was dealt, to perform the good and bad things that seemed to come so naturally.

I rationalized that Melody had no idea who I was, even with my imprudent approach in the convenience store and my passing smile at the gas pumps. In the credits of the movie of her life, I would have been listed as Guy at Gas Station. Frigging Mullet would have had a higher billing.

As I broke the line into the Garden State, I realized I could not equally be in her life and remain anonymous.

The question was: Which way to go?

The answer came to me in the center of the Holland Tunnel: I could do more good in her life—far more—if I remained anonymous.

My selfish desires would be, as Tommy Fingers would say, no good for nobody.

Winding through the lamplit streets of my neighborhood, down the dark alley that led to the reserved parking pad below my apartment, I dropped the mask I'd presented to myself, the one suggesting it was all over, that the curiosity was quelled and that Melody was alive if not well, that she was a big girl and could figure it out on her own—I dropped the mask that suggested I'd never be back to check on her again.

Of course I'd be back, where I would take my experience as Guy at Gas Station and parlay it into more important roles like Man in Produce Section and Stranger on Cell Phone and Jogger in Park, though always being miscast, never getting credited for the part for which I was so aptly prepared, so commonly playing: Stalker. Though that term, that role, was one I did not consider then, for if I had it might have brought my protective compulsions to an end, and the twisted remainder of what actually happened to Melody, what happened to me, would have never come to fruition. Certainly all of the signs were there: large unaccounted-for gaps in time, sudden disappearances lacking instigation, the lies to my family for what my reasons for finding her were. But I argued them away, as my true intentions for Melody were to protect her—protect her from the people I was lying to—and to make sure she was okay. I wasn't following her with some fuel of obsession; I was guarding her life.

Spoken like a true stalker.

And as I turned off my car and pulled the keys from the ignition, I knew the next visit Randall Gardner received from a Bovaro would probably be from me.

SEVEN

And on it continued. Year after year, town after town. Throughout my childhood I so wanted to visit the places I read about in school, to travel the landscape of the United States with my family and see all those mysterious and unusual places. My family ended up giving me that gift, in the form of an endorsement to locate Melody Grace McCartney and put two bullets in her head. My life returned to normal in New York. I embraced the love of cooking I'd found, that my mother had instilled in me in the sweetest way as a child, always offering a warm place to hide when tensions would rise in our household, when uncles and friends would arrive home cut and bloody and doubled over in pain, when arguments were so loud I could not find a place out of earshot, when reticent looks were passed around the room from a question like, "What happened to Mario? I haven't seen him in ages." My mother could read it in my eyes—*it* was the thing missing from my brothers'—and would pull me to her chest, tell me she needed my help in the kitchen. She diverted my attention by teaching me how to make homemade ravioli, pinoli and all, by letting me coat the pork and steak in the salmoriglio sauce before grilling, by explaining how the less spice you add to a dish, the greater the flavor. Her ability to distract me from the chaos in our house created a baseline for my life. I was the only one willing to learn her lesson: You'll be happier if you use your fists for the dough.

I scraped up marginal cash to buy an old storefront in Brooklyn's Williamsburg neighborhood, right off Wythe Avenue. The place was worth a fortune until it mysteriously burned up two days after I mentioned to my father I had my eye on it; I bought the shell for almost nothing, was swamped with free labor and materials for the next nine months. The details of what made the place so special, like a chandelier dating back to the early 1900s and parquet floors from an even earlier age—all gone. But this is how the Bovaros acquire things. Why bother loosening a bolt with a wrench when you can whack it off with a hammer? But they meant well, in their felonious way. It's amazing the things family will do for you sometimes.

In the hidden hours of the schedule of my life, between the enforcement of contracts and delivery and removal of money to those clients requesting financial help and help for those requiring our protection, I rebuilt the restaurant from the ground up. The late nights and random free moments were all absorbed by the tasks of hiring electricians and plumbers and designers; I quickly learned the *other* end of the restaurant business, an area to which I'd had little exposure growing up. As a result of everything in the building having been replaced—virtually a new facility—I took the restaurant to the other end of the spectrum. Instead of trying to recreate the natural history that had burned away, I refurbished and redesigned the place in a cutting-edge, trendy way that could not have been mistaken for anything other than intentional overcompensation, a style just arriving in Williamsburg. Gone were the discs of Sinatra and his peers, in came a twenty-four-hour satellite feed of *trance*, a barely audible track of what seemed like one song that started in March and didn't end until November when the power dropped. The menu, originally intended to replicate Country Italian, the food of my youth, turned into an Italian fusion with more contemporary flavors and unexpected elements; a feast of food as you'd expect from an authentic Italian restaurant, with the twists in flavor and presentation you'd expect from places whose menus defied categorization. I spent the last of my available cash on a restaurant sign designed by a local artisan, a wood and metal creation that spread across the brick surface above the awning—SYLVIA. I named the restaurant after my mother, the woman who taught me not only how to love food, but how to understand it, who after a miserable life of nurturing a crime boss and her hoodlum sons, died of ovarian cancer before she would ever see me complete its restoration. And as the staff was assembled, the tablecloths draped on the wooden tables, and the bar stocked, my father told me we'd be laundering money through the back end of the business, how we'd be bringing in more than vegetables and meats through the back door.

It's amazing the things you will do for your family sometimes.

Even at the time, while working through long nights of spackling and painting and nailing down hardwood, I knew the reconstruction of the restaurant served as a massive distraction, a means for occupying my mind and keeping it off of Melody. I worked myself to exhaustion every day, so that those moments before I fell asleep, even as I slumbered on a discarded couch in the unfinished kitchen, I'd not have a chance to think of her, be one step closer to forgetting her.

But just before Sylvia opened its large wooden doors to the public, around the time the head chef and I started experimenting in the kitchen and assembling the menu, Melody returned to my head *because* of the distance of time I forced between us. The first few months after finding her in Kentucky weren't so bad; I'd just seen her, and though her existence seemed uncomfortable and unsafe, it was fresh. But as the same season approached one year later, those warm early summer days, the thoughts of her became nearly impossible to push away, and the memories of my experience with her became vivid again, even the slightest reminders—the smell of cut grass or greasy, stale convenience store hot dogs—would send me into a tailspin. And as those memories rose in my mind, so did my concern for Melody, my wonder of what had happened over the last year, whether she had dived into promiscuity in a search for temporary connection, or if she had retreated into herself, destined to hide from the rest of the world, watch life pass from behind a family room window.

My memory of her no longer made sense; she was changing, and I began to once again ascend the fixation of finding out how.

There are two hidden benefits to running your own restaurant: abundant food and easy access to booze. Of course, the greatest downsides to running your own restaurant are all that abundant food and easy access to booze. On the food side, the kitchen crew had to come to terms with various guys from the Bovaro crew hanging out in the kitchen, feasting for free, most commonly my youngest brother, Jimmy, who by twenty-one was piling on the weight with monthly regularity, began to take the shape of a tackle, with all the violence and dexterity built right in. That first year, though, I began to pack on the pounds as well, gained ten before the restaurant had paid its third round of bills.

But what really got me was the alcohol.

It became harder and harder to get to sleep. The control and influence from Pop played a part, my having taken a restaurant I had designed and renovated with my own hands and whoring it out to my family's money laundering, allowing it to be pimped by my older brothers. The resentment began to age me. But the real stress was something else entirely. The more successful Sylvia became, the more the guilt kicked in; it seemed unfair that I could have the life

I was given while having cast Melody into the darkness, then leaving her there. The worry returned, could only be quieted by a small glass of Glenfiddich at the close of the day. The problem is, as any alcoholic will tell you, liquor is a pretty effective way to get rid of that leak in your ceiling; cover it in a thin layer of paint after each storm. Soon, you may as well start a little earlier so by the time bed is in view, you're already there. And if it serves you well at night, why not dilute the guilt and shame and worry anytime you feel their burden? Works equally at lunch as it does at dinner.

Took about three months for me to get to the point where it became noticeable—"Anybody seen Johnny?" "Check in the bar"—and one more for it to have become an official part of my day. The pressure of running a restaurant is immense—like putting on a high-profile stage production day after day—but the alcohol wasn't diluting my stress, in fact made that part of my life worse, slowed my ability to multitask. Its only purpose was to cloud, to erase. It did *that* well in a temporary capacity, so I kept it flowing.

My father eventually took me aside and performed a well-planned intervention, went like this:

DAD: "Johnny, c'mere."
ME: "What's up, Pop?"
DAD, violently slapping a glass of whiskey out of my hand: "Knock it off, kid."

It's amazing the things family will do for you sometimes.

And there it was, as I stood before my father, Peter, and a few of the crew: that look. The same look of dishonor and disappointment covered in a ganache of *we'll get through this* that burned to my memory from when I was ten years old. The look that told me I'd screwed up again. I was becoming weak, not unlike the addicted scumbags we dealt with and their never-ending needs for gambling and drugs and prostitutes. In our family and crew, a glass or two of wine with a meal or a pair of beers was nothing, but the third would always raise an eyebrow, and if it became a pattern, guys were dropped down—or off—the list of trust. Like Louis Salvone; one day you party a little too hard, a year later you've got a coke habit and prison cell and a shiv in your gut.

I surrendered the alcohol with relative ease, for it wasn't serving the purpose it did for most alcoholics. One of the guys who supplied Sylvia with quality meats was a recovering alcoholic and very distant cousin of my father. I hardly knew him, but you could tell by looking at the guy that he was living a new rendition of his former self, that his once heavy body had been drained and thinned by alcoholism, his face left sagging, his belt hidden by a spare tire that had lost its air. He lived a sober existence, but with every delivery I could see him watch the bar through the kitchen door, where if someone was cooking with vodka or wine his movements would slow and his nostrils would flare and undulate like a frigging dog. He once told me he couldn't walk past a bar without wanting to go in, that the smell of any booze at all would make him salivate, that he could actually taste it before the bartender had finished the pour. His story never resonated with me; I couldn't even understand it. I never developed a flavor for alcohol as much as I used it to get rid of the bitter taste of regret I woke up with each morning. In my case, drinking had become a casual way to dilute my guilt and concern, like taking Tylenol every day to assuage the pain of a headache that lasted a year.

I needed no help screwing the cap back on the bottle; I knew there was really only one way to make my headache go away.

Once I'd sobered I looked around and realized the fusion cuisine and the trendy restaurant were a natural fit for me, a breath as fresh as that Kentucky air. For all my armchair analysis of Melody and the people around me, it took me some time to realize—or admit—that the restaurant was a way to break out. I believe *contemporary flavors* and *unexpected elements* were the terms I used to describe the food, but they might have been better used to describe me. Everyone on staff at the restaurant always called me *Jonathan*, and for whatever reason I never corrected them, learned to like it, helped me to live my alter ego. I was the Bovaro on the fence, perched high and looking down on the two worlds of my life, not stuck there because I could not decide which way to go, but trying to figure out how to exist in both equally. I wanted to live the fusion, too.

I started taking my health more seriously, started working out—to build muscle but mostly to release tension—and eventually got an on-again/off-again personal trainer who operated out of the gym near my apartment, a talented gal constantly distracted by my last name. Nonetheless, the training worked, and in my family gaining additional strength would never have gone unutilized.

Over that initial year of developing the restaurant, my appearance began to change, and not just from filling out my sweaters across the chest. While in my mildly drunken stupors I had started noticing that almost everything I read was getting blurry, though once free of the booze, things *remained* blurry. I took a trip two blocks away to an optician who'd had a storefront in Brooklyn since the 1950s and was told I was myopic. Translation: I can't read jack from any real distance. The optometrist, so old I feared his final breaths would be wasted on me, handed my file over to his great-granddaughter to help me select frames. The whole time this girl stared at my face like she knew me, except she didn't. I'm not much for self-assessment, but for whatever reason this gal was taken with me. And as I perused the wall of frames all I really wanted was her help in finding something suitable. Can't explain why, but not many people in our household or crew ever wore glasses; I had no starting point. The only two guys who did were in their eighties; one had frames with lenses the thickness of petri dishes, the other had frames with an opening for one big lens and inside was the windshield of a mid-seventies Chevelle. On the other hand, my sous-chef wore glasses, blue and bold and providing a welcome distraction from the plague of acne his face had once fought and lost.

So, the great-granddaughter, eyes still stuck on my face, reached up and pulled down a set and handed the lensless frames to me. I studied them—as trendy as my restaurant and as expensive as its repairs—and as I held them in my hand, they were so light, so delicate that all I could think was, *These are gonna break in less than a week.* I slowly put them to my face, felt as odd wearing them as if I'd slipped on a dress.

"Oh, yeah," great-granddaughter said.

I studied myself in the mirror, glanced at her sideways.

Then she smiled and laughed a little. "Oh, *yeah*."

I returned to the restaurant, wobbling a bit from my newly sharpened vision, amazed at how far away I could read things; apparently, my sight had been on its way out for some time. And as I walked in the back door of the restaurant, Peter was coming out. We stopped a few feet apart from each other, hands in our pockets.

Peter stared at me for three seconds. "Seriously?"

I shrugged, he walked past.

But for the first time in my life—started in culinary school, really—I started being around people unlike myself, unlike my family, for extended periods of time. Once the restaurant turned into a full-time job, the people involved in its operation and success became full-time acquaintances, people of a (non-mob) culture who brought something to the table, no matter how bland or understated, that rubbed off on me. The changes were subtle, things as unnoticeable as wearing a different kind of pullover—"You look different, Johnny"—to a marginally different haircut to those glasses; I knew there was a small audience that would accept these changes. No one on either side could single out what the difference was, and rightfully so, no one really cared, either. The point is the change was there.

Two worlds, on a slow path toward collision.

I found Melody in Kentucky when I was twenty-four years old. I found her there again when I was twenty-five—twice—with the visits spaced apart by the distance between each of my headaches, the same point in every cycle of making sure she was all right and making sure she was *still* all right. And as always, each and every trip fell under the guise of knocking Melody off. I might've even tried to spy on her more than I did, except my excuses for either not finding her or not being able to take her out became flimsier with each return home.

On my fourth trip to Lawrenceburg, Kentucky—I was now twenty-six years old, she was twenty-two—Melody disappeared. I waited for two days, the greatest length of time I could leave Sylvia alone, but her car never moved. More alarming was the appearance that it hadn't moved in a long time. Dead leaves and tiny branches were strewn across the roof, trunk, and hood, debris that would have blown away from regular driving. The front passenger tire had gone partially flat and there were stains on the bottom quarter of each tire where rainwater had washed away the grime from the wheels—wheels that had not turned in a great while.

Having originally planned on returning home by Friday evening, I waited out that second night, went to the Lawrenceburg post office as soon as it opened on Saturday morning, carried in an empty envelope with Melody's—Shelly Jones's—name and address scribbled on it in handwriting purposely written to appear unlike my own.

I handed it to a middle-aged postal clerk and gave him my story: "Hope you can help me. Got a letter I'm trying to get to a friend of mine but I forgot her apartment number. I was wondering if you guys could get this to her on my behalf."

I handed over the letter with her last known address.

Shelly Jones
901 New Frankfort Road
Lawrenceburg, KY
40342

The clerk studied the envelope, squinted a little, and said, "Umm, one second." And as he walked out of sight, he yelled, "Hey, Ron?"

The clerk disappeared for a minute, then returned with my empty envelope.

"I can put it on her stack, f'ya like."

"Stack?"

"Box at her building filled up a month ago. We've been 'cumulating her mail here in back."

"Why aren't you forwarding it?"

"Got no forwarding address. She just stopped picking it up. Soon we'll have to start sending back any new mail f'her."

I started cracking my knuckles. "You guys call the police?"

The clerk paused before answering, like he was waiting for me to deliver a punch line. "Not picking up your mail ain't no crime." He shrugged a little. "Should be."

I leaned on the counter, pointed at him. "Not to have her *arrested*. To see if she's okay. She could be dead in there."

"F'real? People stop picking up their mail all the time for who knows why. Folks leave the country, take extended trips out of town, get called for military service. Sometimes they just leave and don't worry about having their mail forwarded. Cops don't care about that." He shrugged again. "Should, though."

As I drove back to New York, I tried with all the ingenuity my mind could offer to come up with more than two scenarios, but the only possibilities to emerge were the obvious ones: Melody had been killed or Melody had been relocated. And if she'd been relocated... *why?*

I didn't drive back to my apartment. I did not go see my father and my brothers. Sylvia? Not on my mind. The doorbell I was ringing at seven-thirty that Saturday evening belonged to Randall Gardner.

His wife answered the door of their stately colonial in an apron, looked at me like the stranger I was.

"Randy around?"

She paused, wiped her hands slowly on her apron. "What's this in reference to?"

I sighed, pinched my nose as I conjured up an answer. "It's got to do with work. We're having a problem at Justice that only Randy can fix."

Her eyes widened. "Oh! One sec."

Randall came to the door with a near-empty glass of red wine, all dim-eyed and flushed as though that glass had not been his first. When he recognized me he cursed under his breath, glanced around the house checking for family, then pulled the door behind him as he stepped out onto the stoop.

"*Come* on, man. You come to my house with no warning? You

lost your freaking mind? We've got friends coming over in an hour and—"

"Go back in, put the glass down, explain there's a problem with the computers."

Out of the corner of my eye I could see a couple walking their Pomeranian.

"You sound like an imbecile, Bovaro. You know *nothing* about what I do! My work is serious stuff, man. Guy like you could never understand the first thing—"

Blah, blah, blah was all I heard. As the couple looked our way, I nodded and laughed like I loved the story Randall was telling. I let him continue his inebriated tirade, then as the couple disappeared around the corner, I slapped his face like the woman he was.

"You think I'm gonna ask again?" I grabbed him by his collar and shoved him into his door, nailed the back of his head on the hub of the knocker. "Go back inside, make up whatever excuse you like, and be back out here in sixty seconds, or I'm coming in armed and angry, *capice*?"

"All right!" He waited a second, rubbed his head. "I hate you freaking people."

Got to hand it to Randall: He returned in under twenty seconds, his jacket half on already. We walked to my Mustang in silence. I started the car and backed out of his driveway. I drove two blocks, still not a word between us. Then just as I approached the fringe of his neighborhood, I pulled over to the side of the road under a pair of massive sycamores and grabbed him by the back of the neck, twisted his head so we were eye to eye.

"Don't ever make the mistake of doing that to me again, Gardner. Next time I stop by you invite me in, treat me with respect, offer me a glass of your boxed wine, and introduce me as a friend. I don't care if it's three in the morning. And I don't *ever* want to hear your grumblings about me showing up on your doorstep, because

I remember when you showed up on ours, tears pouring down your face and slobber running out of your mouth as you begged my family for mercy, then begged us for more money. Know what Pete wanted to do? Wanted to cut you loose. Said you were a loser. Asked my father if we could drag your ass out to the alley, beat you, and toss you in the Dumpster like the piece of trash you are. Know who prevented that? Me, Randall. I did. I said we shouldn't, that you might serve some purpose for us in the future. Sure enough, you did. And you still got your nice family and nice place out here in the burbs. But understand, Gardner, you need to keep serving that purpose. Because once you don't anymore, I'm gonna let Pete get some exercise on you, you friggin' *minchione.* I'm telling you right now—and this is a promise—you will not outlive your usefulness."

Randall yanked his head from my grip. "You ever think about what I have on you guys, huh? You think you're impervious to punishment?"

"Don't let that wine do the talking for you, Randy, or we're gonna end up taking a different ride in a minute." I could feel the rage building; I needed fast information and he was impeding my ability to get it. I considered taking the quickest way to making my point, but I really wanted to avoid getting his blood all over the interior of my car.

"Think about who I work for!" he yelled. "I make one phone call and—"

"Randy, let me tell you how we've handled gamblers who've troubled us in the past. We had this guy, let's call him Chuck, lived maybe fifteen miles from here, started getting mouthy on us, considered biting the hand that fed him. Drove Peter out of his mind. We gave Chuck a real-life lesson on how odds worked. We took him to a low bridge over the Passaic River in the middle of the night, loosely tied cinder blocks to both of his feet, made him clutch the blocks to his chest as we forced him to jump off."

Gardner finally shut up. Two cars passed us, kicked up gravel that dinged against my door.

"If Chuck panicked," I continued, "those cinder blocks would keep him at the bottom of the river no matter how hard he tried to swim up. If he had presence of mind, he could try to hold his breath and undo the knots and free himself to swim to the surface."

Randall wiped his mouth as he stared past me, lost in the imagery. Then he asked so quietly that I barely understood the words, "Where's the lesson in odds?"

"My brothers and I stood on the bridge, betting on whether he would live or not." I looked in my rearview, then back at Gardner. "Odds were ten to one he'd survive."

Then, louder: "You killed him?"

I stared out the window as the couple with the Pomeranian walked up their driveway. "He would have killed *himself*, Randy. All he had to do was get control of his mind and think about what he needed to do." I turned to him. "This is an opportunity for you to do the same. Presence of mind, my friend. Think, and make the decisions that will save your life."

Randall faced forward and rubbed his face so hard it looked like he was kneading a massive ball of dough.

As I put the car in gear and had us back on our path to the highway, I said, "As for our gambling friend, he beat the odds. He survived. He was underwater for over ninety seconds, but he eventually surfaced. We picked him up at the shoreline, threw him in the back of our car, and drove him home."

Randall began sniffling, wiping his nose on his sleeve.

"Next time you think for even a split second that you can play us, Randall, I want you to imagine what was running through Chuck's mind for those ninety seconds he was at the bottom of the Passaic."

Gardner sighed, stared at his lap, whispered, "I hate you freaking people."

It took significant restraint to avoid turning to him and sounding like a disgruntled child: *I hate you, too!* Guys like Gardner are the ones you toss into the Passaic tethered to an engine block instead of a cinder block. When he came to us in hysterics, at that time in debt by five figures, he made the mistake of thinking all crews in organized crime had interests in pornography; we did not, found no need to infringe on turf already so well covered. Gardner was desperate for money, and for something to make him worthy of our help, he offered boxes—*boxes*—of videos of he and his wife engaged in their bedroom activities that he had accumulated over a period of several years, all filmed via hidden cameras and high-tech equipment, all without his wife's knowledge, filmed with his face away and hers to the camera. This is the way you must understand Gardner, as willing to give up any shred of dignity for his addiction.

Here, Peter and I saw eye to eye. All four Bovaro brothers would have taken turns on him, would have kicked and smashed those demons into submission. But I saved Randall's life, seeing him for what he was, as having one value that would provide more to our family than the release and rush of delivering his punishment: He would do anything to continue gambling. Even if it meant surrendering the pride and trust of his wife, turning her into an amateur porn star. Even if it meant exposing his own intimate moments to the world. Even if it meant his wife and children could be forced into a lifetime of embarrassment.

Even if it meant potentially jeopardizing the entire Federal Witness Protection Program.

As we arrived at his office building, I parked in a distant space; the lot was mostly empty on that Saturday night. We both emerged from my car at the same time.

"Where you going?" Gardner asked.

"With you."

"You crazy? You can't get into the building, never mind the room where our systems are. I mean, c'mon, the place is loaded with cameras."

It just looked like any office building to me, a fifteen-story glass and concrete structure designed by an architect with little imagination, a small metal sign at the foot of the building marking it as property of the U.S. Department of Justice. Could have been a building full of filing cabinets for all I knew.

He started walking toward the facility and said, "Gimme a half hour."

"To get an address?"

He turned around, took a few paces back in my direction. "Look, I gotta run some diagnostic procedures on the servers, make it look like there's a reason I'm badging in on a Saturday night."

"What are you talking about?"

Gardner held up a hand to signal he was abbreviating the conversation. "What do you know about Oracle?" My answer never arrived. And as he turned and walked away, he said, "Gimme a half hour."

I sat and waited patiently—for about twenty-eight of those thirty minutes. But when the half-hour mark came and went, I made the mistake of falling into paranoia the way I did in the convenience store in Kentucky. I imagined Gardner calling some contact in Justice, my car being surrounded by unmarked vehicles, guns aimed at me from too many positions to identify, red dots from lasers swirling in loose circles over my forehead and chest as I exited my car with my hands in the air. I could only hope that Gardner's addiction to gambling was a ruling force, or better, that my lesson on presence of mind would be enough for him to make the right decision.

At the forty-five-minute mark, I started my car, ready to abandon Randall at the facility along with the opportunity for being captured. A few minutes later, I had the car in motion and aimed for the exit when I saw Randall appear at the cluster of glass doors at the bottom of the building. I drove over to pick him up as though it had been my original intention.

Randall jumped in the front seat and slammed the door, his face covered in sweat as though it was the first time he'd gotten us this particular information.

"Go," he said.

"What did you find out?"

"She's been relocated. Just go."

I felt a rush of relief, from not only knowing she was still alive, but being on the cusp of getting her new location.

As we left the lot and returned to the freeway, my mind started spinning a tale of what might have caused Justice to move her, jammed up on the obvious conclusion: I'd not been as careful as I thought while staking her out. I struggled with which questions to ask first.

"How long ago?"

"Little over five weeks."

It had been almost a year since I'd last seen Melody. I couldn't imagine what would have prompted Justice to relocate her again just a month earlier. Unless someone *else* was trying to kill her.

I raised my voice, hoped it might bring a more detailed answer. "Why'd you guys move her?"

"Who knows."

"It didn't say?"

"You asked for an address."

Gardner would never serve as my partner in crime.

"Gimme what you do have. Where is she?"

"I'll tell you," he said, "once you've driven me home safe and sound."

I didn't say another word, not because I was obeying Gardner's demand—I could have gotten the answer out of him while still keeping one hand on the wheel—but because the flood of potential answers to the question *why* had me clawing for the surface to get some air. Just like Chuck.

I replayed every conversation I'd had with my father and brothers over the previous few months, attempted to reread their words and signals and facial expressions. Their disappointment in my inability to complete the mission of knocking off Melody was not exactly hidden; maybe they thought it was time to get it done no matter what. On the other hand, there was really no compelling reason to have her killed immediately, other than to tidy up that loose end and to make a point to our peers that eventually we eliminate everyone who would dare to testify against us.

We pulled in front of Randall's house, his driveway now full of cars, guests visible through the first-floor windows.

"Great," he said, "everyone's already here."

"Where is she?"

Gardner stared at his house, had a look on his face like he was starting to wonder if this was all worth it. He never turned my way, mumbled, "Four twenty-five Sunrise Road, Farmington, New Mexico."

I closed my eyes and dropped my head back to the headrest, thought, *Man, that's a really, really long drive.* All along I'd been fortunate enough to have Melody within a single day's drive. But New Mexico meant overnight stops. I knew I could never utilize airplanes or trains or anything that would log my name to a ticket purchase, anything that could be used as proof I'd been traveling with the intent of locating her. And with the demands of Sylvia,

I wasn't really sure how I could ever pull it off; those trips would require a significant time commitment.

Gardner turned and stared at me as I blanked out and gazed down the tree-lined street of his neighborhood. "You're welcome."

I kept my eyes on the street. "Get out of my car, you friggin' scumbag."

Once he'd left, I broke my trance, watched him stroll to his front stoop, running his hands through his hair, straightening out his clothes, wiping his face. He put his hand on the doorknob and paused a few seconds like he was trying to get his breath instead of his composure.

With data not flowing from the government side, I tried to paint as full a picture as possible by draining my family of whatever information and intentions they had—though they offered not much more than Randall. Over the course of three days, I casually asked my father and brothers and a few of the capos in our crew if they'd had any change in plans or interest toward Melody, but I could read the honest indifference in their demeanor, in their words:

Pop: "Geez, kid, I got other things on my mind right now."

Peter, with a wave of his hand: "She's *your* little project. Clean up your own mess."

Tommy Fingers: "I thought you took her out four years ago."

Ettore: "Not me, Shonny. No way. Not a shansh." (These were Ettore's last words to me. He would die, bullet to the neck, a terribly slow way to perish, in an alley in midtown five days later. My father turned the other way and allowed it to happen, a payback for a mistake Ettore had made against another family, a price paid to keep peace. No one thought to mention it to me until he'd been gone nearly a week.)

I slowly came to terms with the idea that her move might've had nothing to do with me or my family at all, that it could've been something as benign as a budgetary issue within Justice where they wanted to consolidate witnesses to regions, or that Melody had developed an allergy to some native Kentucky weed, or that some health issue required her to live in a more arid environment. No matter the excuse, I found no serenity in it. Something wasn't right. And now my guard was raised, the paranoia so well sharpened that I'd become afraid I'd get cut and not even feel it.

I finally told myself it had to end, eventually convinced myself of it. The craziness served no purpose. And I'm sure the tapes I played in my head were similar to ones Chuck and Randall played, the wake-up-in-a-cold-sweat type where you decide today is the day you come to your senses. You're never doing it again.

But like all addicts and people weakened with obsession, with the passage of enough time the cycle begins again, and you can't do anything to prevent that; the only control you have is your reaction to it. The fantasy of feeling the rush (Randall's issue) or the weight of concern (my issue) comes on full force, and you fight it for a while—a few hollow victories—until the cycle coincides with some other overwhelming impulse—like the notion that this time will be different, or that this time will be the last—and you give it all a second thought. And then a third. And then it runs through your mind with an uncomfortable rhythm.

And then you think, *I could probably get to New Mexico in two days if I drove really fast.*

EIGHT

Wouldn't it seem the purpose of following Melody over and over again was to learn something about her, to gain some sort of intelligence into how she led her life? No matter where I went—she went—I really only learned of the things that affected her, but never how or why they affected her.

On my third trip to New Mexico, sometime in my twenty-seventh year and her twenty-third, I finally understood just how abandoned she was. Certainly, I was to blame for the absence of family in her life, but the spoon-fed circumstances that Justice delivered ensured it would always be that way. I watched her go back and forth from her small rambler on the north side of Farmington to a forgotten sixties-era office building on the south side of the city, and every day was the same: out the door at seven in the morning, coffee at the 7-Eleven, lunch at a picnic table behind the office building, back home by four-thirty, paying pizza/sandwich/Chinese food delivery guy at five-fifteen, lights-out at ten. Justice offered her safety through the guise of invisibility, days and nights so rote that no one might ever notice she had a routine worth noticing. It's odd how one can find someone else's ennui to be so fascinating.

I finally came to the disappointing conclusion that there was only one person who genuinely cared about her well-being.

Me.

All these trips, all the cycles of concern, were to try and ensure that she had not buried herself in alcohol or promiscuity or some other destructive behavior and to one day—what I hoped for most of all—find her in the arms of a man, safe and secure and satisfied. I longed for her to meet someone who would protect her. I thought that if I witnessed her being happy and healthy I could finally bring it all to a close. But through all the years, all the trips, there were no surprises: same scene, different town.

Then, in the dead of winter halfway through my twenty-eighth year, Melody was relocated once again. By that time, I'd modified my methodology of knowing where she lived; Gardner knew to check once a month and update me if her whereabouts ever changed. And one evening in February, while dropping off a wad of cash to cover his latest losses, Gardner also dropped off an address for me.

And with that relocation, Justice did something that altered the course of my life: They moved her only four hours south of New York.

Columbia, Maryland, a suburb south of Baltimore, became Melody's new home, and this address transformed the rules of the game—mostly by eliminating an entire subset of rules. It meant I could watch her way too regularly; if I left New York at six in the morning, I could be in Columbia by ten, stay for a while, and still be back in Brooklyn by the dinner rush.

Her experiences in Columbia looked no different from Farmington or Lawrenceburg or Mineral Point. I rarely witnessed Melody interact with anyone or anything beyond a superficial level. No friends, no lovers. And with the dissatisfaction that stemmed from her not meeting that need for security, my mind began to shift its attention away from that hope; I had sort of given up. Without recognizing it, the way I started watching her, what I longed to comprehend, changed. I wanted to understand what made her who she was. I wanted to understand what made her who she wasn't.

These became my darkest days, for my actions, with every recollection, were more fixated. During the period she lived in Lawrenceburg, I watched her three times before she was relocated. In Farmington, I visited her three more times. In Columbia, I watched her nineteen times.

The one thing that improved: I became a master of lurking. Gone were the poorly planned purchases of necessities (water, cigarettes). I became deft at staking her out, never again made the mistake of allowing her to see me as I did at the gas station in Kentucky. I learned to always watch the bathroom first. I learned the feds aren't tailing her day after day. She existed more in a file on a computer than she did in Kentucky, in Wisconsin, in the vast rural unknown. I began slipping in and slipping out without leaving so much as a fingerprint.

I started to absorb everything about her, making mental notes of the food she ate (coffee over tea, espressos over lattes) and restaurants she frequented (unknown independents over the chains). The subtleties of her actions painted an impressionist image I could hang in the corridor of my mind, the colors and brushstrokes chosen from my observances: that while shopping for clothes, when she would hold a dress or blouse up to her body, the color was almost always blue or dark green or black, and that after she would leave the store I would step in a moment later and read the size on the tag to be a six or an eight or an occasional ten; that even though she lived closer to Baltimore than DC, she read the *Washington Post* instead of the *Baltimore Sun*; that she liked to spend time in card stores even though I never witnessed her purchase a single card; that she sped up at yellow lights instead of braking; that she always crossed her legs at the knees and not the ankles.

The closest I ever got to her in Columbia: We shared time together in a Best Buy; she was in CDs, I was in computers. She browsed the music for an hour before making her way to one of the registers with a half dozen CDs. I grabbed some wrapped wire from the rack in front of me—still have no idea what a CAT 5 cable is—and made my way toward the same register, timed it so I would be arriving as she was departing.

The teenaged clerk swiped my cable over the barcode reader. "Twenty-seven twenty-nine."

I widened my eyes. "Really? For a few feet of wire?" He shrugged, noshed on a wad of gum, looked annoyed when I handed him cash instead of a credit card.

"Listen," I said, "the girl who just went through here, you remember any of the discs she bought? She's a friend of mine and her birthday's coming up and I don't want to get her something she just purchased."

The clerk stared at me, slowed his chomping. "Aimee Mann. Iron and Wine. I don't know, some others. Death Cab for Cutie, I think. That kind of stuff."

I repeated the names as I watched her walk beyond the sliding door of the store. "Aimee Mann, Iron and Wine, Death Cab for Cutie. Thanks."

I tailed her to the parking lot; I stayed behind the sliding doors, watched her get into a Toyota Camry. Her hair was longer and darker than I'd ever seen it, though still short by most standards, and it helped give dimension and shape to her face, a modest shift to a more defined beauty, like a girl exiting adolescence and embracing womanhood. Before she put the key in the ignition, she glanced at herself in the rearview and did that *thing*—the simultaneous tuck of hair behind her ears—then gently wiped the edge of her bottom lip with her thumb. And as she started her car, pulled out, and drove away, I let out a breath I didn't realize I'd been holding.

Once she was out of view, I tossed the useless computer cable into the trash and walked right back inside the store, proceeded to the music section, repeating the clerk's list under my breath: *Mann, Iron, Death, Mann, Iron, Death.* I grabbed a copy of each available disc from those artists (two each) and proceeded to the same clerk.

"Thought you were trying to avoid getting her the same discs."

I pulled out a wad of twenties from my pocket. "Change of approach."

I left the store and walked through the parking lot with my new stash of music. At the time, my car had the best stereo system of any I'd ever owned. Six months prior, I'd traded in the trusty Mustang for a candy apple red Audi S4 convertible, a machine even faster and more luxurious than its predecessor, more in-your-face and un-Bovaroesque than any other car in its class; the status didn't matter here, only the speed and comfort. When I first drove it back to Brooklyn, parked it in the reserved spot behind Sylvia, it brought mixed reviews:

POP, to a smattering of crew members: "Hey, my kid got class or what?"

GINO: "I'm sorry, Officer, all I remember is he was driving a bright red Audi."

PETER, after three seconds of staring: "Seriously?"

I'd positioned myself in the corner of the lot at Best Buy, a perfect diagonal distance from where Melody had parked. I got in and turned the key, powered the cab without turning the ignition, emptied the in-dash CD changer. I started ripping open the new CDs, loading the changer one by one, then started the first disc. And I sat there, the cab growing dimmer from an increasingly cloudy sky, listening to Aimee Mann. The music was unfamiliar to me—quite mellow and gentle, like falling leaves or snow, the words and style both thoughtful and thought-provoking. I'd been exposed to a moderate variety of music in my life: the usual mix of Sinatra and Bennett and their kindred, the hair bands of the eighties of which Peter had fancied himself their chief emulator, and that frigging trance.

But these songs—the tunes and words—held me temporarily captive, seemed to be trying to explain something intended to stick with you beyond a meal in a restaurant, beyond a loud concert, beyond a single play.

I listened to the entire CD.

These were the first words I ever heard Melody say. She wasn't speaking directly to me, but she was definitely speaking.

Within months my collection grew, the first real collection of music I could call mine, expanded into a diverse assortment all on its own; Aimee Mann introduced me to Neil Finn, who introduced me to Jack Johnson, who introduced me to Sufjan Stevens. A friendly, amiable bunch they were. And where I'd once had a drink at my side in those earlier days at Sylvia, I now had headphones affixed to my head almost permanently, drowning out the trance with music that many times threw me into a real trance, and with each and every note of the music, I felt I had a snapshot of Melody with me, like rereading a romantic note from a lost but not forgotten lover.

I found comfort in Melody's proximity. It made it easy to get a fix, though I never got the one I was hoping for. Not even once could I rest in thinking she was safe. I always viewed her as a prisoner with a cell the size of whatever community Justice decided to make her home. I could have existed this way for some time, and did—until just after I turned thirty.

My thirtieth year held such promise: Sylvia's reputation soared, and maintained a solid staff and outstanding kitchen personnel; our family was in the midst of a relatively peaceful and successful time, a period where Justice seemed to have lost interest and my father began relying on a greater circle of trusted and made men, reducing my personal requirement for involvement; Melody was within a morning's journey, and even though she seemed wary, she also seemed stable.

And just as I let my guard down, everything changed.

Turned out Justice hadn't lost interest; they'd been busy strategizing, quietly putting together a battle plan against my family intended to serve as the harbinger for all organized crime, Italian or Russian or Chinese, in New York or Chicago or Miami. We weren't aware of it at the onset, but Justice's Organized Crime and Racketeering Section had taken nearly two years' worth of budget and dedicated it to making an example of one family: the Bovaros.

And to make this plan work, they'd assembled a group of players who were willing to testify against us, each serving up a specific chunk of data that when connected to the ends of the players on either side all looped together into a perfect circle. Their strategy had been this: Instead of nailing the one person with enough knowledge to bring down the entire organization and finding a way to force them to testify, grab all the little people with partial knowledge and weave a fabric of corruption. Instead of one key witness, bring on fifty to a hundred witnesses with something worth saying, *anything.*

This line of attack had a hidden benefit: In prior cases against us, as in the instance of the McCartneys, we had one unified target to eliminate. But here, how would we eliminate dozens of people? Even if we could, how would we ever know who they were? And how would we make them disappear without widening the potential circle of new witnesses?

This plan started to unfold once people we dealt with on a peripheral basis started mentioning to our crew that *some guys came by asking questions*. At first, it didn't matter; that kind of stuff happened on a regular basis. But once Peter and Pop and the rest of us started comparing notes, it became evident the problem was epidemic.

At the same time, my father hinted that he was receiving nebulous information from someone inside Justice about the government's general intentions, someone working with my father—and *only* my father—that the source, while not providing comprehensive data, would be kept strictly to him. My first thought was that it was *not* Gardner; we'd already pushed him for operational data year after year and every time he'd tell us the same thing: that his databases were not within that scope.

Based on the information we were getting from people on the street, coupled with the vague information supplied to us from my father's inside source, it became apparent that a storm was on the horizon—a rain that would last for months, flood our homes, and destroy our land.

I met my father, brothers, and a few senior crew members at my parents' house in Tenafly to discuss the list of potential problem witnesses—the obvious fruit that Justice had picked—and prioritize the ones to be immediately eliminated. Again, killing was never taken lightly in our home, and I could read the stress the event was causing in my father's demeanor, his concentrated focus and near silence. Justice had played their hand well, for we were no longer going to kill individuals; we were going to kill witnesses, and the potential punishment would be all that more severe. This meant choosing wisely, eliminating only those we were certain would be testifying, the ones most likely to want to see us pay.

This team, possibly the largest group I'd ever seen assembled at one time, was spread evenly across my father's den. The Bovaro men, the capos, and a few from my father's growing circle of trusted associates shared our insights into those we knew best, those we could vouch for, those who seemed untrustworthy. I offered up as much as I could, but most of the people I associated with were semilegitimate guys serving Sylvia, though using their businesses for some other illegal and higher-profit endeavor. I trusted all of them as much as I trusted anyone outside of my bloodline, couldn't recommend putting a bullet in a single one. My casual everyone-is-okay-on-my-end position came across as my not having put much thought into it all, and I got the most skeptical looks from the most recent additions to my father's circle of trust: Donny Vingelli, a punk about my age and nephew of my father's sister, whose primary interest lay in jacking cars; and Edoardo "Eddie" Gravina, an associate whose greatest accomplishment was his identical age to my father, a slender guy with snow white hair and a silver mustache who only spoke when he had something of value to offer, words so anticipated that when he spoke everyone froze to listen, the closest thing my father ever had to a *consigliere.*

As the meeting progressed, we spent less and less time discussing each individual, a consequence of there simply being too many choices. The group of us sat far from the wives and children of the family, the content of the entire conversation masked in double meanings. This is the life we led, where someone is usually listening.

My father rubbed his temples. "Sammy Meat Market." *Ted Simone, owner of Brooklyn Meats and Cheeses.*

Peter slowly nodded. "Agreed. Always thought his meat was going bad." *Neither liked nor trusted the guy.*

My brother Jimmy, wanting to bring more to the table than muscle, offered people up by the bushel, hoping the wheat and chaff would separate themselves. "Mickey Roughneck?" No. "Seventh Street Stevie?" No. "Biscuithead?" Confused stares, then no.

Peter offered up, "Maybe we should consider including our buddy in Alphabet City?" *Should we take out Matthew McManus?*

Pop squinted, returned to massaging his temples. "We invite him we gotta invite all his friends, too." *That opens up an entirely new list of people to consider, and everyone on that list carries approximately the same threat.*

"Not to mention," I said, "it would likely offend his friends back home." We'd long suspected that McManus was serving the Irish mob at the same time, figuring he didn't want all of his eggs in one frying pan, patiently waiting to see which family would emerge as the ultimate force in New York. If true, we wouldn't want to take him out unless absolutely convinced he posed a problem.

In came a gap in the conversation, filled with nothing but sighs and audible swallowing. My father scanned the room slowly, moved from face to face as if mentally extracting a list of individuals out of their respective lifetime experiences, and when he finally turned my way, he stopped. We stared at each other for too long a time. I licked my lips a little, my hands slightly cupped and aimed skyward. I was thinking, *What, why am I so interesting?* He tilted his head down as if using it to point and said, "Johnny, you got to take that girl of yours on a date." *Stop screwing around and kill the McCartney girl.*

I snapped to attention like I'd been asleep in class and called on for an answer. Suddenly, each and every nod was exaggerated, the entire den filled with bobbleheads.

Nodding the hardest, Peter added, "Really, Johnny. You got to know how to treat a gal or she's gonna leave you for someone else."

Then only my own swallowing could be heard. I surveyed the

eyes of the room, looks of annoyance and impatience layered upon me like winter blankets, that of all the people who might need to have their hearts stopped, here was a witness who should have long been buried.

What had I been doing all this time? Where my family was concerned, I figured the best I could do was stall, make so much time pass that no one would care about her anymore. But the frigging feds had brought her right back into the limelight. The problem was this: For all I knew, Melody really was planning to use her waning testimony against us. Though what she'd witnessed was thrown out of court all those years ago, they might want to use her for some *angle* of evidence, something as innocuous as acknowledging that she saw my father in Vincent's and nothing more, a piece of evidence that might be linked to someone else who would take the baton and dash forward to the next witness.

Give a paintbrush and a unique color to a hundred different people and ask them to paint an object on the same canvas. What you get in the end is a convoluted mess of different styles and strokes—but when the last painter is finished, there is no denying you're staring at a completed work. You might not *get it*, but you'd probably nod your head and think, *Yeah, I guess that's a piece of art*. Melody would be nothing more than a twenty-six-year-old woman holding a brush dabbed in blue. And the jury would be nodding our crew all the way to the Lewisburg Federal Penitentiary.

And then another realization arrived like a kidney punch: Most likely, the feds knew how aware we were of their operation—in fact, we figured it was probably part of their plan all along, that they hoped to catch us in the act of taking out one of their witnesses, a partial setup at the potential cost of a human life or two. If that were true, my staking out of Melody would have to come to an end, for I would have been perceived as a threat—hunting Melody instead of protecting her—and taken down on the spot.

If it were possible to taste pallor, I would've been swallowing down its sickly aftertaste. I cannot recall any other moment when I felt my anxiety surge as it did in those few seconds. What my family had seen as an annoying hobby of mine—feeble attempts on Melody's life—now had a predetermined, absolute ending.

I smiled a little, wiped my brow; luckily, I wasn't the only one sweating. "Consider it done," I said. "I'll make sure I give her what she needs." The source of my sweat: If I didn't give her what she needed, someone else in our crew was going to. No longer a tying-up-loose-ends issue, Melody didn't stand much of a chance. My father bit the inside of his cheek as he focused on me. "You need a chaperone?"

I could see those words coming like a fly ball aimed directly at my glove. "Nah, this party is gonna be so big I'm assuming we need people cooking and cleaning elsewhere, right?"

Pop squeezed his bottom lip between his thumb and forefinger, his head tipped down further as he stared at me.

"Okay, Johnny," he said finally. "Treat her right, okay?"

I looked down at my shoes, wiped the sweat from my forehead under the guise of a scratch. "I know, Pop."

The conversation lasted another hour, but the last words I tried to interpret were Peter's: "*You got to know how to treat a gal or she's gonna leave you for someone else.*" Not a single thought or idea ran through my head that wasn't an attempt at solving this problem, at finding a way to set that little six-year-old girl free once and for all.

My sisters-in-law prepared a table—a feast—filling the enormous gap my mother left when she passed away. We congregated to fill our plates, then evenly dispersed over the dining room, kitchen, dinette, and sunroom, consumed veal and sausage and pasta and salads and breads. The conversation turned unusually light, in both quantity and quality. No one noticed my lack of discussion; it had become the common denominator. The only perceptible voices came from the women; the men had a lot on their minds.

And on mine: "*You got to know how to treat a gal or she's gonna leave you for someone else.*"

I sat in the corner of my parents' dinette, my seat pushed back against a window that overlooked a crumbling brick patio, its devastation delivered by the roots of maples and oaks that predated the house by decades. I shoved my plate away, took a long pull off a Moretti, and stared at Peter, who sat in the dining room at a far and distant angle from me. He twisted his neck to get a kink out, and when he did he noticed me watching him. We stared at each other for a few seconds, his words still echoing through my head.

And suddenly my mind opened wide, exposing a gush of beauty, like a daylily receiving its initial blast of morning sunlight.

The first and only time I utterly adored my older brother, Peter: that very day—the moment he supplied me with an unintentional epiphany despite himself. "*You got to know how to treat a gal or she's gonna leave you for someone else.*" The *someone else* quite obviously referenced the feds, that her allegiance would be given to them. But the intended resonance of his words did not reach my ears as an explosion, but as the sweeping crash of an ocean wave. I perverted his words to something beautiful and filled with hope, a line better used as a mantra than a reminder.

I wasn't going to kill Melody. I was going to win her.

NINE

The plan materialized later that night, after two full cycles of food consumption, after a few rounds of drinks to ease anxiety and inspire the imagination, after the team had been reduced to seven. The list was created; targets were matched to various members of the crew. I managed to convince everyone to leave Melody to me and me alone, the only person I'd been tapped to tap.

We were dispatched, and within twenty-four hours a few kills were completed, the easy ones, with the intent that it would catch the feds off guard. But the real essence of the plan was this: We knew the hits would subdue the raging tide of other witnesses, create a flurry of doubt that the feds could really protect them the way they had certainly been promised. We were richer in the currency of fear than the feds; we had to abide by far less rules. And as my father and brothers explained, the point could be no better exemplified than through the death of one of their already protected witnesses: Melody Grace McCartney. Do my job, I was told, and the rest of the pieces would fall in place.

And just like that: My hit became the most valuable.

The first witnesses were having their splayed bodies traced with chalk around the time I left for Columbia, a delay required to get things in order with Sylvia; my head chef, Ryan, was slowly becoming the general manager as it was, what with all of my recent random departures to places unknown (but with locales always resolving to suburban Baltimore).

I'd slept little, managed only to squeeze in a shaveless shower before taking to the highways in the predawn darkness. The first opportunity to assemble a plan came as I was exiting the Holland Tunnel. I had four hours to put something together. And as I rode down the New Jersey Turnpike toward I-95, I couldn't stop looking in my rearview mirror for someone from our crew—or from the federal government.

Whatever plan I'd hoped might surface showed no sign of appearing even as I broke the line of the Keystone State. Then again, what choice did I really have?

"Hi, Melody. Sorry for breaking in but let me explain. Yeah, I'm the guy you're on the run from, but look, here's the thing..."

I had to keep reminding myself of the soul of the plan as it first came to my mind: *Win* her. The actions to match that sentiment did not come as I'd hoped, likely due to my having never considered this option; I'd spent my adult life determined to avoid getting in contact with her, from ever revealing who I was, how I was responsible for the way her life had turned out, for the way her life hadn't turned out.

As I broke the Delaware line, I started to ponder the solution to the second part of my problem: Assuming I could gain Melody's trust, what was I to do with her?

Tell her to run? She was doing that already, and other than me, no one was pursuing her. But if someone else put Gardner to work the way I did, she'd be taken out within twelve hours.

Tell her to come with me? Where, exactly, would we be going?

As the exit for Rising Sun, Maryland, came into view, the only thing I could sense rising was rage, a burn in my stomach derived from the ridiculous life I lived, forced into (supposedly) putting a bullet into an innocent woman because of nothing more significant than happenstance. And with the rage came a clouding of ideas, my mind preoccupied and disconnected.

As I drove half the circumference of the Baltimore Beltway, I noticed my heart pounding harder, my seat belt holding it back like a weight belt, could feel the beat of blood through my temples.

I'd started pushing the ideas to the front of my mind with such force that each one arrived broken and disabled. The closer I got to Columbia, at that point seven miles from Melody's apartment, the less I had in my arsenal of possibilities.

And as I wound through the streets that led me to her building, as the suburb stretched and yawned and came to life, I decided I'd use my last remaining time, the final moments as I staked out her apartment, to draw a conclusion, a final scheme.

Except.

Except I pulled into her complex distracted—distracted by the pair of black Ford Explorers with dark windows and meaty wheels that followed me in. I might as well have waved to them: I dropped under the speed limit, a certain signal I was doing something wrong, my New York license plates as hard to avoid noticing as a chancre sore. The massive vehicles were on my tail for too long, inspired me to turn down a different row of apartment buildings—any direction but toward Melody—and when I did, they kept on going, gunning their engines toward some other destination. My instinct suggested they were rushing to box off the exits; my reaction was to keep drifting along in second gear, pretend I was looking for some other address. I drove in a figure eight around two unconnected buildings.

One minute passed. Nothing.

I poked the nose of the Audi out into the lane of the next apartment building like a cat sniffing the scent of an unrecognized animal.

Two minutes. Nothing.

I pulled out a half car length farther to get a look; everything appeared docile. I let the car slowly float forward, had to tell myself to breathe. I sat on the verge of something: capturing Melody, being arrested, death.

As I reached the end of the row of apartments, I gunned the engine and flew between the two rows like a soldier running from tree to tree to avoid gunfire. And when I got to the other side, I crept around to the corner of Melody's building, pulled the car out of gear, and glided along in neutral, attempting silence.

And sure enough, the Explorers sat running and idle in front of her building, the vehicles empty but for the drivers.

Three minutes. Nothing.

Then with a burst through the glass door at the bottom of her apartment came three large men, suited and armed: U.S. marshals. And in the center of their triangle walked Melody, cloaked in a bulletproof vest so large it overlapped the waist of her jeans, hung on her like a football jersey, a small garbage bag in her hand that appeared almost empty.

Two of the men pushed Melody into the backseat of the first SUV, flanked her on each side; the other man got into the passenger side of the second SUV. Both engines raced and their exhaust hung in the air as they disappeared out of the complex and onto the road that led to Columbia Pike.

And as I waited ten seconds, then zoomed from the parking lot in an effort to follow them, my heartbeat was hardly as noticeable as the word echoing through my brain: *Why?*

The three of us—two Explorers and one red sports car—raced down Columbia Pike, onto Maryland Route 32 for a few miles, then onto I-95, heading north toward Baltimore. Whenever I followed Melody it seemed I was always retracing my steps, always going backward. I flipped on my sunglasses and ball cap and punched the accelerator. And as the SUVs briefly separated in an effort to slide over a lane on the interstate, I just barely made out each license plate, the only unique identifiers of these nondescript government vehicles.

J21275
J21263

I didn't have the time (or concentration) to come up with a foolproof pattern for the tags the way I did with Melody's parents' Oldsmobile. My best effort at seventy miles per hour: Both tags started with 212, the original area code for New York. Beyond that, the easiest thing to do was repeat the last two digits of each tag over and over in my head until recalling them became second nature. *Sixty-three, seventy-five, sixty-three, seventy-five.*

All of my experience shadowing Melody came into full utilization, felt like a series of preseason games in preparation for this championship event. I was tailing the feds now, following the very enemies who waited and watched my family from dark Chevrolets in plain sight, for little other reason than to let us know we were being watched; Pop would occasionally send out a plate of bucatini all'amatriciana for them. And now that they had Melody in their possession, I hated them even more. Neither Melody nor the marshals keeping her had any understanding of how unsafe she really was.

I'd become her only hope of holding on to life.

I'd long since mastered the art of keeping a safe distance—the perfect distance—from the car in my crosshairs. Highways remained easy space to navigate; cities were another story. Traffic lights repeatedly posed a problem, creating potential gaps that could last more than a block. Not to mention the obvious intrusions: other drivers cutting you off, delivery trucks blocking traffic, short stops that had me right on top of Melody's car.

So as I followed them down into the center of Baltimore, right in the middle of the skyscrapers, my hands began to sweat; I knew if I lost her then, I'd likely *lose* her. Her life depended on my ability to stay right on the tail of those government vehicles.

Then, the inevitable: We wound down an alley darkened and cooled by a lack of sun, a strip of pavement where natural light had not shone down since those towers were erected. They slowed behind a smaller ten-story building. I waited farther back as they came to a stop at a rear entrance for a gated parking garage. With a swipe of a badge, both SUVs disappeared into the mouth of the garage, and the teeth of the gate quickly closed. Once they were out of sight, I gunned it down the alley, slowed enough to read the small sign identifying the garage as belonging to the Garmatz Federal Courthouse. I suppose one way or another I was destined to be brought to the feet of such a building.

I didn't move, every sense aware, my car waiting for instructions. I stared at the sign for some answer. What could I do? Go find a parking garage and wander back over to the courthouse and hang out, hope I run into Melody in an elevator?

Had I formulated a plan on my way down from New York, it would have gone dim. Were I not truly hunting her, here is where I would've returned home and shrugged, offered up a *better luck next time* attitude as I plunged a hunk of bread into whatever sauce my father had going in the kitchen. But if I returned home right then, it would have been certain doom for Melody. Gardner would probably get her new locale within a day or less, and the *enough is enough* attitude would have been paired with a seasoned killer fast on her heels. After all, this was business now, and Melody had shot back to being one of our top priorities.

So I did what any gambler would have done—Gardner would've been proud: I played the long shot. I parked my sore thumb of a car between two other red vehicles in a parking lot reserved for the medical center behind the courthouse, in a space reserved for a Dr. Bajkowski, and waited for one or both of those Explorers to emerge from the gated garage adjacent to my parked position. I figured the odds of the marshals moving Melody out of Baltimore in the same vehicle in which they'd brought her in were about the same as them transporting her by way of the same marshal: maybe four to one.

An hour of nothing and I called Gardner, figured I'd milk him for any possible data that might offer some direction. Or hope.

"Give me anything you've got on this transition plan," I said.

He gave me this meld of a grunt and sigh, then said, "Hold on."

Three minutes passed along with a series of clicks, and when he came back on the line a hum draped his words, as though he was sitting next to an air conditioner. Then, as if I had just said the words, "What do you mean transition plan?"

"She's on the move."

"Geez," he said, loud enough I was certain he was alone, "can't wait till someone unloads a clip into that stupid scag."

I tightened my fist around my steering wheel, decided not to remind him her life was the only thing guaranteeing his. "Where is she going?"

"You know I wouldn't know that yet."

"What can you tell me? And what is that friggin' noise?"

"I came down to the server room. I'm using a wall phone and

the administrator ID and password, so no one knows who is logging in to the database, so no one could ever track this call to me. And I can't tell you much. You know that."

"How about the vehicle transporting her? License plates? Anything?"

"We've had this conversation before. Everything here is compartmentalized. I don't have access to any of that data."

I stared at the gate, blanked out. "This is a bad time to become useless."

"What's the big deal? The information will get updated a few days after she arrives at her new destination." I could hear him tapping the keyboard, mumbling to himself. "Only thing that might be useful is the name of the marshal assigned to her. Sean Douglas."

I sat up. "What else? What does he look like? Experience level?"

"No, this is just personnel data. I can tell you he's thirty-three, birthday is October thirtieth, makes about fifty-three K a year. Lives in Towson, Maryland. Unmarried."

Randall blathered on with more subpar data, then mentioned something about the Red Sox and coming up short. Something about covering his losses. So the cycle would go for pathetic Randall. I was stuck on the grainy information I had about this marshal, my new foe. An unmarried guy making fiftysomething a year to protect people—certainly a better deal for protection than you might get from my family—could mean only one thing: I was dealing with a true believer.

Yeah, well...so was he.

I remained in that position for eight hours, the car on and ready. I idled through a quarter tank of gas, survived on one bottle of water and two packs of cigarettes, completed all the tasks I could with stuff from my glove compartment: flipped through my CDs, read through my user manual for the Audi, shaved my face with my near-dead electric razor—a decided benefit after looking in my rearview and realizing just how scary and intimidating I looked with a shadow.

Dr. Bajkowski never showed. I kept hoping he or she was buried safely in a kidney or heart transplant.

And over the course of that time, four different black Explorers left that parking garage, windows so dark you'd need X-ray vision to determine the cargo. They could have been simply taking the SUVs out to get serviced; or taking some politicians or federal judges home; or transporting some other witnesses, some other sad sacks who happened to be in the wrong place at the wrong time.

Or: They could have been taking Melody right out from under me.

More than once I doubted if I should follow any of those Explorers. But like Gardner, I was playing the long shot, and as I'm sure he would've counseled me, the only way to win big is to risk big.

The depression set in around the time the evening rush hour came to a close. The flurry of activity around that parking garage as people left at the end of the workday kept my attention. But once the sun set, so did my expectations. I could see through the grate of the gate that the deck was mostly empty. I became increasingly convinced that Melody had left hours earlier in one of the other Explorers. All I had to show for my day was exhaustion and hunger and a cramp in my lower back that wouldn't find relief until I returned to New York with my head in my hands.

But just after six o'clock, a pair of black Explorers left the garage in tandem, and *one* of the license plates matched an SUV I'd just tailed hours earlier: J21263. I had two seconds to decide: Wait for the other vehicle to emerge later, since the other one did the leading last time and likely carried the cargo I was after, or follow this pair and hope and pray Melody rode inside. For all I knew, Melody might not be transported for days, might take a long time to regroup and get her ready to relo, but the fact that two Explorers were traveling *together*—the first time that had recurred since I arrived at the courthouse—coupled with the familiar license plate, I didn't really need to engage in decision making; instinct had me put the car in gear.

And so I followed them, knowing the chance I was taking was my last.

We wound southward through the city of Baltimore in a manner suggesting they were following some playbook pattern to prevent tailing, weaving through a maze of exit ramps and roads that changed names; thankfully, I made a lot of green lights. Had my car not had the acceleration and handling it did, they might've shaken me.

My anxiety dropped as we merged onto the Baltimore-Washington Parkway, then spiked again at the thought we might be headed for Washington, DC, that whatever rode in those SUVs was just being transported from one courthouse to another.

But halfway down the parkway, we returned to Maryland Route 32 and started heading toward Annapolis. Route 32 ended onto I-97, which we followed to its end six miles later, and as the only choices at the end of the interstate were to go east to Annapolis or west to DC, the SUVs split, each going in opposite directions. I wasn't sure if they were following some procedure for throwing off a tail or if it was just coincidence, but the event put a distinct amount of doubt in my head.

The only choice to be made was the obvious one: I followed J21263.

We exited onto U.S. Route 50 and started driving directly east, right for the Atlantic. Though around the time we reached Salisbury, Maryland, and merged onto U.S. Route 13 on our way down the Delmarva Peninsula, I started picking up a middle-of-nowhere vibe perfectly suited to someone on the run, slapped my hand on the steering wheel at my increasingly likely win; my horse was coming from behind on the final turn.

This location, if not her final stop, should have been added to some future list back at Justice. The Delmarva Peninsula hangs off the mainland of the central Atlantic coast like a clump of hair that has broken free of a barrette, so widely separated by the Chesapeake Bay that it cascades down three states (*Del*aware, *Mar*yland, *V*irgini*a*). There is no simple way to get here; you have to go around or over things: to the top of Delaware and down, cross in the middle at Maryland's Bay Bridge as I had, or up from the very bottom at Virginia's Bay Bridge-Tunnel outside of Norfolk. That makes it perfect for hiding.

On the other hand, it makes it hard to get out, too. If the feds wanted to choke-point any fleeing villains, they'd only have three points they needed to choke.

Just past ten that night, the lone Explorer pulled into a Sheetz gas station not far past the Virginia state line. I waited until it stopped near the convenience store, then I pulled alongside an eighteen-wheeler at the other end. My un-Bovaroesque car, far more noticeable in a small-town environment, became progressively more troublesome to camouflage.

That stop served as my only opportunity to replenish water, cigs, and something—anything—to eat. I slipped out, still wearing my ball cap, my head tipped down, and stood by the front of the eighteen-wheeler as though I were its pilot. The Explorer remained running and idle, and only after a minute did someone emerge: a single, bulked-up marshal who looked like he could've been my law-abiding and law-enforcing twin, right down to a baseball cap and heavy jacket and jeans. His walk, his sway as he surveyed his surroundings without so much as a twist of the neck, the way one hand always seemed semi-balled into a fist, his heavy footsteps, distinguished him from the other patrons. Assessing your adversary is not half the battle; it's the entire thing. This guy was not Willie, not a toddler, not a hoodlum. Not someone I would take down with a single blow.

I waited a moment, hoping the marshal was merely checking out the convenience store before letting his traveler enter for a bathroom break. I needed to duck in and out as well, arm myself with the necessary objects to satisfy thirst and hunger and a fierce addiction to nicotine.

Through the glass, I watched the marshal turn a corner near the back of the store toward the restroom, where the length of his disappearance suggested he was using the facility rather than checking it out. He went through the store and grabbed several bottles of water and a few small packages of junk food, did so with a speed possible only by knowing their exact locations, as though the facility was more familiar to him than his own office. He rushed to the counter, paid, left.

As I heard the door slam on the Explorer, now certain Melody (or whoever) was not going to surface, I made my quick play for the convenience store, giving myself no more than a thirty-second delay so I could catch them again. I hustled in, grabbed an armful of junk: pretzels, chips, a trio of energy bars, two bottles of water—and rushed back to the front, tossed my items on the counter. But here is where the weight of addiction becomes so heavy you have no choice but to curse it; my speed was only as fast as the clerk opening the cabinet behind him to get my smokes.

The cashier, an older man dressed well enough to suggest he might be the owner, tossed four packs on the counter next to my pretzels, and just as I reached into my pocket for some cash, the marshal returned to the store. I tipped my head down so that my chin touched my jacket, pretended to count money. My twin walked to a specific spot with purpose, as though he'd left something behind. I held my money in my hand, faked peeling off bills while the fed surveyed a display; he was looking for a product, not a person. And as I slid two twenties across the counter, I could hear the marshal mumbling under his breath, complaining. All I understood was this: *babysitter.*

I nodded when the cashier offered to put all my stuff in a bag, my chin still pressed to my chest, cap down over my forehead, partly covered my face as I pretended to adjust my glasses. And as my purchases were bagged, the marshal made his way up front, the man who could take me down on the spot, legally put a bullet in my head if he judged me to be any threat at all, stood right behind me in line no less than eighteen inches away.

The cashier handed over my bag and change, thanked me; I did not respond, did not want my voice to be heard. I slowly turned around, and the marshal quickly slid up, nearly bumped into me he was in such a hurry to pay. And as I pretended to check the contents of my bag, I tilted my head to catch a glimpse of the lone product in the marshal's hand.

Hostess Orange CupCakes.

I caught and held my breath like I was about to dive into a pool, and though I bolted from that store, my movements tight and swift, those seconds felt like slow motion. Walking back to my car, I looked over my shoulder at the blackened windows of the Explorer parked no more than a snowball's throw away, knowing Melody was nearly in my grip.

And as I turned the ignition of the Audi, I empathized with

Randall, for there is an undeniable rush that comes from having played the long shot and knowing it's about to pay off.

I followed them another hour south on U.S. Route 13, rode through enough small towns to feed the Justice Department a decade's worth of addresses for protected witnesses: Temperanceville, Accomac, Melfa—I couldn't tell you where they began and ended, *if* they began and ended. We stopped again just before the Chesapeake Bay Bridge-Tunnel, pulled into a shabby-looking two-story motel that looked like its heyday came and went before I was born, that nothing had been updated since, not the paint, the sign, definitely not the parking lot. The building sat so close to the bay that you could see the water shining in the moonlight, smell the salt and rotting sea life, taste it in the air. The strip of beach at the edge of the property glowed like a bright beige stripe, three abandoned chairs stared out at the water at equidistant points.

The Explorer drove onto the crumbling pavement in front of what might've been considered the lobby of the motel, pulled forward next to another SUV that had been waiting for them. This particular vehicle was another Explorer—that must have been some deal Justice had with Ford—but it'd been given more attention: trim running along the doors thick enough to be bars, weird-looking roll bar on top, enormous wheels. Everything the marshals did, every swap of vehicles, seemed planned, all part of some larger operation, some organized chaos developed to transport witnesses. I found it hard not to admire it.

Melody was the pea in the Marshals Service's shell game.

I tucked my car at the edge of the building adjacent to where the Explorers rested, their engines still running. I reached under the passenger seat and pulled out a pair of binoculars, an item I'd purchased and chucked under there just after I bought the car, reserved for my pursuits of Melody, though never used.

But that night they were required; between the darkness and distance, I'd never make out any usable details. I pulled the lenses apart, removed my glasses, and pressed the binoculars to my sockets.

Two marshals surfaced, one from each SUV. They talked briefly—all business—then returned to their respective vehicles. The driver of the Explorer pulled his vehicle forward and parked in a space in a poorly lit area of the parking lot. A minute later, he turned the car off, got out, walked to the other SUV, and got in the passenger side.

Then they drove away, leaving J21263 by its lonesome.

And my greatest fear surfaced at what might remain under the shell: no pea.

I stared at that Explorer for five minutes, convinced Melody was still in there. I never saw anyone move her. On the other hand, I never saw her *in* the thing either, had no idea exactly what I was following. And if it weren't for the orange cupcakes, I might've doubted the entire journey.

Then in the sixth minute: The driver's side rear door opened and out stepped another marshal, one I hadn't yet seen, a taller and thicker version of the previous marshal, who appeared to have stopped accompanying his partner to the gym a few years earlier, this one's power being derived more from sheer size than muscle. The guy looked like management. The previous marshal had all the danger and potential of a butterfly knife; this one was simply a butter knife.

He surveyed the area with casual interest, then walked around to the passenger side and opened the rear door.

And Melody emerged.

For those first seconds, I forgot a marshal stood beside her. Her hair ran down the back of her neck, stopped before her collar. She wore clothes that had probably suited her at the start of the day, but now at the end she appeared disheveled. She looked *almost* alive.

From my distance it seemed either Melody was more petite than I remembered or that the marshal was enormous. It took me a second to assess them both, to determine what it would take to manipulate each of them should it ever come to physical means. While her protector looked around, Melody stared at the ground, and when he walked forward to the motel, she followed him like a child.

As they disappeared out of view along the side of the building, I pulled my car around to the far end of the motel and observed them walking down from the other end. The marshal seemed relatively on guard, looking behind all the hidden crevices of the facility—between vending machines, under the staircases, behind the shrubbery—with the level of interest he might have if he were teaching tactical techniques to a class of new recruits; he possessed all the passion of someone completing a checklist. And the entire time Melody's eyes were fixed on the Bay Bridge-Tunnel, watched the cars and trucks crossing over with the sustained amazement of a little kid's first visit to a large city, her head twisted as far as possible before having to turn around and walk backwards.

They moved down the sidewalk next to the doors of the rooms. Without knowing it, they shuffled closer and closer to my position, aimed directly at my grille. I turned off my car before they got any nearer, didn't want my running engine to catch the marshal's attention. A few steps farther, they paused in front of a set of rooms at the center of the motel, stood the distance of their rooms apart, each with a hand on the knob to their doors. I read the numbers on the doors of the rooms nearest me and counted up to determine their locations.

Melody: 130.
Marshal: 132.

They remained that way for a too-casual amount of time. I could see Melody's face, her awkward smile as she made idle chat with him, a breeze making her bangs dance on her forehead as they spoke. She glanced inside a plastic grocery bag the marshal handed her, tipped her head at him like she was waiting for a hug that never came.

Then she opened the door to her room, and two things occurred that really bothered me. First, the marshal did not go in before Melody to scope out the room. It struck me as a significant misjudgment, as though the guy were more aloof than I'd imagined, that at some point he had stopped caring about his job—or this witness. But what bothered me more: Just before Melody stepped inside, she lunged forward and kissed the marshal on the cheek. The whole event seemed weird: the way she looked at him, the hope in her expression like she might finally be safe, his nonbusiness reaction of holding her hand for a moment and returning her glance. I was surprised at how much that scene concerned me. I wanted the other marshal back; despite his clear physical preparedness and attention to the mission at hand, at least I knew who my adversary was. With this guy, I didn't know what I was getting, with all his hand-holding, his stroking-of-the-fur approach to protection, as though he could seduce her to safety. It annoyed me that he wasn't paying closer attention. If my family was thinking I might not be up to the task of offing Melody, they could have sent someone else to find and kill her.

I needed the marshal to protect her as much as she did.

They walked into their motel rooms and closed their doors at the same time. I watched and waited, and with each passing minute my adrenaline waned, my heartbeat and breathing slowed. I opened a new pack of cigarettes, lit one, took a victory hit.

And this is how the race ended, my horse having pulled into first, crossed the line at the photo finish. There was only one thing left to do: Go to the winner's circle and claim my wreath.

In those down moments I tried to consider what I would do with Melody. My instinct was to explain what had led me there, what had brought me to her life at that moment. Talk about a long story. I didn't even have a fraction of the time required to enlighten her properly.

I progressed to the idea of telling her how the government operation was being jeopardized by an addicted employee, and that no matter where they relocated her, she would be found again within hours. But that would make her pass the information back to the marshal she seemed so enamored of, which would make its way back to Washington and permanently cut off our source, leaving her no safer.

The next option was to just get her out of there, explain that she was far safer on the run without government backing, that the least hazardous thing for her to do was run from everyone at once. But if she had lived in fear before, that lifestyle would have been a nose-dive into an abyss of terror. And now that my father wanted her eliminated again, someone somehow would eventually find her; I couldn't stall things any longer.

My final conclusion—the only remaining option, yet the hardest sell—came by way of a lesson taught to me by my father, by Peter, by Tommy Fingers, repeatedly drilled into my impressionable head as a kid: Confront your aggressors *with aggression*. But that night as I sat and formulated my plan, the cab of my car filled with smoke and salty air and lonely ideas, I put their advice into play, knowing the only possible way to grant Melody safety was the riskiest: I had to bring her right to my father's feet, show him how innocent she was, that she could never pose a threat. I understood Pop's human side like no one else, paid attention in those moments when he was buried in thought and concern, watched him darken as he used violence and revenge as a buckler against betrayal and rejection. My plan was to reach out and play on those emotions, to ask him to imagine seeing me at age five in a room with Melody as she is just learning to walk and speak her first words, ask him to fathom the idea that one day he would ask his little boy to put a bullet into that baby girl. I hoped and prayed he might not be able to betray her. That he might not be able to betray his own son.

Yet again, the fundamentality of Gardner's life nudged its way into mine: To win big, you've got to risk big. And as I longed for a better solution, I knew my plan was her only shot at true freedom. And if it failed, her story would wind up with its original ending anyway.

I sat in my car noshing on an energy bar produced several seasons prior, washing each bite down with water, formulating what I would say when I approached her. I couldn't exactly walk in and say, "Now listen, don't yell for the marshal, but my name is Jonathan Bovaro. I'm not going to hurt you." I couldn't think of an approach more surely to elicit a scream. The only thing Melody could reasonably expect from me was violence, and I knew gaining her trust would require me to be true to who I was; I'd have to begin with fear, move backward toward apprehension, and hope to somehow land at dependence. I couldn't allow myself to be distracted from the reason I was there: Remove Melody from false safety and deliver her to permanent freedom and security. I was not there to win her heart or save her soul. She was just a little girl who'd fallen down a well and gotten stuck, and I had come to offer her a hand to finally pull her out.

Yet my greatest weakness that night was my greatest strength: I knew I would have to scare her. Over the span of my thirty-year life, she'd been a distant part of it for twenty, and in all those years she and I had never looked into each other's eyes and connected, never communicated, never shared a thought or idea between us. When the moment came, unlike at the gas station, there would be no way for her to look through me. And to know that the first time she'd read my eyes and mind would be under the guise of violence broke my heart.

Just past midnight, I slipped on a thin pair of leather gloves and stepped out of the car, carefully made my way to the darkest side of the nearly abandoned motel and walked up to a strip of rooms sheltered by the shadow of the stairwell to the second floor, recalled all those slow summer evenings with Peter and Gino as teenagers, the wagers we would place on who could break into a building the fastest—first our own family's, then the neighborhood stores; we rarely stole anything, derived more enjoyment from rearranging things (turning all the cans upside down, emptying the refrigeration units, significantly dropping prices) and then relocking the place. Beating Peter was nearly impossible, but the attempts sharpened our skills.

Once I'd selected the vacant room I'd be utilizing for practice, I glanced at the door for a minute, shook my head in amazement that the Marshals Service would use old motels for hiding a witness; a large hotel with doormen and security cameras seemed brighter.

I pushed my weight against the door and could tell I'd be able to open it with a good shove, but force of any degree would not be the solution; when the time came, kicking Melody's door in would mean a pistol pressed to the back of my neck within seconds. I pulled out my debit card and slid it down three times, each time catching on the lock and jamming. On my fourth attempt my card slid right in—and right behind the door, with it still locked. I whispered a rant of profanity I'll refrain from repeating; I pressed my knee hard against the door until it snapped open with a metallic clang. I quickly grabbed my card and slid into the crevice of the stairwell, waited five minutes: nothing.

I returned to the practice room, relocked it, and started again. It took me six minutes to finally break in using my card.

The second time it took me one.

By my fifth try, I was getting inside within seconds.

I returned to my car and waited, tried to formulate a plan of action. No script came to mind to acquire her trust. I planned to enter, explain why I was there—then the hard part—explain why she would be safer with me, why my intentions were noble. And then...I would set her free. I would give her the option to run toward me or turn away. I would be the first one, the only one, ever to put her in control of her destiny, and I hoped the taste of freedom would linger and have her longing for a bigger drink. I wasn't about to throw her in my car and insist the direction I was headed was the safest. It wasn't. But I wanted her to *want* to come with me, not be dragged somewhere under duress, the modus operandi of the feds.

The risks on my end, though secondary, remained huge. Should I be captured I would take an enormous fall; tampering with a federal witness is a dark corner. I could only hope my father and our crew would understand my motives, that it might make them rethink things, and that I wouldn't spend my life in prison mired in regret. But I was willing to take this risk if it meant finally freeing Melody.

I stared through the windshield of my car for a half hour, waiting for the heart of the night to come before taking action, watching the vehicles—mostly eighteen-wheelers at that hour—cross the bridge and pay their tolls, when an unexpected motion caught my attention. I glanced over to the long line of rooms and the marshal appeared, stepped out of his room, pulled out a cell phone, studied it like he was searching for a signal.

I slid down in my seat and watched as he walked toward the beach, his eyes on his phone instead of the ground. He must have connected, because he put the phone to his ear and held it in place by pressing his shoulder to the side of his head, propped his leg up on the bench of a broken picnic table under a cluster of large pine trees, took off his shoes and socks, and rolled up the bottoms of his pants.

He stood there for a few moments, talking, staring at the water of the Chesapeake, taking a few more steps toward it with each passing minute.

Ten minutes later, he'd reached the beach, a few hundred feet from the motel. I sat back up, pulled out my binoculars, and watched him chat, the occasional smile and chuckle denoting a personal conversation, which I interpreted as a call that would last longer than anything Justice-related.

Without realizing my actions I'd slipped the gloves over my hands again, put on my leather jacket—despite that warm May evening—to darken my body; I knew the moment would soon be upon me.

And as the marshal slowly sat down in the sand and gazed upon the moonlit water, phone still pressed to his ear, I tossed the binoculars aside. I slipped out of my car and quietly clasped the door, tightened my jacket around my body, left the car unlocked.

I dashed down the dark corridor to Melody's room, hunched over and fast in my movements, pulled out my debit card as I got closer. I took a deep breath and held it, placed one hand on the knob, slid my card over the lock with the other, and quietly opened the door, slid in, and pulled it behind me.

Our two worlds, once hurtling toward one another, finally collided.

I stood in the corner and let my eyes adjust to the darkness, and when they finally focused through the grain of black and white, I could see the shape of Melody's body balled up under the covers, could smell vinegary chemicals lingering in the air, the noise of the ventilator near the window humming loud enough to cover my steps.

Everything about who she was, all the innocence, the flesh and the spirit, was trapped under those blankets, and I hated myself for having to disrupt it, for having to toss her into a swirl of fear even if just for a minute.

I stepped toward the bed like a cat positioning to pounce, and with each footstep I could see more of her, watched as the covers rose and fell with each breath, then her nose move each time she inhaled.

All the risks, all the following, all the worrying, all the wonder, every thought I'd ever had about her collapsed like a black hole, and out the other end churned an energy as sharp and bright as a laser.

I closed my eyes and took the final step forward, close enough to reach down and kiss her on the lips, to smell the powdery scent of her skin. How gently I could have whispered in her ear, "I'm here to save you, Melody. You'll never have to run again."

Instead, I reached inside my jacket, pulled out a pen, and pressed the point to her neck with all the strength and intent of killing her.

FINCHÉ C'È VITA, C'È SPERANZA

(AS LONG AS THERE IS LIFE, THERE IS HOPE)

ONE

And then her body stops rising and falling, her nose stops moving.

She shivers and says this: "*Ow.*"

Through all of my years of anger and violence and fist-pounding, I can't muster it here to save my life. There is no faking it. If only she knew: *This is going to hurt me a lot more than it's going to hurt you.* I shake my head in disappointment with myself, quietly mumble, "Oh, sorry," like I just blew a take on a movie set.

I stand up a little, loosen my grip on her neck, and whisper in her ear, "I'm gonna let you go. Do not scream. Do you understand?"

She shakes her head but I think she meant to nod, and as I release her, her fingers dance around her neck as though she's expecting to find a small pool of blood. I pull back a few paces, ready to bolt if she begins screaming; I can only hope that capturing her and so quickly freeing her will provide for a temporary form of trust. Or at least confusion.

As I watch her rub her neck through the grain, see her shake and hear her breathe and force back a nervous cry, I can tell she peed herself. And now I know I could never understand the degree of terror and trepidation she must have been living with day after day for two decades. I stand ashamed; through all my years of despicable behavior I have never despised who I am as much as I do right now.

Melody stumbles out of bed, keeps her distance. We face each other in the dark silence, she energized by panic, I dispirited by disgrace.

I reach in my jacket, pull out my keys, and press the button on my keychain flashlight, shine it around the room until I spot the wall switch. I flip on the light and stare at her and hope she can't tell how hard I'm swallowing. She squints as a yellow hue fills the room, holds her hands to her chest like a praying child. She's wearing a loose-fitting camisole and pajama bottoms, her hair has been chopped short and is two shades lighter than it was just hours earlier, the bangs that danced above her eyes abbreviated to expose her forehead. Then comes a flurry of details I could've never gotten close enough to notice: the exact diamond shape of her jawline, the dark rims of her irises that give her eyes the design of targets, how she actually stands a few inches taller than I'd imagined. The harder part immediately follows, the identifying what never changed, the pieces that verify who she is: the curves of her nose and ears, and the way she is blinking—more like a flicker—she could just as easily be looking up at those skyscrapers again. Today she will not throw her arms in the air. Today she will not spin like a dancer, will not be a little Mary Tyler Moore.

She looks me over, but mostly locks on my face, and I can tell she really did look right past me at that gas station in Kentucky. There is no *you look familiar* statement on its way.

I take a nonaggressive step in her direction.

"You know who I am?" I ask. She says nothing, does nothing, eyes still flickering, hands still clutched to her chest. I answer my own question: "I'm John Bovaro."

My words are a potent weapon, slice her as badly as any knife, put a hole in her wider than from a hollow-point bullet. The blood washes from her face—an inverted blush—and now her fingers are dancing on her chest. Worst of all, as she holds back tears, her mouth turns to a casual frown, as though what's running through her mind is *that's what I was afraid of*, like she's finally being fired from a job where she'd been underperforming.

And then, like she's already given up, she whisper-yells, "Sean. Sean."

I laugh a little, not at Melody but at the odd selection the Marshals Service made for her guardian. If the marshal from the Sheetz was next door, I'd have a serious problem. But *Sean*? This entire event may have been predetermined.

I cast an open hand toward the end of the bed, suggesting she take a seat, and say, "Sean isn't going to be here anytime soon."

She doesn't sit, loses whatever blood had remained in her face, and whisper-yells again, "You killed him?"

I pull out my cigs, flip one to my lips, and light it. "Didn't need to. He's out on the beach, walking the shoreline." I take a record-breaking drag, feel an immediate drop in anxiety, and as I am about to blow out two full lungs of smoke, I catch myself and quickly turn my head away from Melody as the cloud escapes. "He's got his pants all rolled up like he's going clam-digging. I gotta tell you, that guy's a useless fu-huh..."—I catch myself again—"fellow."

Melody keeps her eyes on mine, reaches down to the bed like a blind person, carefully sits. She stares at me—I am no longer a person she can pass over the way she did in Kentucky—and I have become an image that will never escape her mind, that may even appear in nightmares that knock her awake and breathless in sweat-soaked sheets. I feel compelled to fill the silence.

"You know what that marshal makes?" I can't remember but I take a guess. "Forty grand. What kind of protection is forty grand going to get you?" Which might matter if the guy worked *for* organized crime instead of against it.

My words are having no positive impact. I watch her watch me, notice how she can't stop trembling. Every time I have seen Melody, year after year and through every phase of her young life, she has looked different, either through natural maturation or a change forced by the feds. I've never seen her look the same twice, always being modified, preparing for a new role in a new town. She has been an actress, and I her paparazzo. Though every time, I could never deny the natural beauty underneath; you can't cut, color, or restyle inherent loveliness.

I run my thumb around the filter of my cigarette, slowly bring it to my mouth and finish it off, and with the hit still inside me, say, "I like your hair this way." I take the butt, snuff it out on the metal edge of the mirror, and put the DNA-laced filter into the pocket of my jacket.

Melody slips her hands under her thighs in what looks like an attempt to get them to stop shaking, but it comes off like a sign of surrender.

"What do you want from me?" she says. She's not ready for the answer. I pull out my Marlboros, hold the pack in her direction with the offer of one. Her response allows us both to relax: "My parents always told me cigarettes would kill me." My prior attempts to lower the tension were ineffective, and under the circumstances it's impressive that she came out the tempered one. She's a lot stronger than her trembling suggests.

I accept her olive branch and pass her one in return. "The death I can handle. It's the bad breath and yellow teeth I find troublesome."

Melody puckers, tries to bring moisture to her mouth. "Why not try the nicotine gum?"

I shake my head and scrunch my nose. "You can't intimidate people by snuffing out chewed gum on their forearms."

Indeed, that came off a little dark; I was trying to strike a chord, not a nerve. I force a chuckle, then slide up a blade of the blinds in her room, see the marshal still out on the brightly moonlit sand.

"John Bovaro," she says, the first thing she has said this loud, the first attempt at trying to get someone's attention. I walk back in the center of the room and lean on the dresser. "Or, what, you go by Johnny? Little John?"

I slide my glasses up the bridge of my nose. "Actually, if you really want to know, I prefer Jonathan."

She gives me a look identical to the one Peter did when I told him the same thing; he'd responded with a blank stare, followed by, "Seriously?"

The difference: Melody giggles and says, "You've got to be kidding."

I smile, let her know she can feel free to even the playing field however she sees fit. I walk to the chair next to the window, glance out at the shoreline once more—the marshal is still spellbound on the beach—and reach down to the back of the chair and grab her robe and hand it to her. "Here. If you want to slip into something dry." She doesn't immediately take it. I move closer, practically put it in her hands. I read the uncertainty and confusion in her gaze, so I try to cement what I hope she is already thinking. "I'm sorry if I scared you."

There would be no way for her to understand that this moment might generate nightmares for me, too, how close I am right now to possibly losing her forever. Anything goes wrong—the marshal returns, I lose this margin of trust, one of our crew comes bursting through her door—and the result will be one from a collection of disasters.

She takes the robe.

I walk away and keep my back to her, surprised at how aware I am of the sound of the fabric being pulled from her body, the smooth swish of something being dragged against her skin.

"Can I ask you a question?"

"You *may*," she says, my signal to turn back around.

"How'd you know I was on to you back in Maryland?"

"What do you mean?"

I run all of Gardner's knowledge and accessibilities through my head, try to determine which person in my family was next to receive the very information I used. "In Columbia. How did you know I was following you?"

She licks her lips and shakes her head, squints in confusion like she's trying to solve two puzzles at once. "I had no idea who you were until a few minutes ago."

I look down and try to understand what might have happened. "You mean, someone else from my family threatened you?"

"No."

"Then why are you being relocated?"

The confusion in her eyes suddenly disappears and she looks at me like a child deciding whether to tell her parent the truth or fortify an existing lie. "I, uh... I decided I was bored and needed a change."

The truth not only sets you free, it occasionally launches you from your prison. "You mean... you made up a threat to get the government to relocate you, to get you a new identity."

She pauses, then nods. "Yeah, pretty much."

"Because you were bored."

She barely grins, seemingly surprised at her talent for manipulation. "Yeah."

This might be the biggest rush I've ever felt with a woman, the closest I might've ever come to finding a female so closely aligned to my own way of life. She's *almost* a criminal.

"Stickin' it to the man," I say as I offer my palm for a high-five, a move I immediately regret, though we both seem taken aback when she weakly slaps my leather-covered hand, more of a wipe of her palm against mine, but it is the very first positive shared physical contact she and I have had, the first time she reached out to touch me. And I imagine she's thinking the same thing I am: *This person is real.* For these few seconds, I have disconnected, lost an understanding of time and place—certainly lost a sense of urgency; somewhere out there are marshals and Bovaros and bullets. "You're all right, girl," I say, returning myself to the moment.

I need to look out the window again and make sure the marshal is safely distanced, but I can't stop staring at Melody, the way she is trying to read my eyes, the look on her face that shows a sign of hope that the punishment she'd anticipated will not be forthcoming.

"You're not going to kill me, are you."

Her brave statement chops the connection, frees me up. "Please. If I'd come here to kill you, you'd be fighting rigor mortis and I'd be halfway to Brooklyn." Truth: If *anyone else* had come here to kill you. "You think that fed they got protecting you is gonna step in and save the day?"

I pull out my cigarettes and stare at them, realize my addiction is out of control; it takes everything I've got to shove them back in my jacket.

"Sean's a good guy," she says.

"Yeah? Then go have tea and crumpets with him. But don't trust the man with your life. He's not a good marshal." She wipes her eyebrows and forehead. "I think what you really meant is he's *the* good guy, the way you see me as the bad guy... but I'm going to convince you that I'm actually the better one."

She holds her ground, is tougher than anyone I ever had to bang around; I find it really distracting. "I think you're underestimating the situation you're in right now," she says.

I've really got to look out the window again, but I'm playing this hand out, willing to take a real risk if it means leaving an impression on Melody.

"Look," I say, "I've watched a lot of feds over the course of my life. They've lingered around our homes and neighborhoods like unwanted relatives, like party crashers, and I can tell you this guy they assigned to you is distracted, completely uninvolved in your case." I hold out my arms to put myself on display. "Obviously."

"I trust him."

I walk right up to her. "C'mon, you feel safe right now?"

She looks into my eyes, then drops her head halfway down, then finally all the way to the floor. She shakes her head slowly. "No."

I let it sink in, allow a moment to pass before I slide toward the door and say, "Get a good night's rest. I'm coming back for you in the morning. I just wanted to let you know I was here—and that you'll need to leave with me. I'll explain tomorrow, but please understand: I'm your only chance."

One last look out the window—he's still on the beach, but starting to move—and the doorknob is in my gloved hand.

"Wait!" Melody gets to her feet. "What do you mean?"

"What confused you, Melody?"

She looks at me like she just got unexpected results from a pregnancy test. Her eyes are locked on my face and her lips are moving slowly, like she's repeating something to herself; it occurs to me that it's probably been who knows how many years since someone has called her by her real name. It's like I flipped a switch.

Finally, she says, "Where, uh... where exactly do you think you're taking me tomorrow?"

I can't tell if she's trying to pry information to leak to the marshal. At this point I just want her to consider what I'm offering, to think about why I'm here, why I'm letting her go. To want to know more in the morning, to ask me why I'm her only chance.

"A road trip," I say. "Melody, listen—I want you to believe me on one important thing, okay? *I am not going to hurt you.* But you have to come with me in the morning, and we'll have to move very quickly."

She catches me off guard with her response. "Ludicrous. What about Sean? What on earth would I tell him?"

"Nothing. Just have breakfast with the guy and tell him everything is fine. Don't worry. I'll come and find you. I'll explain it all later."

"You seriously don't think he'll find out about you? Please."

I wave her toward the window, flip up a slat of the blinds for her to look out. "Are you telling me that guy is gonna be your hero?" We both watch as he picks up a handful of shells or stones and chucks them into the Chesapeake, one at a time.

The only thing more pathetic than his substandard protection of his witness is Melody's defense of him: "He probably just misses his wife. Marshals are just as human as anyone. He probably needs some time to chill out."

"Sure, whatever. But that guy isn't married."

"He is, actually."

"Actually, *no.*"

"Actually, *yes.*"

Gardner better be right. "He is absolutely not married, Melody. What, you think only the feds can do research or check someone out before getting involved?"

I leave Melody there, slip out of the room without a single tick of a latch or creak of a hinge. I pull the door behind me as she stares at the marshal, her shoulders now slumped, the realization setting in that she is going to be let down again, that not one person in her life really cares about her safety, really wants her to live, wants her to be happy, wants her to escape.

Until now.

I drop down and creep under the window to her room, to all the rooms, sheltered by a burly hedgerow likely planted during the Carter administration. As soon as I open the door to my car and slide down into the seat, I start stripping: the gloves, the jacket, my outer shirt. Down to a T-shirt and jeans, I can't stop the sweat, can't slow my heart, can't catch my breath.

As I watch the marshal, a mere dot in my field of vision, I realize my body's reaction to this event has nothing to do with him, is in no way related to having narrowly gotten in and out of Melody's room, not related to the worry and concern of freeing her from this particular crevice of the country they swept her into. I know this because I can't stop recalling every word Melody and I just shared, replaying every interaction and dialogue in my head. I have spent the last twenty years gradually getting closer and closer to this woman, like a slow journey across the country beginning with the Atlantic, now finally ending at the shoreline of the Pacific. Yet we will continue the journey west; tomorrow, her hand in mine, we sail.

I turn the ignition of my car, thrilled I traded in my former vehicle. The Mustang would roar, a lion entering and announcing its takeover of new turf; the Audi purrs like a cat, hiding somewhere nearby without your knowledge, a nimble blur that flies by when you turn your head. And as the marshal stands and brushes the sand from his pants, I slink across the parking lot and disappear.

I drive south on Route 13, really the only direction I can go; I don't want to retrace my steps to the north, within a mile the east becomes an inlet to the ocean's barrier islands, and I'm currently where the westbound lanes end. The early morning air is thick with salty moisture that my air conditioner works hard to remove. Less than a minute of driving and I hit the tollgate for the Chesapeake Bay Bridge-Tunnel. I wind over to the only manned booth, see not a single car coming or going. I hand a twenty to an elderly woman who makes no eye contact, grab my change, hit the gas and go.

For seventeen miles I am floating above and drifting below the Chesapeake Bay. I do not see other cars or trucks, I do not see land. I drive alone, fast. The strings of lights in the tunnel sections whiz by, flash like an old movie projector, have the look and sensation of a child's version of time travel. I can't help thinking this must be how Melody has lived so many moments of her life, being transported somewhere. Being transported *elsewhere.*

And sure enough, as I emerge from the second tunnel and rise to the top of the last bridge, I see the other side, the land that lines the bay on the Hampton Roads area of Virginia, and for a moment I wonder if I really did travel across time, unsure of how this urban place can reside so near to one of the most rural parts of this country, separated by nothing more than a twelve-dollar toll. As my wheels touch down on land again, the landscape is draped in homes and businesses and multiple distant skylines. I will drive until I fall right into the middle of one.

Norfolk, Virginia, becomes my destination. I drift through the empty downtown streets, crawl between the unlit skyscrapers, and easily make my way through this nightlifeless city. I descend floor after floor of the parking garage beneath the Waterside Marriott—a building standing twenty-four stories, one of the tallest towers in the city—and park in a distant dark corner.

I take the elevator to the lobby and approach the desk. The lobby is paneled and mirrored and well lit, a double-tiered staircase cascading down from several stories up, too nice a place, really, to provide a hoodlum a few hours of rest before a kidnapping.

Behind the desk, one man and one woman stand at attention,

both in their forties, look like they could be siblings or a married couple truly on their way to becoming one, and both stiffly smile as I approach. They wear tags displaying their names—Chad and Melissa—and labeling them both as managers.

Exhaustion is upon me, has me delivering my needs in single words.

"Room," I say under my breath, like I just walked into a quick pillow.

"Reservation, sir?" Chad says.

"No."

"Any preference for room type?"

"Eh."

"We have many rooms available. Would you prefer a higher or lower floor?"

"Whatever."

"North- or south-facing?"

"You're killing me, Chad. I just want a bed."

We go through the usual back-and-forth of their request for a credit card, which I never provide, which they explain is required in case additional charges are incurred, which means I usually fork over a wad of cash to cover it, which embarrasses them and eventually has them give way; this is why the rest of my family crashes in dumps when on an assignment.

"We'd be happy to take your bags up for you," Melissa says. I look behind me like there might actually be something there. "Right," she mumbles, handing over the room card. "Enjoy your stay. Elevators are just past the desk on the right."

I rub my eyes as I walk, press the call button for the elevator, and wait in front of a closed store, a guest facility that carries higher-end clothes for men and women. I stare through the dark window at a headless mannequin wearing a sundress quite similar in style to the one Melody wore in Kentucky the day Willie and his friends pursued her. With a flash, I see Melody in it, and I remember how it fit her adult body, how she could've sold the style to the world by doing nothing more than wearing the dress in public.

The elevator bell dings, and as the doors slowly open it occurs to me that Melody has no more baggage with her than I do. I watched her walk into that motel room with a small plastic bag and nothing else—couldn't have contained much more than a single change of clothes—and some of what she did have were now cold and wet. I recall my memory of her room; I don't remember seeing clothing sitting out on the bed, the dresser, the floor. Nothing.

The elevator doors close.

I walk back to the desk. "What time does the store open?"

Melissa types something, doesn't look up. "Nine o'clock."

"I will have checked out by then."

Melissa glances over at Chad and he scrunches his nose and nods at the same time. "Just ring it all up here," he says to her.

I go back and stand at the store window, stare at the sundress while Melissa walks over with the key to open the place. I wait while she slides over the glass door, disables the alarm.

"No time to pack?" she asks.

I walk in and start surveying. "Not for me, for my . . . girlfriend."

"Okay, what can I ring up for you?"

I point to the window. "That sundress."

"What's her size?"

I bite my lip a little. "Not entirely sure. I don't know her that well." Melissa stares at me like I'm wasting her time. "I mean, I don't know those particular details yet."

She takes a deep breath, prepared to play twenty questions. "Is she tall or short?"

I stare at the dress, recall the tags of garments she'd shopped for—the sixes, the eights, the occasional ten—drop to the low end assuming a likely loss in her desire to eat.

"Size six," I guess.

Melissa opens her eyes wider. "Okay," she says as she reaches for one off the rack. "I'll ring this up for—"

"Wait a minute." I walk deeper into the racks. "And a sweater, she's gonna need a sweater."

She sighs through her nose, turns to the nearest stack of pullovers, holds up some brown thing with a knit pattern that looks like an eighteen-wheeler left its tire prints down the center. "This is very popular right now."

I wave her off. "She'd never wear that." I look around for a second and unfold a green Ralph Lauren sweater and hold it up. "This . . . is something she would wear," I say. "Yeah, this is her."

Melissa laughs quietly. "Okay."

"And jeans," I add.

"Okay, trust me when I say that's going to be a waste of your time. Women like to try on—"

"She's about five foot six or so, got very proportional legs, you know? I mean, not very muscular, but the kind where you like seeing her wear shorts." I stare at the pile of jeans on the table. "And the kind of hips for pulling someone close, that, sort of, perfect place for resting your hands." I drift off a little. "And a full, round . . ." I look up, open my hands to the air.

She grins with a motherly approval. "Sounds like you know her better than you think." Melissa starts getting into it. "Okay, so, like, maybe a lower-waist kind of thing?"

"What about undergarments?"

Melissa frowns a little. "Are you serious? Jeans are one thing, but bras and panties? Women really like to have what works for them."

"You're gonna have to help me out here."

"You two seem to have a real packing deficiency."

"Yeah, well," I say, as I start playing with the sheer fabric of the sundress, "we're running away together."

With two bags in each hand, I slip the card between my knuckles and slide it in the reader to my room, kick the door open and the lights automatically come on. Turns out Chad took advantage of my *I don't care* disposition and booked me a suite when all I really needed was a bed and a shower. The room has a king-size poster bed and a separate seating area with a pair of loveseats facing each other near a gas fireplace. The bathroom possesses toiletries for every possible skin type, a jetted tub, and a shower suitable for a small party. From the twenty-first floor, my window overlooks the Norfolk waterfront, a brick version of a boardwalk lined with shopping pavilions and restaurants and boat slips, a city center so inviting and pedestrian-friendly it reeks of planned development, of a calculated design assembled by some architect who rarely visits the city, who doesn't appreciate the practicality of things like loading zones and alleys.

I stare at the deserted waterfront. In New York dollars, a condo with this view would cost seven figures and carry a thousand-dollar monthly fee, no matter how run-down the building, no matter what street it claimed as its address. Chad probably thought he was doing me a favor by giving me such an elegant and lofty room, but all he did was shellac my already vulnerable and exposed grain of guilt. Such is the nature of Melody's life, of mine: She suffers tonight in a dank motel room, missing all of the necessities and niceties most women would request, guarded by a half-wit protector; I live in prosperity and comfort, will sleep the next few hours in a bed with a plush mattress and a new down comforter, will have a fresh breakfast delivered to my door as I shower. No two lives should be reversed more than ours.

I walk to the bed and sink into its softness as I sit. I set the alarm on the clock instead of requesting a wake-up call, having learned long ago that technology will always be more reliable than any human being.

I check my cell: three messages from my head chef, zero from my family.

I pull back the comforter, and the sheets are stretched perfect and smooth like a pool yet to be dived into. I strip down to my boxers and take the plunge, and within seconds I drown in sleep.

TWO

As I leave the hotel less than five hours after arriving—notably the most expensive per hour cost of sleep I've ever incurred—the city of Norfolk comes alive, the traffic thickening as I narrowly escape rush hour and return to the Bay Bridge-Tunnel. The chilly air seems held in place by a fog that will likely burn off before I get to the other side, disintegrated by a distinct spring-into-summer morning sun that has me reaching for my sunglasses.

On the bridge portions I pass all the vehicles I can so that the single-lane tunnel sections are more bearable, and within thirty minutes I can see the lonely expression of the Delmarva Peninsula, the remaining lengths of the bridge spans stretching out like waiting arms. I say a silent prayer that Melody's are outstretched for me as well. Everything is running out: time, hope, and my last chance of making an escape with Melody. I'll be facing one of three scenarios: (1) Melody coughed up my arrival to the marshal, in which case I will be nailed; (2) Melody tasted what it's like to be free—both from my arrival *and* my departure, and the fact that she can turn me in if she chooses—and suspects that only I can give that to her; or (3) she's already gone, disappeared—or dead.

I turn into the motel parking lot, spotting the marshal's Explorer still in place from last night, and drive around until I find another red car to park next to, the only trick I have to conceal my cherry bomb. I exit my car and slip on my jacket, then my driving gloves. I move in and out of the walkways and crevices of the motel that I'd walked just hours earlier. The facility appears dirtier and more neglected in the daylight than when illuminated by nothing more than the moon. I slip behind the bushes a stretch away from their rooms and stare, watching for anything: a crack in the door, movement of blinds, a cleaning person going in or coming out.

After almost twenty minutes of crouching, the marshal is the first to emerge—*from Melody's room.* I read the numbers on the doors and I am certain of it; I can't help but wonder how close they've become, if Melody's apparent attraction to the marshal somehow evolved—or worse, the possible words they exchanged in what might have been an all-night discussion, how the impression I left on Melody was not as effective as I hoped.

The marshal walks out and stands on the sidewalk, goes nowhere, breathes like he's getting ready to make an Olympic run down a ski slope. Then he quickly returns to his room. Two minutes later he shows again, takes a few paces back and forth while he rubs his eyebrows and temples, then back into his room. He goes through this ritual one more time before he doesn't make it back, bends over like he's looking for something he dropped in the shrubs, then retches all over the hedges, stumbles back inside his room, and closes the door.

This, I determine, functions equally as a blessing and a curse. I'd intended to snag Melody when the marshal left his room to take care of resolving their bill, prepare the Explorer, meet another marshal—whatever would draw him out and away. Now I know he is indisposed, a real chance to get her out of here. Unfortunately, I'll have to pull it off with him one wall away.

I reverse my movements, retracing the perimeter of the facility, keeping my eyes on the doors to their rooms. I zip down the walkway and slow as I come right up on their doors. I pause and listen for voices, hearing only the marshal's muffled vomiting; I make note of how flimsy the structure of this motel actually is, how quiet we will need to be.

I pull out my card and open Melody's door within seconds, a mastered skill utilized for its final time. My eyes slowly adjust to dim flickering light, the muted television throwing gray light upon the walls. I hear the shower running and splashes of water hitting the bottom of the tub in large bursts. Her room is strangely warm, heat still radiating from the ventilator even though it's off. Within thirty seconds, the water stops and the only remaining sound is the vent fan for the bathroom. Its rattling and knocking make it impossible to hear sounds from the marshal next door.

I stand like a statue by the entryway, survey the room like a vandal coming back to assess his handiwork. So many things remain from the night before: the clothes she removed from her body, the chair by the window, the smell of stale smoke once exhaled from my lungs.

And then I start absorbing those things I missed the first time. A Rorschach-shaped, roux-colored stain decorates the pillowcase in the dent where her head had rested. A ripped-open box of hair coloring along with its near-empty contents rests below the mirror on the dresser. One-inch lengths of hair are sprinkled unevenly across the floor like salt on an icy sidewalk. Other than her clothes from the night before, there is so little to know of her. Were I a voyeur or snoop, how disappointed I would be at gaining access to her life. The woman barely exists.

The vent fan goes off. I walk toward the bathroom door and look around for any further signs of life, and as I get nearer I can hear Melody drying her body, the sound of the cotton towel gliding across her skin. I inhale and hold my breath to better hear, put one hand and one ear on the door. Though I'm certain she's lived a transgressive life—her scamming of the government is proof enough—I can't let go of viewing her as an ingénue, an innocent girl waiting to learn what the world has to offer. Granted, my world is not one worth emulating. Even now I disappoint myself, standing only inches away, separated by nothing more than a hollow wooden door, wondering just what that innocence might look like, how smooth and warm it would feel in my hands.

I turn around and sit on the edge of a small fold-out chair. I've made it so close to the end of my lifelong journey of righting this wrong that nothing will stop my completion. If Melody chooses to leave me here, so be it; I'll make a struggled attempt at accepting it. Until then, the only way someone is taking her is over my bullet-filled body.

I stare at the muted television and watch the Weather Channel, try to read the lips of the meteorologists, find out the warm streak will soon be coming to an end. I have my ear trained on the door to the bathroom, shift my eyes on the door to her room. Whichever one opens first will be the decision maker.

Then all at the same time: The bathroom door opens, the mirror lights are flipped off, and Melody walks right in front of me and yelps.

"Oh, geez!" she says.

I race to cover my eyes. "You decent?" I ask softly, implying her loud voice is a bad idea.

She waits to respond. I hear her deep breathing. "You're very polite for a captor, you know that?"

I crack a little space between my fingers, take a peek from the corner of my eye. She's wearing a pair of jeans and a blue T-shirt that casually reveals the shape of her body, a mixture of cheap fragrances follow her out with a ten-second delay.

She backs up a little and turns to the side and I examine her body, note that I may have been way off on the style of jeans she wears, but spot on for the contour they needed to cover. Melissa was right; all these years of watching her left an impression.

"We have to leave," I say. "*Now.*"

Our futures come down to her response to my demand. She slips her hands in the pockets of her jeans, nervously taps her thighs beneath the denim. Her hesitance, her keeping herself together here suggests she gave my late-night discourse some consideration.

She studies me, says, "Today is the last day of the rest of my life."

Having lived an existence of distrust and confusion, she seems to find solace in ambivalence; she's clearly sitting on the fence. Unfortunately, I don't have time to try and talk her down. And as much as I'd love to grab her hand and yank her off, she's been yanked all her life. The decision has to be hers, a choice that will carry a commitment strengthened by the exercising of her free will.

"Get it?" she adds.

I grab the remote and turn up the television to mask our conversation; she's either too nervous to speak quietly or she's trying to send a signal to the puker. At this point it's more important for me to cover our words than to try and hear the marshal.

I step closer; she does not back away. "I promised I wouldn't hurt you, didn't I?"

"But you're a liar. You've been in my life for no more than a few minutes and you wasted it by lying to me."

"What did I lie about?"

"You said Sean makes forty grand a year. He actually makes fifty-three."

I purse my lips; fifty-three does sound familiar. If nothing else, at least I know Gardner's information was on the up and up.

Assuming everything else he gave me was accurate: "He confirm that he isn't married?" She bites the corner of her mouth, shrugs one shoulder, and looks toward the blind-covered window. "If you ever see him again, ask." I walk a little closer to the door. "Unfortunately, you probably won't ever see him again. And if you do, you won't live long enough to ask. You've got one shot at survival here, and it requires you to trust me."

She has enough confidence to look me right in the eye. Her mouth opens, pauses without forming words, as though she's thinking twice about whatever was about to escape. I seem to have achieved one objective: By introducing myself last night and leaving her unharmed, my return has her displaying a different disposition.

I turn to fully face her, drop my hands to my sides, attempt a nonconfrontational pose. "Tell me you want me to leave," I say. "Ask, Melody. You can do it."

"I don't have to ask anything. Sean comes through that door and there'll be nothing more to discuss."

There's that friggin' fence again.

I fold my arms, confrontation arrives anyway and makes itself known, passes my lips in what appear to be words of jealousy. "I find it entertaining that you call your little clam-digging friend Sean instead of marshal or deputy."

She speaks positively but shakes her head in disappointment. "We have a sort of... connection."

I try not to laugh too loud. "Well, expect to get disconnected very soon."

She rolls her eyes as though anxiety has been replaced by annoyance. "Are you going to tell me what's going on? What'd you do with Sean?"

"Sean is delayed. You might say he's having a bout of tummy trouble."

"Oh, clever! Let me guess: That means you sliced his stomach to pieces. You guys are totally awesome."

I need to get her out of here, but she's starting to suck the energy right out of me. I stand back and hold my hands out, far-distanced and weaponless. "Does that seem like my style?"

"What do I know? It was definitely your dad's style."

I look away, would love to explain how that would never be who I am to her, and that I have traveled twenty years to undo the specific actions that caused her all this destruction, to restore her to who she was before we vandalized her life. Unfortunately, we don't have that kind of time. "Yeah, well, that's sort of why I'm here."

"Aw, your daddy send you on errand?" The fear she had five hours earlier seems to have been fully transformed into hatred. Quite unfortunate. For nearly my entire life I've been mentored on the way to manipulate fear into a currency that can be used to make any purchase. Hatred, on the other hand, adds up to nothing, was almost exclusively reserved for the feds and the cops and those we had betrayed.

And now I'm facing a bout of fear myself—the fear I'm going to lose her here. I search my arsenal of possibility; I've got nothing, can't look her in the eye. I've never been defeated easily—at least never *this* easily—but Melody has knocked me down. I'm surprised how much it hurts.

I turn to leave, no longer caring what faces me on the other side, ready to take out that inadequate marshal with a few swift blows, give him a lesson on how seriously he should be taking his job.

"Meet me out front in five minutes." And as I open the door and step into the sun, I say, "And be alone."

"Wait!" she says, then pauses like she had no follow-up. "Should I bring my stuff?"

I stare at her, and with all the intention I can rally I try to drive home my point, that if she chooses the marshal over me, the existence she will condemn herself to: "What stuff?"

I close the door behind me, walk to my car. And wait.

THREE

I keep my promise. I pull next to the rusty overhang at the front of the motel. But now I am fueled, less interested in strategy than in battle; Peter would be proud. A small part of me would love to get face-to-face with her marshal—*Sean*, the lethargic superhero—and put a finger to his chest and a fist to his head, command him to protect her life like his own.

I decide to in-your-face this entire scene: I park my car sideways and block anyone else from driving through the entryway, display the Audi like the only ripe tomato in a struggling Delmarva crop. Then I put the top down and my sunglasses on.

I keep the engine running and watch the path Melody would walk, my eyes so fixed on any movement near the corner of the building that I can't even distract myself with lighting a smoke.

Of the five minutes I told her to wait, four have passed and my heart starts pounding harder. I can't help but consider going back to her room, throwing her over my shoulder and tossing her in the car, taking her somewhere more suited to explaining the whole story; after all, of all the hardware in my toolbox, force has been a chrome Craftsman. But it would be so much more powerful if she makes the choice on her own.

And so I stare and hope and pray. If there are other sounds, other cars passing up and down Route 13, I don't acknowledge them. A storm could be rising behind me: federal agents carefully slipping between parked cars and placing the back of my head in the crosshairs of their rifle scopes; the charge of another marshal as he winds up his arm in preparation to pistol-whip me; the surge of tires over gravel from an Impala with New York plates, then the sluggish exit of crew members, the tap on my shoulder and ruffling of my hair as someone mutters, "We'll take it from here, Johnny."

The fifth minute ends, departs like a train rolling down a dusty track, slowly vanishing out of sight. Can't help but think it's a real shame she didn't make it to the station on time.

Though it appears her decision has been made, I refuse to give up. As much as common sense would suggest I throw the car in gear and return to New York, I'm stuck. In the sixth minute, I repeatedly think, *C'mon, Melody.* In the seventh minute, I start whispering it.

But in the eighth:

Melody walks around the corner, her hands in her pockets again, bottom lip tightly clenched between her teeth. She keeps looking back and around and over her shoulder like a kid about to make her first drug buy. As she slowly draws closer, I try to avoid smiling, but no amount of strength can prevent it; it feels silly when it happens. This must be how a man unsure of his lover's affection feels when his offer of marriage is tearfully accepted. She chose *me.*

Melody approaches like a child having just been offered a piece of candy by a lurking stranger. The closer she gets the more confused she looks. She stops about ten feet away. Though I expect her first words to be *you better not hurt me* or *I demand to know what's going on,* she pops this fly:

"Why not just paint a target on the back?"

The steadiness in her voice surprises me, suggests she's been transported so many times under such terrifying conditions that I am nothing more than a new driver. I wave her closer.

"Meaning what?"

She doesn't budge. "Meaning I cannot think of a more conspicuous way for you to get me out of here." Read: You're an amateur and we don't stand a chance.

"What do I care?" I say. "I've committed no crime." Except, of course, the breaking and entering thing. I clarify. "At least none that would concern the pukemeister back there. And let's be clear: I'm not holding a gun to your head or a knife to your throat. You're coming willingly."

She chuckles as though my stab at wangling her with semantics pales in comparison to the manipulation she's received from the government. "You kidding? The gun or knife is implied, *Jonathan*."

"I specifically told you I would not hurt you."

"And I specifically told you I perceive you to be a manipulative liar."

Still going through the hatred phase, I see. Though I'm now getting the sense she's forcing it. She may say I'm a liar, but as she finally steps a little closer, I can tell Melody wants to know what it is she'd be giving up. She inches toward the car, and once having finally reached it, places her hand on the frame of the passenger door, looks over the interior like a dieter staring down a hot fudge sundae.

"Besides," she says, letting her eyes eventually make their way to mine, "you did have a knife to my throat not too long ago, remember?"

"You mean this?" I reach into my pocket and pull out the pen I'd put to her neck. She stares at the Montblanc, cocks her head as though thinking, *It did sorta feel like a pen instead of a knife.* When I was a middle schooler, Tommy Fingers taught me the art of staying fully armed without carrying a single weapon, achieved by way of everyday things that can cause immense damage—paper clips, pens, a roll of coins, even dental floss. You can wipe someone out, and when the cops arrive they find nothing incriminating on you. Should the marshal have surprised me last night, the last thing I'd have wanted him to shake out of my jacket was a traditional weapon.

I try to capitalize on her doubt. "Hop in," I say, and smile a little, try to suggest that everything is going to be okay, except I'm thinking, *C'mon-c'mon-c'mon-get-in-the-friggin'-car-let's-go.*

She bites her lip again, looks over her shoulder, makes one last attempt to find that fence upon which to perch herself, hoping to size up the other option and what it might have to offer. But she exhales long and hard, like she's uncertain as to the quality of either product. Then, without seeing her hand, I hear the latch of the passenger door quietly click as she opens it. And though she's still looking over her shoulder, I'm hoping it's because she wants to make sure we can make a clean getaway.

She slides down onto the passenger seat slowly, wiggles her lower body into place like she's trying to slip into a pair of tight pants. She reaches over and gently closes the door, rolls her shoulders and rubs her bare arms.

"I'm not really dressed for riding with the top down." She turns to look at me. "I mean, you're wearing a sweater and a jacket."

Her words are phrased in such a way that she is not asking me to *put the top back up.* Maybe she thinks having the top down will preserve the possibility of being seen and rescued by the feds. Or maybe she just wants to feel the freedom of riding out in the open, of feeling the wind whip around her, of *not* being protected.

"Wait," I say, reaching behind her seat and nodding toward the bridge-tunnel, "I crossed over that monster last night, picked up some clothes for you. I figured you weren't going to have much." I hand her a shopping bag—three more are in the trunk—and she peeks inside before she accepts it.

I know I need to get us away from this motel—the urgency

is still buried in my gut—but with her by my side, I am foolishly pulled from concern, feel like I am adrift on the water like a cast-away. Melody gently places the bag in her lap, turns to me and stares.

She's the first woman to corner me like this, to make me feel like I need to fill the gap in silence. "I hope these are your style." How do you like that clever gift of conversation? She says nothing, glances in the bag again. "I was guessing you were maybe a size six?" Yes, nicely played—especially if it turns out she's now smaller than a six and I've implied she's heavier. Apparently, I do not have the magnetism that Sean has, am missing the gravity that might bring a kiss to *my* cheek.

She looks inside the bag as though a dead fish were at the bottom, does not pull anything out. "You... bought me clothes?"

Happy to have her in the conversation, I quickly respond with a flood of useless information: "Yeah, Norfolk's right on the other side, maybe an hour or so from here. I did a little power-shopping last night. For you, I mean. To get you clothes. And stuff."

She widens the opening of the bag, and as she studies its contents, she does that *thing*: She reaches up and runs her fingers around the edge of her hairline, as though trying to tuck imaginary hair behind her ears—the hair was there hours ago, so recently removed it must feel like a phantom limb—and it looks like she's doing nothing more than tracing the outline of her ears. I hate that there is nothing for her to tuck; I fear she may one day stop doing it. I find her delicate motion a selfish, if not guilty, pleasure.

And with that, she slowly reaches in, selects the dark green sweater, stares at it for what feels like a time longer than if she'd seen it in the store herself. Then she brings it to her face, closes her eyes, rubs it against her cheek and inhales a breath of cotton.

Maybe it's the lack of sleep or the torrent of action over the last couple days, maybe it's my fear of Melody being hurt or my narrow capacity to prevent it, but somehow emotion slips inside me, possesses my body like a demon. We should be long gone, but I can't take my eyes off of her, can't move. I'm staring to the point of rudeness. And then I make the ultimate mistake by saying what I'm thinking.

"It matches your eyes."

The problem is this: Her eyes are still closed. She would never imagine how I have them memorized like a poem. The color was what made them memorable, but not in the way you'd notice someone with "bright blue" or "wild green" or "rich brown" eyes; hers are a vague composite, a mixture crafted from a painter's palette. But the intensity of her irises, the dark circle at the edges, the marbled swirl of color, had me forever lost in them. Sometimes the most beautiful and breathtaking objects are those lacking vibrant colors at all, like a fresh snow-covered landscape; not everyone has eyes of autumn leaves and Caribbean waters. And so it is here my words betrayed me. True, anyone could have—*would* have—noticed the glow and hue within moments of meeting her, but I have revealed something more. She and I both detect the oddness of my words the second they pass my lips.

She pulls the sweater from her face, opens her eyes but avoids eye contact. "You've seen me for just a few minutes of my life and you know my dress size and the color of my eyes?"

I can't read her words, can't determine if she is flattered or creeped out. In either case, it wakes me up, has me shoving the car in gear and the wheels in motion at a speed high enough that precludes jumping out. "I got you a bunch more stuff in the trunk, but we gotta get out of here."

I pull onto Route 13, whip an illegal U-turn, and within seconds we're driving northbound at sixty miles an hour. Melody shifts lower in the seat and drags the sweater across her torso like a blanket. She covers her face with her hands and shakes her head, a series of motions that could only be translated as *what am I doing?* I'm glad she's taken the risk to trust me, and though she might be fearing what the feds will infer if they find out she willingly left with me, it would have to be slight compared to their finding out how she manipulated the program for her personal benefit.

The sound of the concrete under my racing wheels acts as a buffer to our talking. The air is still moist and thick, will have us feeling dirty when we finally stop. We drive for a few miles before Melody assembles the confidence or curiosity to glance at me, and even then it is only for a second before she looks away. A mile later, she glances again, her eyes lingering longer. She repeats this as I drive, each time her gaze staying upon me with greater time, greater boldness. We are no more than ten miles north of Cape Charles and she is now officially staring at me.

I try not to look her way, but the harder I try the more impossible it becomes. I meet her eyes and smile, take my hand off the stick and wipe my forehead, reach under the seat and pull out my CD case, hand it to her. "Pick anything you can listen to at top volume," I say, hoping to avoid the silence, the space between us that can only be filled with explanation; I want her to relax before I unload.

But as she unzips the pouch, I realize I've made a second critical mistake. She says, "What do we have here? Bach? Mozart?"

Hardly. It's like the friggin' Melody Grace McCartney funpack. How freaked will she be when she sees a collection of her favorites? Tipped off to her purchases at Best Buy so long ago, I moved from one band to another, inadvertently associated similar artists, likely mirrored her library.

She flips through the collection, studies each disc, slows with each one. "You're a . . . pretty mellow guy."

I shrug, need a cig. "I have my moments."

She frowns, keeps turning the pages. "We have surprisingly similar tastes."

Just one of many surprises to come. She pulls out *Hot Fuss* by the Killers and waves it in front of me. "Funny," I say as I jam it in the CD player.

The car screams up the road, a perfect line to the north, and when I tell her of my plan, I hope it's the only thing screaming. Mr. Brightside I'm not.

Miles pass and so do the tracks. By the time "Somebody Told Me" finishes, it feels like I should be talking myself, that enlightenment on her situation should be forthcoming, that the clean getaway has been achieved and it's time to move on. "All These Things That I've Done" ends and Melody stares into the distance, appears lost in disbelief. I know my delay in explaining is going to create a forest of doubt I'll spend the remainder of this journey axing down. Her imagination is likely producing more terrifying tales than what the future actually holds.

I think.

Even though awkwardness is present, like a passenger in the backseat, I waste tracks six, seven, and eight. Melody seems lost now, props her elbow on the edge of the door and rests her head on it.

I edit the formulated words in my head—a succinct retelling of why I am here, how I have watched over her, how I am watching over her now, how I will set her free to live her life by her own design. "Believe Me, Natalie" begins. And as I drop my speed, turn to her now that we're well distanced from Cape Charles, all deep-breathed and ready to tell her everything, I see she's fallen asleep.

And now it's my turn to stare. I spend more time looking at her than I do the road before me. Her head rests back and to the side, her hands positioned across her chest holding the sweater in place, her feet tucked together under the dash and her legs cocked sideways. It feels like I've taken a girlfriend for a country ride. I get a flash of her and me at the ages our lives first became entangled, me at ten and she at six, imagine for a moment that we'd grown up down the street from one another, the girl and boy next door, realized we'd been in love all our lives, and now we're making a far more innocent escape together.

I turn the music down, even though so many other things might have brought her out of sleep—stoplights, sirens, loud trucks; she's out cold. "Everything Will Be Alright" ends, and so does the disc. I turn the stereo off.

I merge back onto Route 50, begin driving west toward Annapolis, where shortly thereafter I will wind my way to I-95 and begin the journey to New York. The clean, smooth pavement and stretches of highway deliver a constant white noise that helps keep Melody asleep. When I'm not noticing her I'm practicing my words, getting it down to a rhythm, sharpening their meaning and effectiveness. I run through the routine a few times before I get lost in looking at Melody again. With her hair so short, all choppy-edged and irregularly colored, I take in the entire shape of her face. Her smoothly chiseled jawline, the delicate shape of her ears, the lonely empty hole at the bottom of her lobe, the widow's peak at the top of her hairline, a face so soft and appealing and blemish-free it could hardly matter what happened to her hair. Someday far from this moment, after I have set her free to be herself and she has opened her life to another person, some man will get lost in her, look in her eyes and hear not a single word she is saying, he will pull her to his chest in bed and lightly stroke the skin of her face and wonder, *What could I have done to deserve her*, and he will whisper in her ear, *I will never leave you. I will love you forever.*

Until then, I have to open her cage and shake it a little or she's never going to fly.

FOUR

I'm pleased with our progress, having crossed the Bay Bridge in Maryland and wound over the highways that bring us back to I-95. As I pull off of the exit ramp from Route 32 to merge onto the interstate, my foot slips off the clutch and I accidentally grind the gear as I put it into fifth. The car jerks a little and the noise is loud, especially with the top down.

Melody wakes, rubs her eyes, clears her throat. She sits up a little, lets the sun beat down on her and pulls the sweater from her chest, and as she recognizes her surroundings she comes to attention.

"Why are we going back to Columbia?"

"We're not," I say over the road noise. "We're going home." She looks at me like she just swallowed a mouthful of sour milk. "To *my* home."

"What do you mean?"

"My home. Where I live."

Though I'm sure of my plan, she stares at me like she's trying to decipher the words of a foreigner, shakes her head as if to suggest, *This is the basket I put all my eggs in?*

"Please tell me you live in Pennsylvania."

I laugh, throw my arms in the air. "New York City, baby. The Big Apple."

How could I know I was riding beside a loaded gun? I couldn't have, until my words pulled her trigger. As if I'd spoken some code word, she fires: Melody yanks up on the parking brake and grabs the steering wheel, spirals us across two lanes of traffic, narrowly making it in front of a FedEx truck and a Mini Cooper, drops us off on the shoulder of the interstate like a bag of trash crashing at the bottom of a landfill. We've stopped moving and I grip the steering wheel in my white-knuckled fists like the security bar of a roller coaster. As I breathe in dust from the cloud we've created, Melody quickly reaches over, turns off the car, and pulls the key from the ignition. The air fills with a chorus of screeching tires, shrilling horns, and yelling drivers.

This event serves as a teachable moment, helps me to learn my very own lesson: *When violence arrives, it rarely knocks.* It did not tap me on the shoulder, suggest I get ready. It sought to create change by way of confusion.

I never saw it coming.

I'm so panicked, my breath is nowhere close to catchable. I get out what I can. "Are you. Out. Of your *mind*?"

I'm confused by her level of calmness. "Why are you taking me to New York?" I stare at her, my eyes drooping like a dog aware of forthcoming punishment. I almost start explaining, but this is not the right time, *definitely* not the right place.

Cars slow as they pass, most trying to figure out what happened, others yell for us to *go back to New York* and wave fists or middle fingers.

"What's the matter," she says, "can't handle the wet work yourself? Need an uncle or a big brother to do the—" Big breath and scowl. "Oh, that *is* it!" She laughs and shakes her head. "Oh, you were so clever with all your '*I'm* not going to hurt you. I promise *I* won't hurt you.' Yeah, but see that psychotic maladjusted freak over there? Yeah, he might hurt you. He's more of a damage-oriented kind of guy. I'd watch yourself around him."

I really wish I could compose myself. I try to look her in the eye, but fail. "You got me all wrong, Melody."

Her disposition shifts like I'd spoken another code word. Of the six I'd said, the only one that could have packed any value was *Melody.* Her true name is my secret weapon, her kryptonite. She sits with her back against the passenger door, slumps a little, holds the keys in the palm of both hands like a cup of tea.

I finally connect my eyes with hers. "Hear me out, okay?"

She stares me down, lifts the sweater back to her torso, fingers the weave. She gives it a strange look, like she can't make sense of it, can't determine its place and purpose, can't clarify the reason behind my buying clothes for someone facing certain death. Originally an unscripted part of my plan, making those purchases might have saved me, though more importantly, saved her. Right now I may be a blackbird in her eyes, but she's having a hard time explaining that single, bright blue feather.

I wipe my face clean of perspiration and dust. "Look," I say, ready to get out of here before a cop comes inquiring, "you want to grab a bite? Let's get a table and talk. There's a great place nearby."

"You know this area?"

"The ground is very soft and moist, buried a few people here years ago." Neither of us laughs.

She ignores my joke, says, "My nerves are shot...but I guess I should try to eat something."

I put out my hand for the keys. She waits a second before delivering them, but when she does I grab both the keys and her hand at the same time, squeeze them both firmly. I tug her arm a little, pull her in my direction like I'm going to give her a kiss: "You're safe with me, Melody, okay? *As long as I am with you*, you are safe."

She looks in my eyes like she's trying to read something, anything, that might indicate where this is all going. She licks her lips, shakes her head *no* but silently mouths the word, "Okay."

We continue driving northward, avoid Little Italy and head toward the geographic center of Baltimore, through an iffy section of midtown, to a signless restaurant owned but not run by the Bovaros. The unassuming place was the collateral of an unpaid debt to my father some fifteen years earlier, a debt whose makers have long since perished. My folks brought us to Baltimore a few times when we were kids, usually for a baseball game, lots of food and late nights with distant family. On more than one occasion we went to the downtown portion of the city that rests right on the water, would stroll and shop together, almost a normal family. And when we were done we would get in the car and drive to this little hole-in-the-wall. Except this hole had sensational food, could whip up an osso buco that even a finicky child would devour. I do not recall my father ever paying a single bill. We would walk in, eat, and leave without dropping a penny on the table. And as we were escorted to the door by the manager, we'd be thanked for merely dining there, as though Pop were a sitting senator or a food critic for the *Baltimore Sun*. They knew us then. And when Melody and I arrive, they will know of me still. Melody and I will be temporarily safe there, a desolate world belonging to my father's galaxy.

We leave the highway and drive down a street covered in enough rock dust that you can see tire tracks. I make our way to the restaurant and park on pavement that has cracked and crumbled, disintegrated into disrepair so long ago that it feels like we're parking on gravel. I leave the top down and rush to open the door for Melody, but she's out before I get to the other side. She looks at the door, then at me, and says, "Oh." She appears bewildered, and appears tired of fighting it.

The building, an old stone house that somehow survived the blue-collar influx that eventually encircled it, has nothing to indicate it's a restaurant other than the powerful scent as you draw near, an aroma of simmering sauces that makes you want to draw near*er*. A dirty faux grass runner welcomes us, a path we follow until we're standing under a crippled awning in front of the glass entrance. I get the door for Melody. She half looks at me as though a second blue feather has appeared, whispers, "Thanks."

We're so early they're not yet ready for the lunch crowd. The place is just starting to wake up; a server in the back is folding napkins and a busboy is still positioning chairs in front of the tables. I can see an annoyance in the server's eyes as we've arrived before they're technically open—as a restaurateur, I empathize fully—but then his eyes focus on *me*. He throws a quick wave in the air, a signal to stay put, then opens the kitchen door, yells something I couldn't decipher over the speakers streaming Julius La Rosa's "Eh, Cumpari!"

The server rushes to the front and greets us with a smile, and as he walks us to a quiet and cozy table in a far corner of the place, he puts his hand on my shoulder and we exchange a brief conversation of pleasantries spoken entirely in Italian, a stretch for my limited vocabulary. I can almost remember his name from years back—Antonio? Antonino?—so I overcompensate by continuing the conversation longer than I might have considering our circumstances. 'Tone pulls the chair out for what he perceives is my date. As we sit, I push the menus aside.

"Allow me to order for you, Melody." I plan on using my acquired knowledge of her life to provide a segue into how I understand who she is, in every capacity.

She winces a little, like I'm some greaser trying to work my magic on her.

"I don't mean to offend," I say softly, "but I believe I know what you would like."

Melody turns to 'Tone and says, "We've been dating for a few hours." She crosses her fingers and smirks. "We're tight."

"She will have the rabbit in red wine. Three orders again, darling? And make sure Thumper is nice and rare." She rolls her eyes, then looks to the ground, then around the room. I wait until the span of silence grows so wide she has no choice but to look at me. Then I stare at her and say to our server, "She will have the carpaccio of beef with watercress and garlic aioli and eggplant croquettes, and I will have the veal chops with lemon sage sauce and the risotto with arugula and goat's cheese." I quickly glance at 'Tone from the corner of my eye to see if he makes a face; he merely scribbles and nods. A few years ago I ate the veal here, a dish so memorable that recalling it now required no effort. The beef, on the other hand—don't remember anything even close to it on the menu. Not that it matters; they'll be making it today.

Melody turns the corners of her mouth down like she's trying to hold back a smile, but as she speaks, it escapes. "Raw beef was a risk, Jonathan. So was eggplant, especially for lunch."

A *calculated* risk; I saw her eat—and enjoy—the same dish at an Italian eatery two relocations earlier.

"Did I fail?"

She studies me with a look like she's sizing me up for the first time, fights putting the smile away. "Not yet."

I order a bottle of wine and 'Tone leaves us. We're the only people in the entire room.

She takes a deep breath, sits up straight. "You wanted to talk."

Not as much as I feel that I *have to*. All those words, all the scripting I tried to memorize in the car while she slept, have vanished now that she faces me, her feminine voice misguiding every remark and thought that attempts to surface, her eyes sparkling with a hope or need for something real and life-sustaining.

Here goes nothing. Here goes everything.

I nod as I put my elbows on the table and lean toward her, speak at a low volume as if someone is seated at the table next to us. "Do you wonder," I say, "how it is that I knew what was on this menu without even taking a glance?"

She shrugs. "Photographic memory?"

I lean even closer, speak even softer. "We're the only customers in this restaurant because they're not open yet, and will not be open for probably another hour. We were given the best table in the place because they would not give me anything less. We will sit and eat a delicious meal, the finest they will prepare today, and we will drink a bottle of wine, and when we're done with our dessert and cannot finish another bite, we'll get up and walk out of here without paying a cent."

More sour milk. "Should I be impressed?"

"You should be *concerned*, Melody."

She leans toward me, shows no sign of intimidation. "I've been concerned my entire life, Johnny-boy. Every time I start my car, enter my apartment, see some guy standing near me in a coffee shop who looks even vaguely Mediterranean. This is why we're here? For you to explain why I've spent my life in Witness Protection? I know more about it than you ever could."

"No, what I'm showing you is the depth of my family's influence, okay? Are we in New York right now? Nowhere close, yet the folks here will do whatever I ask of them. People think you can run away to Tennessee or Ohio, but the truth is we have a presence in those places, too. I mean, really, you think there are all these Italian families vying for the same chunk of business in the five boroughs? Get real. Forget the Mafia, what about the damn Russians or the Chinese or the Dominicans? Even the fu—*lousy* street gangs are tapping into what used to be our exclusive interests."

"Nice. So you move to the suburbs like everyone else, bringing all your crime and misery with you."

We've gotten off track and I've only been working this issue for one minute. I take off my glasses and rub my eyes. "You're missing the central issue here. You can't hide, Melody. The marshals they assign to you cannot move you far enough away. You can't outrun a sunset." Then, as I unfold my napkin and place it in my lap, I add, "We could have snatched you long ago."

Another server emerges from the kitchen, puts a basket of warm bread on our table, and displays the label of a bottle of Medici Ermete Concerto Reggiano Lambrusco to me. I put my glasses back on, nod in approval, tell him I'll do the pouring. He rips off a few lines in Italian that mean nothing to me; I smile and nod like I get it, then he leaves us.

I take Melody's glass and pour as slowly as possible, prevent even a single gulp of air from shooting back in the bottle and disturbing the sediment at the bottom. Melody looks at me like I don't know what I'm doing.

"I'm leaving the sediment in the bottle," I say. "Keep you from denying the greatness of this wine."

She peeks at the label as I fill her glass. "It's just a Lambrusco."

"Aye, Yankee," I say, my eye still on the red pour. "Trust me."

She takes a breath as though she's about to extend our dialogue on the wine, but instead: "What did you mean when you said you could've snatched me long ago?"

I look up, catch her eye, twist the bottle to avoid dripping, and lift. Here we go: "I've been keeping an eye on you for years."

I let my comment settle along with the wine.

Melody sits back against her seat, her breath now audible. I can see her chest undulate. "What... what do you mean?"

I've seen Melody in some dire moments, seen her weep by the hand of man, by the hand of fate. But this is the first time it will be from my very words, from *me*. I feel the air escaping from my power; I sink in my seat as I deflate. I grab the wine and fill my glass, let it burble and splash down, sediment and bubbles and all. I chug a third of it.

I'd love to win her, but I *have* to save her. And just like I took Ettore down in that muddy field, when I showed him no mercy, blasted him a second time to fortify a point he would never forget, I must do it here.

"Jane Watkins," I say. "Shelly Jones," I say. "Linda Simms, Sandra Clarke," I say. "You want me to tell you the kinds of jobs you've had? The places you used to get coffee in the morning? Your favorite restaurants? The cars you've driven? Places you've worked?"

It was far easier collapsing Ettore; watching her reaction is more painful than any blow my body has ever received. Melody's eyes glisten. Having held her breath through my explanation, she lets it out in a rapid sigh and single tears fall from both eyes.

"That's how you knew my size," she says. I can see in the way her eyes are moving that the remaining pieces of the puzzle nearly assemble themselves. "And my eye color, and the kinds of food I like." She shakes her head a little and more tears drift down. "And what you meant when you came into my motel room and said, 'I like your hair this way.'" She looks me in the eye as she wipes her cheeks dry. "You knew me. You've known me all along."

By the time the food arrives, Melody and I have been silent for a while. She's resisted making any more eye contact, failed to even look in my general direction. As the plates are set before us, Melody composes herself and stares at her dish; it seems like she might actually consider eating.

I nod toward the table. "Please." She reaches for her fork, plays with the tines before she grabs her knife and begins slicing the beef. I wait until she has a mouthful before I ask, "Aren't you curious as to why I've been watching you all these years?"

She continues to ignore me, takes another slice of beef and brings it to her mouth.

I go ahead and answer the question. "I was there."

She slows her chewing, head still down, finally responds to me as she scoops up a forkful of watercress. "Where?"

"At Vincent's."

There's that eye contact I was looking for.

"You should try the risotto," I say, sliding my plate in her direction.

She slides it back. "*When* were you there?"

Considering how desperate I'd been for her to look me in the eye, I cannot maintain it. "That Sunday morning when my dad was gutting Jimmy 'the Rat' Fratello."

There is not as much a silence between us as there is a vacancy. I might as well have just told her she was the princess of some faraway kingdom. Either way it will cause a complete remapping of her life, of the actions taken and the interpretation of events.

I try to fill the hole. A little. "Turns out Jimmy really was a rat. Which is why he got, uh . . . you know. He earned his demise, if that helps."

Keeping her eyes on me, she grabs the Lambrusco and fills her glass, fast. Some of it splashes out.

She says, "You're about to tell me some tragic news."

I prop myself up, put down my fork, clean my mouth with a large drink of water. "I was there with my dad," I say, confirming her thought. "The kids in the family were always kind of around. I mean, where could we go, really?" I take a deep breath that stutters, that shows my anxiety, shows I care about her more than I'd ever admit to myself. I begin the story:

"I was supposed to stay upstairs at Vincent's, play with my cousins in a big billiards room on the third floor. It was a rule of thumb that us little guys weren't allowed to touch the pool tables for fear we'd rip the felt or chip the balls or whatever, so it was supposed to be a big deal for us to hang out upstairs while my father and Jimmy did a little business. Of course, we were all old enough to understand that whenever all the kids were sequestered, something bigger and better was going on elsewhere.

"Well, like any kid, I thought my dad was the greatest, you know? I wanted to see what he did for a living. I always assumed he was in the restaurant business. I mean, we were always eating in the best places, could always pick whatever table we wanted, order whatever food we wanted—and we never paid and stuff."

I glance around the room, realize I just described our current situation. Even though I truly am in the restaurant business, there's no denying I have become too much like my father.

"Well," I continue, "I snuck down when no one was looking and tried to catch a glimpse of his high-business dealings." I get lost for a moment in recalling this event, haven't replayed this tape in a long time. Should I confess that I thought I might see him tasting sample foods or going over an accounting error with Jimmy? Is there any value in showing her I was innocent then, too? That we were, that same day, dragged away from everything that brought us security and an understanding of happiness?

Melody nods in agitation, moves her fork in a circular motion for me to continue, tries to accelerate my story by finishing this particular scene. "You saw him slicing up Jimmy Fratello?"

I take a bite of risotto and shrug. "No... actually, I saw my dad and Jimmy just talking. It was pretty boring, really. I watched them for a little while but lost interest, eventually walked down the hallway and went outside." I gently plunge my knife in and out of my veal, seems the wrong thing to be eating right now. I drop my utensils on the table. "I remember that day: It was cold and overcast outside. I was kicking stones into the sewer near Vincent's, kept staring at the gray sky." I look at Melody; I've got her full attention.

"Until I stopped to watch this guy try to parallel park his Oldsmobile. Would've bet twenty bucks it was his first time."

She releases a sigh and it comes out sounding like *Ohhh.* "Daddy," she says, "he couldn't parallel park to save his life." She starts nodding as though she's just figured out the twist at the end of a film. "You saw my dad."

"And your mom and..." I lick my lips. "And you, Melody. I saw *you.*" I get lost in the indelible image of her twirling on the sidewalk, a tape played *too many* times, an image that morphed from a simple memory to a recollection of invalid perfection. "You had the sweetest smile and the cutest blond curls." She reaches up and touches the back of her head as though I've brought up a sensitive subject, tries to pretend she needed to rub her neck. "Anyway, a few seconds later you all come screaming down the alley, hop in your car, and zoom off."

Melody slides her dish to the left, her wineglass to the right, leans on the table where her food once was. She takes a series of microscopic breaths, small undulations that indicate we're going awfully fast. She has just become aware that a part of her history exists in someone's memory. Melody Grace McCartney is becoming real again.

"Sean told me," she says, "that the police got there long after the crime, and that nothing in my file indicated how the feds found my parents—or how they even knew we were witnesses in the first place." She points her finger at me like she's picking me out of a lineup. "It was *you.*"

I blink instead of nod. "What can I say? I wasn't the thirty-year-old guy sitting before you, Melody. I was just a kid, who wanted to be a grown-up and big and important like my father. I had no idea it was my dad that killed Jimmy. I didn't even really understand what killing *was* yet." I frown at my ultimate decision. "When the cops were asking everyone on the street if anyone saw anything, I told them I saw a family run out of the restaurant."

"And you just magically knew our address?"

"No. But I did notice your car had Jersey tags, and I remembered two numbers and a letter." Fig Newton. Florence Nightingale. "Apparently, it was enough."

She puts a fist to her mouth, stares me down. "So," she says, "*you* are the one who brought all of this pain and misery and destruction into my life. *You* are the one responsible for my parents' deaths!" She rises up, like she's standing to leave. I lift off my chair to match her, let her know leaving is not an option, running is not a possibility. Yet.

"The most I would have had to deal with," she yells, "was some...some post-traumatic stress disorder, maybe some therapy. I still would have had parents and proms and friends and birthday parties and a heritage and something to look forward to!" She pops like a bubble, gushes this tirade as though she'd been waiting her entire life to unload.

"Melody, I was ten years old—just a few years older than you were. Do you have any idea what this did to *my* family?"

"I do not care."

"I turned my own father in—not intentionally, of course—but it doesn't change the fact that I'm the one who did it!"

"Your father is a sick bastard! Who wants a dad who eviscerates people?" She drops down into her chair.

As I slowly ease down as well, I say, "My dad wasn't Jeffrey Dahmer. It wasn't all weird." I finally lower my voice a notch, hope she'll do the same. "I mean, he was still my dad, the guy who took me to Yankee games and taught me how to throw a football, how to appreciate things like this wine." Taught me how to clock my twelve-year-old nemesis and beat him to submission, how to hot-wire almost any car. "He wasn't your stereotypical mafioso, with his Friday-night wife and his Saturday-night girlfriend. He taught me to respect women." Unfortunately, also the guy who coined the street term for a woman he deemed to be half-skank/half-bimbo: *skimbo*. "We attended a Catholic church and he cried when I made my first Communion." And only took the Lord's name in vain three times during that service. "He cheered me on when I hit a homer in Little League and consoled me when I blew a critical double play." And had an interaction with the umpire that involved more than kicking dirt on the guy's feet. "He was a real dad. To me, at least."

"You don't get it, Jonathan. I didn't have a chance to play Little League or dance ballet or anything else. We were always trying to stay out of sight. My dad might have taught me how to toss a ball if he hadn't been so worried about one of us getting plucked off in the process. I mean, getting mail from our mailbox was a stressful daily event."

"Look, I'm not comparing my parents to yours. My point is that my family—and the business we're in—makes people do bad things. But the bottom line is *it's business*."

"My family never did anything to the Bovaro clan."

"Your parents testified."

"And if they hadn't?"

I consider the question, do not consider answering it. I want to illuminate this scene, and her potential future, but it would be easily recognized as artificial light. I simply cannot lie to Melody, the way I cannot be profane in front of her, the way I struggle to light a smoke in front of her. My mother once gave me a piece of knowledge that rang with such truth, even as a child, that I might never forget it: A man finally understands the greatest sense of devotion, knows he has fallen to love's greatest depth, when he voluntarily surrenders all his vices and addictions for a woman. Based on the way my father lived his life, I'm not sure what my mother derived from it. But the concept now scares me, that I possibly have some secondary motivation and interest in Melody's welfare, for if I do it will surely mean her demise. Besides, the toughest vice remains; I may never be able to surrender the violence.

No one wants you to surrender the violence.

I start eating again. It gives me a place to look and an action to complete while I try to think of how to explain my game plan. Despite the tension in our bodies, in the air, we've been finding the food both necessary and enjoyable. Melody returns to her plate after watching me for a minute, and over a five-minute period we each consume half of our meals.

She finally breaks the silence, hits me with an off-the-wall question, one for which I am ill-prepared.

"Where do you rank in your family?"

I take another bite, wish I had a positive answer. Here the reality can't be avoided. "Not high."

"Why?"

I lick my teeth. "The fact that I indirectly turned my father in to the cops embarrassed my family greatly."

She frowns. "How sad."

"You can make fun, but it turned into a real mess. We've been trying to clean it up for years. The truth is the only way I could earn back the trust and honor of my family, of my peers, was to correct the... mistake."

She squints a little and taps the bottom of her wineglass. "Correct it how?"

"In order for me to regain my honor, I needed to kill you and your parents." We stare at each other. "Most kids are worried about getting their driver's license at sixteen; I was worried about rubbing out three people."

Melody slowly reaches for her knife, grips it like a hammer. "*You* killed my parents?"

"No... but I tried." It's official: I've lost any ability to deceive her. And as my honesty enwraps her, it loosens her fingers from the knife.

"I was supposed to do the killings, but I didn't have the stones. I had your folks in my sight, but I could've never pulled the trigger."

She exhales so hard and long that it flows over my face. Her next question is predictable, would have been mine as well. "So who did?"

"My older cousin. He was with me for backup—and sort of a witness, to tell everyone back home. He could see how incapable I was, just... pushed me out of the way and snapped off the bullets that killed your parents. Then he took me back to the car and beat the crap out of me." I point to the mark on my temple.

"Why'd he do that?"

"Because I failed. I failed my family once again. It was like there was no way to honor them."

In comes a brief gap in the conversation that Melody ends with a probable deduction, the very reason—indirect as it is—that I am running toward her. "Except... by killing *me*."

We're stuck looking at each other, which I eventually break by nodding. "I kept going to wherever you'd moved and... waited." I lean in. "I would have never done it. Never. I mean, sure, I used to rough guys up at home when it was necessary. It's the way things are handled in our business, but please believe me: I could never—*will* never—hurt you."

Who knows why, but this particular iteration of my promise of safety seems to stick; she visibly relaxes: Her fingers bend at the knuckles, shoulders droop, a sigh escapes.

"What did you tell your family every time you came back empty-handed?"

"That I couldn't find you."

"But... what made you keep coming back? Why didn't you just say you had no idea where I was in the first place unless you really had some intention of killing me?"

I lean even farther forward, as close as I can get to her without getting up and moving to her side of the table. I slowly move my hand toward hers, curve my fingers around the palm of her hand; she makes no attempt to move it away. I gently tighten my grip, and she squeezes back, closes her eyes a little as though a drug is just starting to kick in. I hope she can't feel my hand trembling.

Then I say, "To make sure you were okay, Melody."

She opens her eyes, but they look sleepy. "I was never okay, Jonathan."

I grasp her hand a little tighter. "You are now."

She breathes slow and full and nods a little. As she analyzes my words, our situation, the nodding gets slower and slower until it stops.

Then, like she's thinking out loud: "But now you're here. No longer hiding." She drags and slurs this word like the little bit of wine she's consumed has suddenly kicked in: "*Why?*"

I hate to do it, but I tighten my grip on her hand; the implied affection all but vanishes.

"Because they finally found you."

She looks down. "Your family?"

"Someone within the organization. Let's just say the urgency's changed, and someone had to take you out. I volunteered." She looks at her hand in mine like she wonders how it got there, how to pull it back.

So I let it go.

"You're safer with me than the feds, Melody."

She pinches her bottom lip, studies me for a reaction, for a sign that my aim is true.

"My family didn't have to try hard to find you," I say. "The information was pretty easily handed over."

"What do you mean? By who?"

I turn away; I know I can't tell her. If she equates her lack of safety to the hole in security at Justice—a wholly valid notion, mind you—she might think one last run back to the Marshals Service would be worth attempting, that she might be able to correct the problem by informing Justice of their leak, that she might really be safe if the leak were fixed. But an even greater consequence exists: If I lose Gardner, I lose her. I lose it all.

"Just trust me that the information is and always will be completely accurate. And if you can try to believe it's possible for a good guy to be in organized crime, you must also believe that it's possible for a bad guy to be in the Justice Department, so the converse is true."

She turns and stares out the front window and the sun hits her eyes directly, tightens her pupils and exposes a layer of color in her irises I had not yet been given the pleasure of noticing. "Actually, it's not a converse, or an inverse, or a contrapositive, or any other geometric derivative. Your statement was just a mess of attempted logic. But I get the point."

I laugh, having not the slightest idea what she's talking about. I love her intelligence and understanding of things beyond my reach, her ability to see things invisible to me, her talent for not just stepping around me, but dancing.

I can't pull my eyes from hers. I get distracted by her knowledge of math and ask her what is was like to be a teacher—a question serving little value at this point in our time together, but nothing could have prevented it. I find myself wanting to learn whatever I can about her, the details I could never acquire from afar.

The delay in her answering is long enough that I assumed she either didn't hear me or was simply ignoring me, but finally the answer comes, her eyes still fixed on whatever is beyond the window, like a sick child watching other kids play. She tells me she requested that the feds get her any job that dealt with math, that the discipline had become an obsession for her as a child, that with all of the moving and changing of locations and names, as all of the uncertainty unfolded year after year, there was one thing she could count on as an absolute truth: math. I've stopped putting my fork to my food, stopped eating, stopped being aware of anything but the woman before me. I listen to every word, sink down in depression like quicksand.

She has me forgetting who I am, where I am.

Melody tells me how she used math as a protective device, that when things were scary and tentative, she would solve increasingly difficult equations—find the proverbial answer—and know she could be certain of something. Her introspection is honest and accurate, but she does not appear to understand the dark, final destination to which her insecurity has taken her. She tells me how on her own she learned it all, that while her classmates in algebra struggled she'd go home and finish off books on calculus, that she'd self-taught herself differential equations and was about to embark on the next level of advanced coursework. But even I, rough hood that I am, can see she will eventually run out of material, that eventually there will be no next class, that she will never find the ultimate truth by way of mathematics.

And then my own final destination is lit like a concert hall, all lights aimed at me. She is with me for one reason only: I can give her the ultimate truth of her life.

I take a few bites of my risotto, which has cooled and coagulated and lost its intensity. Then, like she's checking to make sure she got the better deal, Melody asks, "Why am I safer with you?"

I gulp down the risotto and answer, "My family will kill you if they find you alone. My family will *not* kill you if they find you with me. And if you're with a fed or anyone else?" I shrug.

"But why? Why do they want me dead? You know how many times I sat in my bedroom and imagined that all my running was for nothing, that you guys had forgotten who I even was? I mean, what damage could I possibly do to your family? The government lost all the cases that involved my parents' testimony."

I take a drink of wine. "Yes, but therein lies the problem. Your parents testified—*not you.* It's a long story, but there's a big storm brewing, and—I don't mean this to sound casual—my family doesn't want any loose ends. Your testimony could end up being useful, even critical. It's just easier if you're gone."

She closes her eyes and drops her head. "Just like that, huh?"

I put my fork on my plate and take her hand again, but this time it's limp and cold like the palm of the corpse I'm trying to prevent her from becoming.

"I will protect you, Melody. *Trust me.*"

She looks up, glances in my general direction like I'm the one invisible thing she can't see. And as she glares right through me, I realize I've become *one of them*; I just made her the same promise the feds have been making her whole life, and I'm no more certain I can keep it than they were. And Melody's too experienced to assume otherwise.

We finish our meal with a pair of espressos, sit in a silence that does not feel awkward, a quiet space more common to couples who have lived a full life together, where just being next to each other is its own form of companionship.

And as I predicted, 'Tone never brings us a check, just stops by to see if we need anything else and wishes us well in our day. It shames me.

As I start playing with the key to the Audi, Melody asks, "What're you planning to do with me once we get to New York?"

"I, uh... I want to take you back to my family and introduce you to them."

She flops back in her chair, waits for me to laugh at my own joke. "You're kidding, right? This is your plan?"

"Hear me out, okay?"

"I might as well jam this knife in my gut right now."

"Hear me out."

"Know what might be less painful? Tie me to the bumper of your car and drag me around the beltway."

"Melody, just wa—"

"Oh, better, can you do that thing where you wrap the wire around my neck and strangulate me?"

"A garrote. And no, no one is—"

"This trip is a death sentence!"

I wave my hands in front of her. "Melody! Nobody is killing anybody, okay? Like I've explained, if you are with *me*, you're safe."

She wipes her eyes, then her entire face. "Let's hear this brilliant scheme."

I clear my throat like I'm preparing to step up to the microphone for a presentation. "I'm going to show my family what a nice woman you are"—Melody smirks, wipes her nose—"how you're no threat to them, how you're a *person*."

"I'm no threat to them if I'm a dead person."

"I'm going to show them you are not some file of incriminating evidence they're trying to erase or a rat spilling his guts to the cops, but a real human being with feelings and emotions and something worth—"

"Are you stupid?"

"What?"

"Take drugs or something?"

"Of course not."

"Suffer from any mental disease or deficiency?"

Debatable.

"Because," she says, "I can't figure out what could possibly be running through your mind, what might make you think I stand the slightest chance of survival if you bring me to your home. It's like introducing a deer to the patrons of a hunting lodge."

I stand, motion for her to get up as well. I offer my hand to help her out of her chair. She stares at it, but eventually takes it. We lumber to the front of the restaurant and exit, meander down the nylon green walkway and pause when we arrive at the end. In the bright sunshine, we inhale the lingering dust of ash and stone, gaze at a thirty-foot-high man-made hill of gray and silver rock lining the other side of the road. Trucks drive by and gravel spills to the road as they pass over potholes.

"I'll tell you what," I say. "I left my keys on the table in the restaurant. I'm gonna go back in and get them. If you think you'll be safer with the feds than with me, feel free to leave. If you think you'll be safer with me—and I hope you will—then be here when I come back out."

I look at her, hoping she does not answer me on the spot—either way. I really want her to consider it, be part of the plan for real, to make a commitment. She studies me for a second, just nods. I turn and walk back toward the restaurant.

Of course, I did not forget my keys, fabricated the entire excuse to give her a minute to consider the dump of information under which she's now buried, a pile more weighty than those stones across the street.

'Tone spots me and I wave him over. We share more Italian, loses me near the end so I cut him off, tell him how outstanding the meal and service was, how my father wishes them all well. A quick handshake/hug combo and he walks back into the kitchen. After he's completely out of sight, I reach into my pocket and pull out my wad of bills and toss two hundred in twenties on the table.

And when I return to the front—hesitate while I take a breath and hold it—and exit the restaurant a final time, Melody is waiting for me with a smile. Actually, I think her mouth is turned up from extreme squinting, the harsh sun blasting her face. Either way.

"Thank you," I say.

As we stroll to my car, I put my hand on the small of her back and I'm almost certain she's letting some of her weight fall against my palm. I notice her stealing short glances of me again, like when we were riding up the highway from Cape Charles. I find myself trying to hold her glances, to see the look in her eye and understand the way she's starting to view me. Something has changed within her and I want to figure out what it is, what produced it, how to sustain it. When I finally catch her eye, she slows her pace a little and grins at me, seems like she has something to say, but quickly turns and drops her smile as she looks at the Audi.

I follow the path of her eyes and spot two teenage boys with their backs to us, staring and pointing inside my car. And laughing.

We stop moving. I regretfully pull my hand from Melody's back, yank up my sleeves, and whisper, "Stay here."

"Do it again," I hear one of the kids say.

As I quietly approach them, one of them leans over the door and spits all over the upholstery on the passenger side. I wait for another truck full of rock to roll down the street, use it to mask the sound of the broken pavement and gravel under my feet. I sneak up behind them, say, "What do you little fu"—I glimpse Melody and she's looking down, her interest and hope in me long vanished—"funny guys think you're doing?"

Both kids try to bolt, but I grab the slower one as he passes, my fist full of hair and collar. His knees buckle like he's a marionette and I'm annoyed by his weakness, that this bug is causing a disruption in all I'm trying to do, that I have to spend even a second swatting him away. The product of my emotions has become distilled, and the only essential element remains: rage.

I swing him around, shove his face inside my car, bend his body over so far he nearly falls in the cab. "Funny now? Still funny? C'mon, laugh. I wanna hear the laugh."

His friend stops in mid-escape and returns, does nothing more than watch. I pull back on the kid's collar and wind up for a slam onto the frame of the car door, and as I do I shoot a look at Melody. I'm not sure I've ever so easily read disappointment in someone's face.

She slowly shakes her head, shrugs, and says, "It's just saliva."

Her disapproval sucks the anger from me, hamstrings my ability to take these varmints out. I shove the kid to the ground and say, "Go home and hug your mother."

"Yes, sir," he mumbles, as his buddy helps him to his feet. They both look at me for further instructions.

"Run, you little sh—shysters." Boy, am I longing for some profanity. I start my way back to Melody, turn my head out of her view, and whisper, "You've got three seconds, you little *faccia di merda*."

They both depart so quickly that they slip and fall in the gravel, stumble into one another. As the kids run down the street, Melody and I analyze the car. They must have been at it for a while, because not only are there several gobs of spit on the seats, but some have already dried.

I groan under my breath. "Let me go back in the restaurant and see if I can get some paper towels," I say.

Melody doesn't respond. She stares at the seats but I can sense her eyes are out of focus, her thoughts elsewhere. I've lost her. The weak accrual of convincing and nominal amount of trust I might've secured throughout our meal have been crushed to rubble by disillusionment. I start toward the restaurant but keep my eyes on her with every step. She reaches in the car and pulls out the green sweater, checks it over, starts to put it on. I decelerate as she bunches it up at the collar and pulls it over her head, her arms up and her shirt pressed tight against her frame, the sun detailing the shape of her body as she slowly brings it down and covers and hides her body again. She turns away so that her back faces me, gently shifts her hips so that she's leaning against the body of the car, and slips her hands in the pockets of her jeans.

As I reach the door of the restaurant, I stop. I look at her and want to correct every instance of how I've failed her, from twenty years ago to twenty seconds ago. I fantasize about moving up behind her, gently wrapping my arms around her belly, and whispering in her ear, "It's all right. Everything's gonna be all right." And then she would close her eyes and push her head against my neck and then, for once, we'd both feel a brief wave of contentment, a peek of what it might be like to be at peace, to be safe.

I open the door and walk to the kitchen, explain my situation to 'Tone. He mumbles something about how the neighborhood has gone south, hands me two worn cotton towels, one wet and one dry. Then he shoves a paper plate in my hand and drops two cannoli on it. I nod in appreciation and make my way back to the front. I tuck the towels under my arm as I open the door and half jog into the sun-filled parking lot.

Melody is missing.

Each step closer to the car brings a drop in my pace. Within seconds I am standing in the center of the parking lot, towels in hand, head and body twisting in every direction for any sign of her. I run to the corners of the building, look around both sides of the restaurant: nothing. Then up to the street, look east and west, find not a single person anywhere in my field of vision. I couldn't have been in the restaurant for more than sixty seconds; it's like she truly vanished, no trace of her having been here or having shared a meal and moments with me. My mind races at not only why she left, but how she departed so successfully. Dust from the parking lot does not hang in the air. No racing car engines can be heard, no squealing tires. No voices, no whispers or screams for help. There now exists a void, and I am standing in the center of the vacuum.

Melody is not just gone—she's *long* gone.

FIVE

I jump in my car, toss the towels on the seat and spin out of the parking lot, drive down the road toward the city center. My eyes are peeled for any sign of Melody, but beyond the drivers of cars and commercial trucks, there are no signs of any living thing whatsoever. Even the two kids have disappeared far from view. After a mile, I hang a U-turn in the middle of the street and head in the opposite direction, speed toward the exit for the Jones Falls Expressway and stop just before the ramp and sit on the shoulder, defeated. Too much time has passed now. She could be anywhere, with anyone. It's like looking for a needle across an unharvested field of hay.

I attempt to methodically run through all of the options; only three possibilities surface:

(1) She left on her own, officially having lost all faith and trust in me after my foolish reaction to the spitheads, from my lack of self-control that would eventually implode any master plan I professed to have. I'd never blame her for leaving.

(2) Somehow the feds knew where she was, managed to track us amidst all of my casual absconding, and spirited

her away at the perfect moment. How I criticized Sean and his feeble protections of Melody in Cape Charles, how distracted he was, how his attention was distinctly elsewhere. Did I not just fail Melody the exact same way? Who's to say he didn't slip those kids twenty bucks to spit in my car and create a diversion.

(3) Someone from our crew preempted our successful arrival in New York. This someone figured I would do what I was truly attempting: Keep the girl alive. This someone decided enough was enough and Melody's life needed to end, and now she's riding in the trunk of a large black sedan. The question I can't seem to answer is how anyone in my family might've had the slightest clue where we were; even I had no idea that we'd end up at this particular restaurant at this particular time.

Unless.

I hang another U-turn, narrowly beat a dump truck coming off the ramp from the expressway, and drive back to the restaurant. I barge into the kitchen, corner 'Tone, and ask in English he will fully understand if he has had any contact with my father or anyone else in our crew. He shakes his head like a dog trying to throw moisture off his fur. I scan the rest of the kitchen. "Anyone in here? Anyone call up to New York? Now is the time to speak up!" Everybody stops and stares, every motion frozen.

'Tone puts his hands up in a way that could be read as both *not me* and *I have no idea what you're talking about.* I slowly walk backward toward the door. And when I return to my car, I grab my cell and call my brother.

"Pete," he answers.

"Checking in. You at Sylvia?"

"There earlier, everything's fine. Ryan's got it under control."

Sylvia's head chef has opened for me before—during the majority of my other off-schedule journeys to locate Melody—and I am certain of Ryan's reliability; this is hardly why I called.

"Everything else coming together?" I ask. *People dropping like flies?*

"Pop and Eddie got a close eye on everything, everyone." Eddie Gravina, my father's *consigliere.*

I shake my head even though Peter can't see my reaction. "What's Eddie got to do with anything? Where's Pop?"

Peter ignores me. "You're the only one who's probably going to arrive late to the party." *You're the question mark.*

"You can't have the party without all the party favors, right?" *Pop's not going to rest until every loose end is knotted.* "And I'm bringing mine home shortly."

Peter's reaction is all I care about. Any delay, any slight cough of confusion—any sign that someone else is after Melody—and I'll be screaming into the phone with such furor I'll crack the plastic, returning to New York at a hundred miles per hour.

As much as I would dread this response from my brother, it would nonetheless bring me direction, a place to point my energy, a way to begin again and attempt to rescue her one last time. Unfortunately, he answers me with assurance, with a clear tone of relief.

"My brother," he says with a laugh, "it may have aged like wine, but the flavor is that much greater, wouldn't you say?" Then louder, "I will pass along the news. Can't wait to open that bottle and take a drink."

The most recent time I hated my brother Peter: two seconds ago, when he delivered this weird metaphor implying Melody was something he would consume, how he'd derive pleasure from putting her down, or knowing she was already with the fishes. I can't shake the imagery, the sick look he'd get on his face from opening the trunk of the car and seeing another person lifeless and cold, the proportional punishment for disrupting his world, our world.

I say nothing more and Peter hangs up.

Fury builds inside me and for the first time I *recognize* it. I want so desperately to push it away, to be the man Melody suggested I could be—that she wants me to be—but I've been trained that the better use of a blazing temper is to harness the power behind it. I try to beat it back like a demon attempting possession, but the violence runs through my veins like an amphetamine. But this time—the first time—I pin it down, begin the process of suffocation: I have every intention of finding Melody, and when I find her I'm going to bring her right through the front door of my father's house, and I'm going to present her, the innocent girl that she is, to my father and Peter and the rest of my family. My original plan now has fuel; Peter's asinine metaphor has given me clarity and purpose. I will challenge them to look at Melody, to meet her and touch her, to take in her beauty and honesty and integrity and to try and find the slightest ability to take her life. Call me a hopeless romantic. Just call me hopeless. But I pray my family will see what I see, that they will lay down their frigging weapons this one time and say, *Maybe you're right.* And if one of them—any of them—reach for a weapon or turn her way with evil intent, they will have to kill me first.

Take *that*, fury.

SIX

I sit in my car and face the sun, let the engine idle. Now that I have an enriched goal, I must find Melody and bring it to completion. If there's been any plan to snag her without my knowledge, Peter would've been aware of it.

The next likeliest scenario is she fell—or leapt—into the arms of the feds, which also makes this the best-case scenario. The sooner she's under their care, the better, for within a day's time Randall will be put to good use again.

I start driving in concentric circles. I begin with tight ones, up and down every street near the restaurant, double back and begin again, eyes peeled for any sign of her having been anywhere: an abandoned sandal or clothing item, an intentionally left sign that she was taken rather than having left of her own accord.

As I negotiate the urban streets, I briefly replay the conversation with Peter, try to understand why Eddie is involved in taking all these people out. Eddie Gravina is a good guy, very trusted in our family. But he has two things working against him: He's only been part of our crew for about eight years, and he's never been on the action end of anything that I'm aware of. His purpose and value rests more in giving advice, acting as a sounding board for my father. So why would he be keeping, as Peter put it, a *close eye* on everything—on anything? It's not sitting right with me. His name should have never come up. Last time I saw the guy he was sitting in the kitchen at Sylvia, reading the sports section and slurping a free bowl of Sylvia's version of cioppino, a thin rivulet of broth dribbling out of the corner of his mouth.

As the sun shifts to an afternoon sky I make my way back to downtown Baltimore, hover around the federal building I'd hid behind not so long ago. Dr. Bajkowski is apparently working out of the office today, along with all of his or her associates, as not a single space is free. I circumnavigate the building a few times, not wanting to sit still in case my car was recognized or tagged back at the restaurant. The frigging thing sticks out like a bloody knuckle.

The more time that passes, the more nervous I get, the less in control I feel of the situation, despite the obvious truth: I have lost *complete* control. My nerves get the better of me and I call Gardner. He sighs, hangs up, calls me back from the server room; he's performed this ritual enough times that I've come to recognize the sound of the fans whirring on all of the computers.

"You forget I have a job?" he says.

"You mean the one I just called you at?"

"I've got a meeting in seven minutes, and when that's over I need to finalize a database design and submit the final draft of a disaster recovery plan."

"I'm trying to recover from a disaster of my own."

"Let me clarify: I do not have time."

"You have time for your frigging addiction and to pimp out images of your wife, you have time for me. I cannot begin to explain how this is the wrong moment for you to test my patience."

I hear him typing on a computer keyboard, taking out on the keys what he wishes he could take out on me. He clicks those keys for a solid two minutes, with gaps in his typing about every ten seconds, winds it all up with one loud slap of the keyboard.

"Gimme a minute," he says, and the line goes dead.

And sure enough, it's almost exactly sixty seconds when I get a call from Randall's cell.

"Nine-one-nine Norton Drive, Columbia, Maryland. Goodbye."

"Wait! That's outdated information."

"It's what I have, okay? I don't create, delete, or modify the data, I just tell it where to be stored and how to be accessed."

This does not surprise me. Let's be honest: Melody's most recent address was the passenger seat of my Audi.

"It's probably going to change very soon," I say, "and I want to know when it does—the second it does."

"How would I—"

"Monitor the status of her file every hour and let me know the instant it changes. If it doesn't, you check in with me every four hours to let me know there's no update."

"For the love—I can't keep doing this. They can't track what I'm doing directly from the server, but if they wanted to they could find out how many times the record was accessed, which could raise a flag. I'm not taking this risk."

"Listen, I'm completely finished explaining our relationship. You have a boss?"

"Of course."

"I outrank him, you understand?"

He pulls the phone away from his mouth, yells a few commandment-breaking profanities, then returns with, "I should've never gotten into bed with you whores."

Oh, if I could reach through the telephone line. "Yeah, but you did. And you know what? Consider me your own personal raging case of herpes, my friend. You're gonna carry me around the rest of your life, everywhere you go. You can try and cover me up, but you and I both know you can never—*never*—get rid of me. I will always be right there, running through your blood, festering under your skin, waiting to pop—"

"I'm not doin' it."

I thought my STD metaphor was fairly vivid. I guess I should stick to what I know: sticks and stones; words suck. I wipe my face and speak the language of his native tongue: "When was the last time we gave you a boost?"

Gardner's no longer quick to answer. "Two days ago."

"Then let me put it this way: You don't do this, we're cutting you off." I'm truly trying to avoid the threat of violence, but if turning off his supply of gambling cash doesn't work, I'll have only that card left to play.

He hesitates before carefully phrasing his response. "You're squandering what I have to give, you know. You'll be lucky to get another day out of this."

I *do* know. But one day is all I need.

"Stay in touch," I say as I flip my phone closed, toss it on the seat next to me.

My car rests at the edge of an alley two blocks from the courthouse. Through a narrow slit between the corners of two skyscrapers, I can see a margin of harbor, of shimmering water and motionless flags. In two-second intervals, people pass: the families, the mothers and fathers holding the hands of their children; the businessmen and women shortcutting across the harbor to get to the other side of the financial district or to grab a meal in Little Italy; the couples walking arm in arm along the wide brick pathway. Each of these are snapshots and nothing more—flashes, glimpses—people living simple existences, leading lives of normalcy, living without crime, living without constant fear, living without doubt as to where they are or who they are. It feels strange to witness them. I do not belong here and neither does Melody. We are actors cast as characters in the wrong play. These people live their lives day to day and misunderstand what occurs in the directions they never look, where all the terrible violence and fear proliferates. All around these innocent residents, people are having their names changed, their bodies relocated, living like ghosts among the true and real. They could never know we were even here.

Then, right in the small gap of my vision, in the slice between the buildings, a young couple stops. The boy turns around and says something to the girl and she laughs and slaps him on the chest. He reaches down to her waist and pulls her in and she throws her arms around his neck. They begin to kiss, and though I feel I should look away, I am unable. It strikes me: This is very well a direction *I* have never looked—down the path of the living.

Someday, I will bring Melody here and point out to the harbor and say, "Look. There is something I want you to see." And I will explain how if she trusts me, she will be able to live this way, too. That if she allows me, I can change her from a ghost to flesh and bone.

Whatever captured my attention about the couple now makes me hurt. I feel like a little kid getting a stomachache from one too many candies.

A car pulls behind me and nearly taps my bumper. I pull my foot from the brake and roll out to the edge of the alley, turn northward on Charles Street. I start driving, heading nowhere.

My mind becomes preoccupied with the activities of our crew. Witnesses and other troublemakers are gone, bullets in their heads, weighted and resting on the floors of rivers, buried in beds of loose soil. No one knows they're missing yet, won't know until a family member or fed counts one less bird in the nest.

I carve a vertical line through the middle of the city, eventually end up so far north that I drive right along the edge of the campus of Johns Hopkins University. At the rate I'm rolling, I'll be in Towson within minutes. Staying in motion somehow feels like progress, though I know the logical thing to do is stop and wait. I pull off of Charles Street, parallel park in front of an open meter, flip open my cell and make sure I have plenty of battery power and full signal strength. I drop my head back to the headrest and slowly relax the muscles in my neck, and when I twist to the right I look out the passenger door window and notice the campus bookstore for Hopkins, a Barnes and Noble that stretches across the bottom of a block-wide building. The smooth stone facility has blue awnings and ceiling-high windows, and café tables positioned in front of the windows with more students than chairs.

I play with my cell phone, flipping it open and slapping it shut in rhythm as I watch the students moving in and out of the bookstore; it occurs to me I've never seen a mentally unhealthy college student; the subtle smiles on their faces, the way they interact, their rush from building to building, all imply a sense of well-being that will be sucked from half of them within a year of graduation. For now, though, they study and try to learn more in disciplines that make them happy, of what they think will make them happy.

Once upon a time Randall Gardner walked some campus, studying computer science and cramming for exams, never could have imagined a future where he'd surrender every shred of common sense to satisfy a gambling addiction, where he'd have his head slammed into his own front door by the guy feeding his habit.

I can't help but think the same thing about the cops, the folks at Justice, the Seans of the world—who once sought to serve and protect but later learned that all the stuff in the textbooks was theory, and half of it was crap in the first place, that the two most effective ways to overcome the bad guys are the same mechanisms that've worked so well for the villains: physical force and extortion. I wonder if the cop who worked me over when I was only ten years old, the one who served as the impetus behind the wrecked lives of the McCartney family, ever cracks open one of his dusty texts on the concepts of law enforcement.

For now they hope. For now they study. Accounting, art, architecture. Computer science and political science and environmental science. Law and medicine.

And math.

I stare at the billboard on the edge of Charles Street, the one advertising the variety of programs available at Johns Hopkins, and dial the number listed at the bottom, my ear pressed tightly against the phone for any sign of an incoming call. Three transfers later I'm connected with the math department. I ask one question (barely understand the answer) and hang up.

I drop a handful of coins in the meter and make my way past the café tables and the bicycle racks, keep my cell in my hand as I enter the bookstore. I walk around the display tables holding the phone in front of me, verifying signal strength with every step. It looks like I'm checking for an explosive device hidden in the stacks.

I follow the signs for the textbook section, walk aisles filled with knowledge I could never acquire, pass books on theory that would never lead me to discovery. I have fallen so far out of my depth, I'm outside looking in.

I slip behind a young girl carrying a pile of books nearly half her size and ask, "Does anyone here know much about math texts?"

She slows and turns to me a little, but her face is covered by the books. From behind them she says, "Let me get Diane, she's a graduate engineering student. Wait here."

She walks away, wobbling side to side. As she makes a ninety-degree turn between rows of racks, the top three nearly slide off. I turn and look at the textbooks at my side, organized by subject for their respective courses.

Physiological Fluid Mechanics
Bioelectromagnetic Phenomena
Theoretical Neuroscience

I do not belong here. People tell their kids they can be anything they want to be in life; the optimism is warm but the truth is cold. I couldn't become a mathematician any more than I could become a Chinaman. I may long to be something else, something other than a mobster, but I have no illusions that I should be something *more.* Melody, though... it would be hard for her to be much less. She belongs here, would've been here had I not forced her into a biannual escape. And that's why I'm in this store, in this section. I want to understand her, to know who she was born to be. Through her music I heard her speak; through her study I hope to interpret.

Diane walks my way, has a clipboard in her hand and wears a headset with the microphone aimed at her lips. She's a pretty but oddly petite, small-featured gal, like a nine-year-old who one morning woke up twenty-seven.

She stares at me from a foot below and shines a smile so full of perfect teeth the orthodontist should have signed his work.

"I'm looking for a math text," I say.

She moves the microphone down an inch. "Do you have the course name or number?"

"No. I spoke with dean of the department of applied something-or-other. Told him I was looking for a textbook for someone who had a full understanding of differential equations. He suggested a list of books—stochastical something and combinatorial yada yada. The only thing that stuck was something, like, string theory."

"Which professor's teaching the course?"

"No, it's not for a class. It's a gift. For a friend."

She studies me. "Odd," she says, "but okay. This way." She tries to yank her headset off but the wire gets tangled in her hair. She grunts as we walk to the math textbooks.

"We have a few on string theory, but take it from someone who completed the course here a year ago that this one's undeniably the best." She hands me an eighty-dollar, seven-hundred-page, four-pound monster: *A First Course in String Theory* by Barton Zwiebach. "This wasn't the book required for the course at the time, but I can tell you I'd have never passed if I hadn't bought it. If your friend is trying to understand string theory all on his or her own, this is the one."

I fold my phone and slip it in my pocket, open the cover and hear the binding crackle. As I carefully turn the smooth pages I glance at the writing. The thing might as well have been written in Cyrillic.

"You have friends who like to explore the world of mathematical physics in their spare time?"

Tommy Fingers once explained how to get all the air out of a guy's lungs—displacing the air with fluid—so he'll sink to the bottom of whatever body of water he's being dumped in. I'm guessing this is not what Diane means. Theory is not important in the Bovaro household; success resides in the application.

"I'm trying to make new friends, you might say."

Diane shrugs and smiles. "Enjoy."

I tuck the text under my arm and check my cell as I make my way to the counter.

With no hope of finding Melody on my own—I'm relying completely on Gardner; what a frightening thought that is—I come to the realization that the best position to place myself is on the edge of an interstate. Being in the center of a large city is like being in a cage.

I drive westward to the perfect location, the point where I-70 intersects with the Baltimore Beltway; I can equally go north, south, or west, and all while safely sitting still. Waiting. I park at the border of the park-and-ride, aim my car down the empty interstate like a rock pulled back in a slingshot.

Melody is likely in motion toward a destination with the sole characteristic of being *somewhere far away*; this is one large friggin' country. She has got to be tired of running. At least as much as I'm tired of following.

I plug my cell phone into the car charger and wait. I open the text on string theory and understand pretty much everything on the copyright page. Beyond that, not a clue. The book gives me more insight into Melody than I'd originally imagined, though; intelligence is a sensual thing. The fact that she understands all this stuff, that she could understand what *Motivating the AdS/CFT correspondence* means, that these formulas and Greek letters and strange shapes can be brought together to make sense and be applied to life sends a wave of warmth through me. It's like she knows how to speak another language, except this language can only be understood by very few. Capacity for knowledge is as innate and uncontrollable as eye color, and Melody's radiates.

I sit and hope for the call—ninety minutes pass—and as my ability to control the situation drops to zero, my anxiety climbs. Here I am at that rock-bottom moment that has me finally turning to God. I've come to the realization that I'm never going to do this on my own, that I have no means left to rescue Melody, that *someone needs to help*. And so I bow my head and pray to God, the

One whose wrath seemed so sweet and glorious all those Sundays in Mass. I now pathetically ask Him to throw down a soft blanket of grace upon me, one of the least deserving souls on this earth. Though I can recall so many biblical instances of destruction put down upon the unrepentant, I try to recall the lessons of mercy and come up dry. I just keep seeing Job, poor slob. I rest my head on my steering wheel, whisper out my needs and a final amen.

Within ninety seconds my cell rings.

I grab for it so quickly I send it across the passenger seat.

"Go," I say.

"Your update," Gardner says, "is no update."

I pound my stick with my fist. "Nothing, no activity at all?"

"No update means no update."

I flip my phone shut and stare down the empty highway.

How I would love to testify that God gave me exactly what I asked the moment I requested it. But I have to remember He really did answer my prayer; He just said *No.*

Had I known I would spend so much time sleeping in my car, I would have bought a Lincoln Navigator, an expansive touring machine with bucket seats the size of La-Z-Boys. I can attest to the firm ride my car boasts. I wake up to the sun shining in my rearview, reflecting back against my face. The clock reads just after eight o'clock, which means Gardner is overdue for an update. The gap between his phone calls increased by roughly forty-five minutes each time, until he'd extended an every-four-hour update to every six hours.

I get out of the car and stretch, run my fingers through my hair, and have a Marlboro for breakfast. Cars drift into the park-and-ride with regularity and people pull in the spaces around me, men and women in suits and dresses. In the distance I see the massive building for the Social Security Administration. Of the thousands who work in that facility, I imagine there's at least one clerk or accountant or customer service representative who was deposited there by the feds, at least one person who goes by a name not on his or her original birth certificate. I am starting to see the ghosts everywhere.

I hop back in my car, drive out to find somewhere to grab a quick bite while I wait for Gardner to call. The air is weighed heavy with a humidity found only in urban centers; I put the top down and my sunglasses on. And just as I exit northward onto the beltway, my phone rings.

"Go."

I hear my own voice echo quietly on the phone, then: "Guess who?"

I pull my foot off the accelerator. "I don't know." I check my phone to read the incoming number. "Someone calling from the Mountaineer Coffee Mill?" I've slowed down to forty-five miles per hour. Cars zoom by so fast my car shimmies with each passing vehicle.

"Right," the female voice says. "Now, who do you know who could be so unfortunate to be calling from a coffeehouse in Morgantown, West Virginia?"

I've spoken with Melody so little, yet I recognize the sarcastic downturn in her voice, as true and unique as a fingerprint. "Well, that certainly narrows it down." My nerves are sparking. I do not want this call to get dropped. "How are you, Melody?"

She sighs as though she's trying to hide it from me. "I'm cold, dirty. Exhausted and broke. I'm at the end, Jonathan." Another sigh, louder. Then she whispers, "I didn't leave you. I want you to know I didn't leave you."

Thirty-five miles per hour and falling. "I know," I say, but a more honest voice would have confessed, *I hoped.*

"I was taken. Stolen. Lifted right off the ground and tossed in the backseat, then raced away. Next thing I know, I'm"—long delay as if she's examining her surroundings—"here."

A guy in a commercial plumbing truck pulls up next to me, blows his horn, and yells out the passenger window, "Hey, Granny! The *other* pedal! Press the *other* pedal!"

I turn and answer, "Hey, up yours, you fug-g-gantastic driver."

"Always the gentleman," she says.

I try to get my car moving, except I'm moving so slowly that sixth gear has been rendered useless; I keep the phone to my ear, press my knee against the steering wheel, and shift down to third, punch the accelerator, and three seconds later I pass the truck like it's a tree in the median.

Then it occurs to me how odd it is that her opinion of me—whether in jest or not—would be that I'm some form of a gentleman, that some sheath of honorableness covers the real me. How could a man with so much blood on his hands ever be categorized this way? Her perception of me is only what I've displayed. Why did I not curb my tongue in front of the women I'd dated? Why could I never put aside a cigarette for the girls who detested the habit? My goal is to improve—to fix—her life, but the unpredicted by-product is that she makes me want to be a better man.

Melody makes me want to be that *something else.*

I speak what I'm thinking, speak *without* thinking: "You have an unexpected positive effect on my life, Melody."

I regret the words as soon as they pass my lips. The sentiment had to be from the adrenaline-fueled rush of finding her, of knowing she is okay, of knowing she wants me to rescue her and free her once and for all. That the emotion running through me is composed of something more than excitement, that some percentage of this experience is dedicated to sentiment, alarms me. Except...

"And for some reason you have the only positive effect on

mine," she says, "which is why I want you to know that I didn't leave you. I was taken away."

With her words, my guard drops, falls to the ground and shatters to pieces. I'm afraid to look in the rearview for fear of seeing a dopey smile in its reflection.

"It seems no one wants me to have you," I say. "Not the good guys or the bad guys. It's just one big"—apparently I had a backup guard, because it rises in front of me—"hey, how'd you get my number?"

My instant fear: I'm being set up, that the feds wore Melody down or somehow extorted her, and they're collectively preparing some trap.

Except Melody quickly answers, "Your dad gave it to me."

"No, really."

"Does 718-555-4369 sound familiar?"

"That's... impossible."

"You mean that *was* dear old dad? The Disemboweler of Brooklyn?"

"The better question is where did you get *that* number? That's the private line for his office in Brooklyn. Not many people have it."

"I'll tell you later."

"Wait, no. My father would've never handed out my cell phone number."

"I'll tell you *lay-ter.* Where are you? I'm a damsel in distress here."

"Distress?"

"West Virginia, Jonathan, West Virginia."

"I'm still in Baltimore."

I hear her slowly inhale over the line, then she asks in the sweetest voice, with a subtle surrender that no man could ever deny: "Will you come find me?"

A wave crashes over me; I swim to the surface, to the light, to the air, struggle to remain afloat. I try to formulate the proper response, but no matter what actually comes out of my mouth, the answer could only be *of course I will.*

I bring moisture to my lips, eventually say, "Are you sure, Melody?"

She does not hesitate. "I'm sure."

I whisk across two lanes of traffic, go up the exit ramp for Liberty Road, zoom around two loops of the cloverleaf, and head south. "I'm getting on I-70 right now. What's the address?"

"Two-fifty-four Walnut Street, outside the university."

"Two-fifty-four Walnut. Got it." I punch the accelerator and merge back onto the westward interstate. "Don't move."

Our call ends and I pull in front of a crowd of cars. It takes only a few minutes before I have passed the exits for the roads leading to Ellicott City and Columbia; nearly all of the traffic goes with them. Heading directly away from the city, I have quickly broken free into the sprawling Maryland countryside.

And as I traverse the hills and valleys of western Maryland, I recall my prayer at the park-and-ride. Like before, I'd love to testify God gave me exactly what I asked the moment I requested it. And though sometimes His answer to prayer is *No*, turns out this time His answer was *Not yet.*

SEVEN

If you travel across and out Maryland's narrow western panhandle, cross the steep ranges of hills and mountains that make the ride far longer than it appears on a map, you will eventually come upon Morgantown, West Virginia, a small city that doubles in size during West Virginia University's fall and spring semesters. The university brims with active students and a positive urgency—I see little difference from the atmosphere at Johns Hopkins—an unlikely observation considering the depressed status of its home state.

During my journey, I completed three calls: one to Peter, assuring him things are fine on my end; one to Eddie Gravina, where I essentially gave the same information passed along to Peter an hour earlier; and one to Gardner: no update. For now, I'll let Gardner think I'm still desperate for his information, that I still want to be notified should her information change. If her record updates while she's with me, the appearance of a new and unused address for relocation, this could only indicate she's working with the feds to bring me and my family down. The risk I'm taking is lessened only by a trust in her I can neither deny nor understand. Fools routinely die for inexplicable notions.

Through my various pursuits of Melody, I've seen more of West

Virginia than I could've ever imagined, and I can say that Morgantown is more attractive than the other Blue Ridge towns I've seen. Walnut serves as one of the main drags through the city, and finding the coffeehouse required no reading of address numbers, the silver letters spelling out MOUNTAINEER COFFEE MILL visible from a half block away. The awning above the door is similar to Sylvia's, reminds me of the work back home that I hope is being completed while I'm on this temporary journey.

I pull in front of the café, enjoy the luxury of empty city streets in a place where so many walk. I get out and run my hands through my hair, grab a pullover from the backseat and slip it on to cut the chill in the air. The coffeehouse has good bones, had obviously once become a dump, renovated with care by some prior owner, then allowed to fall into partial decay by the current one. The exterior has been covered in a grass green paint that is chipping near the moldings, and the awning has faded on the sun-facing angles. The windows are fogged by seasons of dust. Through the window next to the door I see Melody. And when she sees me, she stands and wraps her hands up in the bottom of her shirt, walks toward me.

I open the door and Melody collapses in my arms like a dying soldier. She trembles and shakes as though she's detoxing from a drug. This moment tells me my instincts are right, that Melody is acting alone. If not, she's one exceptional actress.

"It's okay," I say, "it's okay, I've got you." I recall that recent daydream when I imagined her falling into my arms in almost the same way. *It's all right, everything's gonna be all right*, I wanted to tell her.

The students and middle-aged hipsters in the café stare at us—her, really—and it pisses me off. I run my hand behind her neck and pull her face to my chest and gently kiss the top of her head. I return each and every stare with a look that implies, *When I'm done here I'm going to go over and rip your throat out*, until attention has been categorically diverted elsewhere.

After Melody has regained her composure and gets back on her feet, we exit the coffeehouse. I open the door of my car and she drops down into the seat, stares forward like she's trying to decipher the words AIR BAG on my dashboard, her hands in her lap, lifeless.

I get in the driver's side and watch her for a few seconds, then reach behind her seat and hand her the bag with the textbook. "For you," I say.

She looks at me and passes a smile that appears forced. "You're always bearing gifts."

"Well, I had time to kill in Baltimore." She opens the bag and pulls out Zwiebach's monster, stares at it like a practical joke she doesn't understand. I rub my forehead, feel like an idiot. "Not as useful as a sweater, I suppose."

But when she turns to me, her eyes are wet. "Are you kidding?" She reaches over the gearshift and hugs me. I slide my arm around her back and slip my hand beneath her underarm, tighten it around her body. She lets go before I do. "You pick this out on your own?"

"Get real. I would have thought string theory had something to do with the clothing industry. I spoke with the dean of math... *stuff*, who told me what the class after differential equations would be. He reeled off a list of titles that gave me a headache. The only one that stuck was string theory, and a girl at the bookstore told me this was the best one for self-study."

She shakes her head and looks at me like she's trying to interpret a newly learned language. "I can't believe you called a dean to research this—and that you remembered I was ready to move beyond differential equations. That's so"—she struggles for the word, is reluctant to use it once found—"romantic."

I swallow, hard. She stares at me, shows no sign or interest in stopping. I look up to the sky, darkening with clouds from the west. Eventually she looks up, too.

"Where's that useless fed of yours?" I ask, half waiting to be pistol-whipped right here on Walnut. Who's to say her tears and sadness aren't those of guilt?

"Who knows, really. I ditched him a few miles back. Last night."

I check all my mirrors. "He managed to lose you twice in two days. That's gotta be a career killer."

I casually watch Melody from the corner of my eyes. She already returned her interest to the textbook. She runs her fingers around the edge of it like she's caressing a lover's hand, smiles as though someone just whispered something sweet in her ear.

She notices me watching her; I cannot look away.

"You know," she says, "your dad referred to you as Little Johnny."

Her having actually conversed with my father appears like it might be true. I try again for closure: "How did you get his number?"

She closes her eyes and dips her head. "I'll tell you later." I don't respond. She looks at me and adds, "I cheated and lied to get it. I deceived some people into getting what I wanted. It's not something you would likely find endearing."

I give her a blank stare. "Perhaps you've forgotten who I am."

She puckers her lips and sort of narrows her eyes at me, rips off an undoubtedly abbreviated, stream-of-consciousness edition: "I called information in New York for Bovaro and they found a listing but it was unpublished to a post office box address so I called the post office in that borough and posed as your mother and insisted the information they had in their system was incorrect because our mail—your father's mail—was delivered to a neighbor's house and that the whole reason we rented a post office box in the first place was to avoid having mail go to a physical address and hey if it's going to go to a physical address why didn't it come to ours so I concluded that their information was out of date and demanded the guy read whatever information they currently had on file to see if it was correct and he gave me an address on Hicks Street along with the phone number I used to contact your father a few hours ago."

She could never know how hard I'm trying not to smile. Turns out introducing her to my family might be easier than I'd imagined; she's already one of us. I don't mean to give my family too much credit; honestly, we're not that crafty. But it appears our motivations and means are quite similar. Though the greatest benefit of her story comes from my ability to drop any worry that she's working in collusion with the feds, setting up my family—and me. I know Melody's had to develop skills at deception and misleading people that I could never understand, but I could never be convinced this elaborate scheme was scripted.

Melody turns her hands out as if to imply, *That's all I got.*

I can no longer restrain the smile, and it bursts through embedded in laughter. "Man, Melody, you really are..." She looks at me like she's anxious to hear the rest, leans forward like she wants to make sure she hears the punch line of the sentence. Instead, I just repeat it, and end it: "You really are." I mentally follow with all the things I'm thinking but cannot confess: beautiful, clever, misunderstood.

She sits back, nods in disappointment: *It's okay.*

I start the car and pull away from the café. Rain begins to trickle, noticeable on the windshield before it can be felt. I put the top up while we're slowly drifting toward a red light. Normally, a few drops of rain would mean nothing, but I use it as an excuse to keep us veiled from the outside world. We roll out to I-68, and as the sun drops and our speed increases, the temperature in the car has cooled enough that I put the windows up. The sudden quietness in the cab makes noticeable how we're not talking.

Melody rests back like she's considering sleep, then slowly turns her head to me. I can sense her staring; I ignore it for a while, but feel compelled to return it. I catch her stare, clear my throat and ask, "Do you want me to take you anywhere?"

She keeps her eyes on me, reaches down and unbuckles her seat belt, carefully leans over and drops her head to my lap, lays her cheek on my thigh, and says, "Yes, take me anywhere."

Within seconds, the heat of her face seeps through to my leg. I glance at her long torso extended across the center of the cab, at the rise and fall of her curves. I try to again remember her as the innocent little girl twirling about the sidewalk in front of Vincent's, but that image is nowhere to be found. I can't deny that the grown woman whose body is stretched before me has developed into a masterpiece, a work of art worthy of study and emulation. It would be easy to dismiss how attracted I am to her, that our history together is improperly skewing my opinion of who she is, but it seems unlikely; isn't the girl next door, the one you've known over too many years, the one usually overlooked? Even if how she's been a significant part of my life and attention for so long is somehow influencing me, it doesn't change the fact that she is genuinely attractive—it just makes her *more* attractive.

I take my right hand from the steering wheel and let it slowly drop to her shoulder and I squeeze it softly, run my thumb gently against the back of it. She takes a deep breath, and as she lets it out, she slides her hand around my thigh and underneath, so that it rests between the seat and my leg.

We drive like this for ten minutes and she eventually falls asleep. Every now and then she makes a quiet vocal sound in her sleep like a newborn. I notice her shirt has drifted up and exposed her midriff and back. I carefully slide my hand over and try to pull her shirt down to keep her warm, but I accidentally brush her skin, and as I do her body shifts a little and rises to meet my hand, and I keep it there longer than I should.

Then I remember why I'm doing all of this, why I want to set her free—and none of it has to do with feeling anything romantic toward Melody. Without question, romance is the worst thing I could offer her. I quickly return both hands to the steering wheel. What Melody needs is unfettered freedom; being tied to me in any way would be more damaging than what she has now.

I'm lucky if I drive three miles before my attention drifts to her again. I look down and notice the smoothness of her neck, fully exposed by her short hair. I bite my lip and carefully bring my hand to her neck and gently caress the skin from the edge of her hairline down to the top of her shirt. I do this for the next half hour.

Self-control has never been a strong suit of the Bovaros.

The sun sets as we retravel the eastbound lanes of the highways I'd covered hours earlier. With the tinted windows of my car and the cloudy sky, the cab has been nearly blackened. Crossing over Braddock Mountain on I-70, the last mountain range on our journey back toward Baltimore, my cell vibrates. I carefully shift to the side, pull it from my left pocket, and flip it open.

Gardner finishes a yawn and mutters, "No update."

Quietly, I respond, "I have to say I'm becoming increasingly less concerned with the capabilities of your employer." Melody wriggles her body a little.

Randall mumbles something out of range, sounds like he may have hit the sauce before heading back to the office to check for new information. "I don't know, maybe they haven't moved her. Maybe she's still in Columbia."

"Stay a technologist, buddy. You have no future in operations. What, you think they'd keep her there forever? 'Got an idea, let's just drive around in a big circle and take her back home.'" Melody shifts again.

"What do I care?"

"I admire your commitment to excellence."

Then, with boozy sarcasm: "No update." When I finally get around to seeing Gardner again, I'm going to beat his head with a nine iron just for the sheer pleasure of it. "Look, the system will catch up, and you'll find her nearby, blah, blah, blah."

"She's probably in North Dakota."

"Listen, I was thinking maybe I could start getting a bigger boost, considering how helpful I've—"

"Yeah, I'll let you know what I find out." I hang up on the scumbag.

"Jonathan?"

Melody's voice startles me and I jerk up in my seat and accidentally slam her head into the bottom of the steering wheel and throw our car across two lanes of traffic. I overcompensate and slide back into the fast lane then off onto the shoulder, then back again.

"Geez," I say, "you scared me to death." Cars behind us slow down as we get back up to cruising speed.

"Sorry." Melody sits up and rubs her neck and head. "How long was I asleep?"

My eyes move from mirror to mirror, make sure no police lights are coming up the rear. "About three hours."

She nods a little. "We must be getting close to Philadelphia."

"Baltimore, actually."

She rubs her eyes and yawns. "Wouldn't it have been faster to take the Pennsylvania Turnpike?"

I glance her way, then back to the road. "We're avoiding Philly. For the moment."

She stops rubbing her eyes. "What's in Philadelphia?"

"Some bad people, who were given some bad information."

I feel like a parent trying to avoid telling his daughter that her puppy got run over. The *bad people* are various members of our crew who had several targets to eliminate in Philadelphia. Two crew members were in DC, taking out one very important target. Baltimore was technically my location, and despite the fact that my target moved, I claimed it as my own—and claimed to have made a successful hit: the *bad information.* My goal for now is to keep us between the two cities, allow the rest of the crew to finish its business—according to Peter all is well—and return home; I don't want anyone trying to check in or meet up with me while they're in the area. I want them all settled and in one place when we arrive back in New York.

"And who knows where the marshals and the FBI are at this point," I add. "They're a completely separate issue." That's no exaggeration. The only insight I have into what they're thinking is the confirmation from Gardner that they know nothing.

Melody doesn't say a word, merely digests everything I've told her. I have no doubt she's wondering what she's done, putting her trust in the hands of a mobster, of a monster, to protect her. I can't begin to imagine how miserable her life has been, though I'm certain it's led her to desperation. It is far easier to embrace hopelessness than hope. I have no delusions of grandeur, no comprehension that I am anything more than what happened to be waiting at the end of her rope. What she could not know is that I have no intention of letting her down, of letting her go. I am going to return her life to her, wrap it up and hand it over like a present. I am going to give her a second chance—or in her case, a tenth.

As if I spoke these words to her, I notice her soften. Her shoulders drop and she does a full-body sigh that suggests relief. I'm not sure what she's thinking, but I'm afraid to ask, to open my mouth and potentially offer up a less convincing version of her future.

Melody makes a subtle comment about how different we are,

yet how amusing it is that we're running together. I laugh and agree, but suggest we aren't different at all.

I say we're nearly identical.

After a long pause, Melody twists in her seat to face me better, says, "Come again?"

I look at her, read the seriousness in her expression. "You really think you and I are so different?"

She squints like the sun is over my shoulder. "Yeah, I think we're totally different. I'm trapped. I have to be whatever they tell me to be, stuck in a life with jobs where no one notices I exist, but you're free—free to do and be whatever you want to be."

I immediately recall those moments in the bookstore at Johns Hopkins and how convinced I was—still am—that we only have so much control over our destinies. I think for a minute to articulate my point.

"How often do you think I'm watched by the cops or the feds?" I ask. "If I get a citation for jaywalking, they'll be on me in a heartbeat, trying to get me to flip on someone in my family. I can't go anywhere without being noticed—and I'm a pretty stand-up guy by comparison. But that's irrelevant. I'll never be rid of the Bovaro tag, might as well have it tattooed on my forehead. I will always be viewed as a criminal or a criminal-in-training. At a minimum, I'll always be viewed as someone with information on other criminals."

"Do you? Have information on other criminals?"

I barely have enough space to store it all. "Sure. I mean, didn't you know the details of what your dad did for a living?" I regret bringing up her father—in the past tense, no less.

"I guess I see your point, but we're still very different. You can do whatever you want with your life. Nothing is keeping you suppressed, forcing you out of the realm of possibility."

"You think I can be a United States congressman?"

"Okay, well—"

"How about a world-class surgeon? Trust your prostate to the son of Anthony Bovaro?"

"I don't have a pros—"

"How 'bout an FBI agent? Think I'd be well received at the academy? Ooh, how about a stockbroker? Want to put your financial investments in the hands of a Bovaro?"

She stops trying to answer.

"How about a disc jockey?" I continue. "Musician? Professor? I can't even be a Little League coach."

When I glance over at Melody, she catches my eye and smiles. I turn back to the road. "Maybe we are alike," she says, then very softly as though only to herself, "Maybe that's why I feel I have this connection with you."

I almost ask her to repeat herself, but I'm afraid to, afraid I misheard or that she'll deny having said it at all.

Then the rationalization begins, that the feelings I'm starting to have toward her are not wrong, and—you know, big deal—what could be the harm in trying to hold her hand? Had she kept that sentence to herself, my hands would have remained where they were—ten and two—but two just lost its grip. I reach over and gently take her hand in mine. She looks down and I fear she might pull it away, but instead she takes her other hand and places it on top, capturing mine. The warmth of her palms sends a wave of pleasure through my veins and into my brain like a shot of morphine. I understand, I do: None of her prior protectors cared about her—cared about her like a father or a husband. That kiss she popped on Sean's cheek in Cape Charles? She wanted some signal he felt *passionate* about caring for her, that it was more than his job, that he was following something other than the command of a superior. I know I should pull my hand away, retract the notion. But: *like a shot of morphine.*

Neither of us looks at one another. We speak not a word for miles.

On our approach to Baltimore, we share vignettes of our family life, begin with guarded generalities and progress to specific embarrassments and disasters of the relative ways we've been forced to live. She confesses how vulnerable she felt as a little girl moving from school to school, how hard it was to make friends, and how she gave up on trying, on putting in the effort to vet and build relationships when she knew she would leave them behind at any moment, and how isolation became as great a comfort as her reliance upon math. I confess how I so desperately wanted to leave behind the lifestyle I was born into: how first I tried to stand out by excelling in my studies, achieving grades never recorded on my brothers' report cards; how I briefly considered the path of the priesthood until admitting to myself that I was marred by a lack of discipline and an incapacity to forgive; how I tried so diligently to find a course of study and career that could have no possible benefit to my family's corrupt operations, how I attended culinary school, how I broke free, and how I returned to my own prison by using my restaurant to launder a large percentage of the money that comes to the Bovaro organization. We pass stories back and forth for the remainder of our time on the freeway. No discussion of murder ever occurs. No doubt we'd love to forget all about it—her far more than I—but getting to know each other turned out to be an unexpected pleasure, her voice in response to mine as sweet and reassuring as a hymn.

The Baltimore skyline comes into view and the particular shapes of the tallest buildings, their erratic rise and fall across the smoggy horizon, are now as familiar as my reflection in the mirror. Baltimore has become a temporary second home. I take the exit that brings us to the feet of the city, winds us down toward the Inner Harbor.

Melody never asks what I'm doing or where we're going. I can't tell if she has an inherent trust in me or if she's come to let everyone else make the decisions for so long that she's unsure of the proper way to integrate her opinion. I suppose, then, I shouldn't tell her I'm crafting this plan on the fly.

Our conversation slows as we reach the core of downtown, ends the moment I pull in front of the entrance to the Renaissance Harborplace Hotel. What we concluded: We are indeed quite alike, with one glaring exception. Melody would give anything to be who she was meant to be, and I would give anything to be anyone but who I was meant to be.

EIGHT

I leave the car running, get out and open the door for Melody. She takes my hand and exits, absorbs her surroundings as I grab my overnight bag and all the clothing-filled shopping bags out of my trunk. The valet hands her the ticket for the Audi and she looks at it like she was given some foreign currency.

I tilt my head for Melody to follow me into the lobby, and throughout the entire walk she remains a few steps behind, looking around the place like it's a museum. The hotel gives off a vibe of money—that it requires a lot to stay here and the patrons have no problem forking it over—but I chose this place for a different reason: It sits directly across from the harbor, with the same view I had when I watched the people of the city through the narrow gap between buildings. I want Melody to glimpse her future.

I drop my bags at the desk and begin fishing through my pockets for all the buried wads of cash. It's everywhere: multiple pockets of my jeans, in my jacket, crumpled up on the bottom of my overnight bag. Melody catches up, stands next to me like a daughter. I can sense her watching me, her eyes never leaving my face.

A lady behind the desk approaches, a refined middle-ager with hair pulled so tightly into a bun it renders her eyebrows immobile.

She welcomes us, smiles like it's been drawn on her skin with a magic marker.

"Have you stayed with us before, sir?"

I locate my biggest wad and pull it out, uncurl the currency. "We have not."

"May I have your reservation number?"

I start counting bills. "We don't have a reservation."

So here's how the process works: I am a grungy guy boasting a thick five o'clock shadow, standing next to his strung-out-looking girlfriend, walking in with no reservation. Prepare for the blow-off.

"Well, sir, there's a convention in the hotel. I'm afraid there're no—"

I chuck several hundred dollars on the counter. "We'd like two rooms, adjoining, facing the harbor. Two nights." I keep counting bills because a second wad will be required right...

"Uh, sure. Let me see." She types for a moment. "Do you have a major credit card?"

Now. I drop a slightly larger wad on the counter. Of course I have a credit card. Am I going to use it so the feds can easily find out where we are? I'm thinking *no.* When I'm in New York, my name does all the work; everywhere else cash acts as the grease. I determined years ago that some hotel clerks are like hosts at restaurants: A wad of cash brings the best room or table. Name and money, the first and second rules of thumb growing up Bovaro.

She prints off the agreement, some paper covered in small print, asks me to sign it. I go to the bottom and scribble gibberish in the spot for my name. I shove the door cards in my pocket, slip a bag-filled fist behind Melody in an effort to guide her, and walk us to the elevators.

I press the up button and a car immediately opens. We walk into what feels like a large coffin with an interior composed of mirrors. Melody catches a glimpse of herself and turns down and away. I put all the shopping bags in one hand, reach over and smile and pull her to me, bring her to my chest. She rests herself against me. I kiss the top of her head, say nothing.

We exit one floor from the top of the hotel and find our rooms. I open the door to the suite on the right and allow Melody to walk in first. I put her bags down near the dresser, say, "These are all for you. Hope I wasn't being too presumptuous."

Melody sits on the bed, bounces lightly on it a few times giving it a little test drive, looks around the room with the slow steady movement of a surveillance camera. For a woman who's spent so much time in hotels and motels, she looks uncertain of her surroundings.

I walk over to the window, open the blinds, and stare out over the harbor. And just as I'm about to call her over and show her what I wanted her to see, I am awash in disappointment: The view is nearly identical to the one from my room at the hotel in Norfolk. Truly, both views display brick-lined harbors, milling pedestrians, an array of skyscrapers, pavilions with shops and restaurants. This could be Columbus, Louisville, Pittsburgh, Des Moines. Another cookie-cutter, master-planned design that she does not need in her life. How often had she been relocated where some guy waved his hand across the land and said, "Look! Isn't this great?" I have become as useless and ineffective as the feds. I turn away, start biting my thumbnail.

"Why did you book two nights?" she asks.

I don't have an answer to offer—at least, not one she should hear. The truth: I want all of the hits to be completed, for Melody and I to be the last to arrive, to return home after all is *well*—not amidst the chaos and concern. Or: If things collapse, I want us to be nowhere near New York, out of striking distance if the feds' plan is more complete and successful than ours. But more to the immediate point, I need time for everyone to return to New York so I can avoid being asked to meet up with our crew somewhere on the way—and having someone else finish Melody off before I can get her to New York safely. I walk to the bed and sit down next to her, keep a distance between us.

I finally answer, "Thought you might like a day in the spa here in the hotel. Figured, you know, you might enjoy getting pampered for a change."

She looks down and laughs a little; it appears to have been the last thing she expected as a response. "I don't know what to say." She plays with the back of her head, rubs her hair up and down in a smooth motion. I slide closer and put my hand on her shoulder; it seems to increase her discontent, the stiffness of her shoulder suggesting a restless longing for better circumstances. I'm the best she's got, and I'm a pretty sizable question mark.

I rise because I do not want to mislead her, do not want her to think in any way that my intentions for her are anything but the best I have to give. I walk to the window again and stare at a cluster of office buildings.

"There's nothing in this for me, Melody. We're not in the same room. You can leave anytime you want, okay?" I turn around and face her. Her knees are bent and her toes are pointed inward, arms crossed like she has a chill. I see the little girl again. "I'll be really disappointed if you decide to leave, but... it's totally up to you. I would never try to keep you here. I want you to *want* to be here. I want you to know that I understand the distance of the narrow tunnel that will set you free. You just have to trust that I can navigate you through it." She looks to me with her lips firmly pressed together, like a platitude is not what she needs at the moment. So I give her something the feds likely never did: honesty. "The tunnel's very, very narrow, Melody. I'm sure you understand that. But unlike Justice, I know what's on the other side."

Melody bites the inside of her cheek, eventually nods. I want her to view me as the solution, not just the better option.

I open the adjoining door and chuck my overnight bag on the bed across the room. "I'm just one knock away, okay?" And sure, as soon as I say it I realize that had to have been the closing line from every marshal she's ever known.

She nods and her eyes fill. She turns away and whispers, "Okay."

"Good night, Melody." I close the door, leave it unlocked. I put my ear to the wall and listen for sniffles or outright crying, but neither ever come.

I walk to my bathroom and flip on the vent and reach for my smokes, hold them in my hand like a gun. I study the corrosive little tubes of relief as two thoughts hit me at the same time: (1) I am a socially acceptable, less destructive version of Gardner, enslaved to an addiction, so lazy and unwilling to give it up that I'm permitting it to destroy me. This thought—the fact that Gardner and I have some trait in common—sickens me, and; (2) if Melody can surrender her life to me, the least I can do to exemplify a man of discipline, a man that can deliver the goods, is give up a ridiculous dependency.

And like any addict, like every loser and scumbag who comes to my family saddled with a need for money to get a fix, I rationalize the *one last time* scenario. Sure, I'm going to give up cigs, but I'll just smoke one more. One final time, and then it's over.

I stare at the pack in my hand for a long time before I squeeze the death out of it, clench my fist so tightly that the cigarette papers tear and tobacco spills out. The smell drives me frigging nuts. I empty it all into the toilet, then empty the other two packs from my overnight bag into the can as well, and flush my addiction right into Baltimore's sewers, down the Patapsco River, into the Chesapeake Bay.

So, around five in the morning I wake up with an unbearable headache and a wave of nausea that I'd liken to salmonella poisoning. There's the sweat, too.

I stumble out of bed and put my ear to the adjoining door—takes all my might to keep from opening it and peeking in—and I swear I hear the sound of utensils hitting a plate and a cup hitting a saucer, the soundtrack of working in the restaurant business; I'd recognize that clinking anywhere.

I turn on the shower, strip down, and get in while the water is still cold, try to wash the withdrawal away. No matter how clean I make my body, how close I shave, or how well I brush my teeth, the misery keeps coming, and introduces me to its not so distant cousin: anxiety.

I dry off and stand in front of the fogged mirror, close my eyes, and inhale steam. As I'm combing my hair, my cell phone rings.

I answer it and hear this: "No update."

"Die! Die, you frigging no-good scumbag *porcaccione. Non me ne importa un cavolo!*" I slap the phone shut, rub my eyes for a second, then slip my cell in my pocket.

I walk out of the bathroom and get dressed, listen one more time for Melody—still with the clinking—then quickly make my way to the front desk.

I walk up to the only person there, an older guy dressed well enough to indicate he's management. "Nearest pharmacy?"

"Yes, sir. Twenty-four-hour CVS up the block." He points as though I can see through the mahogany-paneled walls.

I run across the empty lanes of the street, become the only

patron of the dormant store, buy every box of 4 mg Nicorette they have left in stock (smoking might be cheaper), and pop a few in my mouth as I walk to the counter to pay. It doesn't take long before the comfort of the drug is back in my veins—a partial defeat; were I a smack addict, this would be my methadone—but I still run back to the hotel. The last time I turned my back on Melody, I spent the day sniffing around Baltimore like a dog who couldn't find his way home.

I hurry back to my room, lose my breath on the way. Friggin' cigarettes.

It's nearly seven o'clock, and this time when I put my ear to Melody's door, I faintly hear the turning of pages. I sit on the edge of my bed, collect my thoughts along with my breath, then call down to the front desk and ask to be transferred to the spa. The guy I spoke with regarding the pharmacy tells me the spa does not open for a few more minutes—at seven—but that I can hold.

When I get the lady on the phone, our conversation goes like this:

"I'd like to make an appointment for my...friend," I say. "Female."

"Of course. What day and time?"

"Today, an hour from now."

"Oh, no, I'm sorry, sir. We're booked for the next eleven days, the next opening I have is on the—"

I hang up. What's the point, really? Obviously, this transaction needs to occur in person. Name and money, my friend. Name and money.

Fifteen minutes and a few hundred later Melody has appointments scheduled that run from eight-thirty all the way to four in the afternoon, so she'll be finished around five. I don't even understand what they are, was told women *love them*, even got the pleasure-indicating eye roll as punctuation.

I stall in my room until eight—banging on Melody's door before that seems too rude, after that seems too lackadaisical—upon which I exit into the hall and knock on her hallway door.

Melody opens it and laughs at me, props herself in the doorway. She looks fresh and clean and caffeinated, is wearing the robe from the bathroom. "You could've come through the adjoining door, you know." Then she readjusts her robe—an attempt at tightening it—but when she pulls the left side out to stretch it over, I can't help but notice a margin of her breast that suggests she's wearing *only* the robe.

"It seemed a little...inappropriate," I say. "Like I had some right to be in your room anytime I wanted." She slumps down a little and crosses her calves as she stands in the doorway, and as she does her left leg is exposed all the way to her upper thigh and the V opens up in her robe again, and now I'm certain she has nothing else on. I keep eye contact but my peripheral vision takes her all in, the shape of her body, the smooth curve of her chest, the overcast valley between. I could provide a sketch artist with enough details to keep him busy for a week. The shape of her jawline and the way it casts a shadow on her neck, the delicate question-mark shape of her ears, how her eyelashes gently sway like wisps of wheat whenever she blinks. People often suggest God has a sense of humor; there is no disputing He has a sense of artistry.

I bite my lip, glance down the hall as though something legitimate took my attention away. She slides to the side and waves me in.

"Sorry to disturb you so early, but I got you in the spa at eight-thirty." Her room smells like the kitchen at Sylvia.

"They had an opening?"

I shrug. "I made an opening." She looks at me like she's simultaneously impressed and disappointed. "It's all smoke and mirrors. Bovaro means something in New York. Money means something everywhere else."

"You say that like you have no respect for yourself."

I think for a moment, struggle to make eye contact. "I don't."

She takes a step closer. "You seem like a decent guy to me, Jonathan."

"Let's be honest: What you mean is I seem like a decent guy, *respectively*."

"I've been told a lot about your family over the years. Granted, the people doing the telling aren't exactly your advocates, but you really don't seem to fully fit the profile."

Ask Willie. Ask Ettore (if you could). Ask anyone, really.

"I've never had to work hard at anything in my life," I say. *Except this.* "I'm trying, though. I want to be fair and honest. I mean, it would mean so much more if the cash I was throwing around was money I'd earned from being a talented chef or a successful restaurateur—even if I'd legitimately won it at the track. I mean, most of my income comes from aboveboard sources, but the rest poisons the whole wad." She nods a little. "Do I smell sausage?"

She slinks in front of a room service tray in the corner of the room. "I took the liberty. Sorry, I was famished."

"No, good move. We won't have time to eat before your spa appointments anyway."

"Plural?"

I walk right up to her, rub her shoulder in a nonsensual way. "The whole day is yours. You're getting the works: massage, facial, hair, manicure, pedicure, some sort of upper-echelon skin treatment, and a couple of things I didn't really understand and probably can't pronounce correctly."

She stares at me. "So, I'll be done around..."

"Dinnertime."

The narrow space between us disappears as she stands on her toes and throws her arms around my neck. She closes her eyes and gives me the gentlest kiss I have ever received, presses her lips to mine and keeps them there long enough to knock the power from me, then she runs her fingers up the back of my neck, slowly moves her mouth to my ear and whispers, "Something this thoughtful could only come from the money you *earned*."

I swallow, reluctantly hold her in my arms. As we embrace I squeeze her back, unable to deny how perfectly the shape of her body rests in my hands. I try to breathe but I cannot inhale deeply enough. She pulls back a little, keeps her eyes on me and twists her arms around my neck, and as she drops down from her toes, her robe falls open.

Have you ever walked into a kitchen that smells so good you can't resist having a taste of what's cooking? In our house, there was always a loaf of crusty bread sitting on the counter near the stove, available for anyone who wanted to tear off a hunk and plunge it into whatever sauce had been simmering. In the open space between the left and right side of her robe lies a temptation that could never be matched by any gastronomic allure. I'm not sure I've ever wanted to touch something this badly. And I can't tell if she notices she exposed herself to me or if she's aware and willing to let me indulge, but I know I'm not what she needs. And so, no matter the scents coming from the kitchen, I'm determined to keep myself on a strict diet.

Watch this self-frigging-control.

I lock my eyes on hers, concentrate like I'm trying to read her mind. I carefully bring my hands around to her front, gently grab the edges of her robe—I do not touch her skin—and pull them together. She and I look down and watch me tie the belt.

I press my lips together. "I'm picking up a hollandaise."

She squints, feigns annoyance. "And to think I let you in my room at such an unscrupulous hour."

"Tastes like those bastards used tarragon vinegar instead of fresh lemon. If one of my chefs did that, he'd be at the bottom of the East River. Want me to take the guy out?"

"Have him drawn and quartered."

"Eh, horses are a hassle. Gimme your coffee spoon. I'll file it into a shiv."

We smile at each other, then she tosses a question my way. What I thought would be a pillow turns out to be a grenade: "Have you ever killed anyone?"

I smirk, look up to the corners of her room for a camera or microphone, then answer loudly, "No."

She grabs my shirt, pulls me closer. "You mean, I would've been your first?"

I sigh and grab her hand. My stomach turns at the thought of that once being on my docket, at how close Ettore came. "That was the plan."

She looks at me and smiles. "Well, if you're not careful you'll end up being *my* first, too." As I decipher what that means, she drops her hand and her head at the same time, closes her eyes and shakes her head, mumbles something to herself.

As I interpret her statement—and her own reaction to it—I widen my eyes and step back.

"Wait." I pinch my chin. "You mean," I stutter, "you're a . . ."

Melody drops her shoulders and throws up a hand. "Yes, a *virgin*, Jonathan. What's the matter, you've never killed a virgin?"

"I told you I'm not gonna kill you."

"It was a euphemism. Does the term *deflower* sound better?"

"How's this possible?"

She chuckles, makes a face. "What do you mean? You think there's some rite of passage—"

"How old are you?" All along I thought I knew, but now I'm starting to wonder.

"Depends on which persona you want me to use. If I'm Linda Simms, I'm just about to turn thirty. Shelly Jones? She's a spry twenty-four." She shrugs, rolls her eyes. "I'm twenty-six."

I walk backward, sit on the sofa near the window. Melody sits across from me on the bed and curls her legs up and covers them with her robe.

"And you never...you never found someone you loved enough?" I'm lost again, like in 'Tone's restaurant, forgetting who and where I am.

"I'd love to say I was being morally responsible, but the truth is I never allowed myself to get close to anyone—physically or emotionally. There was just too much risk."

I hesitate before asking, "Risk for whom?"

She stares at the floor, reaches up and clutches the robe to her chest. It takes a moment before she responds. She does not directly answer my question, but exposes her vulnerability, of failed love, through a story of losing a teen romance by way of being pulled from the boy's arms and tossed in the back of a government van.

"There's never been a reason to love," she says, "because it would mean lying about who I am the entire time, only to one day make the decision to either leave that person behind or take him with me and put him in equal danger." She falls back on the bed, lets a leg drop off the edge. "It's a real mess. I've thought about it for years, desperately searching for the loophole." She turns her head and glances my way. "There is no loophole."

My mouth has gone dry. As I speak, I half gag on the words. "I'm sorry, Melody."

"For?"

"Just...everything. For every moment of suffering and heartache.

For every night you went to bed scared and woke up alone." My voice begins to fade. "For there not being a loophole."

She smiles a little. Her look reminds me of my mother, an expression I received as a child when I'd say something cute but of no consequence.

"All of this comes back to my family," I add. "If I had a father who did something legitimate with his life, we wouldn't be here."

Melody sits up a little. "True, but you realize...if he did, you and I would have never met."

I stare at her, can barely ask, "And that matters?"

Her eyes glisten. She answers my question so softly that if I couldn't read her lips I might not have understood: "Of course."

NINE

I escort Melody down to the spa, introduce her to the staff as a means of alerting them that the woman they promised to treat like a princess has just arrived. Earlier this morning, when I demanded it, they assured me they treat all their customers like royalty, to which I chucked an additional hundred on the counter as an illustration of how I do not want her being treated like all their other customers. Round and round we went, though I believe we finally ended at a place of understanding.

I stick to her side through the initial part of the process, the introductions and explanations of treatments she'll be getting. While they prepare a room for her massage, we wait in an area that loosely resembles a lounge or higher-end coffeehouse, a dimly lit cavern with a waterfall trickling out of view and a set of deep, plush sofas. Unrecognizable classical music plays through speakers I don't see. A buffet lines one wall, contains displays of fresh fruits, breads, and yogurts. I do a quick survey and the majority of it passes my typically overcritical nature for food review. I'd eat any of it except an overly green star fruit and a heavily sugared mélange of berries. Melody goes for my recommendation of a fresh hunk of pineapple.

No more than two or three minutes pass before the masseur and one of the clerks come into the lounge to let Melody know they're ready to take her for her massage. This must be the point where the guy usually leaves, because I get a series of strange looks as I follow them into the massage room.

"What," I say.

The clerk says, "Sir, she'll be getting her massage now."

I glance in the room and see the masseur drip a small bead of clear fluid in his hands. He slaps his hands together and wrings them vigorously. His biceps slide up and down the sleeves of his T-shirt, his pecs and traps looking like hunks of concrete trying to rip through his skin. The guy reminds me of Delmo Peretti, a cruiserweight boxer we tried to turn into a superstar (and thereafter into revenue) some twenty years ago. The guy was all muscle—seriously: no fat, no brain, no heart that I could find evidence of. He tried to teach me to wrestle when I was a kid, except for me it was like trying to flip and pin a Pontiac. The real problem with Delmo was I wouldn't have trusted the guy with my catcher's mitt, never mind a woman. And in a few seconds, this masseur's going to have his hands all over Melody. I understand the guy's a professional. But, you know, so am I.

I turn to Melody and ask, "You have to take your clothes off?"

She whispers back, "I think that makes it easier."

The fact that she's so confident, so comfortable with doing it, makes the whole thing much worse. "Well, as your bodyguard, I need to stay by your side and guard your... body."

The masseur laughs and says, "No problem, come on in." Then he turns to Melody, hands her some towel/sheet thing and says, "Why don't you disrobe, put this on, and I'll be back in a moment." Then he slides his hand up and down her lower back a few times and squeezes her shoulder. Friggin' Delmo.

As he closes the door behind him, I sit in a chair by a tray of lotions. Melody looks at me and shrugs, grabs the button on her jeans and undoes them. I quickly throw my hands to my face and cover my eyes—who exactly am I protecting here?—and tap my feet. She laughs a little. Now, here is a curious and confusing element to my individual design: No more than an hour earlier Melody was nearly undressed in front of me—but now *hearing* her undress drives me out of my mind. The slide of her jeans down her legs, the sound of crackling static as the sweater crosses over her hair, the quiet whoosh as she removes her T-shirt. A man's imagination should never be underestimated. I know what's next—and as I hear the tick as she unclips her bra, the imagery from my mind's eye could be nothing less than pinpoint accurate. Then the only thing left; it rushes to me like a fastball toward home plate: the smooth, hushed slide as she pulls her panties off. My jaw hurts from clenching my teeth so hard. I hear her struggle with the towel a little.

"Okay," she says, "it's safe."

Not the word I would use.

I look her in the eye but still capture the softness of her legs and the absence of defined muscle, that her hips are slightly wider than her chest. She does this little pose thing, cocks her leg and throws an arm up as if to say *Tada!* Then she snickers at herself and cautiously crawls up on the table, and though she doesn't seem to be forcing a seductive manner, I hope someday I can confess to her exactly what this is doing to me. She carefully pulls the towel down to her waist while stretching her forearm across her chest, then brings her body to the table belly down and puts her arms above her. Her chest is pushed to the sides and all but completely visible. And as I study her shape, internalize the hues and texture of her skin, I finally understand what inspires a man to put a paintbrush to a canvas.

What I see in her, this pull I feel, is difficult to explain—another confusing element—for she is not the first woman I've seen unclothed; this is not a case of gaining interest in a woman because she is *new*. I've never been so strongly drawn to another person. Is it because I've wanted us to be close since we were kids? Is it because being with her is forbidden? Does it even matter?

"I should wait outside," I say, as convincing and true as if I'd said I was recruited by the Knicks.

Melody frowns. "But how will you guard me?"

She's kidding—but she's right. I really shouldn't take my eyes off her. Every time I do, something bad happens. I reach in my pocket and pull out my nicotine gum and throw a pair of tablets in my mouth.

Melody squints at me, the box, then me again. "Is that Nicorette?"

I shove the box back in my pocket, shrug. "What can I say? You make me want to be a better man."

She laughs a little, brushes her cheek with the back of her hand, watches me chew. Then she squints again. "Are you serious? You stopped smoking for me? I never asked."

"Well," I say, "you shouldn't have to."

Her smile disintegrates as one corner of her mouth turns down, then the other. "You... really are full of surprises." She looks as if she's just received bad news. "I mean, we don't really know how much time we're going to have together."

I lean forward on my knees and nod a little. "That's why I'm stopping now."

Melody looks at me, parts her lips a little, appears like she's saying something to herself, yet the words seem aimed for me. Her eyes are fixed on mine. I can't look away. My chewing decelerates until it comes to a complete stop; my breathing follows suit.

She says, "Have you ever given a woman a massage before?"

I swallow, adjust my glasses. "No," I say quietly. Though I have, what I really mean is, *Please don't ask me to do this.*

"Get up," she says, "take steps in my direction, and stop when you reach the table."

I wipe my hands on my jeans a few times, get out of my chair with all the grace of a colt making its first attempt to stand. I walk over and stop in front of her.

She reaches behind her and slides the towel thing down farther, exposes an inch of cleavage on her backside.

"Place your hands on the small of my back."

I feel like a fumbling teenager. "This is not a good idea."

"Place your hands on the small of my back."

It takes me fifteen seconds before I have the strength—the weakness—to put my hand on her skin, and when I do I press down hard so she's less likely to notice the way it's trembling. She raises her lower body a little and pushes back as my other hand joins the effort. I feel dizzy—nothing metaphorical here; I blame either the withdrawal or my new overdosage of nicotine. I drag my hands across her back and steadily slide them up and down her body, let my thumbs ride the hills and valleys of her backbone. Her flesh is so tight and smooth, so free of scars and damage from the sun. I can't stop imagining what it would be like to press my lips against it, to open my mouth and taste what I'm seeing and touching. But as I force this thought away, the fantasy is replaced with the image of a bullet piercing her beautiful skin—by my hand or anyone else's—something invading to destroy this perfect creation: a bullet, a knife, a tight length of wire. My eyes fill with tears from anger and regret, and as a droplet falls from my cheek and splashes on Melody's back, the masseur reenters the room.

I quickly wipe my face, stumble toward the door. "I'll just... wait... outside."

A few minutes later Melody finds me in the lounge again, standing in the corner by the waterfall, cracking my knuckles one by one.

She's apparently abandoned the massage altogether, now

wearing a different robe, a longer and fuller one that looks like it's meant to be worn over clothes. She walks up and hugs me, whispers, "I loved having your hands on my body."

"There's really no other place they'd rather be." I clear my throat. "Listen, I'm gonna make myself scarce."

"No, I want you here."

"Well, so far my presence seems to have clouded what I wanted to be a day of relaxation for you." I read her eyes; she's not buying it. "Besides, I need to take care of some business." I hate that phrase—usually translates into one of our crew getting ready to go play poker, whack some guy, or cheat on his wife—but it's been programmed into me, ready for instant utilization. And here, in these few moments we have together, I can't use it on Melody. I correct myself: "I need to make some phone calls and lie to my family." She still doesn't look convinced. "I need to buy us more time."

She nods slowly, asks, "Why do we need more time?"

I look away. "We just do." Then I move in quick and peck her just below her ear. "I'll see you at five o'clock, okay?" I turn and step backward out of the spa. "Meet you in the hotel bar."

She watches me walk out, half waves. "I'll be there."

I turn down the corridor that leads me back to the elevators. I fear leaving her alone in that spa, but I'm starting to fear her being with me even more. She needs a rock right now and I'm dirt turning to mud. I have to hope we've hidden ourselves well enough that no one could ever find us in this corner of the country. And now that Melody is safe—around other people and occupied—I can return to my room and begin the business of the day.

The first calls I make to Sylvia end up costing me an hour. I speak with my head chef. Ryan gives me the lowdown on how the restaurant performed last night, team members who are not coming in, an emerging plumbing problem in the ladies' room, a change in appointment from a health inspector, and distributors who fouled up orders or failed delivering on time. I make several calls—livid ones—attempting to straighten things out from two hundred miles away. I call Ryan back and give him the updates, then we organize the menu, select the specials, attempt to figure out which servers we can ask to fill in, who will cover which sections. I ask if my family has been pitching in at all. Ryan tells me they've mostly occupied the kitchen, offered to consume free samples.

As I complete the restaurant-related portion of my call-making, I plug my cell into the rapid charger, gear it up for the dreaded conversations to come.

Around eleven, I try to get in touch with Peter but nothing comes of it. His cell, office phone, home phone: nothing. Having no information feels worse than having bad information. I drop lower on the probability scale and call my dad's office line.

"Yes," the person answers. There's no doubting the owner of this cold, raspy voice: Eddie Gravina.

"Hey, it's John. Where's Pop?"

"Out."

"When's he coming back?"

"Later."

I wait for details, don't get them. "Meaning what? He go out for a morning jog?" I've always liked Eddie, but if his elevated stature in our crew means he thinks he can be vague with Tony Bovaro's sons, I'll escort the guy to the door myself.

"He's taking care of some business."

See what I mean? "Yeah, well, me, too. Where's Pete?"

I hear him take a sip of something. "When are you coming home, Johnny?"

I close my eyes and drop my hand to my lap, and when I open my eyes, they immediately focus on my cell phone. The phone number is brightly displayed; for whatever reason, even though I'd just dialed it, *seeing* it triggers the memory of Melody's story, the way she got the number for Pop's office line. Suddenly, the improbability of my father so easily handing over my cell number to some girl on the phone transforms back to impossibility. I rush my cell to my ear.

"Eddie, how long have you been manning this line?"

"Eh, you know, I've been helping your father here a few days."

"Did you give my cell number out to some strange girl who called yesterday?"

Silence. Eventually, Eddie speaks in an uncharacteristically articulate manner. "I do not know what you are talking about." Good grief, I hope this guy never has to take the stand.

"Why would you give my cell number out like that?"

He breathes in slow and heavy, even the guy's lungs produce a rasp. "Johnny, it's probably time for you to come home."

He's acting an awful lot like my father, except I've got news for him: He's not my father. "Why don't you head on over to Sylvia and grab a snack while you wait for me?"

"Son," he says, "we need to bottle this wine. And you are the late harvest."

Another wine metaphor? Couldn't my family somehow relate what we're doing to curing olives or aging cheese or restoring an old car? Not to mention, what self-respecting Italian makes the mistake of saying wine grapes go from the vine to the bottle instead of the vine to the barrel? I'm concerned by his disinterest in the details, hope it's not viral.

"I'll be home soon"—I roll my eyes—"with the vintage year. Where's Pete?"

"He's around."

Guess he thought that was the end of the conversation, because he hangs up. I have half a mind to call him back, but there's no point in wasting the battery power. And with my father tucked away and *taking care of business*, that means Peter becomes my focus.

Around noon, I slip back down to the spa and peek inside from around the corner of the entrance. Melody sits in a large chair twisted around and cocked back toward a sink where she's getting her hair either washed or colored, hard to tell. But she and the lady doing the work seem to be chatting and laughing. Most important of all, she is still *here*. A layer of anxiety drops away.

When I return to my room, I order a bacon, egg, and avocado sandwich (excellent), a spring salad (fair), and a pot of coffee, and nibble while trying to get my brother on the phone. I turn on the television and flip through various news channels to check for any mention of the distributed massacre instituted by my family. So far: nothing. Halfway into my second cup of coffee, Peter finally answers his cell.

"'S'Pete."

"You've been tough to get ahold of."

"One sec," he says. I hear him chew, then chat with someone in the background. "Yeah, this tastes really good." Then to me, "Man, Ryan outdid himself today."

"Can you guys do me a friggin' favor and find some other clubhouse to hang out in? Ryan's trying to run an establishment."

"Excellent point you bring up, brother. Where's Sylvia's manager? She misses you."

"I'm done here, everything's wrapped up." *Melody's dead, covered in blankets in my trunk.*

"You're bringing it home for us?" *We gotta see it to believe it.*

"Absolutely. I'm bringing it home." He has no idea. "How's everything on your end?"

"It's beautiful, man. This puzzle came together better than we imagined. We're gonna frame it and hang it on the wall."

If what he's saying is true, that's a lot of dead people—of which most have probably not yet gone missing. On the one hand, it would be great to get out of here before the feds start looking for suspects; on the other, more blood will be shed if I leave prematurely.

Peter says, "We're surprised it's taken you so long. We thought you'd be home by now."

The perfect segue to my partial prep. "Yeah, I apologize for the delay, but I sorta met someone. On my journey."

"C'mon, Johnny, this isn't the right time to get your rocks off. Besides, Tommy was gonna try to meet up with you in Baltimore, maybe go visit Alfonse. He's in your area, taking care of a few minor things." Of course he is.

"Sorry, no good. She and I are, uh, spending a lot of time together, you know?" I take a huge mouthful of sandwich, gulp it down half chewed.

"Do what you gotta do and unload her. We got things to celebrate."

"Nah, it's more than that. We've really hit it off. I'm bringing her up."

Delay. "Seriously?"

"Totally. She's...from our area, in a way. She'll be riding shotgun."

"With that huge package in the back?" He laughs. "You're sick. I love it." Then louder, "Bring your freakin' skimbo, love to meet her."

This is precisely why I wanted to give the update to Peter. My father would have insisted I bring the body home immediately and leave the woman behind. I can't yet explain that they're one and the same. Peter, the crazy, risk-taking loose hinge in our family, is the perfect person to drop it in my father's lap on my behalf. A screwup, I will seem. Jokes will be made. A small price to pay.

TEN

At four-fifteen, I make one last journey to the spa to spy on Melody. As I look in, the place is packed, every seat taken—in both the spa itself and the waiting area. Melody, however, currently has the attention of three women at once, all bending over her like surgeons looming above a hemorrhaging patient.

I rush back upstairs and take a quick shower, attempt to make myself presentable, to appear relaxed. As I comb my wet hair in front of the mirror above the dresser, I hear Melody's door open and close, then the noise of her television. I sit down on the edge of my bed and imagine that if this were some parallel world, she and I would be getting ready at the same time in the same room, that we would share idle conversation, discuss the plans of the evening, comment on the way each other looked. Instead, we are two layers of drywall apart, strangers connected by the worst of circumstances. I recall her statement of how we might've never met had it not been for my father's murdering of the Rat. Forget how unlikely it would've been for an intelligent girl from suburban Jersey to run into a thug from the city, but had we done so, would we have shared anything more than a passing glance, an *excuse me* as one moved out of the way of the other? How selfish I feel for considering the upside to the disasters of her life.

Despite what's in store for her tomorrow—for us—I want to take her mind off of it tonight, give her at least one evening of normalcy before the challenges of true escape. And if everything goes as planned tomorrow, this will act as the first of a lifelong series of peace-filled evenings for her.

A few minutes later, her television goes off and her door closes again. As I'm about to walk out the door myself and meet her in the hall—no reason to meet in the lounge if we're both here and ready—my cell rings: Ryan. We resolve two minor issues, but the conversation distracts me enough that I run a few minutes behind; I force a wrap-up of the call on the way to the elevator, end it before I get in and take the car to the second floor.

I stroll around the opposite side of the hotel from the spa, follow a rounded corner that leads me right to the entrance of the bar. From the hallway, I can see the city buildings and lights through the tall windows. The bar is broken into sections, could easily handle multiple large gatherings at the same time. The entire room possesses a sleepy haze, feels like I'm viewing everything through a blue filter lens. I just walked into a giant aquarium.

I push my glasses up the bridge of my nose and study the patrons. At just a few minutes after five the place is mostly empty, but the happy hour crowd is growing, slipping by me as I scan the room for Melody. I finally spot her sitting casually with her legs crossed at a table near one of the windows. I first recognize her by her dress: the sundress I purchased in Norfolk. And though I can't identify the difference in the way she looks, I know a difference exists. I take steps in her direction, and once I'm a third of the way there I notice some man sitting across from her. She sees me coming—she's facing him and looking at me from the corner of her eyes. I can only see the back of the guy's head, but he's motioning with his hands, seems intent on making some point to her.

I slow down as I study him: young, professional type, wearing a suit, sitting in a manner that suggests he's planning to get up at any second. Not a fed. A toddler.

I bring my pace back up to full speed and approach the guy. I've had it with inconveniences. I can't take two extra minutes to finish a phone call without some clown stepping in and creating a hassle?

Melody looks at me. "A friend of yours?" I ask, putting my hand on his shoulder.

She does this thing where she sort of smiles and frowns at the same time, shakes her head *No.*

Then let's take out the trash. I grip his shoulder with all the strength of a firm handshake, yet the guy collapses like I'd smashed his knees with a bat. I grab him by the collar of his suit, lift him out of the chair like a bag of potatoes, and fling him off to the side. He stumbles across the room and knocks over two tables, crashes to the floor and doesn't move.

"Oh, c'mon," I say, "that was a little dramatic, wasn't it?" The room goes silent. All eyes fall on us. Two women at the bar gasp.

I turn to Melody. "You okay? Was he trying to hurt you?"

She glances at the onlookers, then back to me. "You're supposed to ask me that *before* you come to my aid." One of the bartenders rushes over to see if the guy's okay.

All of the changes in Melody's look strike me at once. They made no improvements, didn't need to. No wonder the spa was booked so far in advance; these folks were pros. They simply fine-tuned what was already in view, brought the camera lens into focus. Her hair, now a shade lighter, better matches the tone of her skin. They cut it differently around her ears and forehead, and though I would've never guessed that making it shorter was a good idea, they made the right decision. Her hair appears silky and full and I find it hard to refrain from reaching out and running my fingers through it. I can't place it now, but the colors of her makeup are different, look natural, as if she weren't wearing any at all. Her skin shines and glows. I run my hand along the back of her arm.

"Oh, Melody, you're stunning. Really, words are failing me. I can't tell you how proud I am to be with you, for people to think you and I are—"

"Thanks," she says. "Shouldn't he be getting up by now?"

I wave it off, don't bother looking at him. "He'll be fine." I reach in my pocket, grab a couple bills and toss them on the table. "We should get going."

She grabs my hand and pulls me out of the bar at a pretty good clip, keeps her head down and a hand to her face. She curses under her breath as she glances at the guy groaning on the floor. Everyone watches us leave.

Once we're in the hall and out of view, she smashes me in the chest with her fist and whispers so loudly she might as well have screamed. "This is not your twisted corner of New York. You can't walk into a bar, render someone unconscious, then drop a few twenties on the table like it's some MasterCard with an unlimited credit line for felonies!"

"Look, I can never know who's after you, okay? I'm trying to protect you and give you freedom at the same time." She turns and I follow her to the elevator. "Who was he?"

"Who knows."

"Was he bothering you?"

"Not really."

"Was he hitting on you?"

"Yes. But he was *only* hitting on me. Just like those kids were *only* spitting on your car. There's no reason to overreact, no cause for violence."

We get in the elevator. I stare at my shoes as we drop one floor and are deposited in the busy lobby. After we've rushed across Pratt Street and onto the harbor, we slow to a normal pace. Melody's right. All I did was put us in jeopardy, reveal us in the public eye, potentially destroy everything I've worked toward. What she doesn't understand is how useful the violence can be, how well it performs in a personal economy based on influence. In this case, though, her point rings true; I've been utilizing violence the same way I drop money: wastefully.

My phone vibrates. I pull it out and see I missed a call from Peter. Melody pauses to gaze at a guy who's riding a unicycle, juggling, telling a story. A small crowd comprised mostly of children sit and stand around him on the dirty brick sidewalk. I call Peter back while she's distracted, and as soon as the call connects she turns my way. I spin around, pretend I'm looking at the traffic heading northward on Light Street. Peter and I converse for less than a minute, but the point of the call was to let me know that whatever Tommy Fingers was trying to get or locate in my area was achieved—he's not exactly sure what it is but Eddie Gravina is anxious for my father to have it—and he's now on his way back to New York; Tommy was the last to leave the mid-Atlantic. Melody and I are finally alone.

I turn back toward Melody, can tell she's forcing her attention on the unicycling juggler to give me privacy. To get her attention I sort of brush her hand, slip two fingers into her palm, and she turns around and smiles. She tightens her grip around my fingers but I try to let go. I sense she wanted me to hold her hand, so I regrip, but then she lets her hand loosen. We go through this embarrassing sequence a few times before I simply tighten my hand around hers and jokingly pull her over as if I'm trying to drag her.

While we walk around the harbor I point out various things—Federal Hill, the National Aquarium, the converted Power Plant, the iconic Domino Sugar sign—mostly so she'll look in those directions, for every time she does, I use the opportunity to stare at her, to be able to gawk without making her feel embarrassed.

You'd think after all these years of watching her exist I'd have no problem putting aside viewing her this way—but it's a habit developed and mastered over the course of my life, acts like a drug I cannot surrender.

A breeze rushes over us and causes her sundress to fly up, and though she may have wanted to smooth it back, she shivers and crosses her arms. She looks down at her dress and her sandals and says, "These are lovely clothes, Jonathan. Thank you."

I hold her hand, look into her eyes for a while before I answer. "They're only lovely because they're on you. On the mannequins...just looked like clothes." She swallows and smiles. "I could see you in them, though. Like they were cut and sewn for you."

Melody turns and faces me square. Without thinking I take her other hand in mine as well. We look like we're getting ready to exchange vows. She gazes into my eyes with anticipation, like I have something I'm about to offer—but the offer was already made: Through her freedom I am trying to give her the greatest gift I could conjure, but it's not enough, could never be enough.

As I hold her hands in mine I feel the gentle tug of emotion, temptation disguised in a robe of passion. It may not be what she wants—absolutely not what she needs—but I want to tell her what is building in my heart. I have now drifted beyond trying to correct, fall aimlessly toward trying to inspire. I have no justifiable reason to go there, no right to take her there. Yet here I begin making a terrible mistake, of letting myself drop a guard that I erected with great purpose, spent a lifetime constructing. Here I am about to perform that greatest example of losing self-control, of instantiating selfishness in Bovaro history. I open my frigging mouth:

"You're flawless, Melody. Beautiful, smart, funny. Everything about you is right in every way: your height, your hands, your..." I keep going, talk about her legs and body and lips, snapping off generic compliments like a grocery list. I'm sure I lost her at *flawless.* She smiles like I'm one of her students, a kid with a crush who finally got the courage to confess his desire.

I slouch back, think for a moment, stop trying to drive the nail with a sledgehammer. I finally speak what's on my mind. I look down, stare at her painted toenails. "You know, for the first time in my life I understand every man who's died for a woman." I return my eyes to hers, whisper so only she can hear. "I would die for you, Melody."

She freezes for a few seconds, then bites her lip a little as her chin wrinkles. She drops her head, gently wipes her eyes and sniffles, does that thing where she fake-tucks her hair behind her ears, which dissolves any last thread of hope, of strength I might've had. She moves her head from side to side as if she's trying to sort something out, then looks up at me with wet eyes and wet lips. She circles her hands around my palms and tightens them, stands on her toes, closes her eyes, tilts her head, parts her lips.

Now, the biggest rationalization of all time: I can't abandon her here, with the expectation of a kiss; were I not to deliver, how embarrassed would she be? Forget the fact that I don't recall ever wanting something this badly in my entire life.

I lean down, take in the scent of the lotions on her skin carried upward by a wave of heat rising from her body, feel the warmth of her breath just before our lips meet. Her kiss is as gentle as a drifting feather, as sweet as a candy apple. The rhythm of the movement of our lips, how they fit together directly opposes the way our hands fumbled just moments earlier, as though we've been married for twenty years and have practiced our way to this intimate precision. Her tongue lightly brushes against mine and I pull my hands from hers and move them to her face. I can't believe I've never noticed how pleasurable this experience can be. So long ago my older brothers explained that a kiss served no further purpose than generating the key that opens the door to sexual activity. As adolescents, Peter and Gino would define this as crossing first base. I've crossed first base before, and let me tell you: This was blasting one out of the park at the bottom of the ninth to win the series, rounding the bases in slow motion, being carried across the field on the shoulders of teammates.

I couldn't tell you how long we kissed and embraced, though long enough that a few people stared or smirked at our public display of affection. One passing lady turned to her mate and said, "How come you don't kiss me like that?"

We turn and start walking again, say not a word about what we just did, but clearly some significance follows; the rest of our walk, we hold hands. We have become one of the couples I spied through that narrow gap between the buildings during my panicked search for Melody and from high atop these large hotels in which I have stayed. We have become a pair milling about the casual and carefree. Except we are not carefree.

Ghosts among the real, my friend. Ghosts among the real.

We don't speak much through our walking tour of Baltimore's Inner Harbor. We've both got various scenarios on our minds, though I imagine hers are more significant. She holds on to my arm with both hands curled around it, and though it's a sign of affection, it occasionally feels like she is holding on for dear life.

She stares up at some historic battleship temporarily harbored for tourists, and at this second I finally determine exactly what the folks in the spa managed to achieve in Melody: She looks the closest to her real self that I've seen since she was a little girl. The tone of her skin, the way her hair is pulled away from the sides of her face, how her cheekbones and jawline are exposed. I see images of her youth within her, like a film having random frames of her earlier self spliced in. I visualize her as still having long hair, that it's merely tied up in a ponytail. The little girl stands at my feet, staring up at a large ship instead of the large buildings that framed Vincent's.

We begin to talk more of eating, try to select a place to dine among the few hundred possibilities within walking distance. But during this discussion, Melody drifts back to asking me questions about my family, and the questions are not about personalities as much as they are about criminal activity. Had she and I not just shared a defined level of intimacy, I might've started thinking she was wired.

Finally, she slows her pace and asks quietly, "Have you ever had to murder someone?" She forms the question giving me an out: Have you ever *had* to murder someone, as opposed to murdering for no reason whatsoever.

"You asked me that before."

"I know," she says. "But I need the absolute truth, Jonathan."

I'm not really sure why. As her guardian, you'd think she'd want to be with a guy who's unafraid to fully utilize a firearm.

"I've never murdered anyone, okay? Besides, no family is in the murdering business, per se. It's only used under the worst of circumstances. Like firing an employee."

"Permanently." We stop and she turns to me. "Have you ever *wanted* to murder someone?"

I chuckle and drop her hand, "Sure. Haven't you? What do you really want to know, Melody? Have I ever beaten someone within an inch of his life? You bet. I've done what needed to be done, to protect myself, to protect my family. That's what you do for the ones you love. It's what I would do for you."

Melody flinches, refocuses on my face, hesitates before speaking. I retrace my last few sentences, unsure of what caused a reaction in her. Then it occurs to me that her brain—her capacity for mathematical processing—remapped my statements, broke them apart into smaller pieces and reassembled them in a form that was easier to solve and understand, and she deciphered this: "I'll do whatever I need to protect the ones I love, and because I love you, I'll protect you the same way."

As I open my mouth to backtrack the meaning behind my words, she says, "Tell me the story."

"Of?"

"Tell me the worst thing you can tell me."

I put my hands in my pockets, turn my head, and recede as if being blown by a strong wind. "Why?"

She doesn't quickly answer, wavers like she might change her mind about going down whatever path this is. Finally, "Because I have to sort out whatever these feelings are that I have. I'm only seeing one side of you." She bridges the gap I created seconds earlier. "I need to know what you're capable of."

I don't answer her, but I fully understand what she needs. Though she made it clear what she wants me to tell her, here are the words she left unspoken: "I am trusting you to free me, that somehow you will pull this off—but when this is over, I need to be able to discard you. Help me understand how."

Herein lies the direct result of caving to temptation, the wreckage caused by weakness and a lack of restraint and discipline. My heart shouldn't be breaking, should've never been vulnerable in the first place. I'm thankful she spotted the problem, protected us from my worsening myopia. At some point I started convincing her that freedom included being free of me—and stopped convincing myself.

I'm willing to give her what she needs—what I need—to keep this on course, to make this mission a success.

"There was, uh...one guy in particular," I say. "Turned out very badly."

She closes her eyes and hugs me, whispers, "Thank you."

I return the hug, bury my face in the crevice of her neck, and fill my lungs like it's my last embrace before heading off to war.

ELEVEN

Though we are hungry, selecting a particular style of cuisine does not remain on our minds. We pick the nearest place to where we're standing, a seafood restaurant that's been located on the harbor for as long as I can remember, still standing from our days of coming downtown as kids. We walk in and the restaurant is large but well partitioned into cozy sections, its semicircular shape affording nice views of the harbor and city skyline for the majority of tables. The hostess welcomes us; I reach in my pocket and start peeling off bills. Melody slaps my hand and rolls her eyes.

"What," I say, "it's impolite to tip a hostess?"

The girl grabs two menus and walks all the way to the back of the restaurant, pretty much as far as you could possibly get from the windows, shows us a table right next to the door of the kitchen, adjacent to a booth with two screaming kids chaperoned by indifferent parents.

Melody seats herself. I stare at her like she's lost her mind. I pull out my wad again.

"Sit," she says.

"See, this is what happens."

"Sit."

The hostess asks Melody, "Is there a problem, ma'am?"

Melody shakes her head and the hostess disappears. She looks up at me and says, "It's just a table."

"You deserve better. You deserve the best—"

"Sit."

I regret not taking the longer walk to Little Italy, where I could be around my brethren, my culture. Pick any restaurant there and you have a fifty-fifty shot that the hostess is an elderly woman—likely the wife of the guy whose name is plastered on the sign—whose life experience brings an understanding of the needs of a young couple who appear to be dating, regardless of the truth of our circumstances. And there we would get priority *everything.* If Italians understand any of the essentials of life, they understand food and love.

"Just a table," I grumble as I take my seat. A hunk of carrot goes flying into the walkway from the booth behind us.

We're greeted by a server named Herman. Were this guy applying for a position at Sylvia, I'd give him the job just so I could fire him on the spot. His unkempt, ratlike look is one thing, but the bigger issue is his attention is elsewhere, like down the front of Melody's dress—my companion is modestly endowed and not wearing a bra, which means Herman has to struggle for a glimpse; his extensive effort ticks me off. He hands me a menu without making eye contact, nearly jabs me in the chin with it, asks if he can get us something to drink, but the way he's leaning forward and glaring at Melody's chest I think the question might have been meant for her breasts.

"First the table and now this?"

"Jonathan, it's just a—Oh, for Pete's sake." She turns to our server. "A bottle of Chianti. Go." He disappears.

"This is all wrong," I say. "I just want the best for you, Melody. The best food, the best table, the best server."

She leans forward, reaches over and touches my hand. "You're here, so it *is* the best table, with the best view. You see? I'm not expecting or asking for anything more."

In the kitchen, a tray of dishes hits the floor and the crash echoes out to our table, as well as the loud argument that follows.

I rub my temples. "*Porco mondo.*"

Herman returns with a bottle of Ruffino that's so warm I'm convinced it was stored above the fryer. I grab the corkscrew out of his hands. "Leave us." I open the bottle and quickly pour two glasses, hand her one, and say, "To the best table in the house."

She laughs and we clink our glasses together so hard we spill wine onto the table. "*Porco mondo!*" she says. "Whatever that means."

In the first gap in conversation, I offer to tell Melody the story she requested, along with the opportunity to renege; it's not exactly the kind of thing you'd want to hear before eating.

When we were out on the harbor, I told her there was one guy who turned out pretty bad. Truth: There were a lot of guys, really. I took my own here and there, but more often served as a deliveryman. As I sit before her now at this moment of confession, I am so thankful I never came to taking another life, so relieved that my résumé is missing that one bulleted line of experience. If she only knew how my wrongdoings paled in comparison to the rest of our crew, how far down on the scale of maleficence my actions were.

As I hesitate to confess my worst-case experience, the story I fear may have her vomiting or running for the nearest uniformed officer, I know what she needs is to hear what a monster I am, how I have displayed my own propensity for savagery and a tendency toward evil.

She needs me to be discardable.

I pour more wine and take an enormous drink before I spread my history over our tablecloth like a bag of broken glass.

Gregory Morrison. I like to remember Greg as a complete nutcase, instead of the miswired or underloved man he likely was. Greg first made himself known to me and my family when he was eight or nine—about seven years younger than I was at the time. He used to hang around some of the places we provided protection for, otherwise he would've simply blended into the gray urban background. Far as we knew, his family had nothing to do with ours. His dad was a dentist in midtown, never heard that he'd gotten into any trouble.

Greg, though, upon hitting puberty became loud and obnoxious, from a safe distance referred to most of us as dagos, wops, and guineas. We'd toss him a few Italian insults and laugh it off. But during the summer he would've graduated from high school, his obnoxiousness transformed into criminal activity. He became the leader of a pathetic gang in our residential neighborhood whose big claim to fame was breaking into pharmacies and stealing cigarettes and prescription drugs.

We paid him no mind until the day Peter and I caught him and his loser friends trying to break into one of our establishments. Peter confronted the group, but there were six of them and only two of us. So Morrison rolls the dice, pretends he and his gang are going to rough us up. Peter waved him off, told them all to get lost. But this only fueled Morrison, seemed to insult him that we didn't consider him on the same playing field—so he pushed it, and regrettably pushed Peter's easily pressable button. It didn't help that Pete was bored and looking for some action.

And like all good brawls, it was not six-on-two; it was

one-on-one. Peter beat Morrison something fierce, really humiliated the guy in front of his buddies. I'd seen Peter do this many times growing up, mostly for fun—but something about this time disturbed me. The entire time Peter is pounding away, Greg keeps telling Pete he's going to get him, that this isn't over, that he's going to regret every blow. Were it me, I would have stopped, set Greg free, and ended the event, but Peter thought it was downright hilarious, only made him pound longer, kept going until he grew bored of that, too.

Even as we all walked away, Greg was still rambling on through slurred speech. "You're gonna get it, Bovaros. You're gonna get payback," he muttered between winces and coughs. "Gonna make your whole family pay."

Nearly a week later, I walked into my folks' place and saw my mother rocking in my father's arms, weeping like a child. My first thought was someone on my mom's side had passed away—except my father was staring into the distance with tear tracks marking his cheeks. My next thought was that one of my brothers had died. I remember the lightheadedness and vertigo that came upon me, how I quickly moved to lean on the doorjamb.

My father had a look on his face he's only had a few times. In his look I read that someone was going to have to die.

I was the first to arrive at their house that evening, the first to receive the news: Gregory Morrison had raped my mother in the parking lot of a small Italian grocery store a few miles from our home, attacked her while she was loading bags of food into the trunk of her car. The entire time, all while insulting and slapping my mother, calling her a whore, Morrison kept repeating, "Tell your boys payback is hell."

My father helped my mother up to their room, got her to rest on their bed. I waited outside their door. A few minutes later he quietly came out and took me aside.

"I gotta stay with your mother," he said. "You're the only one who knows about this right now, Johnny." To my recollection, my father only cried five times in his adult life: at each of his sons' first Communions, and as he spoke those words. While he fought the tears—difficult to see on a man who's lost no battle—he grabbed the back of my neck, gave it a tight squeeze. "You go make things right, *capice*?"

I nodded, carefully walked down the creaky wooden stairs of their home, wanted to vomit at the thought of what had happened to my mother. She was—just like Melody—a casualty of being anywhere near our criminal family, another woman virtually destroyed, stripped of dignity and tossed aside, all because the leaders around her were violent, self-serving men.

And in that moment, the violence emerged in me. A lifetime of experience instructed me the one way to correct the situation. With each step toward my car, the fright and anxiety of what had happened to my mother converted over to unabated hatred for Gregory Morrison, the formation of undiscovered wrath.

I sped to the rathole apartment Morrison shared with two of his buddies on the Lower East Side, kicked in his door so hard the bottom hinge snapped off. Five feet away was Morrison, sitting in a torn, stained recliner, directly facing the door like it was a widescreen television, waiting. He lifted a small handgun, aimed it directly at my chest, said, "Payback," and pulled the trigger.

All he got for his planning and patience was an empty click. Nothing. Morrison cursed at top volume, looked down sideways at the gun, reached for the clip—of course, by this time I was in midair. I landed on him square and we both went flying off the back of the chair and onto the fringe of his kitchen, the gun flying across the room toward the window.

Morrison grabbed his rib cage and moaned. I stood as he remained in the fetal position, picked up a wooden chair from under his kitchen table, and smashed it over him again and again until the thing had broken into kindling.

Morrison was not the only one with patience. I sat in his roach-filled pit for over two hours waiting for him to return to consciousness. I would not allow him to sleep through his misery. He was going to be wide awake, he was going to live through the excruciating pain and suffering just like my mother had to be awake and aware through hers. He was going to remember, for every one of his remaining days, the mistake he made.

I cannot retell how I implemented vengeance upon Morrison; for all my claims of strength, I can't confess the truest darkness of my life. Though the images are forever clear in my mind, the taste is too bitter to pass over my tongue. I will say that Greg will never chew things easily again, will forever be taunted and teased by neighborhood kids as *Smashmouth.* He will never be able to provide the proper chemistry to produce children. He will have difficulty turning his head to the left and struggle with bouts of vertigo that will worsen with age.

He will, however, get to live. And this did not sit well with my family.

By the time I returned to my parents' house, all of my brothers were there. After an update on the status of my mother, I gave them all the details of my experience with Morrison, every strike and blow, every word he uttered as he begged for help, right down to how I left him weeping like a little boy—*alive.*

Pop and Peter flew from their chairs almost simultaneously.

"I want him dead!" my father yelled. Peter said nothing, just reached in his pocket for his keys.

I stopped him before he could leave the room, told everyone to sit down, explained my motivations—how I let Morrison live for a reason, that if one of us or one of our crew went and knocked him off, he'd be forgotten in a month and someone would fill his place.

But by leaving a living, breathing example that people would see, day after day, a constant reminder of what happens to those who harm us, the event would never be forgotten. People would learn. After all, was this not the point of most of God's Old Testament examples? What would be the point of wiping out Jericho, or of forty years in the desert, if there was not something to learn from it? Peter was the first to come around on the idea, liked the notion of seeing him on the street now and again, being able to give him the evil eye on a regular basis. Once my father calmed and saw the light of the idea, Gino and Jimmy fell in line.

And then the turn of events in my life: At this moment, this very conversation where I managed to sway the angry, rage-filled determination of my siblings and father, I realized I might be able to one day sway them toward setting Melody free, that if I posed a compelling enough argument, they might be winnable. Even though I was much younger then, I knew I could make it happen—if only I could conjure a way to make everything come together, for the timing and reason to be right.

And now here I am, sitting in a seafood restaurant with Melody, mere hours from putting a plan into play whose origin came five years earlier at the notion that keeping an enemy alive was more powerful than killing him. All I need to do is convince the same group of people of the same thing. One last time.

I pray that one day Melody will be completely free, content and living the life she was meant to live, and that I have *this* story to tell, too. That I can share the details of something beautiful, filled with hope and happiness.

As for Morrison, he now occupies most of his days sitting at the bar of a dive in Brooklyn, cashing in his welfare checks and converting them to lottery tickets, drinking beer through a straw.

But not all things were corrected by my actions. Fourteen months ago, after spending years mired in fear and depression, my mother died of ovarian cancer, the recipient of a painful existence better suited for every other individual in my family.

Melody plays with the rim of her wineglass as she processes this dump of information, seems to be formulating conclusions based on details I didn't realize I'd offered.

She finally looks up and says, "You're a strange hero, Jonathan."

Herman starts heading toward our table. I flick my wrist at him like I'm swatting a fly and he changes direction in midstep.

"What do you mean?" I ask.

"You may not realize it, but you kept Greg alive when anyone else in your family would've killed him. He'd be thankful if he knew." I doubt that—although things do seem different when I view them through Melody's eyes. She thinks for a moment and adds, "So, if I understand correctly, your worst violent act was triggered not because you were evil, but because you were human." She studies me, keeps her eyes on me as she brings her glass to her lips and takes a slow drink of wine. "Man, if you can convince your family of something like that..."

There could be only one way for her to finish that sentence: ... *then I stand a chance.*

I can't tell if her statements are real or simply rationalizations for not letting me go, but either way I can read in her expression that I've let her down—not in terms of the violence, but in helping her find an easy way to discard me tomorrow. It was not the intention of my story, but clearly her look says this: *Thanks for nothing.*

TWELVE

Just after Herman brings the bill, I start fishing for my cash. I'd love to stiff the weasel, but I can never bring myself to short a server, no matter how incapable or clumsy—was brought up that way, but really gained an appreciation after seeing some of the hardest-working folks in my restaurant get shafted.

As I count my money—I'm finally running low, will have to tap into the wad in my car on our journey home—Melody is trying to explain to me what a Fibonacci number is. I appreciate her effort to highlight a fine mathematician of Italian ancestry (weren't they all?), but I have absolutely no clue what she's talking about. Something about how every two preceding numbers become the sum of the following number.

"I see," I lie.

Only a few days around me and she can read my expressions with accuracy, offers help. "Like, 3, 4, 7, 11, 18, 29."

"Lotto numbers."

"Judging by the look on your face, I'm guessing you really weren't that interested."

I lean on the table and smile at her. "You couldn't be more off. You know how cool it is that you understand stuff I could never comprehend? I can barely balance Sylvia's books. I'm interested in everything about you, in all the pieces I could never grasp by watching you from a distance." I lean in so I can speak softer. "You're like a beautiful painting where the colors become richer and deeper and more captivating with every step closer to the canvas."

She smiles, bites her bottom lip. "That is so not something I would expect to come from the mouth of a Bovaro." She looks down and away. "But it's something I will never forget."

I stand, walk around to pull out her chair for her; she smoothes her dress before standing. I plop the wad of cash on the table and we exit the restaurant, walk out into the cool night air. Her sundress may have been appropriate for the sunlit harbor, but within a few steps she rubs her shoulders with her hands, shivers. In an attempt to offer warmth, I sidle up and put my arms around her from behind.

"We should probably head back to the hotel," I say.

She nudges me as we walk. "You're not going to take advantage of me, are you?"

"Actually," I say, wondering if my body-warming is sending the wrong message, "we should probably get some rest. We have a big day tomorrow."

She turns around, tries to read my eyes. "You serious?"

I half shrug. "Tomorrow will be a very serious day."

We walk steadily northward up the harbor, our hotel waiting for us around the bend like Oz at the end of the yellow brick road.

After a long silence, Melody says, "Are you sure you want to do this thing tomorrow? Sure you've thought it all the way through?"

I'm finally at the point of assuredness—because no choices remain. The circumstances—everything and everyone coming together at the same time, along with my own twenty-year need to rescue her—could not be more perfectly designed. The only risk is Melody's safety; I'll need to be awfully convincing. But the risk of her not coming with me, running about in the fields only to be hunted and mounted on the wall by our crew, is exponentially worse. I consider offering a detailed explanation, but at this point I could only lessen her confidence.

"I have." She shivers again and I put my hand on her lower back, pull her my way. "C'mon, let's take a shortcut so we can get you back safe and warm."

We start walking faster, reach the edge of Harborplace within minutes, jaywalk across the east- and westbound lanes of Pratt Street. I suggest to Melody that we cut through a narrow alley between two skyscrapers to shorten the return walk. We slip down the alley and out of sight, start walk-jogging to the other end, when we hear another set of footsteps behind us. This, in any city, would not be an unusual occurrence. But as the footsteps behind us turn into a pace faster than ours—the attempt to catch up—anxiety rises.

I keep my eyes locked on the light at the end of the alley, but I can tell Melody is looking up at me, waiting for me to take control. "Just ignore it," I say.

Could be nobody. On the other hand, could be *anybody*. Maybe Tommy Fingers hung out in Baltimore after all. Maybe her marshal found us and wants to have a word. Maybe a cop wants to nail us for jaywalking across Pratt Street.

"Oh, man," Melody whispers.

I consider turning around at this point, weigh the usefulness of an early assessment of what may be coming, but I will not take my hand from Melody, will not allow her to be compromised in any way by turning my attention elsewhere, even for a handful of seconds.

As the footsteps get louder and closer, we have slowed and steadied our pace—though you would never guess because Melody's now breathing so hard she's on the verge of hyperventilating, the fear on her face as evident as the night I stormed her motel room in Cape Charles.

I run my hand up her back and around her shoulder and she whimpers, looks on the verge of tears. "No one is going to hurt you—not now, not ever. I'd never let it happen."

The person slides up behind us, and while Melody might be panicking, I'm bathed in relief: I can tell by the person's smell, a blend of stale alcohol and poor hygiene, that it's no one from our crew, no one from the Marshals Service.

I feel a giant hand on my neck, brings me to a fast stop. The other hand grabs Melody by the shoulder and shoves her into a set of garbage cans. She goes tumbling over, bashes her arm on the corner of a Dumpster, smacks her shoulder on the pavement. As she tries to right herself, I can see blood on her shoulder and across her wrists from where she tried to brace herself. One of her sandals has come off, and as she twists her body, her dress rides up behind her with her legs apart and bent, leaving her facing us in an immodest position. She tries to shift her body and pull her dress down but it must hurt too much.

A small blade is pressed against my neckline, so thin and incapable I can feel the thing bend as it's pressed into my flesh. I consider smacking it out of the person's hand, but I want to gain an understanding of intention, to see where this is going.

Then I become the recipient of a most atrocious blast of breath, an exhale of sewage that carries these words: "Yeah, that's it, stay just like that. When I'm done taking your man's money, he's gonna watch me take you on the ride of your life."

I see. So it's going *there*.

All I can say is this: toddler. So many crumbsnatchers in this city, a giant urban daycare center.

I feel blood running down my neck—nothing to be concerned about yet—but based on his overcompensation, this guy's judgment is either drug-fueled or he's off his rocker. In any case, bad timing for the guy. He continues to snap off the disgusting perversions he's got planned for Melody. How terribly unfortunate for him that I just had to recall and retell the experience of Morrison assaulting my mother. With every word spoken from this scumbag, I picture Morrison's drooling mouth uttering the same abusive and repulsive things. The images of a loved one being violated in that way are indelible, can never be cut out like a cancer or tumor. I will carry it the rest of my life. And now this: interplay with some bottom-dweller who wants more money for crack or smack or meth and happened upon a couple where he could not only steal cash, but forced sex as well.

Melody's lips quiver. She has tears forming in the corners of her eyes and her breath is clipped. And now I wonder what it is she's thinking, what she wants me to do. Does she want me to stand down? Offer up the cash and plead to leave her alone? Give up the tendency toward destruction the way I gave up the cigarettes? The profanity?

Sasquatch starts grabbing my butt looking for a wallet. "Gimme your wallet! Now!"

I glance at Melody, slowly turn my hands out and up, mime a request for permission.

Melody looks at me with confusion. "What," she whispers.

I mouth these words to her: "Just a mugging?"

As Sasquatch feels my entire body up and down, Melody stares at me, reads my story over and over, seems to finally comprehend the gist. And something in her changes. She wipes the tears away, the breathing slows and calms, her lips cease to tremble and so easily produce her answer: "Do it."

They never want you to give up the violence.

If Sasquatch knew these would be his final words this evening, I'm guessing he would not have said, "Shut up, you ugly slut." For these are the last spoken before I plunge my fist into the toddler's throat. As he falls to the ground, drops the knife to his side, and lunges both hands to his neck, I kick him over with my foot, step down on his hand-covered gullet, and put most of my two hundred pounds on it until he coughs up a little blood.

I turn to Melody and ask, "You okay?"

She rests sideways against a Dumpster, closes her eyes and nods.

Sasquatch's gag-screaming has become quite distracting; I take an old sneaker from behind a trash can and shove the toe in his mouth.

I turn to Melody and say, "I'm gonna make sure he doesn't follow us—or consider running. You might want to look the other way."

She says, "Okay," but keeps watching, gets to see firsthand my sinister capabilities. This is not a softened story from my past; this is here and now, an image she'll recall for a lifetime.

Then it hits me: The stories didn't cut it. My tale of dismantling Morrison was not good enough. She needs to see it happen. She needs to know she could never be with someone filled with such imbalanced rage. She *wants* to watch. Unfortunately for Sasquatch, I must deliver.

I grab a broken two-by-four from a pile of loose trash, look down each end of the alley to be sure his muted screams won't draw attention, and swing the board down on his lower leg, over and over, until I've removed all functionality from his ankle. While the toddler squirms, I find his knife and kick it into the sewer drain.

I look over at Melody and she's paying attention; I could never know what she's thinking, but she's taking it all in. Though it seems so wrong, I have to continue, to disappoint her with who I am, to provide her the mechanism to break whatever chain has her tethered to me. She does not appear bothered my actions, so I step it up another level.

I face no fight in destroying Sasquatch, no regret in wrecking him for what he would have done to Melody were I passive. He is another Morrison. Another loser destined to sip his food through a straw.

I hold the two-by-four in my hand, walk up to Sasquatch's fright-filled face, listen to his muffled coughs. I walk behind him, kick the shoe out of his mouth—the begging instantly begins, a random repetition of the words *please* and *no* that resemble Morse code—put my foot on his forehead and line up the two-by-four against his chin like a driver against a golf ball. "Now we'll give our friend something to remember this moment," I say.

I pull the broken stud back slowly, wind up to swing, when Melody cheers out, "Yeah, give that bastard a souvenir!"

She catches me so off guard, uses a term so unknown to people outside of the tight team of men that comprise our crew, I feel like someone just swung something against my own head. I stumble forward, my foot slipping off of Sasquatch's skull as Melody rushes to cover her mouth—but the way she's propped up makes it hard for her to move, and she fumbles around like she didn't mean to say what she did, tries to pretend the words were never spoken.

I attempt to process the meaning behind what she said, but the confusion has thrown me off course, made me less capable of providing physical destruction. I toss the board back in the trash and watch Sasquatch whimper and grab his throat with one hand and his leg with the other. I hate him. I hate what he would have done to Melody. I hate what he'd probably done to women before, how he'll continue to victimize society with his alley muggings and petty crimes. He needs to pay.

I reach down, grab him by the shirt, and say, "Look at me, look at me. Remember this face." Then I pull him up, lift his meaty chest right off the ground, and whisper in his ear so Melody can't hear. "You stay right here. I'm taking the girl to safety, then I'm gonna come back, and I'm gonna kill you. There's no way out for you, no escape, do you understand? You're gonna stay right here and prepare to die. If you're not here when I come back, I'm gonna find you, and I promise I'm gonna take what would have lasted five minutes and drag it out for an entire weekend. So, I want you to promise me you're gonna wait right here."

He chokes, says, "I promise." Blood trickles out of the corner of his mouth. I dump him back on the ground and he curls into a ball like a frightened armadillo.

"Say it again."

"I promise."

"Remember this face."

"I promise."

I stand above him, let my shadow cast a layer of darkness over him, watch the guy struggle to make sense of what just happened.

I, of course, have no intention of returning. Sasquatch won't stay, either—but he'll consider what I said for maybe an hour. Though those sixty minutes are nothing compared to the lifetime of fear women face after being traumatized by these scumbags, at least it was sixty minutes. My family is in the business of keeping people enslaved to their addictions and under the fearful thumb of our power, and while these people return again and again to repeat the same mistakes, the recidivism rate for those who wrong us is near zero.

I brush off my clothes and return to Melody, help her to her feet. As she stands and stabilizes, I realize she was banged up more than I originally thought, see the bloodstains emerging on her dress. Both straps of her sundress are broken and she has to hold the dress to her chest to keep it from falling. She finds her lost sandal, but the heel has broken off and disappeared. She tries to dignify herself, wipes off her dress and adjusts it over her body with one hand.

"You need me to get you to a hospital?"

She forces a smile. "I've been in worse condition." She tries to take a step forward but her ankle buckles as if hers had been the one I disabled.

"C'mere," I say, as I bend down and pick her up. She throws her arms around my neck and gets a look on her face like she's afraid she's going to fall. I start walking us down the alley and her expression changes. I can sense her staring at me as we reach the well-lit end of the passageway.

We turn back onto the main drag. Cars whiz by as I carry her back to the hotel. We have to endure catcalls and other lewd statements from the occupants of passing vehicles. She doesn't seem to care.

As we enter the hotel lobby, the commentary ends and the staring begins. Melody waves her hand at the desk staff and visitors checking in, offers up, "We just got married." Everyone starts clapping and whistling like they're relieved no weird or criminal activity is occurring in this prestigious facility.

An older couple hold the elevator, stare at us the entire ride to our floor. The man comments to Melody, "You know you're bleeding?"

"He dropped me on the sidewalk," she says, then whispers, "a nice guy, but a bit of a weakling."

As we exit the elevator, I let her body slip a little, then fling her over my shoulder. My hand naturally slides to the crevice between her upper thigh and bottom. I hold her legs tightly, press her against my shoulder to keep her secure and steady.

When I get her to my room—balancing her and opening the door is not easy—I walk in, flip on the light, then toss her on the bed like a suitcase. She bounces across the mattress and giggles loudly, goes flying backward—I forgot about the straps of her sundress, for if I'd remembered I would've never chucked her like that; her dress rises to the top of her thighs and drops down from her chest, exposes both of her breasts.

She covers herself. Except, not really.

Then, my thoughts, like rounds from a machine gun: *No, no, no, no, no, no, no, no.*

Her smile fades. Actually, it dissolves—into a look that implies she wants to continue. She covers her chest with only her hand, props up a leg that makes her dress drift way up, her narrow panties exposing her midriff. I can testify that she is consistent—she's making those look good, too. If I ever return to Norfolk, I'll have to find Melissa and compliment her on her saleswomanship.

"Come here," she says.

I take a deep breath and narrow my field of vision to the floor—no one could ever joke of my being a weakling after performing *this* act. "We should get you cleaned up."

"I'm too dirty for you?" Though I'm not looking, I can tell she's dragging a fingertip across her belly button.

"That's not what I meant." Eyes to the floor, eyes to the floor.

"Okay." She slowly rolls over and gets to her feet. Her ankle still seems to be bothering her, but she's able to walk on it now, takes uneven steps in my direction. I watch her feet as they approach, can't help but notice the contrast of red nail polish against her cream-colored skin. She stops right in front of me. "I'll draw a bath," she says, then slowly raises her arms, and the now strapless dress falls to the ground like a bath towel.

My eyes, still cast downward, study the bloody dress. If I look at her body, I will shed any sense of control I have—I'm only flesh and blood, after all, and mostly flesh, at that. I'll want to feel her against me with such desire that I'll undoubtedly make the worst possible decision, cross a line that will cloud and distort the meaning of tomorrow's big event. I've spent so much time trying to free her of me and my family; the last thing she needs is to want to be around me, with me.

I close my eyes and lift my head, wait until they're aimed at her face. When I open them, I see the hope in her expression, along with the longing for intimacy and the request for not being rejected—which I attempt to assuage.

I step backward to the closet and grab a blanket. "Melody, you do not need to seduce me." As I enwrap her, I add, "I'm yours already." *Have been since you were six years old.* "Let *me* draw your bath."

Melody sits down on the edge of the bed and I walk to the bathroom and pull back the curtain of my tub, run the water and take the first gush of cold water and splash it across my face. I wait as the tub fills with hot water, squirt enormous blasts of body wash under the stream to create a thick coverlet of bubbles, sit on the floor as billows of steam rise to the ceiling. Once the tub is near the top, I leave the bathroom, find Melody sprawled back on the bed, staring at the ceiling, running her hand up and down the seam of the bedspread.

"Your bath is ready."

She props herself on her side. "Will you stay with me?"

"I was gonna tend to your wounds. Just need to get my Dopp kit from my overnight bag. You can go ahead. I'll be right in."

I open my suitcase and grab the leather pouch I've carried with me on all my journeys, the pouch with contents used to stop the bleeding from so many unexpected events. I hear the water move in small waves, can visualize the immersion of her naked body. I wait an extra minute before returning to my bathroom where she waits.

I tap the door and she says, "You can come in."

I peek around the corner. On the floor, I notice the piled-up blanket with her panties curled on top as though she'd just melted like Frosty the Snowman or the Wicked Witch of the West. Steam coats me as I take a half step in.

Her body is buried under the water, protected by a shield of bubbles. I open my bag and start retrieving items like a medic on a battlefield. I analyze her wounds, start looking at her arms and hands and shoulders. I soak a cotton ball in antiseptic and gently dab it on an open cut on her forearm. Melody closes her eyes, grimaces. After a few iterations, she gets used to the pain, begins watching me instead of the wounds.

"You're good at this," she says softly.

"Well, I've got a lot of experience fixing wounds—my own, at least."

She watches again, the only sound between us the noise of the bathroom fan. Then a few moments later, she says, "Show me one."

"One what?"

"Wound."

That's like trying to select the most significant battle of the Civil War. But if I had to pick, it's probably the one she's been able to see all along, the one Ettore imprinted on my temple, the one that speaks every time I look in a mirror, reminds me why I'm doing all of this. But Melody needs to see more, to see what's behind my curtain of clothes. I'm not sure where to begin, but I'm hot from the steam, so I don't hesitate to pull my sweater up and expose my stomach, display a six-inch scar that healed into more of a valley than an indentation, the result of a wayward knife when I was ten years younger.

Melody opens her mouth but nothing comes out, leans up and slowly reaches for my abdomen, runs her finger lightly across the scar. "Oh, my…" She swallows. "How terrible." Honestly, the thing looks far worse than it ever hurt. Alternatively, I have a small puncture wound—can barely see it—right at the center of my left deltoid, a poorly healed perforation that sends a blast of pain all the way to the base of my neck anytime I have to lift something above my head. Melody keeps her fingers moving, leaves the six-inch carving and moves to a smaller question-mark shape near the center of my chest. She raises my sweater as she gazes at the remnants of battles gone by, my own collection of *souvenirs*. She lifts the sweater even farther as the look on her face turns to queasiness, and

I realize I've been handed another opportunity to show her how life with me has a discordant translation, that if she has any emotion for me running through her, sustaining it would have to be worth *this*.

So I pull off my sweater and T-shirt completely, expose my torn and blemished upper body to her like a prize catch pulled from the ocean. She slides back down in the tub as she lets out a sigh, says, "Oh." She actually turns and looks away, says to herself, "There are just so many."

Then I quickly put the T-shirt back on as I realize the potential mistake I made: My wounded body may have reinstated the fear of what she could face tomorrow. "Well, all wounds heal, you know? I mean, most of them do, I guess. You can get through pretty much anything. Remind me to get rid of this DNA-soaked sweater, by the way."

The bubbles are disappearing so I step up my tending to her cuts. I finish her arms and shoulders, ask her how her ankle is feeling.

"Still a little sore."

I carefully reach into the water, find her knee with my hand, curl my fingers underneath her leg as I run them down the length of her calf. I gently lift up her leg, hold her calf in one hand and drag my fingers to her ankle, rub it softly to check for swelling. I massage her foot—it seems so small and delicate—and ask her how it feels.

She just stares at me, nods quickly, like *keep doing that*.

The bubbles are gone, her nude body concealed by nothing more than a cloud of soapy water. I walk over to her room to get her terry robe, then open it for her to step into. She backs in, like I'm helping her put on a winter coat, then pulls the sides together and tightens the belt.

I leave her there, walk out to my bed, and sit on the end and drop my head to my hands. She emerges a few minutes later, comes and sits next to me.

"Beating up that guy take it out of you?"

I look at her and smile. "*You* take it out of me."

She slides over so our thighs are pressed together, puts her hand on my jeans, slides her hand between my legs. It feels intimate but something's changed in how she leans my way and touches me, like the surge of passion has dissipated and her interest in me is more thought out, almost preplanned.

"Listen," she says, "I'm tired, Jonathan. I'm tired of waiting and I'm tired of lying and I'm tired of not living and, I... I'm just going to come out and say it." I can feel her hand trembling between my legs. "I want you to sleep with me tonight. I mean, I'm not even sure what I'm really asking—as you well know—but I want it to happen."

While what she's offering is the greatest gift I might ever receive, her honesty and ability to express her feelings this way are what drag me down harder than any pair of cinder blocks. I clear my throat to rid the obvious lump in it, and say with no hesitation, having lost—surrendered—any further ability to deny my feelings, "I want you, too, Melody."

She studies me, pulls her hand out and rests it on a less intimate spot near my knee. "But."

I lick my lips, shake my head. "I can't take anything more from you."

"You're not taking it, Jonathan; I'm giving it. I want you to have it."

"But I don't deserve it. More importantly, you'll regret it the rest of your life."

She smirks. "What?"

"What if, after tomorrow, we have to remain apart?"

Melody passes me a look I don't recognize, some blend of being hurt and being confounded. Her voice starts off at normal volume but fades so abruptly I barely understand the finish: "Why would we have to remain apart?"

I bite my lip, feel like I'm watching her collapse and die alongside her parents. I might as well have put the bullet in her back then. I hold my breath for a few seconds. "I may be the unpredictable one," I say, "but I come from a long line of capricious and impulsive people." I reach over and glide my hand up the back of her neck, gently run my fingers through her hair. "I know what I'm doing. No matter what the feds told you about my family or how they think we operate or what our motivations and responses are, no one understands my family the way I do. I need you to trust me; I'm just preparing for the worst."

"The worst being...?"

I laugh through my nose. "You haven't considered the worst?"

She turns to face me more directly, pulls her leg up, and I stroke it with the back of my hand. "I thought I hit rock bottom some time ago," she says. "Turns out it's a sliding scale downward." She reaches over, rests her hand on my shoulder, then slowly slips it around my neck. "But I have a really big reason to want to stay alive now. Do you understand?"

I nod. "Don't worry, Melody. I'll never let anything bad happen to you again. I made you that promise and I intend to keep it. I'll always do what needs to be done to keep you safe. Always."

Right. That and you're *flawless*. My superlatives have to go.

Except something inside her changes this time. Melody stares at me, gives me the same look she gave in the Italian place in Baltimore when she first genuinely considered my words, started feeling the sway. She keeps her hand behind my neck and pulls me to her, rests her forehead against mine and looks down. We stay like this for a long time, paralyzed.

"Will you sleep with me?" she finally whispers. "I mean, literally."

I know: terrible idea. It's like pulling our hands from the wheel, careening off into a ditch, left with no more than the remains of a totaled automobile and a lifetime of scars and bad memories. But between us we share a mixture of fear and loneliness and hope, and I can't ignore the potential pleasure of feeling her warmth throughout the night. I know deep down that if I do not sleep with her, feel her against me for one night, I'll regret it for every remaining moment on this earth. Where every addict attempting recovery battles the *one last time* scenario, they followed the path of addiction with this first step: *One time can't hurt.*

I slowly nod.

"I'll be over in a minute," I say.

She walks back to her room through the adjoining door, pulls it behind her but does not close it. I quickly brush my teeth and run a wet hand through my hair, change into nothing more than pajama bottoms. I wait behind the adjoining door until I hear the sound of her faucet go off and the door to her bathroom open, and I walk in.

Melody stands next to the bed twisting her fingers together over her chest, looks down at herself. She's wearing nothing but a camisole Melissa convinced me every woman needs in her bag—indeed—and panties. "I hope this is okay," she says. "It's how I sleep." She curls her toes, twists her foot on the floor like a little girl. I nod like it's fine, then harder, like it's perfect. She brings a hand to her face, covers a smile, and shakes her head.

She walks up to me, takes me by both hands and leads us to the bed, sits on the edge and pulls me down. She slips under the covers, her eyes on me the entire time. I consider turning around and fleeing to the safety of my room, but her look demands that I remain. I get in next to her and take off my glasses. She turns off the lamp and I'm thankful I don't have the light to reflect the color and design of her soft and curvy body.

She snuggles up against me and we kiss, what she probably meant to be a peck but somehow transformed into that seemingly practiced intimacy again. The kiss lasts for more than a minute, manages to progress beyond our only other encounter, enhanced by the freedom to explore away from onlookers, the ability to moan and caress in the privacy of our darkened room. And as if she read my mind, she pulls back and throws a finger to my lips, is out of breath, holds her finger firmly against my mouth. I can feel her breath on my face. Finally, she whispers, "Keep me alive, Jonathan."

I nod, try to pretend I'm not equally winded, attempt a look of certainty despite a heart of cold confidence.

She slowly turns over and slides my direction, pushes her lower back and bottom against me, hard; a layer of heat emerges between us, stays trapped under the sheet. She reaches back like she's trying to find the blanket, but grabs my arm and pulls it over her instead, takes my hand and places it on her belly, holds it there for a moment, then slides it up under her camisole so it rests just below her chest; I can feel the soft edge of her breasts against the side of my hand. I lean my head forward, get my face so close to her head that I could count the hairs.

In any other situation, I might have found this the perfect way to fall asleep, but I cannot deny it being the most intimate way I've ever held a woman; I've had many in my arms, but never before wanted one in them so badly, never so greatly regretted how I must eventually release her.

With my hand on her torso I can feel her heart slowing, yet still pumping hard. I think of how my father asked me to make it stop, bring her life to an abrupt ending, slap her shut and toss her aside like an unfinished book. This recurring reality of my life and family drains away the pleasure of the moment. My hand starts to shake and I'm afraid she'll feel it; I don't want to move it, either. My emotional stake in her well-being has grown exponentially, my approach to saving her shifting to the more reckless and desperate; my family better make the right choice. With each breath

I see how easily Ettore would've dropped her in the parking lot of the A&P, how he would've simply walked away, returned to his motel room to clean his guns. How he could never know what he destroyed, and how my father could never grasp what he actually requested. Like taking an unseen Monet or Rembrandt and torching it, no one would've ever comprehended its magnificence, ever knew it even existed.

I think of the first night I met her in the motel in Cape Charles. As her body now rises and falls with each breath, I remember just how gently she slept then, how peaceful she seemed until I pressed my pen to her neck, began the long journey toward gaining her trust. And then I remember what I witnessed before I even entered her room, an image that had gone missing during these turbulent days but comes upon me now with the weight and worry of a forgotten deadline.

I gently jar her body with my hand. She stirs, turns her head halfway.

"I saw you kiss Sean," I blurt.

The rising and falling stops.

"What?" she says. "Wait. Who?"

"Your useless fed. And I saw him leave your room the morning I came to get you."

She turns her head all the way to mine, her back flat against the mattress. She stares at me and thinks for a moment; her inability to recall what I'm talking about declares the memory's insignificance. I wish I hadn't brought it up.

"It wasn't that kind of kiss," she says. "It wasn't what you and I just shared."

I smile a little. "It's okay."

She turns all the way so we face each other squarely. "No, it's not. I was just... I don't know what I was doing. It was nothing. You have to know that. And I don't know what you think you saw, but he was not in my room overnight. I did not see him until the next day, he simply checked in on me in the morning."

"Okay." She runs her hand up my body, stares at me. "Seriously."

She smiles a little, turns back to her original position. After a moment, she says, "You were right, by the way. Sean is *not* married."

Gardner may be an inconsistent human being, but his data sure is reliable.

Then she adds, "I asked him about it after he stole me away from you in Baltimore, wanted to know why he wore a wedding band. He told me his wife had died years earlier and that he leaves the ring on because 'there will only ever be one Mrs. Douglas' and he will never remarry—his words." She chuckles quietly. "Then he told me it helps to fend off the ladies, too."

What a pretentious, self-congratulating piece of—

"I liked that about him," she says.

Oh.

Then, as she yawns, "It was one of his two redeeming qualities." When I don't respond, she continues, "The idea of someone knowing when real love has come and gone from this life, how that person can love the memory of someone more than they could ever love again." She pushes back against me again. "There's no truer sign of love, nothing more beautiful, than sacrifice."

She takes a deep breath, holds it the way I used to when inhaling my first hit of nicotine for the day, then lets it slip out as a sigh.

"So," I say, "what was his other redeeming quality?"

She shifts her body a little. "He seemed to have his finger on the pulse of what was going on even though he appeared aloof, like it was easy for him. Like the way he found me in the parking lot of the Italian restaurant." She turns a little. "I wasn't happy about that, as you know—but he always seemed in control, even though he appeared out of it."

Just what I wanted to hear. To me, he was the distracted bumbler tossing shells in the Chesapeake; Melody's depiction indicates that my interpretation might've been wrong all along.

"He really that different from all the other marshals you've known?"

She gently brushes her cheek, thinks. "He was more talkative, but that's not saying much. Every marshal I've known has been incredibly focused, not easily diverted." I mentally shrug. Then: "I don't know, maybe it's because he came from the FBI."

Now *my* body stops rising and falling.

"What do you mean?"

"He said he used to be with the FBI, was there for most of his career, moved to the Marshals Service not too long ago."

My conceptual sketch of Sean, the abstract drawn and colored by my limited observations, turned out to be an impressionistic work. And useless. As I start to hear Melody's breathing deepen, I know she's seconds from sleep. Me? Not a frigging wink anywhere in my near future. Her breath stutters like she's going to say something else, that there's more to the story, but she either forgot or is too tired to continue. I twist my arm up and over her head, begin lightly stroking her hair, run my fingers back and forth across her hairline at the top of her neck.

Then, barely audible, she asks, "Do you speak Italian?"

I know some, mostly general greetings and small talk, gastronomic terms, and slang no one would ever want translated. "A little."

Her final words: "Whisper to me."

I am preoccupied with Sean now, racked with concern that he's been one room away this entire time, so in control of the operation that he's grabbing a cup of coffee and a croissant before dropping by. But Melody's effect on my being, her steady and strong pull on my life like I have my own personal gravity, has me succumbing to her command. I wrap my arm around her body, outside of her clothes, outside of the sheet, and pull her in, move my head to hers, and whisper all the things I would want her to know, that I could never say for fear she would not have the will to leave me. I whisper in broken Italian how she is both a princess and an angel; how I love what she's done for me, how when I'm with her I want to be a better man; how it does not matter if the world ever views her as imperfect because she's perfect for *me*; how these days, these moments we've shared are so brilliant it's been worth living the other thirty years of my life just to get to experience them.

Melody's body becomes limp and warm, her breathing heavier as she falls into a sound sleep. I keep whispering anyway.

THIRTEEN

I managed to nod off at some point, long after vetting every scenario through my head while I stared at the ceiling, mentally running each play over and over like a coach the night before the championship game, and with all the anxiety; you spend an entire season—in my case, years—trying to get to the big game, only to eventually face down the stress of turning it into the final win of the season. If we triumph, Melody goes free; if we lose, Melody never gets to play again, gets kicked out of the league.

The moment the sun breaks through the slit in the curtains, I open my eyes, destined to remain awake. I slip out of bed and return to my room, leave Melody to sleep off the bruising and trauma from the night before.

I sit on the corner of my bed and watch the news and wait, drift into a daze as the talking head rambles on about newfound long-term complications associated with steady consumption of carbonated beverages. I begin reading the news ticker at the bottom of the screen and it makes me numb, hypnotizes me like a metronome. Until, scrolling across:

> INVESTIGATORS ARE LOOKING INTO THE SUDDEN DISAPPEARANCE OF MANNY PASTULO, LONG ASSOCIATED WITH THE BOVARO AND RICCI CRIME FAMILIES.

And so it goes. If I recall from our family meeting, Pastulo was being handled by three crew members, his takedown led by Tommy Fingers. The reality of our grand plan—the first evidence it actually occurred other than term-encrypted cell phone conversations—brings an alertness no amount of caffeine could ever deliver.

I call Pete, wake him up. He answers with a one-word grunt, something between *yeah* and *what.*

"Everything still looking good?"

He yawns. "When you coming back?"

"Be there shortly, this afternoon. Everyone happy and healthy?"

I hear a woman groan in the background, then she says, "I gotta pee."

"Who's that?" I ask.

Pete takes a deep breath, rustles a little like he's sitting up. "I don't know."

Of course he doesn't. "We come straight to Pop's, right?"

"Yeah."

"We gonna have a full house?" *Is everyone going to be attending?*

"Eddie put together the invitations." *We're having an official family meeting.*

"There gonna be cake?" *Good news or bad news?*

"With extra icing. Pop says he gets the piece with the flowers on it." *All good. Especially once you bring the dead girl home.*

"Yeah, I figured. I just wanted to make sure he's gonna be there, that everyone is gonna be there." My eyes remain glued to the news ticker. "I'm thinking we'll be there early afternoon."

I've become quite in touch with the rise and fall of adrenaline in my bloodstream, this most recent wave caused by the assurance that the final event will occur. How much easier it would've been if something went wrong, that my family muffed the grand plan, that we'd just have to continue on the course of a less risky plan offering no closure whatsoever, no mandate for completing the mission.

As I hang up, I hear Melody moving around in her room. Since the adjoining door remains partially open, I go through it—still feels like I should enter through the hall door—and find her in the bathroom, her mouth filled with toothpaste foam. She glances my way, spits quickly. We sort of hug and share a peck, move like a pair of actors running through their first take of a love scene. My phone vibrates in my pocket: Pete again.

"You still bringing the skim'?" Yes, short for *skimbo.* I hear him flick a lighter, take a pull off a cigarette.

"Yeah."

"Huh. Figured you would've grown bored with her by now." A few days equals a decade in Peter years. Then through his exhale of smoke: "Got off the phone with Pop. Thought you'd be interested to know he says he's 'looking forward to meeting both of your girls.'"

I rub my eyes. "That's great." I slap my phone closed.

"What's great?" Melody asks.

"Uh," I say, looking down, "my whole family will be there today. Just as I'd hoped."

She sits on the bed, presses her knees together, stares at the floor as well. "They know I'm coming?"

"Not exactly."

She doesn't flinch. "They know what you're about to do? What you're about to ask of them?"

"No."

She stands and walks to me; my eyes are still on the floor. She tries to catch my eye, looks like she needs reassurance, and in the absence of my offering it, she says, "Remember, you're the unpredictable one. They should be prepared for something surprising."

As I kiss her forehead and hold her, I say, "They can be surprising at times, too."

Melody and I return to our separate rooms to shower and dress. I finish first, continue watching the news ticker—only the Pastulo item, so far—and wait for her to finish. She peeks her head in the door and asks what I think she should wear to meet my family. I suggest armor. She suggests one of the skirts and a blouse from the shopping bags from Norfolk. I counter with something more practical: jeans and a light sweater. She nods and half pouts, probably thinks practicality translates into *in case we have to run.*

Three minutes later, she shows me how she looks in my picks. The jeans look good, but the sweater is what captures my attention. She's wearing a tight-fitting red sweater, a pullover that Melissa recommended. As we were quickly perusing the store that morning, Melissa said, "If your girlfriend has the frame you describe, this'll look perfect on her." Except she got it backward: Melody looks perfect *in* it. We make our way down to the outside café to force down breakfast before our journey to New York. With visions of Sean the Magnificent in my head, I hold her hand the entire time, grip it with no affection, keep it clasped as though I might pull her in a different direction at any second.

We find a table with an enormous umbrella for us to hide under, order coffee and juice and a table of food: eggs, bacon, French toast, sausage. The only thing I really want is a smoke. The nicotine gum, as it turns out, only rectifies the chemical part of the equation; the mental part remains unsolved. What I want—sadly, need—is the slapping of a fresh pack against my palm, the shaking free of a single cigarette, the feel of the smooth paper as it rests between my lips, the sterile taste of the filter against my tongue. I need the crackling sound of the match as it ignites, the flicker of the end of the cigarette as it lights and the wincing at the short blast of fire, that first deep breath of earthy heat, the curls of smoke, the cloud that forms from my mouth as my lungs empty, the temporary fumes that overwhelm every other scent in the air. Such is the curse of any addiction: Part of the rush exists in performing the act that produces the other part.

Melody dives in, eats like we skipped dinner last night, picks up with the feasting. I can't get beyond playing with the yolk of a broken poached egg. I reach in my pocket, pull out the small box for the nicotine gum, shake it and realize it's empty. I stare at it, crush the box in my fist, start brutally stabbing it with my coffee spoon. Melody stops chewing, says with a partially full mouth, "I find this... disconcerting."

I drop the spoon and cover my face with my hands, realize the lack of gum and cigarettes are not my problem; the issue is with finding a way to overcome the fear of potentially failing her again. "I wish... I wish it could be easier for you."

She swallows her food, takes a drink, puts her utensils down. "What do you mean?"

"Here I am asking you to face the people who put all this misery into your life. You shouldn't have to go through this. It's not right."

"What choice do I have? I mean, geez, you're the one who helped me realize that." She takes my hand, becomes the stronger one. "I agreed to your plan because, well... I really had no place left to go. I couldn't run anymore, couldn't wonder what was waiting around the corner every moment of my life."

I look up at her. I am struck with a disturbing realization: All the anxiety I've been feeling for the past few days, feeling right now, wondering if Sean will be pouncing on me from behind the bushes, if a bullet will be shot into my unshielded flesh, these are the precise worries and fears she has faced every hour of every day. *For twenty years.*

It is inhuman, this punishment. No one should have to live this way. And I'll never permit my family to threaten her again. This surge of clarity is far better than any cigarette.

I will die for her if I have to.

Sometimes a superlative embodies the truth.

Melody tightens her grip on my hand and says, "But more importantly, I've come to trust you, Jonathan. I know you'll take care of me. I truly believe it—and no one could be more surprised at that than I am. You let me be myself these last few days. I was Melody Grace again. How else could I have had her back in my life?"

How she speaks of herself in the third person, her implication that it will come to an end, breaks her comments into two distinct pieces: that I will *take care of her*, but that she will *never be free to be herself.*

My final act will encompass the truth—and will culminate in four hours.

We return to our rooms, and while Melody freshens herself, I pack all of our clothes in my bag, can barely zip it closed. We check the rooms for anything we could possibly be leaving behind, talk only in short requests and answers, like we're cleaning up the scene of a crime.

We return the door cards and check out, walk outside as we wait for the valet to return the Audi to the front of the hotel. Melody and I stand side by side, eyes cast down like married lovers whose vacation has come to an end and the notion of bills and childcare and unmowed lawns returns to the forefront of our minds.

I hand the valet a twenty and open the door for Melody, toss our bags in the trunk, filling the very spot where my family envisions Melody's body is wrapped in blankets and waiting to be buried. As

I pull onto the empty city streets on this Sunday morning, Melody watches the hotel disappear over her shoulder.

We break free of the lights, zoom toward the interstate, past Camden Yards and up an exit ramp built like the first hill of a roller coaster; it twists us over to the northbound side of I-95. Within minutes, we're through the Fort McHenry Tunnel and out past the Baltimore Beltway. I shove a Death Cab for Cutie disc in the player and we listen to the gentle music without a word between us. We've been on the road for fifteen minutes before I rest my hand on Melody's thigh and say, "Three and a half hours and you'll be in the presence of the Bovaro clan."

She places her hand on mine, raises an eyebrow, and asks, "Anything I should know?"

A far different question from "Anything you want to tell me?"

It takes most of the journey from northeastern Maryland to central New Jersey to explain the details of each member of my family, what it was like to grow up around them, share the embarrassing nuances that make each of my brothers who they are. I tell her of the miserable life my mother had to live, how her only reward was a husband who remained faithful to her, how I was the only one who could tell it could've never been enough, how she needed more and didn't live long enough to receive it. I explain how my father had periods of normalcy, could've been a good man, but swam into a sea of crime that eventually engulfed him.

I try to tell her things that might make her think the Bovaros are a real family—the true G-rated vignettes—to ease her into what's about to happen. As we pass the exits for roads leading to Atlantic City, I tell her a story about a family vacation gone awry, right down to the flat tire and food poisoning from bad shellfish.

What I avoid telling her is that we stopped in a housing development on the return ride home, looked at houses under construction, listened to my father and Peter make jokes of how loose all the dirt seemed to be. From that trip came the genesis of a Bovaro trade secret: One of the best places to bury bodies is in a community under construction—not in the concrete foundations, but in the landscaping. All those tree-lined streets? Those are new plantings, easy to move, and the soil underneath is typically rock-free. At night, when all the construction teams are gone, the Bovaro crew arrives, moves a tree from its spot, digs a deeper hole, puts a body in it, covers it with dirt, then puts the tree right back on top. When was the last time someone moved a tree to look for a body? I'd imagine some of the heartiest maples and oaks in New Jersey are being fed by those who've betrayed my family.

After two hours of briefing, it turns out she'd been patiently waiting for me to discuss one person in particular. I never brought him up on my own.

"Will your cousin be there?" She swallows, is trying so hard to be casual. "The, um, one who killed my parents?"

I look at her for a second, turn back to the road. "Uh, *no.*" The one good thing about my cousin's terrible death is being able to deliver some semblance of good news, of relief for Melody. "He was killed a few years ago. Bullet right through the throat, choked on his own blood for a long time before Peter eventually found him. Pete just let him die right there in an alley in midtown Manhattan."

So much for keeping the topic of my family nice and light. Melody's reaction forces an understanding that she's not one of us; where I expected a fist in the air, I instead get a flinch and slouched shoulders, like we're all nuts, cannibals feeding off our own flesh.

"Why didn't Peter try to save him?"

"Uh... it's kind of complicated, but we let my cousin get killed.

It was payback for a mistake we made—*he* made—against another family. The whole thing's sort of ridiculous."

"*Sort* of." She rolls her eyes, turns and stares at the road. "Well, I can't say I'm sorry he's dead."

"You shouldn't be. But in terms of your folks, the truth is he just pulled the trigger. As crazy as he was, my cousin really had no more stake in the murder of your parents than the bullets that killed them. All he did was follow orders." Mr. Roboto.

She glances sideways at me, slides her hands down the length of her thighs like she's wiping sweat from her palms. "Whose orders?"

I shrug and sigh. "My father's."

And then, not another word.

We're closing in on my father's house with such speed we're likely to arrive early. Near Bayway, New Jersey, Melody stares out her window as I fly past the exit for the Staten Island Expressway. "I'm probably not the greatest with New York geography," she says, "but wouldn't that have been the shortest way to Brooklyn?"

"Sure. Why?"

She scowls a little. "Doesn't your family live in Brooklyn?"

"No, no—*I* live in Brooklyn; my family lives in Tenafly."

She turns in her seat, pulls her knee up and faces me. "*Tenafly?*"

"It's in Jersey, just north of the George Washington Bridge."

"I know where it is. Tenafly is barely twenty miles from where I lived before my parents and I went into Witness Protection. You kept saying we were going to New York."

"Melody, my father's house is, like, a mile and a half from the Hudson."

I don't understand why, but this causes a swell in her anxiety.

She starts wiping her hands on her jeans again, takes deep breaths like she's going into labor.

"You never said Tenafly. I'm certain you said Brooklyn. I mean, man, a New Jersey address would've stuck in my head."

"Well, my folks grew up in Brooklyn. Maybe that's where you got it from. Or maybe because you called my father's business line in Brooklyn. Or maybe we just got our signals crossed." Now, this is probably the wrong thing to say, the wrong moment to mention the brevity of our acquaintance, but it comes out of my mouth anyway: "I mean, we've only been together for a couple days."

Melody throws up all over her floor mat.

We clean her face the best we can (bottled water and convenience store napkins) and dispose of my floor mat (jettisoned onto the shoulder of the Jersey Turnpike). She accepts my offer of some Nicorette from the stash in my glove box—to freshen her mouth and calm her nerves.

By the time we get to Englewood she's starting to relax, says, "I haven't been back here since I was a little girl." She chews the gum slowly, gazes out the window like a kid spying the entrance to Disney World. "I'm so close to home."

I begin to steady my pace, catch glimpses of Melody taking long looks across the suburban landscape, her head twisting to keep a lock on various buildings and places and signs. I attempt to provide her with the opportunity to reminisce in whatever way she can. These very roads may have been the last she traveled with her parents on that cloudy morning twenty years ago. I hadn't anticipated the emotional toll it might take on her; to me it was nothing more than pavement leading me to my father's home.

And as I stare at her, watching her try to recapture pieces of her stolen youth, for the first time since she and I have been together I get choked up, really have to fight back tears. I recall my own uneasy youth, the nights I stayed awake praying that the McCartneys would be safe. I want to set her free, yet I lament having to make it happen at all. The whole *if you love something set it free* thing serves as nothing more than a platitude for personal liberation. Over the course of one's life, the odds are the things that were set free weren't very difficult to let go in the first place. The stuff you truly love you fight to keep by your side, right to your final breath. But even Melody comprehends the higher concept better than I—*nothing can ever be more beautiful than sacrifice* were her words—and it's clearly not only what she needs, it's what she wants. And I'm the deliveryman.

As we drive through the sleepy streets of Tenafly, creeping closer to my family's home with every stop sign and crack in the pavement, I glimpse the normal residents as they make their way—the couple loading golf clubs instead of a body into the trunk of their sedan; the minivan that empties boys in soccer uniforms instead of cases of weapons; the lazy, numb stroll of men pushing mowers—and for a fleeting second it feels like what Melody and I are doing is real, that we arrived here through aspiration instead of condemnation, that I really *am* taking home a girlfriend to meet the family, that we'll break the ice over a bottle of wine and a table of food, progress beyond the nervous excitement to becoming a larger family.

I wind us toward our home, to the section of our neighborhood built first, where the lots are bigger and more wooded than the newer homes closer to the highway. The streets remain in moderate disrepair, and the car shakes as we roll over broken branches strewn across the road from a recent storm. A few hundred feet later, I see our home near the end of the block, a Tudor built with so much wood and stone it could never be affordably replicated in today's market. The dwelling predates me by forty years, went from a home to a house after my mother died. My parents bought it to escape the city—escape people like us, my mother would later joke—and they turned it into a grand entertaining space, though it quickly fell into poor condition once my father lost his only love and all of the emotional capacity that came from sharing a life with her. One day when we're all dead and buried, little kids will ride their bikes down the uprooted sidewalk out front and point and say it's haunted. They will be right.

I nod, indicate to Melody which house is ours. She begins nosh-ing on the gum a little harder, and when she sees how many cars are scattered around the circular driveway she starts lightly tapping her feet.

After surveying the array of vehicles, I do the math, say to myself, "Looks like everyone's here." I aim our car directly at the front door, park at the bottom edge of the semicircle. She and I stare at the house, motor running.

Melody takes a deep breath and says, "What did you use as an excuse to get everyone together?"

"I didn't really have to make an excuse," I answer. Then unspo-ken: "It's a celebration of murder! *Salut!*" Melody could never comprehend the jubilant manner with which some in my family celebrate the abuse and disposal of humanity, and I pray they do not tell stories in her earshot, for she could only imagine the same conversation occurred after her parents were leveled. Instead, I offer this: "It's Sunday."

"What's that mean?"

"My family tries to get together for a big meal here. My father, he, uh...he likes to cook. It seems to have a calming effect, so we indulge him as much as possible." I stare at the house. "It was a long-standing tradition when my mom was alive—she was the culinary master in our family—and I think we all want to see it continue...you know, to honor her."

We sit and stare ahead like we're waiting at a red light.

"Part of me wants to kill your father," she says, "and the other part wants his acceptance." I break my lock on the house and turn to Melody. She continues, "This whole thing is a ridiculous long shot, and were I not at the end of the line with this life and the way I have to live it, I'd have never taken the risk. It wasn't that big of a deal a few days ago, when I had nothing left inside of me. Problem is, now I want to survive—to be with you longer." She drops her head, looks at her lap. "I'm resting my hopes on two things, the first being that you've really thought this out and that you understand your family better than I ever could."

I wait, but no part two. "The other?"

"I'm assuming somewhere inside your dad is a good and decent man, like you suggested." She looks at me again. "He raised *you*, after all." She puts her hand on my shoulder. I respond with a smile. "I'm sure he would've done anything to protect you over the years."

My smile vanishes; my father may have helped raise me, but he also raised Peter. And the good and decent man hasn't come around in a while, been kept under submission by a life no longer tempered by the warmth of a woman.

Then Melody adds this: "I'm sure your father would have left the world of crime if he'd needed to for one of his sons, right?"

My eyes fall and land on the dashboard, though I'm seeing nothing but memories of my mother begging him to break free in the desperate and broken days after her attack by Morrison. I was there when she said it, pleaded for it. I was there when my father said, "Anything for you," and I was there a week later when he told Tommy Fingers, "You put two in Agata's head, and I mean today," and then a month later when he told my brother Gino that "the hole left by the Cuccis means we'll be picking up a big chunk of business." (My father became obsessed with taking over the Cucci turf and eventually won the Cucci Coup). Soon after, I witnessed my mother's reluctant acceptance of my father's offerings—jewelry, expensive clothing, and cars—to appease her, offset the crimes set against her. The more she longed for him to abandon this life that was riddled with risk, where no one was safe, the more money he dropped on her. And now I realize why my throwing bills around with Melody bothered me so. What was it *I* was offsetting? Was I merely paying in advance for an upcoming crime? Who exactly had I become?

I can't lift my eyes, neither to her face nor the house. "My family has never been very comfortable with the notion of sacrifice," I say. Then, all at once: I see our odds dwindle, our horse fade as it rounds the last turn. But I'm not giving up, not letting Melody down. I'm not tearing up that ticket yet. I turn off the ignition and grab the keys and pop my door open. "Let's do this."

Just before my door closes, I hear Melody say, "Wait, I—" As I walk around to her side of the car, she flips down the visor and checks her lips and face and hair, spits out her gum into a wrapper, takes a deep breath and forces it out in a blast.

Melody takes my hand as soon as she gets out. Her hand is cold and wet, trembles a little. I hold it firmly as I take broad steps to the front of our house. She walks behind me but speeds up to get to my side. We walk the long brick path covered in debris from months past, each step a crunch of leaves and twigs.

Melody whispers so softly I'm not certain the words are for me: "Are you sure?"

I just keep walking, hold her hand like a child's while crossing through a bad part of town, my eyes leveled at the front door like I'm looking down the barrel of a gun.

"Are you sure?"

We're within a few steps of the entrance, greeted by the enormous two-inch-thick oak door with its rounded top, beveled panels, and small cut glass windows in the upper sections, the product of some long-dead craftsman's time and attention and artistic capacity. It takes all my strength, all my will, to keep from kicking the thing right off its rotting frame. As we step upon the stoop, I feel Melody tighten her hand around mine. With a held breath, I reach down and grip the handle and latch in my hand, and gently open the door.

NELLA VITA—CHI NON RISICA—NON ROSICA

(IN LIFE: WHO RISKS NOTHING, GAINS NOTHING)

ONE

Of all the things that could strike us as we walk in, it's not the smack of a sibling's hand on a shoulder, not the lilting sound of my father's soundtrack of Sinatra or Mario Lanza or Dino Crocetti (he refuses to call him Dean Martin), not the sound of loud voices bouncing off the scarred maple floors of the entryway; it's the smell of the Sunday gravy. I would argue that Sylvia has some of the best chefs in Williamsburg, if not all of Brooklyn, yet our kitchen never captures a gastronomic aroma as powerful and warm as my father's Sunday gravy, the veal- and pork-based red sauce that simmers all day long and serves as the base for most other dishes to be made. The scent asks you to come in and have a taste, grab a glass of wine, sit and tell it about your day. It has a comforting effect—one that might be working on Melody as well; she looks around the house like a child glimpsing a museum for the first time. Her eyes move from object to object, from the paintings on the wall to the pictures on the piano in the study. She catches a fleeting look at my father and mother in happier days, images of my brothers and me in younger, less intimidating stances and sizes.

We pause here in the entryway as I survey the scene; it appears everyone has congregated in the kitchen, as much a tradition as the meal itself. My mother could never "shake people out of her cooking space," and eventually she and my father gave up, blew out the adjacent laundry room and increased the size of the kitchen by 30 percent.

I pull Melody down the hallway to the back of the house, her hand still cold, still trembling. As we break the fringe of the kitchen, a dozen or so people are milling about and various conversations are under way, the largest being where Peter stands before a small crowd of listeners. With his back to us, he says, "So I told him, 'Hey, relax; you still got nine fingers. That's nine more lessons!'" Peter's blatant copyright infringement of Tommy Fingers's material brings a smattering of laughter, mostly from Gino's and Jimmy's wives, gazing adoringly at Peter with their heads cocked, wishing they'd somehow landed the dashing mafioso instead of the also-rans.

I slap Peter on the back and say, "Yeah, except what you really meant was he had seven fingers and two thumbs left, right?" The same response I used to give Tommy when I was a kid; if Pete can recycle old material, why can't I?

He turns around and hugs me hard and fast, whacks me on the back. As I reach to return his hug, Melody is reluctant to release my hand. When I slide over, Melody slips right behind me like she's hiding in my shadow, peeks her head around the side of my neck.

Everyone turns to look at me and Melody, and all of the conversations come to an abrupt end—except for the one occurring in the far corner of the kitchen between my father and Eddie Gravina, a manila folder positioned between them like they're singing from the same hymnal. In my peripheral vision I can tell they're staring at us. My father gets up from his chair slowly, grabs his pants by the belt, and pulls them way up to compensate for the down-drifting that'll occur with each step toward us. He carries the manila folder with him.

I can feel Melody slink behind me again as my father comes our way. I wonder what's running through her mind, wonder if she recognizes the now gray and overweight man who once acted the lead role in her night terrors. The only way this will work is if she faces him. The only way this will work is if he faces her.

No one says a word as Pop approaches us, not my three brothers, not the wives, not Eddie, not the extended crew.

Pop stops at the edge of the counter, leans on it with one hand, studies Melody. "Who's this?"

I move to the side, expose Melody to the villainous crowd, as vulnerable and exposed as though she were standing naked. "This," I say, "is my new girlfriend."

Jimmy, mouth full of meatball sub, jabs Peter in the side. "Fibby bucks, tol' you he wudn't gah." *Fifty bucks. I told you he wasn't gay.* He takes another bite before swallowing.

"Those friggin' glasses," Peter says. "Had to go with the odds." Peter finally gets the laughter and admiration he so desires. He steps toward Melody and smiles, says to her, "You're way too pretty to be with this clown." He offers his hand to her and as she weakly shakes it, he says, "Peter Bovaro."

She swallows twice, can't seem to get the lump down, can't seem to get the words out, though eventually it escapes.

"Melody McCartney," she says.

Peter smiles wider, releases her hand. You can count the seconds of silence—one, two, three—before everyone breaks into laughter.

Everyone except my father and Eddie Gravina.

I scan the room, the faces and expressions and levels of expectation.

My father squints at Melody, opens the manila folder again and studies its contents, closes it slowly and chucks it behind him on the counter.

Peter shoves me, says, "You friggin'—you thought you'd pull one over on us like that?"

"Good one, Johnny," Gino yells from across the room, then gulps down the remaining contents of a Peroni.

"C'mon," Peter says, "let's go to your car. Show me the real one."

Melody laughs a little, too, wipes her brow and looks at me.

"Stay put, Pete," my father says, his eyes locked on Melody. I can tell she feels him studying her, can read the anxiety in the pallor of her face. Pop says to her quietly, "What's your name, sweetheart?"

Silence again.

Melody looks at me, her expression pleading for another rescue attempt. I can hear the whisper: *Are you sure?*

"My name is, uh..." she says.

I purse my lips and slowly nod.

She takes in a deep breath, her eyes bouncing from face to face across the room, landing on mine last. She lets out the breath, slouches her shoulders, puts all her weight on one leg.

"My name is Melody Grace McCartney." She pauses, watches the faces before her contort into expressions of confusion. "I'm exactly who you think I am."

More laughter—but now from only one: my father.

I move between Melody and Pop. "Yeah, this is Melody Grace McCartney," I say, making sure everyone can hear me.

She's just a little girl.

She is six years old.

She's a scared child.

How could she hurt you?

I say, "She's not a kid anymore, but just as innocent. Surprised she managed to live this long?"

"That's enough, Johnny," my father says. He rubs his eyes, leans his lower back against the counter; the cabinets underneath it creak. "Have you lost your friggin' mind?"

Then Peter: "What the hell have you done, Johnny?"

"I haven't done anything but fallen for an amazing woman." My eyes still on Peter, I sense Melody quickly turn and stare at me; I hadn't intended on her knowing how I truly felt about her, figured my feelings were safely encrypted in whispered Italian she could never translate. I didn't want her to have anything in her mind that might prevent her from discarding me, but even though she shouldn't have known the truth, my family needed to. She moves closer.

Peter chuckles. His volume increases with every sentence: "Oh, so, wait—you really *did* bring your girlfriend home? Very cute. Did she ride in the trunk, too? A hundred million available women and you pick one that wants to take us all down? Are you and I even distantly related?"

Melody turns to my father, seems determined to take her case directly to the highest court. "All I know is I adore your son, Mr. Bovaro."

Now it's my turn to be caught off guard. I'm weakened by her speaking those words, that my love for her might not be unrequited. And now my hope is that this toppled apple cart self-corrects, that somehow it will work—that *we* will work. I hope and pray her words are true. I hope and pray she's not just acting.

My father catches my eye, has the same look on his face as the moment I suggested we keep Morrison alive, the look that can only be read as *you are a dreamer.* And like that day so long ago, I hope now that my sense of hope and purpose are as welcome as the peace and calm my mother once brought to him, that he needs this balance.

But then he slowly shakes his head. His expression changes to that of complete and utter disappointment, that maybe he shouldn't have trusted me all those years ago with Morrison either.

"You're a good liar, young lady," he says, but the words are meant for me; he might as well have said, "She lied to you, Johnny."

Melody cocks her head a little and stands taller, says very carefully, "I'm not lying."

I slip my arm around her back and pull her next to me. "She's telling the truth, Pop. You think I'd bring her here if I wasn't convinced she'd never hurt us? She just wants a *real* chance at a normal life, *her* life." Then, as though it will add some level of comfort for my family, some assurance that she'll remain closemouthed, I add, "With me."

Pop sighs, says, "I believe the part about her wanting a normal life, but not the part about it being with you. She has every reason to want us to pay for what we did to her, and she's played you in getting sweet revenge." He turns his body so he's square with Melody and says, "And I'll tell you, kid, you're tough"—he slams his pointer finger down on the counter—"for coming into my house and thinking you could pull this off."

Melody and I reply with mirrored frowns and words: "Pull *what* off?"

"Pop," I say, "look, I don't need you to teach me a lesson here, okay? I'm a grown man and I know what I'm doing. I—"

Now the fist hits the counter. "This isn't about teachin' a lesson, Johnny; it's about serving life in prison. I'm an old man. I'm not letting things end that way. And you've got to think about your family, your brothers and their wives and their children."

I shake my head, conjure a way to start over. "Melody's not going to—"

"Melody's not going to *what*, Johnny?" He snatches up the remote and aims it at the stereo like he wants to kill it. The music ends and he chucks the remote so hard against the wall the plastic cracks and the batteries fall out. He runs his hands through his wiry silver hair, wipes his face, crosses his arms. "Why don't you ask the love of your life what she did yesterday."

I answer with annoyance. "I know *exactly* what she did yesterday."

"Yeah?"

"Spent the day in the spa at our hotel in Baltimore."

"Yeah?"

"I got five women who'll testify to that."

"Well, I got something better than your five women." Pop

turns sideways and snaps his fingers. Gravina slides the manila folder back down the counter. My father empties the contents into his hands, slams a stack of photos against my chest, bends half of them in the process.

My father and I do not take our eyes from each other. I slowly reach up to accept the pictures and he backs up. Melody glides to my side, puts a nervous hand on my shoulder, peeks over to see what I'm holding. No one says a word as my eyes fall to the first image.

The picture is underexposed, yet the subject unmistakable: Melody in the arms of Sean, her head resting against his chest, the backdrop the front end of a black vehicle parked along an empty cornfield, the corner of an old red-painted church sticking its nose into the frame of the image. From seeing her this way, I'm tossed about by a wave of blended disappointment, jealousy, and rivalry, though it's not cause for concern; I saw them in a similar situation the night I followed her to Cape Charles, as she and Sean stood outside the doors to their motel rooms. But then the room spins, tosses me into a vortex of real disorientation as I make an observation—and Melody must make the same observation in the same instant, for her hand drops from my shoulder: In the picture, her hair is already cut and styled from the spa, and she's wearing the clothes I purchased for her.

This picture was taken less than twenty-four hours ago.

Eddie moves up next to my father and says, "Your girlfriend spent the day cooking up a serious deal with the feds. They took her to some operations center and apparently offered her the deal of her life. Any town, any job, any money. Isn't that right, dear?"

I turn to Melody and she stares up at me, head shaking, mouth ajar, eyes filling. "Please, no, Jonathan."

I'm looking at her but remembering Peter's words to me on our last phone call, the relief I felt when Tommy left the Baltimore area: *Whatever Tommy Fingers was trying to get or locate was achieved—not exactly sure what it is but Eddie Gravina's anxious for Pop to have it—and he's now on his way back to New York.*

Peter chimes in: "Geez, Johnny, please tell me you did not discuss what this family does. Did she ask you about our family? Did she ask you to cough up information about our personal business?"

My memory serves up every instance where she probed me for information about my family; the recollections drift and stop in front of me like I'm being dealt a hand of cards. Though most obvious, her simple command—"Tell me the worst thing you can tell me"—was a demand I met with such ease, an offering surrendered with a harmony of heart and mind. I gave her everything she wanted. Worst of all: As I stare at her now, I have no choice but admit I was powerless all along, that no matter how I might rewrite this story, it would always end the same.

"No, Jonathan," Melody pleads, "this isn't right. They're not right."

But the pictures cannot be denied, their proof as convincing as a bloody shoeprint. Melody reaches up to try and claim my hand, tries to gain my attention, but my eyes are locked on the image again. I drop the picture to the floor, look at the next one: Melody in Sean's arms, looking up at his face. *Drop.* Melody and Sean getting out of the black vehicle. *Drop.* "Souvenir," I whisper. Melody being escorted into a larger black vehicle. *Drop.* "That was how you knew what a souvenir was." The vehicle disappearing down an empty, dusty road. *Drop.*

I feel the collective weight of my family's shame bearing down on me; I can barely breathe, yet the only regret I have is that Melody had not been genuine with me. I wanted her love so badly I would have lied to myself, to everyone, to get it. Turns out I lied in spite of it.

"Oh, God, Jonathan, no," Melody says. "*No.* I didn't make any deal! I—"

"How did you pull this off?" I ask. "I thought you were at the spa." She becomes a blur as my eyes fill with tears. "I thought you were waiting for me."

Her voice shakes. "I *was*. I *was*. They came and found me and took me to some place called Safesite. I was only gone for a couple hours. They wanted me to play you, they did, but I told them I wouldn't do it!"

"Then why didn't you tell me?"

Her head shakes like she's nervous, like she's saying *no*. It takes her too long to answer, and when she does: "I don't know."

Pop laughs so loud it startles me, turns to my family, and says, "She doesn't know! She's quick, this one." Nervous smiles fill the room. He turns to Melody and says, "What you mean to say is you tricked my son into thinking you were at a spa all day, managed to sneak out with some federal agents for a bit, then slipped back in before he ever knew you were gone. And this didn't seem *shifty* to you?"

Melody looks across the range of faces in the kitchen, gets a glimpse of her tenuous future from each and every one, different scenarios that all arrive at the same denouement. Her eyes land on my face last; they're wet and red and dim with exhaustion. She shrugs and says softly, "I just... I—I don't know why I didn't say anything, Jonathan. We were living minute to minute and I didn't..."

I toss the remaining pictures—all unviewed—on the floor; Peter bends down and picks them up, starts flipping through them and comparing each image to Melody, passes them along to the rest of the crowd.

I can't convince myself that Melody had been disingenuous, that my interpretations of her words, of her touch, were anything but real. I don't believe the way she kissed me and held me and looked at me were false; the intimacy between us that felt so practiced was anything but manifest. Yet my father is right: Her hatred for my family has to have been so severe that she could've acted her way through this, a performer taught to lie and deceive her entire life by the government, professionals whose careers are dedicated to the livelihood of people just like Melody.

I step back, lean against the wall. I got nothing. I am nowhere. I pray God helps me understand, to make sense of it all, to *know.*

Put it together. C'mon, map this out. What's going on here?

Peter shakes his head, impales the silence with profuse profanity.

My father wipes his face over and over. Each guy in our crew groans as he fumbles with the pictures.

My father says, "All the days of planning, all the sleepless nights rife with worry, everything we did this week, every action perfectly executed, right to this moment we should be celebrating—and my own son takes everything and flushes it right down the frigging toilet."

The fact that my father made that statement in front of Melody means there's absolutely no chance of her seeing another sunset. She's as good as buried.

C'mon. Map it out. What's happening?

Melody grabs my arm, sinks her nails into it. Her crying becomes audible, her body jerks as she begins to plead: "Jonathan, please—I love you. I *do.*" My eyes fill again and I look down so no one can tell; whether her words are true or not, I want to believe them. "There's nothing I wouldn't do to protect you. I just want us to be happy." When I do not drop my arm for her, she slowly pulls her hand away and wipes her eyes. She steps toward my family and yells, "You freaking people. I hate your frigging guts, every single one of you, can't believe for a second I wanted your approval. All I ask is that you forgive me for making a mistake, for even talking to those pricks at Justice. Forgive me, okay? Yes, they'd been watching me and could tell I was getting close to Jonathan, and they promised me the moon if I'd try to get information from him, to trick him. It didn't matter because I told them to screw off. I never told Jonathan about meeting with them and I am *sorry*. I don't want to hurt any of you. Please, just forgive me!"

C'mon, c'mon, c'mon. Figure it out. God, please.

Melody drops to her knees and sits on her feet, becomes hysterical. "I mean, I forgive *you* for having murdered my parents, for ruining my entire life, for making me this wreck you see before you. Can't you please, *please*, give me one more chance? I just want one chance!"

I narrow my eyes, study every face in the room. My father's angry scowl is aimed at Melody; Peter looks at me, shaking his head the entire time; Gino and Jimmy and the rest of the crew look at me then close their eyes and turn away; the wives look at me with saddened eyes, mouth the words, "Oh, Johnny."

But when my gaze lands on Eddie, he catches my stare for only a second before he quickly drops his eyes and looks down. I feel a heat rise up through my chest. I keep my eyes locked on him, will stay like this all day if I have to. He looks up, his eyes taking the long way around the room before he catches me staring at him, then drops his face again, fast.

"Please," Melody begs one more time, "I promise I'll never hurt any of you."

Peter hands over the last picture to Gino, takes a step forward and says, "That sounds like the plea of a woman facing certain death."

My father waves his hand downward a few times, sends a signal for Pete to relax.

I can't stop looking at Eddie. He makes one final attempt to lift his head, but now he's unable to look me in the eye at all.

Then the projections come into focus: Gardner could've never supplied this information to anyone in my family. Being the whiner he is, I'd have been made fully aware if more than one Bovaro was requesting information of him. Though more importantly, I know Gardner didn't have access to this particular kind of data—"no file information, just addresses"—so the insider information was being supplied from another source. Gravina is somehow involved, and the fact that he can't look at me implies the story is more complex than anyone here comprehends; I've known Eddie for years, and if he were simply reporting evidence, he'd have the same look on his face as the rest of my family. Some deeper betrayal exists that I do not yet understand.

The amount of adrenaline running through my veins makes it nearly impossible to keep from outing Gravina right now, forcing him into a corner to make him play his hand, to get to the real details behind how he'd know where Melody was and why no one thought to mention it to me prior to this moment. I'd volunteer to help my brothers dig the hole that would soon house him—but the outcome would not change Melody's own future: dead and buried right next to Eddie.

I promised Melody I would keep her safe, that I would do whatever needs to be done to protect her. To keep that promise, there's only one play I can make, only one that matters: Get Melody out of this house. *Now.*

Melody looks up, holds her breath, fights the tears.

My father glances at Peter, walks to the stockpot on the stove, gives his sauce a stir with a wooden spoon. Then, to no one in particular, "Take care of her."

Peter steps up to bat, but Melody tips my way and grabs my leg and looks up at me, tells me she loves me like it's the last thing she might ever say, uses her final words to assure me that no matter what this looks like, her feelings were genuine, that she wants me to know it was all true. I give Gravina one final glance, and with him still looking away, his line of vision ending at his shoelaces, I believe Melody.

I will never doubt her again.

Pop puts the lid back on the gravy. "Take care of it, Johnny, okay? Enough is enough. We've let you play this game for years." He walks my way, says in a tone that none of us would mistake for anything but genuine sincerity, "No more." As Melody clings to my leg, I hope somehow he sees the little girl, the child I brought home for them to meet. How could he look at this innocent woman and want her dead? How does someone's sense of humanity devolve this far? I pray he sees it, understands, and agrees. He looks down at Melody, watches her breathe hard against my leg and suffer at our hand one final time, sees her get to live the nightmare from which she spent a lifetime running. And as he tilts his head and stares at her, for a few seconds I think he might see it, he might understand what I was trying to do, he might see the virtue, the beauty, the perfection in who she is. But then his expression turns to one of slight contentment, and my last thread of hope falls from the frayed end, drifts through the air, and vanishes. He turns to me and stares me down and says, "Put. A bullet. In the bitch."

Though I hear the words, I cannot fathom them, cannot comprehend how he could ask this of me. He has created a finality, has officially calcified my softer life of tiptoeing around the darker crimes and keeping away from the blood spatter. His words are the mortar binding the bricks in the new wall between us. I am no longer one of them, no longer know who they are. I am a stranger in my own home.

I wipe the moisture from my eyes, know that if I display the slightest hesitation, that if I do not play the part of an infuriated, determined killer, she will be put to rest by a more seasoned member of our crew. So *I* must become the actor, must hurt Melody in a way that convinces not only my family, but her as well.

And now the most difficult moment of my life: As Melody looks up at me with her tear-soaked face and says, "Please, Jonathan, I love you," I reach down and grab her arm and twist it, yank her up to her feet, then slam her against the wall. She squeaks as her back hits the edge of the doorframe. I feel like I'm going to vomit as she crumples to the floor and covers her face, overwhelmed by how many times she's been failed in this life, how she interprets my betrayal now as one more failure. As I lift her back up only to slam her into the corner of the room, I have to tell myself I am saving her life.

"Come here," I say, as I grunt and grab her by her other arm and haul her to the door. She lets her body fall limp, feels like I'm dragging her already dead body. My family watches the spectacle like a boring rerun. My objective is that they view my actions as determination, though the people I need to convince most are my father and Peter. As far as Gravina goes, I'll one day release the pressure from my newfound self-discipline and self-control upon him, make it last for hours.

I open the front door of the Tudor so fast and hard it slams against an antique coat rack, sends it to the floor in slow motion. I yank Melody to the Audi; she stumbles and falls the entire way. I open the passenger door and shove her inside, run around and hop in, lock the doors.

As I start the engine, I say, "Geez, Melody, I hope I didn't hurt you."

I back out of the driveway, whip the car around in the middle of the road, and fly down the neighborhood streets at twice the speed as when we drove in. Melody rubs her shoulder, tries to collect her thoughts.

"I'm so sorry, Melody." I ignore all the stop signs, pass idle cars. "Are you all right?"

She turns and looks at me, holds on to the door grip with all her strength, wipes the moisture from her face with her other hand. "I'm okay, I... think. Wait, you're... you're not mad?"

I wave my hand at her. "Look, here's what we're up against: If I didn't convincingly act out the part of the livid mafioso back there, they're going to send someone after us, make sure I close the deal."

"Kill me?"

"Yes. I don't have the greatest track record, if you recall. And being the guy who thought it was a clever idea to keep Morrison alive, they aren't going to let this slide unless I really appeared like I was going to take you out."

She swallows, hard. "But you're not going to kill me?"

Despite our need for escape, I turn and look at her, pull my foot off the gas. "Melody, it's hard to admit, but I love you. And I promised I would never hurt you—*never.* Do you remember? I promised you that when we first met."

"Yeah," she says, rubbing her shoulder again as if to imply, *Well, this kinda hurt.* She smiles and says, "But that was only, like, three days ago."

I turn back to the road and accelerate. "Yeah, well, it's a promise I've been keeping for twenty years."

She stops rubbing her wounds, stares at me.

"Look," I say, "I don't know how or why you met with the feds or how you managed to get to their operations center, but I know in my heart you love me." She doesn't respond. "Right?"

She reaches over and touches my knee, and as she is about to say something, I catch a glimpse of a familiar shape in my rearview mirror. I shake my head and say, "Predictable."

"What?"

"Guess I'm not taking home the Oscar. It's Peter."

If my father's insistence that I take Melody's life was mortar between the bricks, Peter's tailing us is the wall's capstone. Their reluctant tolerance of my defiance over the years, my loose rebellion and incapacity to conform to the full Bovaro stature, has come to a close. Only time will tell if they've lost their love for me, but for these it is now too late: They have lost their faith, and they have lost their trust.

Everyone has made their choice.

I know what was running through my father's mind: We've come too far, worked too hard to get through this nightmare to have one loose end get pulled and start the unraveling process. Peter begins closing in, speeds up the road in his massive black Chevy.

"I'm never gonna outrun him with that monster engine he's got." Melody turns around, watches the black mass fast approaching. "Though we do have one advantage." I check my rearview again, see him whip around a Honda, the body of his car tipping as he sweeps back into our lane. "We can outmaneuver him."

I quickly turn down a side road, drop the car from sixth to fourth and begin passing cars, take turns at speeds I know Peter could never replicate, would have him flipping the massive sedan off the street and into some suburban front yard.

Melody grips the door with both hands as we cross over a series of small hills, become airborne with each crest. Peter begins to fade as he slows on the turns behind us, pulls to the left each time he comes over a hill.

Peter and I both know these side roads well, have traveled them countless times, can anticipate every twist and turn, every unfilled pothole and blind corner—which means he knows where I'm heading: the Palisades Parkway.

As we hit a mile-long stretch of bends closely lined by century-old oaks, he's all but vanished.

By the time I get to the Palisades, he can't be seen. I drive so far above the speed limit that we're passing cars like they're static randomly broken-down objects in the lanes of the freeway. I care not about the other motorists, about cops, about careening across three lanes at a time; I care only about escape.

We get right back off the Palisades, hop on the New Jersey Turnpike driving south. Peter has disappeared; we've officially lost him.

We slow to the speed of traffic, about seventy, and try to merge into the masses, to blend. I stare ahead and begin trying to formulate a plan.

"Now what?" Melody asks.

I keep driving, keep staring: This is the exact reason emotion had no business influencing the course of her rescue plan.

"Now what?" she tries again.

"Why do you love me?" I ask.

She turns my way, studies me. "What do you mean? There's no *reason*, I—"

"No." I stare at the speedometer, watch the arm of the dial move counterclockwise as we slow. "You love me because I gave you freedom, Melody." I look in her direction, wipe my nose with the back of my hand. "I freed you from the chains and locks that have held you down your whole life. That's the only reason, because I gave you freedom." The dial steadies. "And it's okay."

She touches my leg. "That's not true. I love you because of who you are, the man you—I mean, look, because of what you're doing right now. You don't think I see what you're all about? You're risking everything for me." She squeezes my thigh, casually trumps me: "I will never doubt *your* love for *me*."

I have to get her to safety, have to throw together a plan—fast. I can't just return her to the Witness Protection Program, to the nationwide waiting room of death. "Oh... what are we gonna do?" I accidentally say loud enough for her to hear.

As our speed holds at sixty, she calms, leans over and kisses me on the cheek. "If we got married I couldn't testify against you."

I laugh. "That's cute in a naïve way. The feds would be watching us twenty-four hours a day—welcome to *my* world. And you'd still be able to testify against my family, which would guarantee a bullet."

I'm jammed up trying to understand how to sustain her newfound freedom. Everything's gone wrong. I don't see any more options left. The party's over. And we're the last to leave.

I quickly pull into the slow lane and exit the turnpike, wind us onto a side street and up against a curb. I take the car out of gear and pull up the emergency brake, turn to Melody. Her eyes are so full of hope, she wants me to deliver the next play to the offensive coach, pull us up from a fourteen-point deficit. Unfortunately, the clock has only five seconds remaining, and this is our last time-out.

I take in a slow breath, and in the exhale I say, "We just played the only hand we had, Melody. It's over."

She shakes her head. "What do you mean? What's over?"

"This. Us. It's over."

Her lips quiver; she purses them to keep me from seeing. "Over? It just started. I don't understand."

"Don't you see? You had two days of freedom and you became a new woman—the woman you should've been all along. Don't forget I've been watching you your whole life, Melody, and I saw the change, I know it was there. You're about to lose it all again."

She wipes tears away before they have a chance to run down her cheek. "We could get married," she offers again.

"You know we can't. No one will ever leave us alone. The feds. My family. Everyone will be hunting us down. There won't be a single day that passes where you won't wonder if your car's gonna blow or I've been murdered."

She reaches for my hand, lets the tears fall now, says more earnestly, "Then let's just run away together. Trust me, we can run. No one will ever find us. I feel safer with you than the feds."

I reach over and caress the back of her head and neck with my hand. "Melody, you've been running for over two decades, and you had professionals helping you. How long before they find you—*us*—again?"

"Then we can both go into Witness Protection together. You can testify against your family and—"

"Melody," I say, pulling her to my chest, "it's *over.*" I hold her tight, rock slightly as she cries. I stop praying for her and I to have a life together, begin praying I can simply find a way to rescue her, get her out of here and set her free. "Don't you see? If I go into Witness Protection with you it'll be even worse than before, with more lies, with an even bigger threat of getting killed. Double the risk. It'll never end, Melody. You'll never be free."

And what of testifying against my family? Where and how would it begin? That type of ordeal could never be contrived. I know the price for betrayal in my family, have helped force people to pay it; survival is not included in the fee.

Yet how one-sided it truly is. My family betrayed *me*, asked me to surrender a woman I not only wanted to protect, but claimed to have loved. Except business always comes first—over love, over family, over anything; sacrifice, remember, is poorly practiced within the Bovaro family circle. Were I to testify, where would the line be drawn? Behind me, with an arrow at the end pointing to a chalk outline.

As I hold Melody I get grainy glimpses of myself in Witness Protection, imagine the joy Gardner would get knowing where I was, how I'd fallen prostrate to the very program I spent years undermining. How Randall would so easily hand over my whereabouts to my family, exchange my address for a credit against losses incurred at the hands of the Vikings or the Lakers or the Red Sox. How he'd routinely check for any updated information on Melody and put that on the offering plate as well. Now she is forever doomed. My inside source just became the assurance she'd never be safe in the program again. I can't shake the image of Gardner having the most satisfying revenge against me, how quickly he'd return to pornographically capturing and selling his wife, gambling his salary right into my family's communal fist while I rot in a program with walls nowhere near high enough to protect me. My imagination takes me to the farthest edge of survival, how if I had to spend one second in the program, the first thing I'd have to do is out Gardner, serve him up to Justice on a platter with a frigging apple in his mouth. Oh, the repercussions of doing such a thing.

Of course: the *repercussions*.

This time God didn't make me wait, laid relief upon me like the hot sun upon Noah's saturated face.

I get the answer—and I *get* the answer.

I'm a chess player, envision the path of moves that will lead me directly to checkmate; my opponent could never see it coming.

Melody says something, her words muffled as she speaks them against my chest.

"Wait," I say, "hold on." Everything comes together, like a lifetime of research culminating into great discovery, a cure for the hopelessly diseased.

As the concept gets launched skyward like a firework, I follow it in my mind until it explodes, watch each sparking strand of potential outcome until every instance fizzles out completely, make sure not a single piece of hot ash hits the ground and causes a fire. I replay it again.

"What can we do," I think she says.

"Hold on."

Then again: The play unfolds. Like standing at home plate, I see every face from the opposing team watching my stance, trying to determine where and how I'm going to swing. But we've got men on base already. As much as I'd love to smack one out into the parking lot, I know the right thing to do is get my teammates home safe, to get them over the plate and raise the score. What choice do I really have? I'm going to have to sacrifice myself. I'm never going to make it to first base. Here comes the squeeze play.

I am going to rescue everyone—except Jonathan Bovaro.

TWO

Now that the reality of my only choice clarifies and crystallizes, I know I have mere minutes left with Melody. And once they expire, I will never see her again.

I fill the cab of our car with the fumes of false influence, do what I must to convince her that being with me is the worst thing she could ever want. "My family was gonna make me kill the woman I loved. Peter wasn't just following us to make sure I got the job done." I reach over and wipe her tears away with my thumb. "You see? We're running already."

She sits up, looks at me, then down. I put the car in gear and get us moving; she watches the landscape as we return to the interstate. "What're you going to do?"

I look over my shoulder as I merge into traffic, smear the moisture from my face on my shoulder in the process. "I'm gonna do what I promised you, Melody. I'm gonna *do what needs to be done.* I'm gonna keep you safe and free forever."

She holds on to her door with one hand and the center arm rest with the other, clutches them like she's in a dentist's chair, preparing for the drill. "Why are you driving so fast?"

"Because Peter and others from our crew are probably heading for my house and my restaurant to see if they can find me—and I need to beat them to my restaurant."

My desperate driving displays how I have not a single care left except getting Melody to safety, my own well-being safe-harbored in what will be my final act. I glance at my speedometer as I slip between two cars; we're going nearly a hundred. I slow only for tollbooths.

I fly over the empty roads, thankful for how easily we're traveling on this Sunday morning. Melody clenches her hands and teeth, winces as we fly by everyone and everything, holds on for dear life, her tears dried by fright. We cross the George Washington Bridge, quickly make our way to the BQE. By the time we wind down into Brooklyn, I begin slowing to a safer pace, and as we enter the Williamsburg section I've switched my preoccupation from speed to checking for familiar cars.

I turn down Grand Street, park in front of Sylvia and block a fire hydrant. I check every mirror, look up and down the street, keep the car running.

Melody stares out the window toward my restaurant, looks at nothing else, studies it like she's trying to memorize it. "This is your—"

"Stay here. Keep your head down. If I'm not back in sixty seconds, you drive away. Understand?"

She says nothing, swallows, nods.

"If I'm not back in sixty seconds."

Nods harder. "Okay."

I iterate through the mirrors and street views again, then bolt for Sylvia's front door. I whip it open, run by the tables where a dozen couples and families are dining, the smell of lasagne Bolognese growing in strength with every step closer to the kitchen; had I no knowledge of what day it was, I could tell you by the Bolognese, served only post-Mass on Sundays. This unedited masterpiece recipe was passed down from my mother, developed who knows how many generations ago, involves handmade noodles and layers of sauces and cheeses (the key is using a béchamel instead of ricotta). This creation, perfectly suited to a lazy Sunday and requiring the entire morning to craft and assemble, usually sells out by three in the afternoon. I will miss Ryan's perfect rendition of this dish.

I blast through the door to the kitchen, hurry through the bustling prep area, get a mix of distracted *Hey, Jonathan*s as I run to the very back where we accept deliveries, look out the door for Peter—or anyone else. Nothing.

I rush to my office, open up the safe and stare at the stacks of thousands of dollars waiting to be laundered, grab the small stack in the front, the clean, laundered batch waiting for Paulie's pickup. I go to the closet in the corner, pry open the disabled door and pull out an old dusty leather bag, shake it empty of the dried-up deodorant and toothpaste I used while the restaurant was under construction, fill it with the laundered stash. As I slam the door to the safe shut, reset the digital PIN and spin the tumbler, Ryan comes up behind me, says, "John, can I get sixty seconds?"

Problem is: I only have twenty left.

I brush by him, wave for him to follow. "Listen, I'm not coming back. It's all yours, Ryan. You're the talent here, turn this into whatever you want."

He stops in his tracks, shakes his head, and sighs like the disaster he always knew would befall the restaurant has finally arrived. "Wait—"

"You're already doing the hard part, Ry. Just pay the bills, keep the staff happy. I want to read about this place in the *Times*." Though, no doubt, he'll see me in it first.

"But, wait, don't—"

I put my arm around him, slap his back a few times. "You have not seen me at all today, *capice*?"

I look out the back door as I pass it on my way through the kitchen, see Peter getting out of his car, Tommy Fingers pulling up the alley.

I run out the front of the restaurant, hop in the car and toss the bag behind me, pop the clutch and have all four wheels squealing. Melody looks at me with uncertain relief. "They were coming in the back," I tell her. She slinks down in her seat, turns and watches the door of Sylvia as we speed away.

I push the Audi to its limit, speed around cars waiting at lights, cascade from side to side like a speed skater. I take the well-memorized maze of streets that will liberate us, liberate *her.* Berry. Metropolitan. Meeker. The BQE.

Melody seems certain I'm taking us to LaGuardia, her head twisting to watch the planes approach and depart in the far distance. But confusion shows on her face as she realizes we've turned in the opposite direction, intensifies as I pull off the highway and eventually wind us onto Livingston Street, and when I stop the car in front of the Greyhound bus terminal, Melody turns and squints.

"What's going on? What are we doing?"

I turn the car off and throw the flashers on. I get out, reach in the back and grab the bag with the money, walk to her side and pull her out of the car as I scan the area, watch every position, every angle.

Melody stumbles a little as I lead her inside the terminal. "Wait, are we—"

"You wouldn't get anywhere on a plane without identification. This is your only route of escape. Not to mention my family would never think to come here." Then, quieter, "Though I bet they sent people to LaGuardia, Kennedy, *and* Newark."

I hand her the bag. Melody looks inside, closes her eyes and slouches. The money implies the end as much as a suicide note.

"Should be about nine grand," I say. "That's all the money I had laundered; it's totally clean, untraceable. Not a lot, but it'll get you started."

She drops her hand to her side, holds on to the bag, and stares at me, waits for me to deliver the final blow, knock her out.

I can barely get the words out, swallow a lump so large I nearly choke. I look away and stare at the ticket counter, but I know I have to look her in the eye when I say this. I turn back and say, "Just go away, Melody. Just leave."

She shakes her head and cries, drops the bag and balls her fist up in my clothing. "No, Jonathan. I can't."

"Go somewhere you've never been before. Move to a town where I'd never guess you'd go, in case I weaken and try to find you."

She keeps her fists twisted up in my sweater, bangs me in the chest three times before falling into my arms and weeping. "Please, Jonathan, I'm begging you. I'm beg..."

As I feel my eyes fill, the burn in my nose, the thick paste in my throat, I have no idea how I manage to utter these words into her ear: "Never call me or my family again. Never call the feds or the marshals again. Never use any of your aliases again. Do you understand?" She weeps so hard I can feel the vibration of her jerky breathing against my chest. "Do you understand?"

Melody stops fighting, buries her wet face in my sweater. She goes limp, slips down as if she'd just died in my arms, her weight supported entirely by me. I feel her nod her head a little. Then, finally, "*Yes.*"

I kiss the top of her head and whisper, "This is the last time you'll ever have to run, Melody. I promise." I sigh with relief, feel composure returning as it seems she comprehends—and plans to comply with—what must happen.

All of a sudden, she regains her footing, pulls back, and stares me down. Her eyelashes are wet and clumped together, her eyes red, her cheeks pink from rubbing against the weave of my sweater.

"You knew, didn't you," she says. "You knew I might not be free to make the decision to leave if we'd made love."

And in that second all my composure vanishes. Can't explain why, but her understanding of this notion brings a wave of tears to me; one falls from each of my eyes at the same time. I swallow, step back a little. "I didn't want it to cloud your judgment. I just wanted what was best for you in case the worst happened." I shrug, smile a little as I wipe the tears away. "And the worst happened." She closes the gap between us and hugs me with whatever strength has yet to be sapped from her.

"You'll never be ripped from a lover's arms again," I say. "This will be the last time."

Melody looks at me, studies every detail of my face, of my expression, like she's trying to record an elaborate likeness, planning to repeatedly recall this detailed memory. Then she kisses me and I cannot draw back. It's not the aggressive, passion-fueled kiss of lovers leaving, but gentle and measured. She presses her lips against mine so softly I might've otherwise mistaken it for her first kiss, but then she presses slightly harder and I can feel the pressure of her tongue against mine, she runs her hands up under my sweater and shirt and slides her fingers up my back.

Then she stands on her toes, moves her mouth to my ear and whispers, "You were my first, Jonathan. You will always be my first." She looks at me and smiles, shows me who the tough one is right now, gives to me what I could not accept on my own.

And there it is: the image of Melody I will never be able to shake, the ineffaceable stamp in my brain, a memory that will never be erased or replaced. The image that every other woman over the remainder of my life will be compared to, the one to which they will suffer in comparison. The image of what could have been. The everlasting image, for I will no longer be able to watch her mature and age; she will remain twenty-six and beautiful and strong. The image that will run through my mind as I stare blankly out the window when the girl beside me asks, "Where are you?" and when I do not respond, she will further ask, "Is there someone else?" and I will let out a quiet sigh before eventually offering my answer: "Not the way you're thinking."

I hold Melody's hands in mine and begin to step backward toward the door, our arms lifting as the bridge between us lengthens. I smile and stare at her but she's so blurry now, the tears fogging my eyes and drifting down the sides of my face, that I can barely keep myself under control.

"No matter what's about to happen," I say, "this was all worth it." And as the tips of her fingers break free of mine, as I keep walking backward, she puts a hand to her mouth as she begins to cry again. "*It was all worth it.*"

As I turn and walk out of the terminal, Melody does not budge, watches me through the hazy window, her saddened and dead expression as apparent as when I saw her staring through the window of the A&P on the day her parents were murdered. I get in my car and sit there for a second, glance over and see Melody drop her head, pick up the bag, and slowly blend into the crowd of the terminal. She gets smaller and smaller until I can no longer decipher her from the other patrons in the busy building. How hard it is to keep from running back inside and stealing her away, allowing my selfish love for her to override her safety, to preclude her having any chance at a real relationship with a man who can give her the stability and care and innocent love that I could never offer.

I know I'll never see her again. For the first time in her life she's been truly emancipated—from my family, from the feds, and finally, from me. As the man protecting and stalking her for two decades, it makes me sick to permanently cut these ties, to know the woman I had always loved will open herself to be loved again by another.

I start my car and drift forward a car length so I'm positioned closer to the Enterprise Rent-A-Car next to the terminal. I stare out my window and watch mothers taking their children into Cookie's, a store dedicated to toys, clothes, and school uniforms for kids, and in my mind's eye I see a sequence of images of Melody taking her own to get measured for school uniforms, envision how her children would leave the store, stare up at the city around them, and spin in circles and smile with so much hope and happiness. Little Mary Tyler Moores, they would be. I drop my head to the steering wheel and bawl like a little kid who fell off a bike, all sloppy and wet and jerky. Looks like I may be a toddler after all.

When I eventually look up and gaze into the distance, as I face the looming future, I know I must finish this mission, complete this journey I've been traveling for most of my life. My family will never know where Melody is. The feds will never know where she is, and therefore Gardner will never know where she is. And the only thing left to do, the thing that will preclude any of them from trying to look for her, is what should've been done a long time ago.

I need to kill her.

THREE

I dry my face with the arm of my sweater and bottle my emotions, feel like I could burst at any second, as tightly pressured as a shaken soda. I drive away from the Greyhound bus terminal and realize I haven't moved this casually in some time. It feels strange to linger, to drift; I hesitate drifting *away*, for these are my final moments of peace, the last minutes I'll get to myself for some time.

I glide down the bus lane and watch for any familiar cars in the off chance my family figured out my plan. It takes a bit before I can clear my head enough to begin thinking practically; I must remind myself that although Melody has been released, she will not be free until I unfold the rest of my plan. I watch the buses pass and wonder if she's on one, wonder where she's going, fight not randomly following one in the way I followed the marshals to find her in Cape Charles.

As a bus disappears in front of a cloud of its own exhaust, I flip open my cell and call Gardner at home. It rings six times before he answers, and when he does he never says a word. I hear him open his front door, discernible by its squeaky hinges, hear the tap of the knocker as he closes it behind him. He takes loud footsteps down a sidewalk.

"Geez, *what*?" he whispers loudly.

"Bad time?" I ask. "I'm sorry if I interrupted your day."

"Yes, it's a bad time. Of course it's a bad time. It's Sunday aftern—"

"Randall, stop. You need to start recognizing sarcasm and ridicule."

He mumbles something profane, then: "I am *done* with you. You understand? Done running around and getting you information like some administrative assistant."

"Your addiction available? Put it on the phone. It has a far better sense of judgment."

He presses his mouth against his phone, says, "What would you say if I told you I'm making new friends, that I might not need you and your washed-up father and your nutcase brothers anymore, that I went to a competitor and they were interested in my product."

Poor Randall. He has no clue how useless he's become, how expendable he now is, how he should be enjoying every last moment he has with his family. "Best of luck with that," I say. "And let me give you a heads-up: My obvious indifference should concern you. Any chance you're bright enough to finally realize I was your lifeline all these years?" I hear a car drive down his street.

"Any chance you realize another family might be interested in what I know about all of you?"

I wish he could see the contorted face of annoyance I'm making, wish he was within my grasp so I could toss him around a little for old time's sake. "You know nothing, you *cacasodo*, but let me explain something: I kept you alive. Any other family's gonna take what they need, then toss you in the waste bucket."

"Yeah? We'll see. I'll just—"

"Look, I don't really care, Gardner. In fact, I hope whatever family you plan on working with is patient when they finally free your wife and children of the burden you've cast upon them for all these years." I take a deep breath and remove my glasses, wipe my forehead with the back of my hand. "I need one final piece of information from you and then we're done. This'll be the last thing I ever ask of you."

Big pause. "What do you mean?"

"C'mon, man, I got things I need to do."

"So this is it? One more thing and I'll be free?"

I didn't say *that.* I clarify: "Free from me."

"And my account will still be available?"

I roll my eyes, put my glasses back on. "You need help." He waits for a real answer. "I don't know. I don't care."

This seems to satisfy him. "All right, what is it?"

"Think back a week. Sean Douglas. The guy who was watching over my friend, the one whose information you located for me?"

"Yeah."

"I just need to know his office address and a number to reach him directly."

"Hey, Jim," he says to someone. A dog barks in the background. "That's easy enough." I hear him taking footsteps again. "That really all you need?"

"Yeah. And it's important I get it right away."

I hear the slam of a car door, the *ding-ding-ding* right before he starts the engine. "So what else is new?"

I sit and wait on a tree-lined street adjacent to Fort Greene Park, a half dozen blocks from the Greyhound station, stay sheltered under a pair of horse chestnut trees whose branches and leaves have blossomed and grown into one another like lifelong lovers, watch mothers stroll children along the sidewalk in front of brownstones to the west side. A coolness fills my body at the awareness of how I'll be leaving this area for good, that the unique architecture of these brownstones, of these areas where I spent my youth, will be available only through my memory.

Forty minutes later, Gardner calls, gets all excited about providing me the same information he gave me a week ago. I can sense the anticipation in his voice at my impending disappearance from his life.

"Sean Douglas," he says. "Birthday, October thirtieth. Current age, thirty-three. Home address is 453 Michaelson Lane, Towson, Maryland. Based out of the Baltimore office, 101 West Lombard Street, Baltimore, Maryland, Room 605. Marital status: unmarried. Current salary—"

"Four-fifty-three Michaelson," I repeat quietly, then to Gardner: "How about a phone number? Any private number, like a home or cell?"

"Only a pager."

Gardner says it slowly and I commit it to memory, have him repeat it twice to be sure.

"Why are you looking for the marshal?" he asks.

I sit and stare at my odometer, can't believe how many miles I've accumulated since I purchased this car. With the exception of the distances driven in and around New York, every mile traveled occurred during some pilgrimage of finding or hiding Melody. "You don't want to know." He doesn't respond. "But you'll find out soon enough."

He grunts and mumbles, could be translated as *whatever.* "So, that's it? I'm done?"

I back out of my spot and carefully pull onto Washington Park, begin winding my way toward the south side of Brooklyn, the opposite direction from the neighborhoods my family typically drive in or near. "Yes, Gardner. You're finally done." Though if I were being more honest: "Yes, Gardner. You're *finished.*" I hang up, drop my cell next to the gearshift.

I speed over to the Gowanus Expressway, cross the Verrazano and cut through Staten Island, pick up I-95 near Elizabeth, and begin the return voyage to Baltimore. With every mile southward the worry of being spotted by my family decreases, is replaced by the anxiety of what I'm about to do, with thoughts of wondering where Melody is heading, where she's going to live, how she's going to live, how she'll manage on her own. Having spent my adult life mapping and tracing, I can't stop formulating a way to find her, to figure her out. But my plan has already proven to be effective: I severed the tie with her and with Gardner's scope into Justice simultaneously; I'd have no idea how to even begin finding her now, no hope for knowing where it could end. I berated Gardner for his gambling addiction, yet I was so willing to ignore my own, and now that Melody is out of reach and out of sight—now that she is *out*—I'm getting the early indicators of withdrawal.

In an attempt to balance the fear of being caught against the anxiousness of wanting my plan in full motion, the farthest I make it is central New Jersey. As I pass the exit for New Brunswick, I call Peter's cell phone. It rings only twice.

"Johnny," he says, followed by a sigh. "What's goin' on?"

"You alone?"

"In my car, driving around. Wondering where you went. Why the rush, brother?"

"You're not gonna find me. Look, I can only talk for a minute."

"About the girl."

"She's gone, Pete. Gone forever." The absolute truth, though his interpretation will be: *I killed her.*

He doesn't respond right away. "Is that so."

"Our parting did not go well. It was a struggle to let her go." *She fought me to her death.*

Another delay. "Where was she relocated to?" *Where'd you dump her?*

"Lower East Side." *The East River.*

"She moved in the middle of the day, just like that?"

He's right: Dumping a body in the East River on a Sunday afternoon is not the easiest thing to do, especially alone, but we've done it before, being well acquainted with the most concealed spots, the trash-filled and polluted places so rarely visited. He knows it's possible, and if I had to dump a body fast, it would be there—especially now that he knows I don't really have the stones to carry a dead body around in the trunk of my car.

"Problem is," I say, "she left all her stuff in my car." *Her blood is everywhere.*

"No big deal, John. Come on back, we'll get all her—"

"I gotta get out of here, Pete. I don't think I can live without her." *I can't handle what I just did.*

"Relax, there's plenty of other fish out there." Not sure what the direct decoding of his statement is, but it comes across as a near-literal, so many dead bodies on the floor of that waterway. I hope they don't ever try to drag the East River, for my family's sake.

"I can't do it, Pete. I can't live with it. You know I was never built for a relationship like what I had with her." *You knew murder would be too much for me to handle.* "I'm out of here. I'm gone."

"What do you mean?"

"It's just too much."

"Slow down, let's talk. Where are you? Let me catch up with—"

"I'm gone, Pete. You're never gonna see me again."

"Wait, wait, wait—"

"Listen to me. This is real, okay? I want you to hear and comprehend every word I'm about to say."

My brother's sudden silence, his unexpected compliance, indicates he knows something sobering is forthcoming, something that will impact his life. The white noise of his car disappears; he has pulled over.

"All right," he says.

I take a deep breath and begin. "Understand this: No matter what you see or hear over the next few days, you trust me, you got it?"

Nothing.

"I need you to trust me, Pete. Pop would never go for what I'm about to do. And if this works, you won't just be a kid in a candy store; you'll be running your own chain. No matter what, you trust me."

He sighs quietly. "Why me? I'm the least trustworthy person in this family."

"Exactly. Now break Pop's trust for me and convince him what I'm doing is not going to hurt anyone." Except me.

I can hear Peter rub his stubbly chin, breathe off to the side.

"Also," I say, "I may give you a name in a few days. And if I do, I want you to take it very seriously." *Very seriously* was one of the first terms I learned as an adolescent, used to imply someone falling under our clumsy version of surveillance, followed by the inevitable slaying.

"Someone nearby?"

I don't have time for him to start guessing. I redirect: "Just remember I am not the bad guy, okay?"

"The candy store thing. I don't follow."

I contemplate whether I should declare this key component of my plan, how potentially empowering my solution may be for him, but I know it could only jeopardize it. "You'll understand soon enough."

"I'm not so sure—"

"Goodbye, Pete."

It feels weird to hang up on my brother—but not *unreal*. I'm like a snake that just shed a layer of skin. There are so many more left. I can only hope that if I shed enough layers I'll turn into something better than a slimy reptile.

I wipe the sweat from my forehead, take a series of deep breaths, wish I had a bottle of water to chug. I drive for miles and try to think of anything except where Melody is right now.

As I pass the exits for Trenton, I call Sean's pager, punch in my cell number, and wait.

Upon the first exits for Philadelphia, I finally get the call.

"Marshal Douglas," he says. His voice comes out strong, but weariness seeps through like he could use a nap. Or a drink.

I lick my lips, utter the first of my last words: "This is Jonathan Bovaro."

He doesn't respond, like he's waiting for a punch line. Then I hear him fumbling around as though he's trying to locate something—a pen and pad, a recorder, another person; who cares, really. Then he says, "Come again?"

"Jonathan Bovaro. Don't worry, I'm not going anywhere. Get what you need."

I stare to the side as I drive, notice how the setting sun is cut into slices by the towers in and around the metro Philadelphia area.

"What can I do for you?" he asks.

"You lose something recently?"

"Not exactly." He sighs. "I just lost, in general. Right?"

I can't decipher what he means; seems like he expects me to have some piece of information I don't possess.

"Where are you?" he asks.

I hesitate before answering, wait until a road sign with mileage estimates comes into view; Baltimore is eighty-nine miles away. "I'm roughly an hour and a half from downtown Baltimore."

"What's in Baltimore?"

"You are."

He hesitates like I might give more insight. "Okay. When and where?"

"I'll meet you at the top of Federal Hill, nine o'clock tonight."

"Federal Hill."

"I will not be armed, and have no intention of causing you any harm, okay? And please be alone."

"Nine o'clock."

I know he won't be alone, that others will be waiting in unmarked vans within a distance of accessible capture; they'll have to survey us among so many others in this popular public park.

Just after crossing the Susquehanna River in northeastern Maryland, I exit from the highway and drive toward the small water town of Havre de Grace, casually slip behind a strip mall distanced from the center of town, and pull up to a half-filled Dumpster.

I open my trunk, grab my overnight bag, and carefully remove Melody's bloodied sundress and place it on the front seat of my car. I empty all of her other clothes onto the ground—the jeans, the blouses, the undergarments—then pick them up and toss them into the Dumpster. I reach over, grab two bags of wet trash, and toss them on top of her clothing. I zip up my bag, toss it back in the trunk, and return to the highway.

As soon as I emerge from the southbound side of the Fort McHenry Tunnel, I exit onto Key Highway, creep toward downtown through the back streets of South Baltimore, and eventually land at Federal Hill. I park at the foot of the historic hill, slide my cell phone in my pocket, grab Melody's sundress, and climb the steep steps to the top.

I take a seat on a crumbling bench near the edge of the hill and stare down over the masses milling about the Inner Harbor, face the city in the exact opposite direction from when Melody and I stayed at the Renaissance. This spot, this view so high and unobstructed, is likely the location where 80 percent of all images of Baltimore's skyline are taken, the massive buildings curling around the harbor forming a steel and concrete comma, the lights reflecting off the placid water at the center to create a living postcard.

I watch the families and couples strolling and turning randomly, like ants crawling across a sidewalk. I sink with emotion when I realize that only twenty-four hours ago Melody and I strolled these very walkways, our minds filled with hope and possibility. I stare down at the harbor, now inhabited by two less ghosts.

To my right, a young family is sprawled across a large blanket. To my left, a drunk is passed out on a bench in better condition than mine. Three kids sit on their bikes and stare out over the water before departing to the south side of the city. Behind me, a group of men load furniture into a U-Haul from one of the historic row homes on Warren Avenue. Others walk up and down the staircases to the south and west sides of the hill. Then in the indistinct distance I see Sean come into view. With each step he emerges, first his head, then his body, then his legs. He scans the park until his eyes fall on me. He walks in my direction with a slowness that suggests exhaustion more than caution. And even now, as much as I need him to be one, he does not strike me as a marshal—neither tough nor serious enough. Were he a true marshal I could see him pouncing on me, despite my not having done anything overtly illegal, immediately setting the boundaries. Instead, Sean walks casually and glances once or twice at the harbor as he approaches. He's wearing jeans and a Towson University sweatshirt and scarred Doc Martens, looks like he hasn't shaven in a while, his hair all bent up and to the left as if it's been growing toward the sun.

He approaches, then stops and stands in front of me, blocks my view of the city, shadows me like a tree.

"You," he says.

"Have a seat." He does not comply. I stare at him for a few seconds before my words cripple him: "She's gone. I killed her."

I feel a dizziness at having confessed to something that, if the rest of my plan goes awry, might have me executed—but I can't unring the bell: I reach over and hand him Melody's bloodstained sundress, the result of her being tossed among garbage cans in the alley barely a mile from where we are at this moment.

Sean reaches for the dress and sits at the same time.

"I don't believe you," he says.

"She was trying to get information from me, wanted me to give her all sorts of details about my family. I tried to reason with her." I lower my voice as a couple passes. "She just wouldn't listen. It got... out of control. I just lost it."

Sean looks at the dress, spots the biggest bloodstain, avoids touching it. "I don't believe you," he repeats weakly. What he really means: *I can't believe it.*

"You keep DNA samples on all your witnesses?"

He sniffs hard, then mumbles, "Of course."

"It's gonna match. This is real." I take a deep breath, can barely speak the lie because it could've so closely been the truth had I not spirited Melody away. "She's spread all over the East River. She's gone."

To the dress, he says, "You're full of it. You don't have it in you, Bovaro." Then to me: "Anyone else in your family, but not you."

"Why do you think I'm here talking to you? I can't live with this. You think I'm confessing for entertainment?"

Sean studies the stain again, slowly turns the dress and sees another red blotch. He swallows and looks away, focuses on the drunk. I read his demeanor as nothing other than his own perceived failure, a witness lost because he couldn't contain the danger, couldn't sell the dream.

I swallow, almost gag on my request: "I want to talk to Justice. I have information they'll want, but one thing in particular they'll *need.*" Sean does not seem moved. "I'll confess to killing Melody, no reneging." Fake sigh. "I have to live with what I did. I'll also give up all the details on how the McCartneys were killed. I was there, and I'll tell them exactly what happened. But most of all, I'll supply you with information that will give Justice headlines for a year straight. I'm not exaggerating." And then, another ring of the bell: "But I want to go into Witness Protection. I want to start over."

Sean turns back and looks me in the eye; it takes so much strength to return his stare, to convince him that my actions are genuine. Though I quickly realize that the way he's looking at me might have something to do with my poor choice of words: *Start over.* My guess is the utmost concern of any witness entering the program is *being kept safe*, not getting a new identity, the mere means for achieving the safety. He stands up, gently places the dress over his shoulder, waves for me to get to my feet. His repugnance for me has carved a sneer into his sullen face; I recognize when an adversary can barely contain himself.

"Let's go," he says. I slowly stand, feel a little vertigo at the realization that I've not only surrendered Melody, but I'm about to surrender myself, that whoever I become, Jonathan Bovaro will soon disappear forever.

Sean glares at me, for the first time comes across as something more than an unqualified marshal. "I hope your family kills you," he says, "I really do. I hope you don't make it another twenty-four hours."

He turns slightly and waves his hand for me to walk next to him. As we get to the edge of the hill, one of the streetlights catches the metallic edge of the handcuffs clipped to the side of his jeans, partially tucked into a back pocket. The fact that he's not using them is a bad sign.

We descend the staircase together, not a word between us. When we arrive at the bottom of the hill, he escorts me to my vehicle, doesn't have to ask which is mine.

"Last shot," he says, staring off and away. "Get what you need."

I look at the Audi like I'm leaving a dear friend at the airport. I open the trunk, grab my bag, then slam it shut. As we're halfway to Covington Street, en route to his black government SUV, I say, "Wait!"

I run back to the passenger side of my car, open the glove compartment and pull out the CD case, and take with me the entire library of discs that served as the soundtrack to my finding and protecting Melody, the discs purchased when I followed her through Best Buy, the discs that will allow Melody to speak to me forever.

Sean stays close, watches as I take the case and jam it into the pocket of my overnight bag. I gaze around the perimeter of where we're standing, where his vehicle is parked, tucked in an angled spot across from the American Visionary Art Museum. Turns out Sean kept his promise: He came alone. No one is around to help him. No one is around to watch him open the back door of his Explorer for me, and no one is around to see him check up and down Covington before he slams my head into the doorframe of the SUV, twice. There is no backup, no other marshals, no one else who took an oath to protect and serve as he punches me three times in the face. No one to see that I let him do it, that I merely curl up in a ball and allow his fists to hammer me. No one to notice that I never ask him to stop.

FOUR

Sean shoves me into the men's room on the sixth floor of the Garmatz Federal Courthouse, pushes me so hard I go sliding across the floor and bang my head into the pipe under one of the sinks. Just as the door closes, he says, "Clean yourself up."

I right myself by holding on to the sink. The thing shimmies and shakes, feels like I might rip it right out of the wall as I use it to pull myself up. When I finally see myself in the mirror, the damage doesn't look as bad as it feels. Sean apparently learned as I did that the best way to bruise someone is behind areas covered by clothing: the blows to my body. I have a large lump across my forehead from where he rammed it into the door of the Explorer, blood crusted around both nostrils, and three cuts along my left cheek from his punches to my face. But the real soreness resides in my chest and sides from where he rained down blow after blow until a tour bus turned the corner near Covington and startled him out of his rage.

I turn on the faucet and let the water run over my hair and face, into my mouth. I spit out a pinkish pool of fluid, wipe myself dry with a handful of paper towels, gently dab some of the dried blood from my skin. I rub my rib cage where the pain is most intense, wince as my fingers brush my left side, wonder if I have a cracked rib.

I walk out to the hall and Sean is standing with his back against the wall, staring at his cell phone. The building is quiet and empty at ten-thirty on this Sunday evening.

Sean ignores me, takes another minute to finish whatever it is he's doing, then suddenly snaps his cell shut and looks up. "C'mon," he says, and starts to walk down the hallway.

"Can I get something to drink?"

"Shut up. You're not in Witness Protection yet. If you think I'm gonna wait on you, you're out of your mind. You want a drink? Go stick your head in the toilet."

We make our way to the end of the hall and he opens the last door before the stairwell, flips on a light to display a conference room that could seat fourteen people around one long rectangular table. He flips another switch and the blinds drop across all seven windows and the lights of Baltimore's skyline slowly disappear. At the farthest end of the room is a one-way mirror wide enough to house an entire Hollywood film crew behind it.

I take a few steps toward the table, rest my hand on the back of one of the plush leather chairs. Sean walks to a computer in the corner of the room, spends a minute typing something, then disappears through the door leading to whatever is on the other side of the one-way mirror. For a marshal, he seems awfully comfortable around the facility and its components. I'm not really sure what I expect of him, but it's not this: a man with the keys to the kingdom, able to run the show.

I sit down in the chair at the end of the table and sink into the seat. I rest my damp head against the back of the chair, and just as I close my eyes for a few seconds, Sean reappears through the first door again. As he walks my way, he chucks a bottled water in my lap.

"This room will be full by daybreak," he says, then sits down several seats away from me. "People coming from all over—New

York, DC, Baltimore, of course. You better have something really interesting to say." He stares at me like he might lunge toward me, give me one more round.

"It's gonna be bigger and better than anything they could imagine."

He wipes his face. "This is your big moment, Bovaro. Enjoy it. People are going to care about you, really love you, all the way through getting you deposed. Then you'll return to being nothing. Same loser, different name."

I sit up a little, want to help him understand that his annoyance has more to do with the fact that he'll be ushered out when the real dealmaking and information transfer begins. Instead, I rest back again and say, "You don't like us much, do you?"

"You *who*?"

"Criminals who flip on their own."

Without any hesitation: "Hate you. Really takes all my strength to provide even the thinnest protection. The few witnesses in this program that are innocent—people like Melody and her parents—I love 'em. They're braver than anyone you know, possess a willingness to sacrifice and a commitment to doing the right thing that you'll never understand."

I wish I could correct him, want him to know he and I might have more in common than he thinks. I spent twenty years of my life committed to successfully protecting Melody—something he failed at after only a few days.

I stare back, spill my thoughts. "You know you're a terrible marshal."

He narrows his eyes and grins slightly, then drops his eyes, spins his wedding band around his finger.

"When you phoned me," he says, "you asked if I lost something. I didn't lose anything." He looks back up at me. "She walked away."

Melody's fast confession in the kitchen of my father's house floods my mind. I so easily recall the panic on her face as she offered up the scattered details of those loose hours lost from the spa.

I slide down in my chair. "You guys offered her a deal to turn on me," I say. Everything she said, all genuine. I hate that I let even the slightest doubt cross my mind, feel a deepening of sadness at losing her forever, knowing her love for me was so real that she gave up having the best of everything the government could offer in order to remain with me.

Sean nods a little. "They were going to give her the ultimate incentive." He goes back to spinning his wedding band. "Any town, any job, any money."

I stiffen. That precise definition of her deal wasn't just Gravina's general description of what'd been offered to Melody; those were his *exact words*: any town, any job, any money. I process the information over and over, my eyes dim and mouth open like I'm about to sneeze, except something far more jarring is brewing. I lean forward, put my elbows on the table, intertwine my fingers and start cracking knuckles, need to find a way to call Peter and tell him *the name* he needs to take *very seriously*, give him the proper direction to vent his impending indignation.

"But," Sean adds, "once you'd brainwashed her into thinking you cared about her, and by the fact that she'd truly grown weary from being in this program her whole life, she apparently wanted nothing to do with it any longer. Wouldn't even listen to what they had to say." He leans forward, points a finger. "And the result of her decision was her own murder."

"If only she'd had a marshal capable of protecting her."

Sean leaps out of his seat like he's going to grab me by my shirt and toss me out the sixth-floor window, but he merely reaches in his back pocket. I assume he's grabbing the cuffs, throwing a tantrum by suddenly going by the book and locking me down to the table. Instead he pulls out what looks like a wallet and chucks it against my chest.

It bounces onto the table and falls open backward, displays a gold badge and identification bearing his picture and name—for the Federal Bureau of Investigation.

"I'm with the Organized Crime Unit. Have been for most of my career." I leave the badge on the table, try to assess his angle, the second time today I've been forced to reevaluate everything I thought I understood—though this assessment requires far less analysis. And as I quickly comprehend what has happened, how things have been so badly manipulated, I don't even realize I've left my seat.

"Wait a minute," I say. "Melody was set up." Sean slowly reaches over and takes back his identification, slides it in the pocket opposite the cuffs. "You used her."

"It was an experiment," he says. "And it failed."

Sean sits down, points to my chair, and I do the same. He explains how he was a member of a small group of pioneers within Justice (those who carried disdain for the group termed them *rebels*)—a hybrid of its divisions and offices, but mostly comprised of FBI agents—who proposed breaking the rules, and some laws, to infiltrate three principal areas: child pornography, drug trafficking, and organized crime. He tells me how he started working to bring down child pornographers and pedophiles, how it made him sick enough that he had to move on, generated an anger and rage in him that he redirected toward the Mafia. He studied and learned everything he could about the Italian organizations, memorized every chart and every member of every family operating up and down the East Coast.

A year earlier, the group conjured the idea of manipulating a single witness in WITSEC—the United States Federal Witness Protection Program—into unwittingly becoming a lure, as bait to draw the Mafia closer, to catch them acting on a federally protected witness, with the notion that it would create a frenzy of one member folding on the other. The small group viewed the countless bad guys turned witnesses as a bucket of juicy worms to hang from their giant fishing pole. And all they needed was one worm. The idea was to take a single witness who'd been a member of one of the families, someone they callously viewed as expendable from *both* sides, and set the mousetrap.

Except.

Except they could never find the right witness at the right time, waited years for the perfect scenario to present itself. And during these years, two things occurred simultaneously: an increasing angst at nailing the largest families in New York, and annual federal budgets where funds were increasingly redirected from organized crime to terrorism. They became desperate—I argue it was an issue of job security, but Sean explains it was truly about bringing justice—and they decided they were going to pull in a prizewinner without getting a fishing permit.

And then: little Melody. The woman with whom I fell in love grew bored of her surroundings at the absolute wrong time. The nadir. When Melody called in to the Marshals Service and the FBI was notified, the handler she'd dealt with most of her life explained—lied—that he was going to retire and a younger, more able marshal was going to take her case.

In walked Sean Douglas, a strapping and powerful man who, while fully capable of protecting her, played the part of the aloof buffoon, the only marshal in the history of the service who didn't fit the part, who didn't possess the power to take your life with a punch to your face, the red umbrella in the sea of black ones. The toddler.

"When you found her in Cape Charles," he says, "you think we didn't know you were there?" I feel like I could throw up. When I don't answer, he adds, "I mean, c'mon, I kept making excuses while driving down Route 13 to let you catch up."

"No way. I saw the marshal with your caravan who ran into the convenience store on the Delmarva. That guy was the real deal."

"Indeed, he was. Had no clue I was undercover."

I clench my fist so hard my nails dig into my palm. "I hope one day you have to be protected by the guys you duped."

He ignores me, continues, "When you were so cleverly sneaking into her room in Cape Charles, I sat on the beach on my cell phone talking to agents parked a hundred yards out, who were giving me each and every detail of what you were doing."

I take a deep breath, attempt to suppress the desire to make my first kill. I utilize my last strand of self-control as this realization washes over me: "But...you let me enter her room. I could've killed her right on the spot."

He takes a deep breath and lets it out in measured pulses. "It shouldn't have been Melody. I was against that."

"Oh, *you were against that.*"

"It was a poorly estimated risk. But we did what we had to do."

"And to get to my family, you would have let me kill her?"

"I didn't say that."

"But you knew it could happen."

"Not with you. Part of estimating the risk was knowing that you, of any member of any crew in the five boroughs, had virtually no capacity to kill. You were the ultimate actor for the part, Johnny. Like I said, this was the perfect scenario, and it was handed to us."

I wave him away with the back of my hand. "But you knew it could happen."

He keeps his eyes on mine but licks his teeth like his mouth is getting dry. "We knew." Now he looks away. "It should not have been Melody." He bites the inside of his cheek, then adds, "I really liked her." An entire minute passes before he completes whatever memory of her he's recalling. "I mean, I really did." He looks up at me again, repeats, "Shouldn't have been Melody."

I look at the clock and notice midnight is approaching, feel exhaustion setting in, taking over. "But it was. She was an innocent witness. Where's all the *love* for innocent witnesses you spoke about earlier?"

He raises his voice as his justification becomes as fatigued as I am. "We can't play by the same rules. You get to break the laws and we have to capture you while abiding by them. We're both playing football here, but Justice isn't allowed to have a passing game."

As the hatred returns, I get the notion that what my family does is bad, but only notable because we're higher up the scale, that we aren't the bad guys; we're the worse guys. This entire exchange with Sean brings the anguish back to my mind, has me recalling the very day I inadvertently made Arthur and Lydia and Melody McCartney vulnerable, how that cop manipulated a little boy to get what he needed, a scared kid who wanted to do the right thing to protect the girl with the blond curls and make sure she and her parents were safe, how the cop lied to me, said whatever he had to so he could gain my trust. So he could break my trust.

Maybe Sean is different—his anger and violence toward me at the notion I'd killed Melody certainly seemed genuine—but his remorse does not displace the risk he thrust upon her in the first place. I stare at him, see his pathetic look of regret covered by an opaque, synthetic smugness.

He bores me with a tale of his true incompetence, how they really did lose her in West Virginia—I never confess to where we were all that time—and how it became nothing more than a matter of "coming back to Baltimore to regroup and wait for further instructions from DC."

I'm tired and hungry and in need of a rush of nicotine. I haven't wanted to destroy someone this badly since Gregory Morrison. I take a drink of water, slowly twist the cap back on, and say, "I think it'd be in your best interest to put those cuffs on me."

FIVE

I wake up slouched over the conference room table, my arm asleep and head pounding from dehydration. I take a drink and notice two men sitting at the far end of the table, pads out and already scribbling, too blurry to decipher anything distinct about them; they're all the same anyway. The clock reads 4:23. I rest my head on the edge of the table again and immediately fall back to sleep.

Just before six, I wake to chatter occurring at full volume. Sean wasn't kidding; the room is filling with professionals of every age and size, all requested to arrive early on this Monday morning. At quick glance I count seven people, but two of them, one man and one woman, are the folks running the show, the pair everyone goes to for answers, to receive orders and direction.

I sit back and yawn, take the last sip of water from my bottle.

Someone asks over the din of conversations, "Can we get you some coffee? Can't smoke, unfortunately—this is a federal facility."

I see: We can risk the lives of protected witnesses, but heaven forbid someone picks up a lungful of sidestream smoke. Good thing I gave it up or we'd be having an argument.

"Coffee, yes," I say, rubbing my eyes. "Lots of caffeine."

As I speak these first words, people look my way and stare. It takes me a minute to realize they're looking at Sean's handiwork, the bruises likely reaching full autumn colors. I've taken worse beatings, nothing worth noting.

One of the younger guys in the room pours a cup from an insulated canister with a Pfefferkorn's logo on it and carefully places it before me. As I take a sip I recognize the flavor as genuine; Pfefferkorn's supplied the coffee for the Italian restaurant where I lost Melody the first time, when Sean scooped her up to see what information she had to offer, when they were going to pull the plug on their misshapen operation. What they didn't plan on was her allegiance swinging my way, could've never imagined it—and ultimately losing her for real. It makes this coffee all the richer.

As I slowly drink and wake up, people take their places. Sean sits in the far corner away from the table, looking more distraught and burned out than he did at midnight, his beard having thickened in the time we've been in this room.

The size of this group confuses me. I've heard countless stories of folks in our clan being pinched, and in the most extravagant instances never more than two or three guys were working them over at a time. I might think Sean somehow orchestrated this scene, brought together as many people at once, to record every word I have to offer, to carve it in stone and make it irrefutable—except I catch him occasionally staring at the group and failing to hide a sneer, an eye roll.

As the seven take their seats—who knows how many are behind the glass—the guy who got me the coffee stands and points to the person next to him and begins introductions. "To your left is Alison Margrove, assistant to the—"

"Please," I say, "no offense, but I could care less. Who's in charge?"

The man and woman—*the two*—look at each other. The man says, regarding the lady next to him, "This is Ellen Mayes. She's representing the Office of the Attorney General." He pauses like I'm going to say *nice to meet you.* I shrug. "I'm William Ciacco, Department of Justice."

"Pig," I say.

Everyone turns and looks at me, a few gasps slip out.

"How's that?" he says.

"Ciacco"—I pronounce it authentically, correct their leader's Americanizing of the word: *chock-oh*—"means pig." But with a name like William, it's unlikely he was brought up on the streets of New York or Philly. "*Non è stata colpa mia, Guglielmo.*"

William rolls his pen between his fingers a few times, bites his lip a little, mumbles, "I don't, uh..."

Of course he doesn't. "Aye, Yankee."

"Should I have a translator join us?"

I sit back in my chair and rub my chin, catch a glimpse of Sean sitting forward with his elbows on his knees, looks like he is equally annoyed with both me and Ciacco, disturbed by this entire setup.

"No," I answer. "Let's just get this over with, Pig."

He puts his pen down and shifts in his seat. "Just to set our boundaries here, the people in this room control your fate, your future. I think an environment of mutual respect is in order. And I'd prefer that you call me Mr. Ciacco, even William or—"

"Not likely, Pig. The people who control my fate, the real people running this show, are behind that mirror. Here's the real deal: I control *your* future. Already have. What time you get out of bed today? Have a nice ride up the BW Parkway at three in the morning?" Ciacco clicks his teeth, looks like he might want to hear what I have to say before bullying. "I'll bet those forthcoming headlines and commendations are making it hard to keep the drool from dribbling out of your mouth." I roll my empty water bottle down the center of the table in his direction, it stops a foot short of his notepad. "Now, how 'bout you turn that into a San Pellegrino for me?"

By eight o'clock I've spilled the entire story of how the elder McCartneys met their demise, gave them all the details of how crazy Ettore was, how I could barely stop him from killing Melody, too—but how I was equally to blame, having taken part in the planning and ultimate execution of those federal witnesses.

The Pig and his minions were equally aggravated and uninterested in my story of how a man already in his grave performed these murders. Even more so at this:

CIACCO: "Your father, Anthony Bovaro, ordered these hits?"
ME: "Who knows."
CIACCO, frustrated: "We're assuming you do."
ME: "I was too young. And Ettore was a loose cannon, probably took it upon himself to kill them to impress my father. Did my dad want the McCartneys dead? I don't know. Did he want them to keep their mouths shut? Absolutely. Do I have proof? Not a lick."

Now at nine o'clock, as I am falsely confessing to Melody's murder, the folks around the table are getting more and more excited, their writing suddenly fervent, whispering in each other's ears, occasionally shooting glances toward the one-way mirror.

Everyone appears to be buying it. I have them all captured, hand them details of murder and disposal and evidence (the blood-spattered dress) that could only be offered up by someone who had lived around it all his life: how to clean up a bloody scene, how to wrap a body to keep the trunk of a car free of evidence, the places on the river where the current's pull is the strongest. The only person who seems elsewhere is Sean; his eyes are locked on me, I can see him in my peripheral vision. He appears to be the only one in the room who might've detected how my retelling of Ettore killing the McCartneys bothered me more than the fictional story of how I murdered Melody.

But after an hour of offering particulars and evidence of so many sorts, it has become incontrovertible; I nearly convince *myself.* Ciacco could never be ticked at his early arrival after this event. He's so enamored with the details unfolding that neither he nor his team attempt to refute a single fact. And why would they? What could be better than a mafioso too weak to handle the crime he's committed? How could it get better than this?

Oh, but it does.

I've become so hungry I'm truly getting weak and distracted; acting remorseful for Melody's murder might be more exhausting than if I'd had to face real remorse. And our proximity to Little Italy, just a few blocks away, has me all the more preoccupied.

After all the questions regarding Melody and the McCartneys have been exhausted, Ciacco immediately starts probing about my family, about what I'm prepared to surrender for a government-paid relocation and the respective protection.

"I need a notepad," I say, "and a half hour to think. I'm gonna write down every name that will matter to you. I don't want to forget anybody or anything."

Ciacco sits up like a kid who's just been told he's having pizza for dinner instead of boiled Swiss chard. The implication is that I'll be offering up every murder that just occurred up and down the East Coast, the full story behind my family's attempt to preempt Justice's full-blown takedown of the Bovaros, that I'll be handing them the ace in the hole that my father would've never anticipated.

“Very well,” Ciacco says as he pushes his chair back and stands. “This is a good time to take a break.”

Before he takes a step, I say, “There’s a corner deli in Little Italy that sells fantastic pepper and egg sandwiches. I recommend a dozen of those.” Ciacco slouches, had no intention of pampering. I turn and look at Coffee Guy. “How about you? You like a nice grilled panini?” He does this smile/shrug/nod thing. “Treat yourself to one. I tell you what, I’ll write the address down for you.” I turn back to Ciacco. “Now where’s that pad?”

A big glob of wet scrambled egg falls from my sandwich onto my notepad as I scribble away. Coffee Guy groans a little as he swallows a large mouthful of his snack, a panini pressed together with roasted porchetta, provolone and Locatelli cheeses, and enough basil for a pot of marinara. His bite forces a chunk of tomato out the other side and he quickly scoops it up and shoves it in his mouth like an addict unwilling to waste a single milligram of his drug. This is the quietest the room has been since I arrived here nearly twelve hours earlier. Everyone chows—even Ellen and the Pig are fairly distracted with it—except Sean, who merely sips coffee and watches me. I can sense he wants to finish what he started out on Covington. Well, if he hates me now . . . just wait.

As the clock approaches eleven, my stomach full and my palate satiated—let’s call it my last meal—I tell them I’m ready to name names and confess to crimes committed. Everyone cleans their area, tosses their trash into a metal can in the corner. The room smells of olive oil and stale coffee.

I look down at my pad, satisfied with everything I’ve written, provided enough information to blow their minds. The fuse is set, and I light it as I hand my pad to Coffee Guy. He takes it but does not look at it, merely hands it to the lady next to him, who hands it to the guy next to her. The pad slowly moves along the table, the fuse burning down with every body closer to Ellen and Ciacco. And when it reaches Ellen, she places it evenly between her drink and Ciacco's.

The Pig studies it, turns a hand up in confusion, starts flipping pages to read all the notes I have on this solitary individual, everything I ever knew, addresses, dates, conversations.

"One name," he says. "This isn't a list. Where's the list? This is one name." He looks down at the top page, with the single person's moniker on it, and says, "And who the hell is Randall Gardner?"

Kaboom.

From the corner of my eye, I see Sean lean forward and put his coffee cup on the table, slide to the edge of his chair, stare and frown at me.

Within seconds everyone in the room is startled by a tap on the mirror—from the other side. Ciacco gets up and walks through the adjoining door, disappears for five minutes. I don't say a single word. Everyone follows suit.

By eleven-thirty the energy that once crackled around the table has fizzled to the intensity of a sparkler. Ciacco and Ellen sit and stare forward in defeat as the room empties, like two teenagers caught throwing a party by parents who arrived home earlier than expected. No one is behind the glass anymore, the door wide open, the lights off. Ciacco, Ellen, and Sean are now joined by each of their respective superiors: the people from behind the glass. I unravel the entire story, elaborate on the details covering the subsequent pages beyond Gardner's name. I explain how his gambling addiction was firmly in place before Justice promoted him to handling more sensitive data, how the salary they provided was not enough to offset his recurring losses, how I became as dependent on him as he did on me.

When the doubt and disbelief begin to emerge—the denial that their system would permit this to ever happen—I ask the simple questions, turn Socratic to help them understand.

How would I even know who Randall was or what he did for a living?

How could I supply such detailed and correct information, like addresses of the specific buildings where he worked, the specific database system they utilized, and details of what he did and did not have access to?

And best of all: "How could I have possibly known so many locations where Melody had been relocated at exactly the right time?"

Ciacco sighs with his teeth clenched, makes a whistling sound. "So that's it?"

"Sorry?" I say.

"You have no other information you'd like to share about your family? Perhaps starting with the recent disappearances of Manny Pastulo, Salvatore Foresi, or Vic Panella?"

"Oh, no. Nothing like that."

Ciacco taps his fingers on the table a few times, then scratches his head and says, "Rest assured we'll be interviewing Mr. Gardner in short order, and discipline will be applied as needed. However, what you're offering us as far as *information* is a pair of murders committed by someone who's already deceased and a confession of a murder committed by you." He laughs a little as he stands. "I'd say you're not a likely candidate for the Witness Protection Program." As he walks toward the door he adds, "I'd find yourself an excellent lawyer."

I stare at the guy at the end of the table, an oversized gentleman in a well-tailored suit, and ask, "Where's he going?"

He stares back, keeps his fist to his mouth, but Ciacco answers, "I've got more important things to do."

As his hand finds the door handle, I say, "Sit down, Pig."

Ciacco steps back into the room, points a finger in my direction, but Oversized Guy throws his hand up, taps his fingers in the air, signals for Ciacco to take his seat again.

He hesitates but reluctantly obeys, flops in his chair and folds his arms like a scolded child.

"Are you all paying attention?" I ask the group, but look at Sean. Only Oversized Guy nods.

I take a sip of cold coffee and tell them exactly what I'm offering in exchange for being put in the Federal Witness Protection Program: absolutely nothing.

Before I had Randall wrapped around my finger, he slipped, bragged about the new details he could suddenly offer me and my family for a lousy six grand. And Gardner, having the particular personality God gave him, made the mistake of using that offering to imply he was on even playing ground with the Bovaros.

Do you recall the visit Peter and I made that day, when my brother slammed Gardner's face against the keyboard and the plastic keys stuck to Randall's forehead? After our point was made and Peter and I walked out toward the car, I stopped in my tracks, startled by a fantastic revelation. I turned around and told Pete I'd catch up in a minute.

I knocked on Gardner's door, and the second he opened it, I shoved him inside. "I want the whole list," I said.

"What're you talking about?"

"You want a free ride with this family? You want protection? I want the list. The entire list."

"I gave what you want"—referring to Melody's name and location at the time—"there's nothing else."

"No, you don't get it. I want the list of every person in the program. I want their names and addresses."

Gardner gagged, skin white and sweaty like a little punk caught in a lie. "I can't do—"

"Sure you can. You already have. I've got Melody's address—and you can supply the rest."

"Are you insane? That's thousands of—"

"I don't care. I want that list."

I remember the look of regret on his face, the last time I ever saw a shred of remorse come over him, the look that suggested his entire life just got flushed down the toilet.

Then, weakly: "I can't."

"You will."

"Every name, every address, every witness," I tell the group.

"Impossible," Ellen says.

"Thousands of witnesses. Honestly, I can't believe how many people you have in this program. Though it hardly matters now. Randall's addiction got the better of him and here we are. Would you like me to tell you how many copies I made?"

The group has become so quiet I can hear Ciacco breathing through his nose. Every eye before me is filled with either fear or fury. Two hours ago I was beloved, hidden treasure found and ready to be converted to currency; now at least half of them are wondering how they can take my life without anyone finding out. Only Jesus could have felt more loved and despised than I have today.

Sean abruptly breaks into laughter. "You gotta admit," he says, "that's pretty funny."

"That's enough, Agent Douglas," Ciacco says.

"You freaking losers."

"Remain calm, Sean," Ellen says.

Sean gets up from his chair and points at his bosses. "I'm talking about *you* guys. Do you see yet? You will *never* take them down unless you break the rules. If this isn't proof I don't know what is. You've got to do whatever it takes to make it stop!"

And then, clarity: This is why he came alone to Federal Hill. He wanted no record that he ever met me, no one else to know what might happen. Who knows what his original intentions might've been.

"You want to become like them, Douglas?"

Sean wipes his face, continues his hands right through his hair. "Golly, I guess you're right. I'm sure an injunction will do the trick." Then, to me: "Mr. Bovaro, sir, would you kindly hand over the data and cease any plans for distribution?"

"Enough." Ciacco gets defensive like he's the guy who wrote the law, puts his frayed edges on display: "We've been bending the rules as far as we can. For years. Do you have any idea how long it took us to get inside their crew? The things we had to do, to promise?"

I snap to attention, flip a finger in Ciacco's direction. "You mean Eddie Gravina?" I say. Every eye comes my way, the most certain sign that my hunch was right on the money. "I'm afraid Eddie won't be with us much longer. Hope you got everything you needed out of him."

Sean kicks his chair back and throws his Styrofoam cup across the table, but because it's empty it just floats up in a circle and gently spirals to the ground. Even his anger is impotent.

Sean walks to the mirror and leans his back against it. Oversized Guy stares at me, leans forward and says so quietly it seems like he wants no one else in the room to hear, "So, where are we right now?"

I think for a moment and carefully select my words. "You got two choices," I say. "You can meet my demands—I only ask three simple things—or the list goes public, which I imagine would result in you having to relocate every single person in WITSEC at the exact same time, seems like the only option you'd have after I made sure the list was widely disseminated."

"You're out of your freaking mind," Ciacco says.

"How much does it cost to relocate a witness?" I ask.

"That information is classified."

"About a hundred grand," Sean says, rubbing his temples. "Minimum."

"Wow," I say. "So we're talking about hundreds of millions of dollars in relocations. Does Justice have that kind of extra cash in its budget?"

Oversized Guy responds calmly again, though his voice is slightly louder. "So let me get this straight: You're trying to extort the Department of Justice?"

"Don't patronize me. When we do it, it's extortion. When you guys do it, it's leverage. I don't care what you call it. It's real, either way."

Ellen rests back in her chair, covers her mouth, and mutters, "There are women and children in this program. The lives you're risking."

I smile a little. "Shameful, isn't it."

"You psychopath," she says. "How can you do this?"

"I'm not. I'll bet you a dollar you meet my demands."

The room falls silent. Even the ventilation stops blowing air. We can hear one another swallow, can notice the rustling of fabric whenever someone moves.

Oversized Guy finally summons the courage to ask the question that suggests they might consider my request: "What is it you want?"

I stare at him, clearly the only person I need to convince. "One: I want to be put into the program. I want—"

"Why?"

His question catches me off guard. I see no value in being dishonest with them, so I summarize: "Because I want out. I want the chance to start over. I love my family, but being a member is going to be the death of me. I'm sick of the day in and day out of it. My entire life has been spent with my father trying to 'find my place' in the organization. I want to build something that's more than just a means to advance criminal activity. I want a shot at normalcy."

"You will not live a normal life in the program."

"Normal enough." I look around the room, would never want to be in this place under any other circumstances. "And as part of being put in Witness Protection, I want it stated—publicly—that I'm turning on my family."

Oversized Guy squints, tries to figure my spin. "Why would you want that?"

I wave my hand and run my fingers through my hair. "I just do." The truth ends here. I cannot explain this component of my plan, that despite how it will confuse my family, I need some way for Melody to find out what I've done, to read it in a paper or see it on television, that I claimed to have killed her—that she is forever free.

"What else?"

"Two: Protect Gardner's wife and kids. He told me he started working with another family in New York, which means he'll be dead in a matter of weeks. No one else could ever tolerate Randall the way I did."

"And let me guess: Your third request is to put Gravina in the program?"

"Nope. Should he survive beyond this afternoon, you've got my endorsement to have a field day with that bastard." Everything that went wrong in Tenafly I can map back to him, how he was tracking Melody and using a federal witness—Sean's precious rule-breaking—to bring us down, and nearly to her death. "My third request will be the bitterest pill: You lay off my family. You stand down." And Pete gets his chain of candy stores.

Everyone sighs and groans and shifts in their seats.

"We're done," Ciacco says, stands again.

I turn to Oversized Guy and say, "Since he's not really a player, I'm gonna ask that the Pig be excused. He's going to get a lot of innocent people killed."

The big man takes a thick breath that sounds like a snore, says, "Everyone knows we couldn't possibly relocate thousands of people at one time. Feasibility aside, the cost and exposure would bring this program to its knees. You're willing to jeopardize a system that's been working successfully for over six decades to protect your family? What about the next person who needs it? What happens when we need to put your father in it?"

"You shouldn't have hired addicted people to handle sensitive data."

Sean speaks up: "You shouldn't have exploited him. How about we just take you out to a field and put a bullet in you."

Even the two silent superiors at the table tell Sean to calm down and watch his tone.

"No," I say, "see, that's how *we* handle business. You guys aren't capable. Besides, I'm sure everyone in here knows that if I die, that list will surface instantly. I'd say you might've never tried so hard to protect someone as you will with me."

Ciacco put his hands on the back of his chair and pushes down. "You honestly expect us to let the Bovaro crew do whatever they want?"

"You're doing it right now, waiting to find evidence. Consider this a lifetime of never finding it."

Sean takes a few steps forward, stretches, walks to the door. "There's no list."

Just before he leaves the room, I say, "Sean, would you agree Gardner was, in a sense, an employee of both the Department of Justice and the Bovaro family?"

He doesn't respond immediately. "I suppose."

"Which organization do you think is more effective in dealing with problem employees? You still don't see it, but Gardner had enough sense to know he was safer turning on Justice."

He stares at me like he's looking at a dead body in a coffin, licks his lips and purses them a little. "There is no list." He pulls the door behind him gently, does not return.

"I want the list of every person in the program," I demanded. "I want their names and addresses."

Gardner gagged. "I can't do—"

"Sure you can. You already have. I've got Melody's address—and you can supply the rest."

"Are you insane? That's thousands of—"

"I don't care. I want the list."

I remember the look of regret on his face, the last time I ever saw a shred of remorse come over him, the look that suggested his entire life just got flushed down the toilet.

Then, weakly: "I can't."

"You will."

Gardner shrunk into himself, curled up like a snail into its shell. He sat down and put his knees together, quickly calculated the consequence of such an act.

"That's the line."

"The line?"

"That I will never cross." He sat back, went completely pale, looked as pained as if he'd been beaten with a club. "Do what you have to do, knock me around, but you will never get that out of me. Never."

His reluctance did infuriate me, had me stepping toward him with a tightening fist. But as he sat in his chair, not even throwing up a hand to block me, doing nothing more than turning his face and wincing, I loosened my hand and stepped back. I stared at him for a few seconds, then walked to the door. I paused with my body halfway out, turned back and looked him in the eye.

"But, theoretically... you *could* get it. Right?"

I can lie, can break the rules and break the law, just as Sean suggested. I suppose that's the difference between me and Justice: The Bovaros have always had a sensational passing game. Watch now as my Hail Mary drops gently into the center of the end zone.

Like it matters. We're already ahead by twenty-eight points.

SIX

I haven't been driven by someone in close to a year. Like the family member who takes all the pictures, I am rarely *in* them. So as Sean shepherds me from under the courthouse in a bulletproof Explorer, its interior lined with dials and gadgets and weapons, all designed for apprehending or killing people just like me, this transport feels more peculiar than comforting, sends a shiver through me to know the rifle locked down between us might've been used to send a round through the back of my head. How strange it seems, now that I'm safely wrapped in their protective arms, that I finally understand just how cavalier I acted in those overlapping moments when I spirited Melody away, what they could've done given the opportunity, how I was likely spared by the casting of Sean's ulterior motive.

As we turn onto the alley, I see the parking lot where I waited for Melody to surface—Dr. Bajkowski's parking space. And once we're on Hanover, I glance at the front of this government facility, recall the scene just two hours earlier when the feds drove me around the block, circled back to the front entrance of the courthouse, then escorted me out of a Suburban, my hands cuffed behind me, and walked me right back in the building in front of a crowd of tipped-off journalists. This act, of course, was performed at my request. We walked at a sluggish pace, allowed them to take pictures and footage as they yelled questions that were never acknowledged. How conquered I appeared, my unshaven and bruised face cast down from the flashes.

I can visualize Peter standing in front of his television as my story unfolds on the news, arms crossed and eyes narrowed as he says to no one: "Seriously?"

And I know the tension that will come to Peter's fist as he checks the voice mail on his cell phone, hears the single word I uttered from the conference room phone the first moment I was left alone for thirty seconds, waiting for someone to fetch me a fresh drink while the others chatted in the hallway: "Gravina."

Sean doesn't say a word, has managed to peeve the two marshals in the vehicle—both relegated to the backseats—by forcing his way into the operation.

Baltimore claims everything that was left of who I am: my car and the few belongings in it, my stashes of money, my name. I have only my overnight bag full of toiletries and dirty clothes, and a case full of CDs that I will play over and over until I have memorized every note, that I will use to remember every intricacy of Melody, every iteration of every word, the texture of her skin and the curves of her soft shape.

As we drive down I-95—I've had my fill of this interstate—the cab is silent. Around the time we break the perimeter of the Baltimore Beltway, Sean says quietly to me, keeping his eyes straight ahead, "You know they're never gonna honor your third request, keeping your family free of prosecution."

Of course I know. "We have an agreement," I say anyway.

Clearly my expectation on request number three was loose. Back at the courthouse, we spent hours hammering out the pre-procedures of getting me transitioned into the program and how they would approach protecting Gardner's wife and kids; we spent maybe five minutes discussing the protection of my family. Went something like this:

ME: "My family gets a free ride."
OVERSIZED: "We all know that's not going to happen."
ME, ECHOING ELLEN: "But the women and children."
OVERSIZED: "It's logistically impossible. Let's say we catch your father or one of your brothers engaged in some illegal activity in the course of pursuing some *other* organization. What, we arrest everyone in the room except those in the Bovaro crew?"
ME: (silence)
OVERSIZED: "Best we can offer, and this is a one-time deal you need to commit to right now or it comes off the table, is we'll *keep it in mind*."
ME, AFTER WATCHING FOR A SIGN FROM OVERSIZED GUY THAT HE'S UNWORTHY OF MY INDEFINITE TRUST, A SIGN THAT NEVER OVERRIDES HIS ICY GLARE, HIS OVERT HATRED OF THE MAN WITH WHOM HE IS DEALING: "Keep the list in mind, too, yeah?"

Neither side carved a line in the sand, never agreed to anything other than looking the other way. The most I could hope for is that they'll think twice before pinching anyone, that they'll be dead certain they have airtight evidence before making a move. My prayer is that any of the men in my family—even just one of them—figures out why he should break free of his criminal existence and discovers the path toward doing so, finds the corridor that never appeared for me.

The sun falls to the edge of the horizon as we leave the interstate and ride the roads not far from where Melody had her apartment in Columbia. The roads are too familiar, remind me of when I was so close to having her within reach; my mind replays the tape of my attempt at abduction. We depart from the main drag, take a quiet parkway that leads us to Howard County's countryside and has us driving by Baltimore's wealthiest suburbs, past sprawling horse farms and manses tucked thousands of feet behind gates. As the land eventually converts back to agriculture and our vehicle is shielded by walls of unharvested corn, I begin to wonder if Sean's comment—*How about we just take you out to a field and put a bullet in you*—is about to become the first sentence of the last paragraph of my Witness Protection story. I can't imagine what might exist out here in the middle of nowhere.

The few roads that intersect our abandoned path twist and bend at right angles as though following the original property lines of the farms, delineations set a hundred or more years ago. Right before the road looks like it will narrow into a lane wide enough for only one vehicle, Sean pulls off and parks in a gravel parking lot facing what was once a Baptist church, a dilapidated, red-painted wooden structure missing all its windows. The dust from our sudden appearance curls up into the air and drifts through the gaping holes of the church. Something about this place seems familiar but I can't immediately place it.

In the distance down the one-lane road comes another SUV, a huge cloud of gravel smoke following it like the vehicle is trying to outrun a twister. As it stops right before the church, the cloud catches up, washes over the SUV, and dissolves as it drifts our way. The vehicle remains stationary for a half minute while Sean communicates with the other driver via dashboard radio. Once the SUV, a glossy Excursion, finally rolls forward and pulls next to us, the picture, the familiarity of this place, takes shape: the black SUV against an empty cornfield with the corner of the red-painted church. I'm staring at the exact spot where Melody was photographed in the arms of Sean, the very first picture in the stack viewed in my father's kitchen, the image that turned my stomach, that turned my world upside down and shook loose all the dirt and dust.

She was here. So they really did try to convince her. And she really did tell them *no*, truly came back to me. And now I'm going wherever they took her, having swapped places with Melody in under forty-eight hours.

Then, a blur of commotion: Sean gets out of the driver's seat, is replaced by one of the marshals from the backseat. The second marshal gets out of our SUV and stands beside it on my side. Sean jogs to the Excursion on the passenger side, which reverses and pulls up next to us on my side. And as the back door of the Excursion opens, the marshal standing outside yanks my door and I'm pulled from one SUV and thrown into the other. As I try to get myself together, the vehicle I arrived in has disappeared behind a new cloud of dust.

Before I'm correctly positioned in my seat, the Excursion is shimmying down the road; I can't tell our route because I can't see a thing. The only means of glimpsing the outside is through the windshield—and within seconds it's blocked from my view by a glass divider. The windows on the side and rear of the vehicle are not darkened, they're *black*. No light makes its way in at all. I'm not dead but this sure feels like a coffin.

I hear a switch click and a small beam of light appears overhead. As I snap my buckle, I look up to find Sean sitting next to me, his hand resting on a rifle.

I curl my lip like I just pulled a hunk of rotting meat from the fridge. "You're still here?"

He stares at me, flicks open one of the brackets that was locking the rifle in place. I wait for some kind of response but he just gives me a look implying hope—that he might find a reason to turn that weapon on me.

The SUV picks up speed as we rumble over the country road. Despite being buckled in, I am being tossed around, jerked forward and backward; because I can't see outside I'm unable to anticipate curves and hills and braking. A few minutes into our rural ride we take a sharp turn—I go flying into the door—and the road softens to where it feels like we're floating on air, only the hum of the tires indicates we haven't actually left the ground.

We drive for another ten minutes before we finally slow, take a few rounded turns before coming to a stop. I hear the marshal doing the driving exchange very muffled words with someone outside the Excursion. Then we're in motion again—and suddenly drop like we're riding down a steep hill, drive in a circular pattern until we've descended to the bottom of some structure; the squealing tires suggest a parking garage.

We finally stop and the engine goes off. I hear the doors start popping open; one of the marshals opens mine. And as I step out, two men in suits and loosened ties offer their hands. One of them says, "Welcome to the WITSEC Safesite and Orientation Center."

They turn to walk toward an entryway and I notice Sean looking around like it's the first time he's ever seen the place. Just before I take steps to follow the two men, I turn to Sean and say with forced glee, "Well, I guess this is goodbye."

Sean walks back to the Excursion. "Hardly," he says.

SEVEN

This facility, buried underground and likely roofed by a blanket of corn or soybeans, is actually a factory, an assembly line plant not unlike Ford's. Though this place is rich with luxury, right down to plush carpets (soothing tones to calm the witness), smoked glass (to instill the notion of safety and privacy), and crown molding (reflects the traditions of home), the object—*me*—moves from one station to the next, being altered and enhanced until a finished, polished product is ready to be released.

When I walked through the door, the first thing they asked was whether they could get me anything. My answer: a place where I could crash for a few hours; I wanted clarity for all that was about to come. Instead of a couch next to the coffeepot in the break area, I was escorted to a private room—*my* room—complete with a private bath and king-size bed and television (with no cable or satellite access, used solely for watching DVDs); the only thing missing was the view: not a single window.

Now that I've slept—crashed through the night, woke just before dawn—and showered, I emerge from my room. I'm immediately spotted by a lady behind a large circular desk. She gently rises and comes to my side, asks me how I'm *handling the adjustment* and if I rested well; I suppose most people brought here are frightened into insomnia. As she speaks of the weather, tells me of pending rain that I will neither see nor hear, I follow her down the corridor where she deposits me in a small meeting room. I sit alone, start noticing the general theme of their interior design. My room, the halls, this meeting room, all alike: beige paint, large plush chairs, prints on the walls that always speak of hope and peace—impressionist views of vineyards and flower-filled hillsides, mallard ducks flying over fields and forests free of hunters and retrievers; seagulls nipping through oceanfront sand devoid of a single human body.

After a moment I'm greeted by a pair of coordinators, two women in their late fifties who speak with such calmness and smile so genuinely that it would be impossible, were I actually a witness on the run, not to absorb some sense of optimism from them. I've never met two people more suited for their jobs, for the roles they need to play in such a critical and stress-saturated environment.

I spend an hour with them, mostly chitchatting while I sip a cup of coffee and work down a bran muffin, though their true purpose is to give me a brief overview of my next week—*week*—at the facility, what to expect, who to contact for questions or health issues, what I need to do if I want to *reserve the gym*, and so forth. They ask my clothing size and assure me some apparel will be available for me by the end of the day. They inform me that this place is capable of housing many witnesses and their families at one time, and while our use of various parts of the building will overlap, I will never see them and they will never see me.

Then they explain each station of the assembly line.

I sit and listen as they unfold Justice's grand plan for making me someone I was never meant to be, describe the specifics of how I'll truly become another person right down to the legal documents that prove it, how Jonathan Bovaro is gone and can never return.

Day one: Psychology

My first full day at Safesite has me meeting with the psych team (one psychiatrist and one psychologist), who spend the first portion of our time administering surveys to determine my personality type—could have told them: mafioso with willing spirit and violent tendencies—to better plan my future in a world that will not recognize me. For the five hours that follow, they explain the impact of being in Witness Protection, likely the real reason this team was assembled, utilized not to only quell fears and concerns, but to help head off potential misgivings once the witness is already in the program.

The process of self-analysis exhausts me. Once they're done, have smiled and shaken my hand and patted me on the shoulder, they set me free. As I lumber away from the center of the facility, thoughts of all the repercussions of my actions arrive and stick in my mind. Right now Gravina is bleeding, begging for some form of mercy, confessing his wasteful mistake, confirming that my intentions are real and true.

And after eating a meal in my room, alone, I lie back on my bed and stare at the ceiling and wonder where Melody is, what she is doing, pray she made her way.

Days two and three: Relocation Coordination

Imagine visiting a travel agency and being given the option to journey anywhere you'd like for free, with one condition: It must be bland. You might think a few hours would do the trick here, except this station I'm told is the most critical component from Justice's end—the core cost center of the program—for some witnesses have made the mistake of relocating to parts of the country that mismatched their true needs. Beyond obvious preferences, like climate, they cover things that might not occur when looking at a map of the country, like crippling allergies specific to a region, or arthritic concerns (the Southwest is highly recommended). After completing yet another survey, they determine I'd pretty much enjoy any part of the country, as long as I'm placed near areas that offer fresh produce, cheeses, and meats year round—which means the entire West Coast or the Deep South. They inform me that any of these choices are fine because they are outside of the *swell*—the circle whose center point marks the position on the map where the people who want to harm me most reside, whose radius extends three hundred air miles.

They show me videos of these different sections of the country, forty-minute DVDs that put each area on display, provide all the statistics for populations and school systems and major employers, show summer and winter scenes, offer profiles of quiet towns and villages. As I watch them, I can't help but be amused; they've covered these places in chocolate and whipped cream. I've visited many small corners of this nation in my pursuits of Melody, and by watching these videos you'd think the most attractive places in the country are the ones I never visited. I'm sure they have appealing videos of Michigan and Kentucky, too, absent the depiction of Willie and his *cafoni* trying to assault a young lady in a public park.

Much of the following day covers my preference for a career. Eventually, Kirsten, the young woman who's been assisting, asks me what I like to do, what my skills and interests and propensities are.

We stare each other down. What exactly would I say? I know how to launder money. I know how to manhandle information out of people. I've become fairly adept at tracking people down, breaking into buildings.

Eventually, with a shrug: "I like to cook."

Kirsten raises her eyebrows and nods a little like I just made her workload a lot lighter, as if to say, *Well, that'll be easy.*

Then back to my room, alone, with a meal, staring at the ceiling, wondering what Melody is doing, if she could ever know the best part of being in Safesite is that it distracts me from thinking about her every minute of every waking hour. And some of the nonwaking, too.

Days four and five: Legal

The legal team generates what they call a Memorandum of Understanding, the specifics of what was agreed upon with Justice—both ways—so that everyone knows what they're getting and giving, but mostly so the witness can be certain of the details of his future, right down to the last penny of the monthly subsistence checks. My MOU confuses the legal team, has various members running in and out of the room to contact Justice to get broader details of what I'm giving back. They do not broaden much, pretty much stop at *information against current dealings and relationships within the existing Bovaro organization.*

On my end, I will receive: no advance bonus money; a full-time job that will be no less than a 65-percent match to one of my preferences as generated out of the meetings with the relocation coordinator; a guaranteed annual salary that will be augmented by subsistence checks of one thousand one hundred dollars per month for the first year and seven hundred fifty the following two years; a rent subsidy of five hundred dollars per month for two years. A lot for someone offering nothing, nothing for someone offering a lot.

By the end of day five I'm desperate to get my blood moving and ask one of the fiftysomething gals if I could reserve the gym. She tells me it'll be free after dinner; I take it for an hour.

I'm escorted to the far end of the facility into a gymnasium half the size of a high school basketball court without the bleachers. I'm left alone, my shoes squeaking as I walk across the polished wood floor. I grab a basketball off a rack near the door to a small weight room and start dribbling, each bounce echoing through the room, the ceiling so high it makes me realize just how far underground we are. I take a few shots, begin moving faster, and progress to jump shots, try jamming it in a few times to no avail. As I hold the ball under my arm and catch my breath I look around the empty gym, wish I could borrow someone from the staff for a quick game of one-on-one.

I stare at the basket, put the ball on the ground and sit on it. And the realization arrives: I didn't just swap places with Melody; I am becoming Melody. This is how it will be, countless months of enduring loneliness and isolation. I've been in Witness Protection for four days and I already feel it.

Melody felt it for twenty years.

I pray right now she is in someone's embrace, despite how badly I wish it were mine.

Day six: Authentication

I don't fully understand who comprises the authentication team, seems like some hybrid group of psychologists and technologists, but their critical function is to generate and explain the details of *who you are becoming*, from your name to a pseudo-history to the creation of documents—driver's licenses, social security cards, college transcripts. Then they take me into a room and apply makeup to cover what remain of the cuts and bruises so recently delivered by Sean's hand. I have my picture snapped seven times, each with a clothing change and modification to my hair, some with glasses on and some off, two taken at the end of the day with a full five o'clock shadow. The result: a collection of images that appear to have been assembled over the course of many years.

After the last flash lingers in my vision, I change my clothes and wash the makeup from my face and return to the gym again, intensify my workout, get my blood moving as best I can. I walk into the tiny exercise room and assess the equipment—older models that still look brand-new—and wall coverings, framed movie posters of films that could only bring light and carefree thoughts: *You've Got Mail*, *Doc Hollywood*, half of Jim Carrey's earliest work. No signed prints of *Casino* or *The Godfather* here. I lift weights, beat the side of a dust-laden heavyweight bag, run on the treadmill, and listen to Melody sing to me via a small portable CD player on the floor in the corner: Aimee Mann.

As I get down on a mat and begin doing sit-ups, I recall the night Melody and I shared a bed, how our bodies were wrapped together between the sheets, how we conquered and surrendered to temptation at the same time. I replay the kiss—do so with regularity—that almost crumbled our commitment, would have dismantled her escape. I remember how I felt her giving in, the way she moaned as our lips moved together like it was the first time she had felt the rush of a drug. I remember how she was the stronger of the two of us, how she honored my request, how she held a finger to my mouth, how I felt her breath on my face. I reach for the words she spoke to me.

But then, even with all of the blood moving through my body and my brain, my memory stumbles, falls to the ground, and fractures: I can't remember what she said. *Don't let me go, Jonathan.* No. *Save me, Jonathan.* No. *Rescue me, Jonathan.* Nothing. I can't remember. The words are so distant, almost gone. A sudden panic comes upon me at the notion that someday I will forget her, that the memories of her will be altered, incorrect. That I might one day look back and think, *She was just a girl I was trying to protect, I guess I didn't really know her the way I thought I did*, instead of the truth: that no greater thing will ever come and go from my life, that the moments between us were the exact minutes and hours and days that define me, that my life is worth living if for no other reason than to recall what we shared.

I get to my feet, grab a towel, and run it over my face and hair and neck as I quickly make my way back down the hall to one of the coordinators. As I ask for a pad and a pen, she studies my look of alarm. I wave her off. "Don't worry, nothing to do with the program."

I enter my room and kneel before my bed and start writing everything I can remember from that night in Baltimore, narrate everything that occurred. Never mentioning her by name, I document every detail from the moment we returned to our rooms: her falling back on the bed and the smooth form of her body, her reluctance to cover herself and my desperate desire to cave in to her suggestive pose, helping tend to her wounds in the bath and how I caught indistinct glimpses of her naked body after the bubbles had popped, how we agreed to sleep in the same bed. Three pages later I'm still writing, approaching the sentence that is slipping my mind. I record the kiss to paper, take nearly an entire page to describe it, the way it made me feel, the sensation of the first kiss with the only woman I truly loved, even before I realized it. I write down how she pulled back, put a finger to my lips, looked me in the eye, breathed against my face, and said to me...said... whispered...

Keep me alive, Jonathan.

I write the first three of those four words on the pad and collapse on the floor in relief.

Day seven and part of eight: Procedural Consultations

The procedural team explains who to contact and what to do in case you're ever spotted, and to offer general behaviors and lifestyle choices to avoid the public eye.

The combination of having to watch too many videos about counteraction and veiled survival and the fact that I've not seen sunlight in a week is starting to take a toll. I've been living underground in a facility that could be confused for a hotel, but all of the high ceilings and wide walkways can't prevent it from feeling like what it is: a big tunnel.

I spend each remaining evening alone, exercising, then journaling. Now on my second notepad, I've documented each event from the few days that Melody and I spent together, written down every conversation, every experience, every observation we shared. The way her body looked when it moved, how she would purse her lips to suppress a smile, how the hue of her irises would change when her eyes filled with tears. And in the pursuit of writing down all of these memories, I can't believe how much I actually noticed.

I've been here for well over a week, completed the mandatory steps and ingested the indoctrination to the point where the knowledge of how to handle myself will be second nature—though it hardly matters. Who exactly would be coming after me?

In the dead period where they're finalizing the details of a job, a car, a residence and furnishings, I am restless. Now that the amazement of what's achieved here has faded, I realize that this place, this entire operation and division of the Department of Justice, was born out of protecting people from the likes of my father, of Peter and Tommy Fingers, of me. When I was a kid and I'd help unload the back of an eighteen-wheeler my brothers had broken into, it was presented as a crime where no one got hurt. But people were getting hurt every day—financially and physically—and once I was old enough to understand what my family really did, a different kind of indoctrination had occurred, one built on acceptance and apathy, along with a sharper focus on retaliating against those who *wronged us* or *had it coming*. But here, in this sanctuary built to safeguard the innocent and brave defectors, you see what is required for true protection. The government had to do *this* because of *us*.

Upon arrival I was told Safesite could house several families at one time, and throughout my entire stay I have yet to see one person who was not an employee of the Department of Justice.

Until.

Until this very moment: As I leave my room just past seven o'clock on my thirteenth day, I catch sight of a little boy who could not be more than seven years old, standing far down the walkway with his hand touching the corner that faces an intersection of hallways. He gazes up and down the corridor with a nervous look on his face, then turns and stares at me for a few seconds, as if he might ask me where a certain person or room was, faces me squarely from fifty feet away like we're preparing for a duel. He takes a half step in my direction before being snatched up by a woman and pulled away. I see nothing more than a forearm and a bangle-covered wrist before he disappears.

I shift a few paces to the left and lean against the wall, sense my face becoming cold and wet at the notion of another young child getting dropped into a program that will never set him free, the next Melody to suffer through a life of fear and loss and misery. I slide down the wall until I'm sitting on the floor, my face in my hands. I try to imagine who the woman and child are, wonder how many more family members are waiting in another room, why they are here, what crime family or drug dealer or gang they're running from. I rationalize how I've manipulated the system to truly free one of its witnesses, and I hope and pray that that frightened little kid down the hall will one day be free, too, that the sacrifices he and his family are making now will bring them peace.

Part of me wishes I could bring my father and Peter to this place and have them look around, show them what has been created to protect people from their type of brutality, how the few tax dollars they ever end up paying are contributing to their own eventual demise. Yet I'm the one who bought them more time on the clock. And to what end? Were they to walk these halls with me and see these panicked families, would they turn themselves around? When they catch a glimpse of the little boy scared and shaking and looking for help, would they stop and question, "Why do we do these things?" Would they look at how the government has invented this ingenious operation to give men, women, and children far braver than anyone in our crew a way to survive? My existence, my three decades of living among these men, offers the one true answer: *never.*

I slowly get to my feet, feel the same exhaustion as if I'd finished one of my evening workouts. I wander toward the place where the boy stood, know my decision to free myself of my family was the right thing to do—to give up everything, including who I am. But let my honesty be known: the *if you love something set it free* concept is nothing more than a platitude.

Now, Melody? She may be free, but I'll never let her go.

I pass the place where the boy stopped and stared at me, gone now like the ghost he's become, another apparition to exist among the living and real. I take small steps toward the desk and wipe my face of cold sweat, face the lady behind it.

She looks up and smiles, but I can't return the sentiment. I stare at her, can barely utter the words: "How much longer?"

On my fifteenth morning, I turn on the water in the shower, strip down and shave as I prepare to officially depart from Safesite. I've packed all the things I'll be taking with me, which took less than five minutes. The overnight bag I brought and the clothes that were in it are gone—"You'd be surprised how often a witness is recognized by the shirt he's wearing or the suitcase in his hand or the backpack over his shoulder"—been replaced by government-supplied versions. The odd fit and inferior quality, I am told, are intentional; if a witness wore expensive and/or fashionable clothes in his former life, he gets junk now—and vice versa. On my unmade bed rests a small gray overnight bag with their temporary clothing selections and toiletries by companies I don't recognize. Beyond that, only two other things remain: a small stack of notepads that chronicle and detail my every memory of Melody, and the case of compact discs that act as the soundtrack for those memories. I take all these things and place them on a small table in the corner, in case the cleaners service the room while I'm showering: the bag, the discs, three note-filled pads stacked in chronological order.

I take a long time washing myself, and as I turn off the shower and grab a towel off the rack, I realize I left my comb on the dresser adjacent to my bed. I open the bathroom door and swear I hear the latch to the door of my room click shut, though it happens so quietly I doubt myself. I step into the bedroom and feel a sweep of swirling air, as though the door had closed as I imagined. My naked skin comes alive with goose bumps at the change in temperature from the steam-filled bathroom to the chilled bedroom and I realize I'm jumping like a witness who really has something to fear.

No matter: I leave the door to the bathroom wide open as I towel off and finish getting ready, take a few final minutes to examine myself in the mirror, notice the last traces of bruising from Sean's released anger, see the long gray blemish at my hairline where he slammed my head into the doorframe of the Explorer—indeed, a *souvenir*—the permanent mark that will be the newest addition to my collection of scars, and I wonder if any other woman will assess my face and body the way Melody did.

I slip on my new pair of glasses, same prescription as determined by a contracted optometrist, but different frames—big round frames that could only have been intended for use as sunglasses. I look like a movie star trying to draw attention instead of evade it. But the actual lenses are perfect, clear and scratch-free, so large I can see clearly from the widest angle. These glasses, like the new me, are unscarred, undamaged.

I stare at myself.

I stare at Jonathan Bovaro while I still can.

This is the moment I turn and walk away from him forever, have a permanent out-of-body experience. I will from this day forward begin to read and hear about myself and refer to it in the third person. I will look at pictures of myself and perhaps say, "That guy's a dead man," or "I hope someone takes that scumbag out." Down the hall are marshals waiting to escort me away, to push the boundaries and walls of Safesite to a distance far away. When I walk from my room, everything about my former self will disappear, will be a collection of memories that will define some other person, like a distant relative or soon-forgotten loved one.

Here is where I should feel the panic. Here is where I should say goodbye.

Right before I turn off the bathroom light, I instead say this: *Good riddance.*

I walk to the table and collect my things, still lined up in perfect order, all neatly assembled.

I open the overnight bag and toss in my comb and toothbrush, gently place the CD case into the open slot on the side, and as I pick up my perfectly stacked set of journals and prepare to protect them, sandwich them between two pairs of unfaded and unworn jeans, I stop in mid-motion, do a double take: The journals are out of order.

I make my final walk down the hall and approach the central desk to find out who would've been in my room, but I stop short, notice someone fast approaching from the corner of my eye. I turn and look—Sean slides up to me with a warped grin and a hand on his holster.

I drop my bag on the ground and say, "Okay, when does *this* part end?"

He keeps his smile and shakes his head, looks me up and down, studies my baggy banana-cream-pie-colored sweater, my jeans that are an inch too loose and a half inch too short, my loafers, my movie star glasses. "Smokin'."

"You're not a marshal. You're not even—I don't know, what are you, exactly? Why are you here? Please tell me you're not my contact in WITSEC."

He crosses his arms and says, "I'm not. I'll be the first to admit I would not have your best interests in mind."

"You think?" I say, rubbing my scarred forehead.

"Just here to see you off." He leans in and adds with a whisper, "Though you never know when our paths might cross again."

I wince. "I'd say you have an overactive imagination. I don't plan on ever seeing you again."

"You shouldn't be so quick to blow off the security and protection of the FBI."

"Yeah?" I tilt my head a little. "How's it working out for Eddie Gravina?"

His eyes circle around and back to me, exaggerating his indifference like I just guessed the PIN to his ATM card. "You don't know the first thing about—"

"You're the one who doesn't understand, Sean. I mean, really, after all these years of supposedly mastering an understanding of organized crime? Gravina's either resting at the bottom of some body of water and getting nipped at by various forms of sea life, or"—I gesture my hand about the facility—"he's right here, might have even been escorted to this place by you, yeah?"

He turns as if he's going to walk away, like a little kid whose mother told him the best remedy for a bully is to ignore him. "You're just a street punk, another thug costing a working system a fortune. I'm glad I'm not marshalling you this time, glad I don't have to pretend to care about the guy I'm protecting with my life."

And as he walks off, attempts to flee before I can get the last word, I say loud enough that the lady behind the desk looks up, "Did you care about Melody?"

Sean stops, turns, and stares.

"Did you care about her," I say, "when she kissed you outside your motel room in Cape Charles, when she stood on her toes to reach you?"

He glances at the lady behind the desk—she quickly looks back down—then aims my way, does not walk back or tell me to lower my voice, slips his hands in his pockets and studies me.

"Did she ever know you weren't really a marshal? That you never possessed the capabilities those guys have? That instead of protecting her life, you were risking it?"

Sean looks at me for a long moment, no longer seems to have the bottled angst and fury. It takes him some time, but when he finally answers he speaks softly, out of everyone else's earshot, intends the sentence to be shared only between us: "Strange questions from the man who took her life."

For my benefit—or for those who might be eavesdropping—it sounded like that sentence was altered and forced, for his intonation and glare suggested this unabridged version: "Strange questions from the man who supposedly took her life."

A marshal leads me to an empty conference room where I sit and wait while an incoming witness is processed and taken out of sight. I wonder for a minute if it's Gravina—except the odds are maybe one in four that he would've made it here. My money is on him being protected by the program offered by the East River.

I wait in the same conference room as when I first arrived, study the same hopeful art on the wall. I rest back in the chair and close my eyes. For forty minutes.

When I'm finally claimed, two marshals lead me out of the core of the building, past all the desks, past the ladies who processed and helped me. I pass Kirsten as she exits the ladies' room. She gives me nothing more than a nod and practiced grin. I get no gauntlet of hope and well-wishing; this is not an exit from a recovery program. I am not leaving a store with a big purchase, not a welcome customer. They need to get me out so they can get the next one in.

So many ghosts haunt this land.

As I leave the facility and return to the underground parking garage, a third marshal is added to the mix; I recognize none of them. These marshals are bigger, more intense than they ever seemed at a distance, even the one behind me in line in the convenience store on the Delmarva Peninsula. So easily I confirm that Sean was never one of them, does not have *it* in him. They are not comic book heroes, yet possess the same infrangible composition, armed and angry and hoping to find trouble the way Peter always did; they're just not looking to cause it.

One opens the back door to an older Ford Expedition, points to the seat. I toss my bag on the floor and secure it between my feet as I sit. The marshal flips on the interior light and closes the door. I wait, can see nothing through the panes that once held glass. After three or four minutes the other doors open in concert and the release of pressure from the cab makes my ears pop.

The other marshals take the remaining seats, and the driver turns back and says as he points to himself, then around the car: "Marshals Wilhelm, Broadview, and Caposala. Any questions before we rendezvous with your travel team?" Wilhelm asks, though he might as well have phrased it as, "You don't have any questions, right?" He's already facing forward, turning the ignition. As I consider asking how long before we meet up with the travel team, the divider between the front and back seats goes up and the interior light goes dim and just like that we're in motion.

So here I sit, protected by the very foes I once fought. How they must hate my guts, yet they promise to protect me like I'm their collective newborn.

The vehicle speeds over the cement floor, reversing the journey I made here over two weeks ago: up the ramps and out the garage, over smooth pavement, slowing past the gate, and back out to the countryside. The drive is longer this time, twists far more than I remember. The marshals don't speak to me, to one another. The only voice heard occurs when the driver responds to someone calling over secure radio transmission.

After twenty minutes, the SUV comes to a rest, jerks back and forth as the transmission is put in park, is so well insulated I can't hear one of the front doors open and close again, but I feel it. Caposala says, "In just a moment your door will open and I want you to immediately follow the marshal."

I stare at my door, aim my answer toward it: "Okay."

I slip my fingers around the strap of my bag, curl it in my fist. Within a few seconds my door flies open and a blast of hard rain—drops inaudible as they crashed against the insulated steel shell of the SUV—cascades against me and floods my side of the cab. I turn and wince, my glasses covered in droplets of moisture, and two hands heave me from one vehicle to another the same way my brothers and I would unload all those eighteen-wheelers in the middle of the night; that's what I truly am: cargo.

I adjust myself in the back of what should be my last government SUV and watch the Expedition vanish, study the farmhouse and silo we're sandwiched between. I search for something to dry my lenses—really, they're big enough that they might as well have installed wipers—but I'm so relieved to see the outdoors again that I don't pursue cleaning them.

The light coming through the windows of the SUV is dim, the glass still bulletproof, but they—the two new marshals now shepherding me—no longer care about me seeing my surroundings, allow me to observe where I'm going, where I'll be ending. We wind along a dirt and gravel lane with a grass strip down the center where tires never touch, a country path lined by Leyland cypress trees. We stop at the end next to a mailbox and a small sign that reads WINDSWEPT VALLEY FARM.

We pull onto an unmarked road wide enough for one and a half cars, then onto a lined street that bears no sign to identify it, and finally to a four-lane highway. I do not recognize where we are until we cross over the beltway for Washington, DC, and loop back around to the exit for New Hampshire Avenue. We drive south at the speed of traffic, blend into the mix, and within minutes we are south of the city, driving down I-95: my second home.

These silent marshals, cab drivers with guns and permission to kill, take me on my last journey. I drift off near Richmond, sleep on and off through the Carolinas, officially awaken while we're gassing up somewhere near the northern border of Georgia. When the marshal gets back in the SUV, I'm struck with an adjustment in temperature and humidity that I know will be part of my lifestyle change. When I used to travel to these corners of the country hunting Melody, I knew it would not be long before I would leave; now I am a stranger moving in from out of town, feel like an expatriate. Jonathan Bovaro is disintegrating, a memory that will only fade over the years.

EIGHT

My name is Michael Martin. My friends call me Mike. I grew up outside of New York, which is why you might, on rare occasion, hear me pronounce some words with a peculiar down-turn. I have no siblings, parents deceased at the hand of disparate cancers. My wife and I lived up in Poughkeepsie, where together we operated a small produce company until she died giving birth to our first child a few years ago. Having lost the love of my life and my child at the same time, I could no longer stand to return home to an empty bed and a nursery that would never house a child; I had to relocate and start over. I sold the house and most of my belongings and started driving south, ended up here in central Florida.

Such is the general overview of the story provided to me by WITSEC, the one I memorized before I left their underground facility, the one I practiced in those hours I remained awake on my journey to Florida. The external employment service utilized by the professionals at Safesite is twice removed from the actual person hiring the witness, who in 95 percent of the cases has no idea who they just put on their payroll. No one here will ever know me as anyone other than Michael Martin from Poughkeepsie.

And how could I not notice the clever digs in what ultimately became of my future? The first: To meet my request of always being near fresh produce and meats, the feds decided to relocate me to Florida, the least expensive option over California or Oregon. The second: I was given a job as a cook in a small Italian restaurant—in the Villages, the largest retirement community in the United States if not the world, which spans three counties and multiple zip codes, has over eighty thousand residents with an average age of sixty-five. I could've been relocated to some hamlet in Sonoma County where I'd work as a farmhand, bursting vines and crushing fallen pinot noir grapes with careless footsteps. Instead they delivered me to a noncoastal section of Florida to sweat over a hot stove day after day.

But within one week of moving here, I realize the joke is on them. They might have imagined my misery at preparing salt- and fat-free meals for people in nursing homes, my frustration in not seeing a woman within thirty-five years of my age, my melancholy at building a life where people come to die. But the truth is this is where people come to live. These folks, many as young as fifty, have more energy and verve than I ever saw in people like Paulie or Pop, seem to know more about wine and food than some of the guys from my old neighborhood. These people start their days with a softball game, return home for a swim in their lanai-covered pools, then freshen up before nine holes of golf. And the women here are significantly more interested in their health and well-being than the gals who drifted in and out of the Bovaro establishments.

But the most notable difference between Brooklyn and the Villages is the noise. At least half of the residents travel by golf cart—everywhere: the grocery, the doctor, friends' houses. They drive beside cars at nearly the same speed on protected and tunneled side roads, buzzing around like ants up and down the water-lined pavement.

I'd been given one week to assimilate to my surroundings

before reporting to work, spent five of those days settling into my one-bedroom apartment on the outskirts of the Villages—a palm-tree-shaded flat with white walls and low popcorn ceilings and shades that are always drawn, a double bed, a ten-year-old television, a small stereo, a dresser, and a dinette table sized for two next to a kitchen sized for a ten-year-old—and perusing the surrounding areas in my late-model Hyundai Accent (arguably dig number three) and blowing my first subsistence check on replacement clothes and glasses.

Every day is the same: awake at seven; whip up coffee, peppers, and eggs and toast; read as many papers as I can stand online (Justice, regarding my assistance: "We're still currently accumulating evidence." Regarding Melody: chirping crickets); go for a long run through the neighborhood, shower, watch the news on TV and see the feds fumble about the recent string of Mafia-related killings. This gets me through midday, right around the time I start to daydream about Melody, which eventually becomes fantasy. I have every page of my journals memorized like scripture, realizing now the things I should have done and said, the minor modifications to that script that might've made things perfect, might've made it impossible for us to separate. Now that she's been set free, I am unburdened, liberated to wonder what might've happened if we took the risk, if we'd run off together, if every night she slept in my arms. I have a lot more time on my hands—like, all of it—and the only thing on my mind is Melody. Do I think of Pop and Peter and my brothers? Am I concerned for my family? Of course I am, the way Angelenos fear Los Angeles may tip into the Pacific; it'll probably happen eventually, but not *today*. My concern and interest in Melody, though, is as much a part of me as my Italianness. For twenty years, I masked my distant love for her with the disguise of trying to right the wrongs. Now that she is free and safe, there is nothing left but the love, nothing but the desire.

I count the hours until I start the job acquired on my behalf, desperate for something to take my mind in another direction, any direction. On day eight, I meet my new boss, a guy named Chuck Mullen, a second-generation Irishman who runs an Italian restaurant at the center of one of the so-called villages, the sole proprietor of a thirty-two-table establishment named (heaven help me) Mulleno's. The eatery is nestled between a Ralph Lauren store and a boutique wine shop in a town center that could easily be confused for historic Charleston or Savannah, right down to the preserved live oaks covered in wisps of Spanish moss, each building a perfect replica of architecture and style but with all the conveniences of a modern complex. The restaurant looks better than it smells—the polar opposite of the place in midtown Baltimore where Melody and I shared our first meal—with high-backed booths and serene lighting and crimson walls. I walk in at the peak of lunch hour and less than a third of the tables are taken.

Chuck, a tall and slender guy in his late fifties with wild gray hair, meets me at the front and offers a firm handshake, looks over the top of his glasses at me.

"Michael?" he asks, the first to call me this name.

And away we go: "Please, call me Mike."

He introduces me to the hostess on duty and the kitchen staff, offers an overview of the menu and their approach to cuisine.

Which is: none.

Chuck bought the restaurant as an investment when he retired from NASA, then subsequently lost all of his management and kitchen staff, ended up having to run the place himself and learn about the restaurant industry in the process. And by the end of our first conversation, when he smiles and offers his hand again, seems thrilled at the idea of having someone in the kitchen who understands its components no matter what a hack I may turn out to be, I know I should probably contact Justice and let them know this place will never survive—I'll be needing another job within six months.

My first full day on the job, I enter the kitchen from the rear of the restaurant, am tasked with chopping tomatoes and onions. I grab the only eight-inch chef's knife from a canister across from the prep area, twist it in the light and look for a sign of hope—a marking that reads Henckels, Wüsthof, even Victorinox—but find nothing more than *made in China.* I place it atop a pink hothouse tomato and attempt to slice through it, but the knife is so worn I nearly crush the tomato; juice spurts out where the stem once resided. I look out the corner of my eye, see the guy who would be loosely defined as the sous-chef close his eyes as if to say, "That's only the beginning." I grip the knife firmly and attempt to whet it, have never found a hunk of steel so incapable of possessing sharpness. Trying again with a yellow onion, I see its skin bend up at the sides as I press down. It'd be easier to rip the thing apart with my hands.

As I walk toward the stove in search of a better knife, I see another cook begin making sauce—what might act as their base for anything red—and I watch in horror as a gallon-size can of orange liquid is poured into a large stockpot.

I scowl and look at the cook. "What is that, V8?"

He frowns back, says through a thick accent, "Might as well be."

After many hours of slicing (bending) and mincing (crushing) and preassembling salads (don't ask), I take my break, fold my apron, and head to the front door. Chuck spots me on my way out and says, "Smoke break?"

I pause and smile. "Nah, I don't smoke." I leave off the piece from my true past: *anymore.*

"Where you heading?"

"Just walking down to TooJay's to grab a quick bite."

He turns and looks at the kitchen, then back at me. "But... you can eat here for free."

I bite my cheek, say gently, "I know." I turn and slip out the door.

Work has really helped. Instead of thinking about Melody all of the time, I am cutting onions and peppers and tomatoes and cutlets and thinking about Melody all of the time. Some days I wonder where she is, others are consumed with wondering if she's settled her life, if she's found a lover, if she's finally happy.

As I live my existence here, away from my friends and family, away from everything I know, I rest—can fall into the deepest sleep—knowing she has finally been rescued. I hope and pray she is living the life meant for her.

A little over one month later, just after I finish cleaning up my station for the day, I walk past Chuck in his office, a fist to his mouth and staring off into the distance. He says, "'Night, Mike," without any attempt at making eye contact.

"See ya, boss."

I have one foot out the back door when he says, "What am I doing?" One more step and I would have made it out, could've reasonably pretended I never heard him. I sigh and turn around and walk back in, make my way to his office but do not respond. "What am I doing," he says, then adds, "wrong?"

I bite my lip and scratch my chin as I shrug. He finally twists and looks my way, stares at me for a minute before he fakes a smile and says, "Well... never mind. Good night."

As he spins around in his chair and looms over order sheets, I sigh and run my fingers through my hair, tip up my glasses so I can rub my eyes. I step out of his office and say, "Come here."

He turns and looks at me, eventually gets up. When we get to the kitchen, I turn on the lights, open the chiller, and pull out a five-pound package of links.

"What is this?" I ask.

He looks at it, then me, then directs his answer to the meat. "It's sausage."

I hold it closer to his face. "It's *turkey* sausage. With cherries and nuts."

He half shrugs, offers a response that sounds like a question: "It's gourmet."

"It's crap. This is Thanksgiving dinner in a synthetic casing. If sausage isn't full of pig, I don't understand what it is. The flavor everyone wants comes from the fat. Pig fat."

I toss the sausage back in the chiller, pull out a plastic container of Caesar dressing purchased premade from a distant distributor and hold it up. "No."

"Why?"

I point to the listing of ingredients. "This is mayonnaise flavored with chemicals. And really, Caesar without anchovies?"

"People hate anchovies. People always say no anchovies."

"People don't know what they're talking about."

"I hate anchovies."

"No you don't."

"I don't?"

"You like Worcestershire sauce?" Chuck blinks and nods. "Read what's in it. That flavor you like so much? Anchovies.

Trust me: Crush the anchovies and mix them into a fresh dressing and people will be talking about your salads all the way to Panama City. And please—you gotta explain to the guys who work in this kitchen the difference between Pecorino Romano and Parmigiano-Reggiano." Blank stare. "Which is..." Nothing. "*Pecora* is Italian for sheep, hence Pecorino Romano is made from sheep's milk; the Parmigian' from a cow. Not even close to the same, and absolutely not interchangeable."

I walk to the storage area, wave for him to follow. I flip on the light and hold up one of the twenty 128-ounce cans of that V8-like fluid. "This," I say. "I'm speechless."

"Sauce?"

"Because the people in Bayonne who canned it tell you it is? Do me a favor: The distributor who sold you this can also sell you the same gallon-size cans of crushed tomatoes. Get those instead and we can cook the tomatoes down into a nice marinara. Or better yet, buy me a twenty-dollar tomato press and I'll make fresh sauce for you every morning out of those hothouse jobs you're tossing in the trash every day. I'll even do it on my own time." I've got plenty of it to spare now—what do I care? "And please, no more bottled lemon juice. Isn't this the friggin' citrus capital of the world? I mean, you've got six-hundred-dollar pendant lights hanging over every table but you can't swing a three-dollar bag of lemons?"

Chuck rolls a shoulder like he's loosening a kink. "You know a lot about Italian food for a guy with an English heritage."

I flinch a little. Ah, right: *Martin.*

He sighs and rubs his temples. "How do I know what people like? No one ever says anything. I go to the tables and ask how they like their meals, but they just nod and smile, just pay their checks and leave."

"They're telling you every day, Chuck. Take an hour each night and stand at the door to the kitchen and watch what remains on the plates when the busboys bring 'em back in. Your customers are gonna eat what tastes good." He nods a little. "Tell you what, you let me make *my* Caesar, anchovies and all, and we'll serve it to one half of the room, while the other half gets the chemical mayonnaise, and let's watch what makes its way back into the kitchen." As we walk out and turn the lights back off, I add, "And if I win, you gotta agree to buy some new knives."

The playful competition between me and Chuck, between my homemade offerings and his cost-cutting factory-formulated food products, has served as a wonderful distraction from my obsession with Melody. Every night and every morning remain the same, but when I arrive at work, if for just an hour, I focus my attention on something else, indulge in the camaraderie of the kitchen and my subtle instruction (tear the basil, I tell my peers; don't cut it or half the flavor remains on the knife and cutting board), enjoy the task of cooking without having to worry about things like personalities and profit and paychecks. Over time, I plan out what I'll be trying next, what imitations can be replaced with the real thing.

I've had some great successes. My Caesar had an 88-percent success rate (that remaining 12 percent still baffles me) and a near 100-percent success rate with the sausage we began having shipped down from Satriani's, a place in Brooklyn that used to make biweekly deliveries to Sylvia, a tip I gave to Chuck after pretending to randomly find them on the Internet.

Now, at the end of my third month, Chuck sits me down, opens a pair of icy Heinekens, and hits me with, "How would you like to manage this place?"

I swallow a mouthful and look away, wipe the moisture from my lips.

He hits me again: "I'll give you a thirty percent increase."

I take another drink to avoid answering, but the gap in silence wears me down. "I'm just a cook."

He sits back and drops his hands to his lap, seems genuinely surprised at my apathy. "You've got to be kidding. You know everything about this industry. I don't know how a produce guy could have such a broad grasp on the ins and outs of this business, but you're a natural. I mean, I've never seen someone take the remainders of the day and turn them into salads and antipasto the way you do. What nonurban restaurant gets busy at nine at night?"

Chuck's referring to an idea that morphed into a decided success about a month ago. I suggested that instead of preserving or tossing the vegetables and meats and breads opened for the day, we use them up, make salads and antipastos and bruschettas—and serve them free to folks who just wanted to stop in and grab a beer or bottle of wine. The first night I took an eggplant left unused from eggplant parmigiano and diced it up and sautéed it in olive oil, then added all of the ill-fated chopped vegetables—onions, green peppers, olives, celery, tomatoes—and a cup of the gravy that had nearly thickened to paste, a little salt and pepper and there you go: caponata. Folks in the bar scooped it up and piled it onto hunks of bread and drank alcohol until closing. The next day: sliced tomatoes with garlic and fresh basil and oregano. Every day it was something else. Last week, there was no room in the bar after nine for five consecutive days. The only cost to the plan was my time, and by this point I was so miserable without Melody that I spent every waking hour at the restaurant, could only fall asleep at night by passing out, wanted so badly to numb myself that it was the only alternative to a full-blown depression and the self-destructive behavior that would soon follow.

I smile a little and drink again, already halfway through my beer. Then I shake my head slowly. "I'm just a cook."

He leans in a little, speaks softly. "It's okay, you know. You can move on. Start again. Let yourself be open to finding someone."

Though he's referring to my nonexistent, now dead wife, Chuck has no idea how true his words are, how badly they bother me. I stare at him for a long time before I finally respond. "There will never be anyone like her." I take a drink to avoid getting choked up. "You have no idea how much I miss her." I look down and wipe my eyes, then my face. "I'm just a cook."

Chuck wrinkles his chin, droops his shoulders. "You can have the thirty percent anyway," he says, then turns and looks out the front window. "Just . . . please don't leave."

I place my beer between us on the table, cover my mouth with my hand. I suppose his request is the one thing I can't promise. Though I have no real reason to think I'd ever be yanked away, the chance exists, the possibility that Chuck will one day open the restaurant without me and I will never show, will never call in, will never return. Another solid relationship and assumption of trust to one day be thrown aside, never explained. Another story that ends with the line: *and we never heard from him again.*

So the rut begins, working all morning and day and most of the night, seven days a week, because I can't stand the idea of being alone with my idle mind. Chuck institutes a daily regimen of begging me to take a long break, fearing I'll burn out. What he will never know is that being at home with the images that run through my head before I drift into sleep, the first that enter when I open my eyes the next morning, will destroy me far sooner than the long hours and being on my feet thirteen hours a day. Avoiding those thoughts is like avoiding a hit man; no matter how many times I duck around a corner, he'll find me eventually.

And today I ran out of hiding places. I run through my morning routine today, a day the same as all the others. I shower and brush my teeth and drag a razor across my face, make one full swipe through a lather of shaving cream, leave my cheek looking like a yard of snow with a shoveled sidewalk down the side. And that's it; I can't lift the razor again, can't move. I open my palm and let the razor fall into the sink. I stare at my reflection in the mirror until I no longer recognize myself, the view of my face distorted from tear-filled eyes.

I fall back to my towel rack and slide to the floor, rest my back against the wall and drop my head to my hands and pray in a manner that would too easily be confused with begging.

Through my sob-laden requests, I ask God to free me of Melody, to finally let her go, to feel the freedom that she now feels, to help me stop wanting her and loving her, to stop wondering how and where she is, to complete the process of becoming the new man that Justice created.

I sound so desperate, I'd convince any onlooker of my genuineness, though I'm so unsure of what I really want, of what I really need; I pray for ten straight minutes for freedom, then end with this: "Unless, God, I might possibly one day find her again."

I am doomed.

"Please, God. Help me find her again."

His answer isn't *No.*

As I make my true request, I sense a darkness falling upon me, a creation made of my own hand, composed solely of possessiveness and passion.

His answer isn't *Not yet.*

All those moments, beginning when I was just a child, I prayed that I could keep Melody safe—and that one day I could set her free. God answered those prayers, gave me precisely what I so badly wanted. Here I am asking for more: I want Melody to be free *to be with me.* This request is no longer about Melody; it's to fulfill the desires of my own selfish soul.

His answer seems unequivocal: *Never.*

MALE E BENE A FINE VIENE

(EVIL AND GOOD COME TO AN END)

Two years and nine months later

ONE

Maggie Mullen swirls a glass of wine she started aerating an hour earlier, stares at me and laughs and says, "You're so funny." I can't remember the words I just spoke, distracted with tidying up the kitchen of her father's restaurant. "You can really make me laugh when you want to." *When you want to*—the point of her statement. Over the last couple years, women have drifted in and out of my life, relationships where the strongest bond occurred the first days of our meeting and slowly dissolved over the course of weeks or months, where we shared a mutual warmth that I eventually chilled over like a berg of ice; Chuck's daughter has yet to *drift out*, seems committed to trying to make something of our intense friendship. A decade ago she might have been my ideal companion—a soft-spoken, sweet-natured gal who inherited the bulk of her family's Irish genes, down to the red hair and fair skin and a face that readily blushes and carries a perpetual smile. But I know now how this will go. Her words will reshape as they did for the three women before her, will shift from *you're so funny* to *you're so distracted*. Maggie and I are partners, in a sense. We open the place, close it down at night, are together through the full bell curve of activity that any successful restaurant experiences over a day's time. She and I are not just friends; we possess a rhythm, offset each other's abilities and deficiencies. We keep the tables full and the customers happy and the restaurant well reviewed while her father completes his long recuperation from back surgery. And every night after we step out the back door of the restaurant, I walk her to her car, where she leans forward and gives me a peck on the cheek and pauses, wonders if tonight is the night I will turn my face and capture her affection in the form of a kiss on the lips, take the first step toward a physical encounter that could lead to love.

As I wind down the last few chores before we leave, Maggie picks up the bottle of Syrah and wiggles it a little as she catches my eye. I wave her off while wiping the counter. She stares at the wine like it has failed her, frowns as though I didn't notice she was wearing a pretty new dress or had gotten a new haircut. She swirls the wine in her glass less vigorously, then gently empties the contents of her glass in the sink.

Chuck and Maggie, this ready-made family for me to join, meet every requirement I could've wanted, a tidy package comprised of warmth and security and attraction. Yet the table of contents suggests more than the chapters provide.

After Maggie steps outside, I set the alarm and lock the door. I walk her to her car, perform what has become the final task of my day. She stares at me a second longer than usual, feels like minutes. She stands on her toes and I can smell the wine on her lips as they meet my skin. And now I see: The offer of wine was not to loosen me; she required the loosening. This moment was planned if not practiced. She lets her peck linger a few seconds and exhales against my cheek, to which I cannot respond, feels as though I am about to cheat on my spouse. She drops her body back to the ground and gently turns my chin so I face her.

"It's okay to let her go," she whispers, referring to April Martin, the wife who lived and died without a single breath, created to fill a gap in my fabricated life.

But there was no April; she could've never been on my mind. That last image of Melody had recurred through my head instead, my final glimpse of her as she disappeared into the center of the Greyhound station. I tell Maggie, "I'll never be able to let her go. She was the best part of who I was, of who I am. How do you let go of what makes you stronger?" She could never understand how the person I have become these last few years is a replica of my former self, made with better parts and stronger materials; Maggie would not recognize the cursing, smoking drunk with bloodied knuckles and a bruised body and an anger toward mankind, the man with a disbelief that anything pure and innocent and good could exist, could survive in this world. She slips her hands behind her back and cocks her head as I try to explain in the simplest terms: "Whatever it is you like about me, whatever you're attracted to, it's because of her."

My name disappeared from the news almost two years ago. Justice bored the media into not caring anymore. In fact, not much information surfaced at all about any of the families in and around New York, those few stories usually buried beneath the mire of reporting about terrorism and financial disasters and foreign affairs. And just like me, those few guys who got pinched seemed to show in one or two articles, then quietly vanished. Either the *Times* and the *Post* found no more information to report or stories about the Italian Mafia were not helping sell newspapers.

And since I've been living in my little apartment in the Villages, I have never again seen the name Bovaro in print unless used loosely in reference to me. Peter's chain of candy stores most likely remain in operation—and thriving. I hope he's saving his money; someday all that sugar is going to riddle him with decay. I know, even in my seclusion, that my father is still the balance and power in the operation; when Pop passes and Pete inevitably takes the reins, I give my family one year before my brother bullies his way into territory that my father had respectfully left to other crews.

But with all their flaws, with our entire combined corrupted DNA, I miss my family more than I'd imagined when I bolted from New York so abruptly. My first Christmas alone was the most difficult. I recalled the tables so brimming with food you could barely find a spot for your wineglass, remembered the camaraderie as we seemed to eat and drink for days on end, shared unusually carefree moments with the outer edge of the family—the wives and children and outcast crew members. That week between Christmas and New Year's Day felt as close to normal as our strange unit ever could. We would toast one another around the table at the start of our Christmas feast, would give thanks and honor those the way most do at Thanksgiving. I wondered what was said when the chain stopped at my empty chair, at my obvious absence. I wondered if a toast was made, if they hoped I was surviving.

Each year, I raise a glass, pray they're surviving, too, then try to sleep straight through to December 26.

I still miss the subtle things about my family that I'd overlooked, that I'd taken for granted as I lived as one among them. I miss the way Pop would put his hand on my neck and rub it when we walked together, then ruffle my hair like I was an eight-year-old instead of his grown son. I miss how Pete would opt to give me a quick hug when we saw each other instead of a handshake or a *what's up*, instead of nothing at all. I miss the beauty of hearing the Italian language every day, its sweeping flow and gentle lingering vowels, how its structure and sound could make the most violent and hateful things sound as sweet and soothing as a lullaby. I miss being around people who would lay down their lives for one another, no matter how terrible and flawed they are. I miss being recognized, being called by my name, being able to share a memory from prior to three years ago.

But for all my longings, for these things I miss and wish I could bring back into my existence, they had to be surrendered, were far easier to surrender than what still, to this very moment, occupies me, possesses me less like a demon than an angel: memories of Melody, from my first sight of her as a child to the way it felt when we let go of each other in the bus station. Every woman is compared to her, ranked in order of similarity, noted as poorly drawn knockoffs of a perfect work of art. I've memorized not only every conversation, every possible word, but the way the words were pronounced, the direction the corners of her mouth turned as she spoke them, how many times she batted her lashes when she told a story, when she looked directly in my eye, when she could not face me. She is my favorite movie; how I long for a sequel.

For everything I have given up, I still miss nothing more than I miss Melody.

TWO

Today ends the same as any other day, can be differentiated from two days ago or four days ago or six months ago only by the clothes beneath my apron, by the specials fading on the board in front of Mulleno's. The kitchen is still hot on this Thursday evening at just past ten-thirty, steam rising from sauces and boiling water. Though the kitchen is technically closed, I plan to spend the night experimenting with a potential new offering: braciole. I finish wrapping thin slices of boneless beef round in plastic wrap, then pick up a rubber mallet and gently pound the meat as close as possible to one-eighth-inch thickness. The art to braciole, a traditional Sicilian dish that my mother had perfected by the time she was a teenager, is getting it to roll up evenly and stay together while being browned. Braciole is like a big Hostess Ho Ho, except the chocolate is beef and the creamy filling is a mixture of Pecorino Romano and parsley and garlic. My goal is to test it out this evening, and if a success, order the ingredients next week and have it on the menu one week after that. Once I've finished the browning, the meat has to cook in a sauce of tomato and basil for some time—enough time for Maggie and me to go over the day's numbers.

I cover the beef rolls with a sheath of prosciutto and tie them with kitchen twine, heat a long turn of oil in a large pot, and just before the oil begins to smoke I start browning the first set. I wipe my hands on my apron and quickly walk out to the bar to find Maggie and see if she knows where the order sheet for our produce distributor disappeared to; I need to determine if we'll get enough artichokes for stuffing for one of tomorrow's specials.

The bar is quiet, holds three couples in golfing attire throwing back a few after what must have been a late afternoon tee time, which became a late dinner and nightcaps. Three men sit at the bar, evenly spaced like birds on a wire, heads cocked up and to the side, staring at the highlights of a golf match on a widescreen television in the corner.

"Hey, Mag," I say, touching her lightly on the back, "you seen Atlantic's order sheet?"

She reaches up to a top cabinet and struggles to slide a pair of whiskey bottles beyond the edge of the frame. "Next to the printer in the office," she says as she grunts. "I put it over where—"

"Johnny?" says a voice from the bar.

"—the other statements are from last month. We need to talk to Atlantic because there's a discrepancy on the last—"

"Little Johnny, that you?" I flinch, struggle so desperately not to turn. I clear my throat and lick my lips, pretend the name means nothing to me, that the term *Little Johnny* is as inconsequential to me as it is to Maggie.

"—invoice. We were being charged the same price per pound for asparagus as we were for Vidalias."

"Johnny, that's gotta be you," the man at the bar says.

Maggie doesn't even glance toward the bar. I stay locked in her direction, my face now coated in sweat though I'm so far from the heat of the kitchen. I swallow, twice. "By the fax, you said?"

She closes the cabinet, drops back to steady feet, stares at me, and smirks. "I said the printer."

"Sorry," I say, wiping my brow. "Um, which one?"

She folds her arms, narrows her eyes. "We have more than one printer?"

"Right, okay." I slowly turn in a semicircle in the opposite direction of the bar and begin walking out with all of the natural movement of a robot.

"Johnny Bovaro, I can't believe my eyes."

I freeze; the *Bovaro* is a showstopper. I turn my head toward the bar, but from the corner of my eye: Maggie's attention goes to the man, then to me.

I look at this gentleman in his early seventies, a small-framed fellow with an unusually large bald head adorned with oversized spectacles. He lifts his beer glass to his mouth, condensation rolls down the side and drips on his shirt as he polishes off the remainder. I've never seen this guy before, not even around my old neighborhood. Someone as oddly and memorably proportioned would have quickly acquired a nickname: Nicky Toothpick, Sal "Spider" Salzone. Ted the Head.

"I'm sorry," I say, fingering my own chest, "were you talking to me?"

He wipes his mouth with the back of his hand, opens his wallet, and drops a five on the bar. "Wait'll I tell the boys who I saw today."

My mind floods, and through the water I search for a single fish. Though I'd never be concerned with being taken out by someone in my own family, this guy might be from a different crew, might pass along the information to others and topple the apple cart I have so carefully arranged, throw my name into the news, news that Melody would eventually see, indicating that nothing is what she thought it was—again—that she is not forever safe, that she will again have to run. His utterance of my last name unlocked and opened a box filled with secrets, poisoned the air to the point I can no longer breathe here, and I will have to move on.

I will have to disappear.

I glance over at Maggie and realize this will be the last glimpse I'll have of her, of this place: the final memory.

I wish I could stop the sweat. I give it one last shot. "I'm afraid I'm not—"

"Do me a favor," the man says as he turns to leave, "give your *babbo* my best."

I watch him walk away, grab a stack of cocktail napkins and run them over my forehead and neck. When I twist and look at Maggie, her gaze is one of bewilderment and disappointment, her face pale, her mouth ajar and asking no questions. She knows that I have, best case, lied to her about who I am; worst case, lied to her about who I am and potentially put her in danger, put her father in danger.

I back out of the bar as I eloquently offer, "Um."

I walk into the kitchen and pace around it, confused and disoriented. I try to recall the procedures, the secure and unstored number to dial should I ever get spotted, the name of my handler. I haven't contacted anyone in the longest time.

I stare at the pan and turn the braciole as though I can somehow work my way through this. The meat sizzles and the oil spits and burns my wrist as I try to make some sense of what is happening. The adrenaline rushing through my veins now feels as if it's of some other variety from what propelled my hunting down of Melody all those years; this is an imposter.

I know I've got to go.

I've got to run.

I undo my apron and toss it on the prep area as I bolt for the back door of the restaurant.

I try to recall the number for paging my handler: 904-568—*No.*

I cannot comprehend the wake I'm leaving behind, cannot yet fathom the people here I will miss as well: Chuck and Maggie and the kitchen staff and the regulars who always wanted to visit with me when I had the time. I've betrayed them all. Could I have remained Michael Martin, I would have been just a man starting over. Now that I'm Jonathan Bovaro again, I'm nothing more than a liar, a phony.

904-856—*No.*

When I left New York, it was by my own hand; I knew what was being surrendered. This time it's unexpected, feels as unsure and disturbing as being woken up in the middle of the night and told the house is on fire. How could Melody have done this so many times? How did she survive?

As I open the back door and step out to the loading area, I glimpse the future: Chuck returning early from his recovery, Maggie telling him the story of how I was a man they never really knew, how a stranger called me a different name and I ran from them without saying goodbye, how I vanished. *And we never heard from him again.*

904-658—*No.*

Through the dark and humid night air, I plunge my hands into the pockets of my pants, dig for my keys and my cell phone at the same time. And just as I reach my car, I hear a familiar voice—but instead of nails on a chalkboard, it's like nails digging into my skin.

The voice says this: "Who you calling, Johnny?"

I stop, shoot a look back at the rear door of the restaurant, then back at the man. "Agent Douglas," I say, trying to understand exactly how his timing could be so right. Or so wrong. I wouldn't say the last three years have been good to him, but they've changed him. His hair is very short now, and he somehow managed to move ten or so pounds from his gut to his chest. I might have doubted his identity at first, but his voice is permanently recorded in my memory.

He opens the back door of an SUV. "In."

I jog up, get in and slide across the seat, steal a glimpse of the back entrance of the restaurant again. Sean closes the door and gets in the driver's side. The only signs that this is some official event are the black color of the vehicle and the weaponry and gauges in the interior. Other than that, little else gels. There are no marshals, no one else with us at all. Sean is unshaven, wearing a white T-shirt and jeans like he just finished weeding his garden. He drives away slowly, waves other cars in front of him as we limp out to the quiet town center.

I look over my shoulder, out the rear window of the car. Though it's hard to see through the heavily tinted windows, I see Maggie finally emerge from the back door of Mulleno's and stare at my abandoned Hyundai, then around the area for me.

Just before we turn and drift away, she drops her head and goes back inside.

Right about now the braciole is setting off the smoke alarm.

THREE

Sean doesn't bother to raise the divider as he drives us out to Route 301. I've run the scenario through my mind enough times to come to only one possible conclusion:

"So," I say, "someone recognized me in the Villages, you guys were somehow tipped off, and then you rushed down here to snag me before anybody—"

"I don't think rush is the right word, Bovaro." Sean looks off to his left. "You mind if I pick up a burger real quick?"

I must be on a different plan than the one used for Melody. I lean forward. "I'm thinking... you might want to get me a little farther away first?"

He pulls into the drive-thru for a McDonald's that's minutes from closing, puts his window down and orders, turns back to me. "You want anything?"

I sit back, wave my hand.

After he pays and pulls out, I say, "You have no business pretending to be a marshal, not even at Hallowee—"

"No one wants you, Johnny." He brings a handful of fries to his mouth. One misses, falls to his lap. "Let me rephrase," I think he says, "no one wants you *dead*."

"Who was that guy at Mulleno's?"

"I don't know. I didn't ask."

I squint, look at him in the rearview mirror. "Ask?"

"Just some guy." He opens a straw, submerges it in his soda. I can hear the ice rattle in pulses as he gulps it down.

I lean forward again. "What crew was he with?"

"No crew, possibly a bowling league." He laughs, then repeats, "Just some guy."

"I don't follow."

"Saw him come out of a pub down the block, looked like maybe he was one and a half sheets to the wind. I offered him twenty bucks to play a practical joke on you." Sean takes a bite of burger equal to one-fifth of the sandwich. Then, muffled: "Wouldn't even take the twenty. People are friendly down here."

"I don't—wait, why?"

"You know, get your name out there, expose who you really are. It was something fake that I knew you'd make real by panicking, by doing what you're doing right now: running."

I put my hand on the front seat to steady myself. "Confusing new protection technique Justice is using."

"Not Justice. *Me.*"

"Even worse. Why? Seriously, man, what the—"

"I did it so you could never go back. So that your life in the Villages was wiped out."

"What is this, some sort of punishment? You want me to understand what Melody went through, is that it?" I punch the back of his seat. "I had a life there!"

Sean lurches forward a little, ignores my anger, takes another mouthful of burger. After a few seconds, he says, "That was no life. An existence, maybe. Not much more."

"This doesn't make any—"

"We're moving on to bigger and better things, Johnny."

I sit back and begin my tirade. "I want to know right now what's going on. I still have my cell, you know. Maybe I should just—"

"You still keeping up the writing?"

I shake my head, slow my breathing while I decipher what he means. It hits me: my journals.

He was the one who read them, who left them out of order.

Sean holds the steering wheel steady with his knee, grabs more fries with his right hand and puts up the divider between us with his left hand. I reach forward to try to hold it down but it reaches the top before I can leverage my weight, closing the space between us.

"Why are you doing this?" I yell, then punch the divider with the side of my fist, crack the knuckles of my pinky and forefinger. I shake off the pain as he picks up speed.

We drive through the darkest hours of night, see no light other than passing streetlamps that drift by us like shooting stars. Through the smoky glass of my window I can barely make out the well-lit sign that reads WELCOME TO GEORGIA as we cruise by it at close to seventy miles per hour, realize we passed I-10, the connector to Jacksonville that would have returned us back to I-95, back to the Washington, DC, area. As bungling as Sean has appeared, I've been fooled every time, realize he always has some other plan in mind, acting the part of the marplot to fulfill an ulterior motive. And what else could I assume now: He's gone *rogue*. His rage-filled partial confession in the conference room in Baltimore echoes in my head. "You will *never* take them down unless you break the rules," he said. "You've got to do whatever it takes to make it stop," he said. The only thing I don't understand is the angle. I rest in knowing—trusting—that Sean's tale of the old man playing a practical joke on me means Melody is still free, still safe. I'm just not sure what all of this means for me. One-in-five chance he's driving me far away to make good on another of his comments from the conference room gathering: "How about we just take you out to a field and put a bullet in you." But three years is a long time to hold that kind of anger, not to mention that even Sean would see the Everglades as the obvious choice for dumping someone—which would've been in the opposite direction.

I spend an hour trying to determine how many pages Sean could've read while I was in the shower my final morning at Safesite, what he might have determined by reading nothing but my handwritten adoration for the woman described in the text, the woman who can so easily be identified even though she is never mentioned by name, how the details and words she spoke just before her escape had seemingly replaced the dark ending I claimed to have dealt her.

Worse yet, the journals are now gone forever. My past and all of its documentation will never again be within reach.

FOUR

I wake up when Sean takes an exit ramp too fast and I tip over and my head smacks the window of my door. The morning sun barely illuminates the dark glass that encircles me. I slowly sit up, attempt to get my bearings, can smell the sour remainders of his fast food, even with the divider still closed between us.

I try to catch a glimpse of my surroundings through the window. Over my shoulder I see a sign for the highway we just exited: I-85. Even with all my cross-country travels, I can't remember where this interstate is on the map, have no idea where we are or where we're going.

As I rub my eyes and try to make out anything that gives me an idea of my locale, I finally glimpse a sign for the road we're on: South Carolina Route 187. Another two-lane road lined with more farms. More middle of nowhere. With a half stretch and a yawn, my conclusion is drawn: Sean is taking me directly to my next home; he's relocating me, bypassing Safesite and all of its comprehensiveness. This is what rural America has come to mean to me, its only possible purpose.

As we merge onto a wider road, we wind around the edge of a small town marked as Pendleton, South Carolina, which looks like a first cousin to all the other country towns I've come to know over the course of my life, barely different from those in Kentucky and Virginia, right down to the clusters of small churches, the Dollar General, the Dairy Queen. I bend and twist my body as best I can, attempt to loosen the muscles and joints that have tightened from a long night's ride in a vehicle.

We continue for a few miles before I make my first request. I tap on the divider between us, yell, "Gotta hit the head." Not true, actually, but I want him to stop anyway, want to get out and move my legs and get a cup of coffee—and corner him, get answers no matter how I have to force them to the surface.

My body pulls forward as Sean drops his speed. We enter the next town at a slower pace, and the town mirrors us; the few people who are milling about walk with purpose but without haste. I tap on the glass again after Sean passes by two opportunities for public restrooms. In the distance I can see he has a few more chances before we ride right out of the other end of this village, but instead of stopping at the Citgo to our right or the 7-Eleven on the opposite side of the road, Sean pulls to the left and down another road. And just as I think he's about to hang a U-turn in the middle of the street, he turns ninety degrees and drives straight: right through the main entrance for Clemson University.

The campus appears quiet in these morning hours, the only movement coming from those few ambitious students who registered for the earliest sessions or the freshmen who had no choice but to take what slots remained. Giant Georgian buildings perched atop modest hills cast shadows upon students racing to meet the start of their eight o'clock classes.

Sean parks in the first lot with an open space, a lot for which we clearly do not have a parking permit. He gets out, opens my door, and finally speaks: "Let's do this." He reaches in the side compartment at the bottom of his door and rummages through a stack of hang tags until he finds one that has some seal at the center, the words *official government use* printed at an angle across the emblem. He slips it over the bar for the rearview mirror, then closes his door and mine at the same time.

"The Citgo would've been fine," I say as I arch my back. It cracks, loud.

Sean turns and walks away. I follow him, literally—he makes no attempt to walk with me; I remain three paces behind, struggle to keep up. We stroll along a curved path that takes us into the pedestrian-only portion of the campus, not a parking lot in sight. We look like a couple of unshaven, burnt-out collegians arriving a dozen or so years late from an all-nighter. Sean takes us around as though he's been here a hundred times before, as though this might be his alma mater.

"C'mon, we've passed two buildings already," I say. The sooner I can feign my use of the restroom, the sooner I can get answers.

We arrive at our apparent destination, Martin Hall, one of the more contemporary structures on the university grounds, looks like it was likely designed around the time I was born and does not match the Georgian style of the majority of the buildings, stands above an amphitheater and a large reflection pond with a dozen fountains spraying skyward. A young girl with an overstuffed backpack holds the door for us. Sean goes to the stairwell, takes us up two flights, down the hallway, past sequential classrooms—*past the restrooms*—and stops just before the far end.

"Wait here," he says.

My annoyance at his nondisclosure is cast aside from trying to decode his strange behavior. Sean slides against the wall and peeks through a window no more than one square foot in size, embedded inside a giant oak door. He becomes motionless, watches whatever is occurring within the room. He keeps his eyes to the glass, waves me over without turning my way. As I walk up behind him, he steps to the side and into the center of the hall without saying a word, without indicating what requires my attention.

I gaze through the window, the image crosscut by the grid of old shatterproof glass, blurred by a swirl of dust and fingerprints. I see: twenty or so wooden chairs with pull-up desks, a dozen of which are occupied by nineteen- and twenty-year-olds, their backs to our door. At the far end of the classroom are green chalkboards lightened by smears of erased chalk and an old wooden desk near the window with a lady sitting on the corner of it watching a young guy try to write some formula on the chalkboard. The kids are silent; I can hear the chalk tapping against the board as he attempts to complete the problem. The lady on the edge of the desk has her back to me, is wearing a short blue dress, a long braid of auburn hair hanging past her neckline. Propped on the edge, she swings her leg a little while the student hesitates, stares at the problem he's trying to solve. He stops and drops his hand to his side, and after a few seconds the lady says something and the class erupts into laughter; the boy laughs, too, and returns to his seat. The lady goes to the board and steps partly out of view. She finishes the problem—three lines and she's done—then tosses the chalk on the ledge of the board, claps her hands free of dust, and spins around to face the classroom.

I inhale so hard and fast I might have robbed Sean of anything to breathe.

It's Melody.

I pull back from the window as though someone punched me in the face, cling to the wall like I'm trying to avoid a surveillance camera. I peek from a farther distance. Three years have passed since I last saw her, yet she seems to have grown younger, looks like she's twenty-five instead of approaching thirty. I feel like Scrooge, except I'm seeing the past, present, and future all at once. I'm spying the version of Melody she was always meant to be, almost unrecognizable, the beaten woman who finally escaped her abusive environment and has completed a comprehensive restoration. Her face is full and tanned, every word that escapes from her lips makes its way past a peaceful smile. She crosses her feet as she stands in front of the students, tucks a few hairs that have broken free of the braid behind her ears—the move pulls a sigh from my lungs with such force that my shoulders slouch as the air escapes. She says something else and the class laughs again. As she smiles at the students, I drop down on my knees, make it look to Sean like my movement is intentional instead of the truth: I'm on the verge of collapsing.

Sean stands across the hall, back to the wall, one knee bent and foot propped up. I can barely move, barely look up at him; he frowns in my direction. This has hit me harder than I've ever been hit in my life. I stare up at Sean the way the guy in the alley in Baltimore looked up at me, with the knowledge that destruction is moments away.

I slowly pull myself to my feet. I glide along the wall until I can once again look in the classroom. I watch Melody speak, still cannot make out any words, cannot hear the true sound of her voice. She motions with her hands as she explains something, large round earrings swing next to her face with each movement. Half the class raise their hands at the same time and she points toward a girl, listens as she rubs her lips with the back of a finger, then nods her head and comments on the girl's answer.

Her skin is darker then I ever remember, from any year or age, still showing the remnants of a summer tan, and her hair holds the color of amber ale, so rich and red you couldn't help but stare to the point of discourtesy. She pulls the braid over her shoulder and plays with the end of it as she listens to a student speak.

I could spend the day here, might never look away. Melody's face brims with contentment, her smile so pure and perpetual; I could've never made her this happy.

But then a thought occurs to me and I correct myself: *What I did* made her this happy.

I say, "It worked. Everything she and I went through, all of the risks and things we surrendered, it all worked. I saved her."

Sean smirks. "Saved her? You *wrecked* her." He walks up behind me, looks at Melody over my shoulder. "Look at her left hand."

As she slides it up and down her braid, the unmistakable shimmer catches my eye: a diamond-studded wedding band.

Second only to the notion of never seeing her again, this is the darkest moment of my life. All those days of wishing she would find someone to love again were false; I'd be a fool to deny I wanted anything other than for her to find me, to love me. Though for all the darkness, I am awash in relief, in knowing the safest route was taken: Now I *know* she's happy and full of hope, embarking on the best moments of her life, with a man I hope and pray will protect her and please her and allow her to open up, to survive.

Sean should understand this, too; his comment makes no sense. "Wrecked?" I say.

Sean backs up, walks down the hall, and peeks through the classroom windows until he finds an empty room, then waves me down. I follow him inside and he closes the door behind me.

"Guess who she's married to?" Sean asks.

That I could possibly know the answer is troubling. She's supposed to be dead, meaning everyone I've ever known would think the same thing—except...

I can barely speak it: "You?"

He chuckles. I stare at him for a few seconds before I sit down in one of the classroom chairs. Sean leans back against the instructor's desk, narrows his eyes, and says, "I knew you didn't kill her. I knew you couldn't. Even before I read your sappy journals. Mr. Sensiteevo." I rest back and fold my arms, comprehend the magnitude of Sean knowing she's alive. "You're a lying sack, Bovaro. You lied about killing Melody and you lied about that list." He lowers his voice. "I would've rolled the dice and called your bluff."

"Yeah, keep that dream alive, Sean." I wave him off with the back of my hand. "How did I wreck her? She looks happy to me."

He sighs and rubs the stubble on his chin. "I found her eventually, some time after reading your journals."

I close my eyes and shake my head. It feels like I've spent years climbing to the top of Mount Everest only to have someone tell me I've topped the wrong mountain. I keep my eyes shut as I say, "So Justice knows where she is? That she's alive?"

"Not Justice. Just *me.* Locating her was more of a pastime than a mission." I look up just as he brings his hands to his hips. "I... reluctantly agree she's better off outside the program, and the program is better off with her not in it. As much as I hate to admit it, you did give her her freedom, no matter how risky and poorly thought out it was. But it really didn't take that long to find her. I didn't even have to use any resources at Justice. I left no trace that I ever looked for her, found her the old-fashioned way. She could've been located by any half-wit detective. I caught sight of her shortly after she purchased that wedding ring at a jeweler just outside of UCLA."

"*She* purchased it?"

Sean nods. "Jeweler said he thought it was quite unusual as well, but she'd told him such a story of sentiment about why she was buying it that it stuck with him; he'd already retold the story a half dozen times before I got to him."

"Which was what?"

Sean takes a long look at me. "She's not married to me," he says, then points his finger at me like a gun. "She's married to *you*."

I open my mouth, try three times to form a question; I'm not sure what to ask.

Sean shakes his head and sneers at me, struggles to utter the truth, hates having to speak it at all. "She told the jeweler that she 'can't be with the one she really loves, but wants to remember him forever, be faithful to him forever'...and partly to send the message to other men that she's not available."

Sean looks away and bites his cheek. I try to twist down a smile; he likely doesn't know that Melody told me how he once confessed to her that this is the exact reason he still wears *his* wedding band, and that she was impressed by this side of him—apparently impressed enough to emulate his actions.

"Now," I say, "where would she get an asinine concept like that?"

"Screw you, Bovaro. My wife and I were married for eight and a half years, she succumbed to cancer and suffered miserably for two of them, died in my arms. I've earned the right to live out this little peculiarity." He turns back my way. "But you two? C'mon, how many days—how many *hours*—did you spend together?"

"Twenty-three years," I quickly answer. "She's been the focus of my life for twenty-three years, Sean. She's my first thought every morning and my last thought before I fall asleep, the main character in a quarter of my dreams. Still, to this very day."

We stare at each other for a minute before he breaks the silence. "But for her, Johnny. Days, you know?"

My response to him, as valid as it may be, is generated solely out of hope, constructed by the strongest forces within my heart: "How long does it really take? How many days passed before you knew you were in love with your wife?"

"We dated for nine months before we got engaged."

"What, you got engaged the day you fell in love? That wasn't my question. How long before you were certain you loved her?"

He doesn't say a word, eventually purses his lips and shrugs as if to imply, *Whatever*—except his silence means he's not much different from me after all.

I look around the room and think of how Melody spends her days, how this is her domain. "How'd you track her here?"

Sean's face goes sour. "Geez, what do you think I do for a living?"

"I was never all that sure. You suck at it, whatever it is."

He wipes his face with both hands, gives me a condensed version: "She was a student at UCLA. Records office told me she tested into their adult education program, shaved off over two years of coursework, got her bachelor's degree in mathematics in less than two years, then her master's one year later. Then she came here, to Clemson, where she's a teaching assistant under some professor emeritus while studying for her PhD." He laughs through his nose. "Someday she'll be Professor Felicia Emerson."

I repeat her name to myself, the words forming on my lips but the sound never escaping. *Felicia Emerson.*

I stare at the clean chalkboard behind Sean, imagine Melody filling it with shapes and numbers and rules I could never understand. She has truly created a life for herself, on her way to becoming a doctor. The feds could've never provided the means for this. She is free. Finally. And my presence here can do nothing but take it away again.

"So why all this?" I ask. "Why now?"

"Because you need to fix the situation. After finding out about the whole wedding band thing in Los Angeles, I thought she'd eventually forget all about you. But I wasn't kidding when I said you wrecked her. She's wasting away, Little Johnny. Pining for her pathetic Prince Charming. Look at what you did: You ruined her life *twice*. Not many men can claim to have done that to a woman."

"How—"

"Ruined it the first time by stripping away all hope from her childhood, then you ruined it again by *giving* her hope—hope that she might one day find you." He shifts his weight and the desk cracks. "I won't deny you gave her freedom. But what good is it if she won't take it?"

That this could be true sends a warmth and a shiver through me at the same time, though I know I have no choice but to reject it. "Give her time," I say. "Someday she'll fall in love with—"

"Three years, Johnny. Three years. Take it from someone who knows: I understand what runs through her mind every morning when she gets out of bed and consciously slips that ring over her finger. You think you set her free? I know you're not very intelligent, but you should be smart enough to see she's shackled to you by that diamond band."

I lick my lips and try to say something, anything. I can feel the mounting desire of wanting to see her, to hold her, to accept Sean's words as truth even though I know it's the worst possible thing I could do for her, for me.

Then Sean says, "You gave her the freedom to be herself, but it turns out this is actually who she is. It kills me to say this—and please know I'm saying and doing all this for her *only*, that I still hate everything you are—but... the only way she can ever be truly free is to fulfill her wish to be with you."

We stare at each other but I'm looking right through him. What runs through my mind is the misery Melody faced these past few years, the risks she had to take and how she managed to manipulate a system that expects you to have a history, some proof of who you say you are. I comprehend how hard she worked, the long nights of studying, the determination and effort, the pleasure she received from her achievements and accomplishments, from earning those degrees. This is the first time in her thirty-year life she has something that is genuinely hers, something she built by her own means. And I know deep down I can never take the risk of pulling it away from her. Would I be nothing more than the feds?

Sean can read my indecision, says, "No one else knows she's

alive except me. And as for your disappearance?" He sniffs hard, cocks his head a little. "I'll take care of it."

"You've got to be kidding. You think I forgot that operation back in Maryland? The program is massive. And let's be honest: You're inept. You're not—"

"I'll take care of it." He steps forward, folds his arms. "You'll both be off the map for good. This secret will be only three people deep, not an organization deep. No more chains. No more weak links. No more Gardners. And I promise I'll keep my end of the bargain, I'll keep the secret." He takes one more step forward, waits until he's certain he has my full attention. "But you owe me."

I get up from my chair, tip it over in the process. "I knew it. You bastard. You're going to hold Melody's existence over my head now? Is that why you really tracked her down? To reverse everything I set up with Justice in Baltimore? The protection of my family?"

"I got news for you: Your family was never immune to prosecution."

"I see. So Justice has just sucked at acquiring evidence against our crew for the past three years."

He smirks as he walks to the door. "C'mon, let's go wait for your bride's class to finish."

"No."

Sean opens the door and gets one step into the hall before I put a hand on his shoulder, say quietly, "No."

He turns and looks at me, makes a face that asks the question *Why*.

"It doesn't matter that she's known around here as Felicia Emerson," I say. "Can't you see it? She is Melody Grace McCartney. This is it. She's finally home." Sean turns and faces me directly. "Will she love me when we have to disappear one day? When she has to give up everything she's worked for?"

Sean gives me a look I've yet to see on his face, one of coolness and realization, like something triggered a hidden multiple personality to take over. He squints a little, turns his head to the side but keeps his eyes on me, seems to suddenly accept—or at least understand—my genuine concern for Melody, that even though I'd given up everything for her already, that doing it again right now, while she's mere steps away, is the truest sign that I want her to be happy, that I could never hurt her.

He shakes his head slowly and says, "Man, are you sure?"

I take in a deep breath and it comes back out in a blast. "Yeah."

Sean slowly walks out into the empty hall and I follow. From the corner of my eye, I spy the door to Melody's classroom, know she's separated from me by a single wall, know I could have her in my arms within seconds, could fulfill any number of fantasies that I've perpetuated over the years. Sean notices my preoccupation; I sense him studying me.

"I'll get the car," he says, "and pull it into the parking lot in front of the building—I mean, you know, if you want to wait here, see her for a few more minutes."

And of course: Like any addict, like every loser and scumbag who ever came to my family saddled with a need for money to get a fix, I rationalize the *one last time* scenario. I don't answer, merely slow as I get closer to her classroom door. I peek from a distance and see Melody marking up the chalkboard, hunks of chalk dust drifting into the air and down to the floor.

"Meet you out front in five minutes," he says.

I don't say a word, move toward the window and watch Melody's body wriggle and sway as she fills the board, the fringe of her dress swishing back and forth, her earrings shimmying with every slight movement, her braid gently swinging behind her like a chestnut pendulum. She keeps writing while reaching down to scratch the back of her lower thigh, and when her dress rises I recognize the topography of her legs; an outpouring of memories comes to the forefront of my mind. I tip a little toward the wall. I want to touch her so badly, would give almost anything to have her in my grasp for just a few seconds, to be certain she is real, to have her arms around my body, to feel her warmth and her heart beating against my chest. Almost anything to feel her lips against mine, to experience just once more the way she could part my lips with hers and breathe life into me. Almost anything to whisper in her ear how I will love her forever.

Almost anything. But not her freedom.

As she continues toward the bottom of the board, she hesitates, stops in mid-scribble like something doesn't seem right in her solution—and at the same time, I'm struck the same way. I've overlooked something big. I drop my gaze to the floor as Sean's words echo in my head: "I'll get the car and pull it into the parking lot in front of the building."

The winding paths, the amphitheater, the reflecting pond: *There was no parking lot in front of this building.*

I turn and run so quickly I stumble to my knees, fall against the wall as I get myself to my feet. I race down the steps, crash through the door at the bottom of the building, and rush out into the morning sun. I run back out the paths that brought us to Martin Hall, go flying toward the road that led us onto the campus just in time to see Sean escape the university grounds, turn back onto Old Greenville Highway, and slowly disappear.

I stand on a patch of grass at the front of the university and watch him fade away, hands on my hips, my breath nowhere to be found.

I am abandoned. I am dirty and unshaven, still smelling of chopped vegetables and seared meats and Sean's fast food. I am tired and sore from a night's rest in the backseat of a car. I have no change of clothes. I have no means to shower. I do not have my wallet, do not have a single penny on me. I am a baby left in a basket on a stranger's front stoop.

I stand still, long after I've caught my breath and regained my composure. I watch kids come and go, watch the campus show more signs of life as it approaches nine o'clock.

I can't stand Sean. I hate that he did this to me, that he left me here with nowhere to turn, that my only hope of food and shelter will have to come from Melody, that he stripped everything away from me, from my possessions to my free will. He's a pompous bastard who used his knowledge and investigative skills to disassemble my life and put Melody's back in danger—all because he thought he knew better, that he knew what was best for everyone.

As I twist my body around and face Martin Hall in the distance, I realize I should be hating myself as well, how Sean and I are more alike than I'd ever care to admit, more like cousins than Ettore and I ever were. Did I not do the same thing to Melody? Did I not toss her in the direction I thought would most suit her, most protect her? I left—abandoned—Melody in the Greyhound station because I thought I knew what was best. Is Sean not doing what he thinks is best for me?

Not a chance. He's doing what he thinks is best for Melody.

What Sean just delivered to my existence might as well have been the most violent event of my life. It didn't knock. It didn't tap me on the shoulder, suggest I get ready. It created change by way of the most capable tools in the toolbox: confusion, humiliation, destruction. And now it's my turn to feel the world shift beneath my feet, to utter those simple words: *I never saw it coming.*

I walk slowly back toward Martin Hall.

FIVE

I hold the door for a line of students, a group more alert and talkative than the eight o'clock crowd, follow the last one in and make my way to the restroom. I wash my hands and arms and face with astringent antibacterial soap, run wet hands through my hair until I shape it back into something recognizable, gargle with tap water. There's nothing I can do about my thickening five o'clock shadow, my wrinkled clothes, a neck stiff from sleeping against a car window.

I quietly make my way back to the classroom where Melody had taught just moments earlier, except she and all of her students have disappeared, their replacements now getting situated in the desk chairs. Melody's equations have been erased, nothing left but a white smear of chalk dust, no proof she ever stood at the front of the room and instructed the class, that she ever took a portion of the brilliance inside her and transferred it to those young minds. No proof. Vanished.

I walk down the hall, check each successive classroom to see if Melody is teaching another course elsewhere: nothing. At the end of the corridor, I open the door to the stairwell. Echoes of voices and lazy footsteps bounce about the cement walls, float their way down to me. I begin quietly walking up to the next floor while two males discuss the solution to a math problem. I hear their words but can make no sense of them, like strangers speaking in a foreign tongue.

But then Melody's unmistakable voice reverberates throughout the concrete spiral: "Your methodology is sound, but you're missing the gist. The infinite sum of terms calculated from the values of the derivatives is at a single point. If that single point was centered at zero then, yes, you would have a Maclaurin series—except in your case the center is not zero. Which means?"

No response, only footsteps and the opening of a door.

Finally, one of the boys answers, "A Taylor series?"

Melody says, "Bingo," and the door slams shut, leaves me alone in the wake of its boom.

I run up the remaining steps and gently open the door to the top floor, know she must be on the other side. I take a deep breath and hold it, move so slowly I'd be able to avoid triggering a motion detector. From behind and to the side I see Melody leisurely stroll down the far end of the hallway, flanked on each side by the students, two textbooks pressed against her chest. Near the end of the corridor three more students wait on a bench between two large wooden office doors. They look at Melody as she heads toward them.

I can no longer hear her voice, but I can see her lips move as she turns and unlocks the door to the first office, the boys nodding every now and again as she speaks. She struggles with the door, leverages her weight against it with a shoulder, and as it opens in a burst she disappears out of view. One boy follows her in, the other sits down on the bench.

I step into the hallway, close the door behind me, hold it back so the sound of the latch is nothing more than the tick of a clock hand. Then I lumber down the hall, pretend like I'm supposed to be here, that I'm one of them, though nothing would indicate such a thing. I have no texts, no book bag, no clue where I am or what I'm doing, hope I somehow appear to be a graduate student. I'm at least ten years older than every kid on the bench, yet as I approach with obvious hesitation, the girl at the end picks up her book bag and puts it on the floor, slides over a few inches so I can sit.

She looks like she could be my brother Jimmy's daughter—long midnight hair in a ponytail, pudgy tanned skin, large nose and eyes—right down to the faded sweatshirt and black Chucks. As I sit next to her, she turns and addresses my apparent awkwardness.

She nods and says, "You here to see Ms. Emerson?"

I stare at her. *Felicia Emerson.* "Yes," I say, but the lack of moisture in my mouth makes it come out as a whisper. I clear my throat and say it again. "*Yes.*"

She nods some more, says, "She's awesome. I don't understand a thing Dr. Ames says when I attend the main lecture. But Ms. Emerson . . . I'd be failing this class—again—if it weren't for her."

I smile a little and look beyond her, at the closed door to the office.

The girl nods again, appears to be a tic that accompanies every word she says. "I really love her."

I lean forward, rest my elbows on my knees, and drop my chin between the knuckles of my fist. "Yeah," I say, "I love her, too." I look back at the girl. "She has a way of explaining things, of understanding things."

"Yeah, yeah," she says.

"Makes you want to just be around her all the time, learn everything about who she is, you know?"

She squints a little. "I . . . guess." And that's the last she says to me, never looks my way again.

After ten minutes, the office door opens and the boy finishes a sentence as he walks out, smiles a little and waves as he heads down the hall, is quickly replaced by the next student. I've apparently arrived in the middle of her office hours or tutoring slots, or both.

I sit idle, wait as the students come and go. I'm not on the unseen list that Melody uses for meeting with these kids, yet the students seem to understand their order, their appointment times and predetermined lengths. Melody never surfaces from the room, remains concealed behind the door like a doctor seeing her patients.

Ninety minutes later the bench has cleared. Jimmy's daughter is Melody's final appointment, eventually meanders out of the office and studies a paper marked up with red ink, does the nod thing as she scuffles toward the stairwell, her Chucks squeaking against the tile floor with every step.

I wait until she disappears.

The hallway is silent; I am its only visitor. I stand and take baby steps to the door of the office. I swallow twice but can't remove the lump, take two deep breaths but can't find any oxygen, wipe my hands against my jeans but cannot dry them of sweat.

I reach the doorway and look in from the side, see Melody standing in the far corner with her back to me. The room's dim light is supplied by a pair of matching desk lamps, one on each of two old oak desks facing opposing walls. Posters of ancient mathematicians are affixed crookedly on the center wall above a green seventies-style couch covered in books and overstuffed folders. Melody looks down, leafs through a stack of papers. I can hear the snap of each sheet as she iterates through the pile.

I step inside and face her back, am overcome with a sense of her presence. I can smell the mix of fragrances that compose her unique formula, immediately recall the way scents change once they've touched her skin, no matter the original essence—roses, powder, apples—they all become her distinctive version. Today, vanilla. And with this awareness, everything resolves at once: The lump gets swallowed down, the hands go dry, the air fills with all the oxygen I could ever consume.

I lick my lips and quietly speak to her: "Felicia."

She does not turn, but her leafing slows. She shifts her feet a little and I can see her torso inflate as she takes a deep, slow breath and holds it. The only sound between us is her page-flipping.

I say it again: "F-Felicia."

Keeping her back to me, this time she jumps a little, as though I'd caught her by surprise, as though it was my first word spoken. One of the papers from her stack drifts to the floor as she riffles through them at a slower pace. She does not turn, does not say a thing, does not try to pick up the fallen paper. I hear her release that deep breath as a second page falls to the floor; she doesn't bother to pick that one up either. The pages rest on the tile like the first fallen leaves of autumn; they're hard to ignore, signal the official start to the change of season.

I say so softly it might only be audible to me, a whisper so faint I might have confused it for a thought: "*Melody.*"

She stops ruffling through the pages and carefully places them on a small table in front of her, slowly turns her body around and faces me, puts her hands behind her as she rests back against the table, a single tear running down each cheek.

"Oh..." she whispers. She says something else but I can't make it out, only see her lips move in an attempt to form words, then slightly quiver just before she puts her hand to her mouth. She sighs and laughs at the same time while she studies me, a pair of fresh tears dropping from her eyes.

I take a small step forward and offer my hand and say, "My name is Michael Martin."

She doesn't budge, never shakes my hand. I can read her lips as she repeats my name to herself a few times, tries to affix it to the man before her. I drop my hand. She looks into my eyes like she's trying to put me in a trance, or has somehow fallen into mine, finally says, "Nice to meet you, Michael."

"I was wondering if—"

"Close the door," she says.

"I..."

She brushes her bangs with her left hand and as her fingers cross her forehead, the diamonds in her wedding band sparkle and form an arc like a comet, leave a series of dots in my vision like spots from the sun.

"Close the door, Michael."

Without turning away, I step back, reach behind me, and push the door shut.

"Lock the door, Michael."

It takes me a second, but I eventually pull my eyes from her, find the lock and turn it.

She walks to the couch, puts her arms behind the stack of books and slides them off. They go crashing to the floor, spill into an even spread like fallen dominoes. She sits down and stares at me.

I feel like a little boy, don't know what to say, can't find the right place for my hands.

Suddenly, she covers her face and bursts into tears.

I walk over and kneel in front of her, rest my arms on the couch along each of her thighs and lightly hold her lower body. "You're not in any harm," I say. "You need to believe me. You're safe."

She looks up and wipes her nose and eyes. "I don't care."

"Everything you've built, all that you've worked for is safe, okay?"

"I don't care."

"I will never let anything—"

"I. Don't. Care." She brushes her bangs to the side again. "I love what I do. I love this place. I love all I've learned and all the students. But you know what this is? All of this? This is what killing time looks like. I've been killing time waiting for you." Melody looks at me and touches my face like she's not convinced I'm who she thinks I am, then throws her arms around my neck and pulls me in, holds me and shakes. I slip my hands around her frame.

"But the risks," I say. "You know the risks."

She whispers in my ear, "Every relationship has risks, Jonathan. Not a single one is safe." She takes a deep breath and pulls back to look at me. "I practiced this moment a hundred times, the things I would say if I ever saw you again"—she laughs a little and more tears fall—"but I'm so unprepared, can't think straight."

"I—"

"I realized it too late," she says, touching my face again, "but once I got settled out west I finally understood how I'd blown it, nearly crushed me when I realized what I'd done." She swallows, runs her fingers through my hair and holds the back of my head. "You were my loophole."

I study her expression, her eyes wide and searching mine for an understanding. I try to remember what she once told me, the way she defines *loophole*.

She can read my confusion, clarifies without my asking. "Do you remember? I never allowed myself to love anyone because I'd have to lie about who I was, could never be myself, and always feared having to one day leave that person without notice when I was pulled away by the feds. And if I chose to be honest and bring that person with me, I would've opened them up to all the danger of being on the run and in the line of fire, being with me. That would be the case for any man I would ever meet in my life." She gulps hard, wipes her face, and says, "Except you."

I shake my head a little.

"You," she says, "knew who I was. You would always know the real me. And if anyone could handle the dangers of being on the run, it would be you. I blew it. Realized it all too late. The one man I ever truly loved also happened to be my loophole. By the time I understood, I'd already seen what you'd done on the news, what you'd surrendered to keep me alive and protected. I loved you all the more after that, was determined to be faithful. I waited and prayed you would come to me. I... waited." Melody's chin wrinkles and before she starts crying she pulls me in, says softly, "Never leave me again. Never, do you understand?"

I reach around her body and run my hands up her back and pull her against me, try to hold her firmly enough to stop her trembling. She does not yet know how I longed for her every day, how I waited and prayed as well, but that our circumstances, our outlook on what could've ever come of us differed in one major way: I lost faith. Melody, with no hope and no sign that we might ever find each other, believed in something beyond my ability and comprehension, kept her eyes open to the light while I collapsed into the cold darkness.

But now, as we share the same space, our bodies intertwined, I relinquish all power and control, allow them to be replaced with optimism and intimacy. I'm going to neither look back nor question what lies ahead. My hope exists in her grasp, in her command.

Melody and I are not heroes, not victors by any means. We are two terribly damaged individuals, cripples suffering from the same disease, cured only by being in one another's arms.

We hold each other so tightly that neither of us can draw a breath.

"Never," I promise.

And as with a flash from a camera, I am blurry-eyed and startled, realize Melody fulfilled my hope and prayer from so many years ago when I spirited her away from Cape Charles, that she would one day set herself free, that she would open her life to another person, that some man would get lost in her, look in her eyes, and hear not a single word she is saying, that he would pull her to his chest and lightly stroke the skin of her face and wonder, *What could I have done to deserve her*, that he would whisper in her ear, *I will never leave you. I will love you forever.*

That man is me. That moment is now.

"I promise," I say. "I love you, Melody. I've loved you all my life. I will never leave you. I will love you forever."

We loosen our grip on each other and her cheek scrapes against the stubble on my face as her lips slowly find mine.

There is a song I have never forgotten, a favorite. I heard it too few times many years ago, listened to it with a careful ear and memorized every nuance, every beat, every note. A haunting melody paired with carefully chosen words, a tune that defined a moment in my life and shaped the man I was, the man I became.

As time passed, I never experienced the joy of hearing it again, could find no station to play it, no person who could emulate the artist. How lucky I was that the song was etched in my memory, that enough bits and pieces remained so I'd never forget what it meant to me, so I'd never fail to recognize it should it return to the airwaves.

That music swirls around me now, and as it drifts through my brain it brings elation, a euphoria I thought I might never know again. This woman, the composer, so deft at her manipulation of every instrument and the intonation of every word, so easily hits the high notes and the lows, has me humming along. And as she finishes, completes the performance and waits for my response, I wipe the tears from my cheeks and close my eyes, have only one request on my lips. "If I begged, would you play it one more time?"

SIX

I am not the man I once was. I am not the *person* I once was. I look in the mirror and see a familiar toothbrush going into a familiar mouth, wash a face with scars from events I can still recall, but I might as well be staring at a departed spirit. All those years ago when the government recreated me, people would call me by a name I did not own. I would walk right by these folks as though they did not exist, as though I did not exist. But now, having lived in Clemson, South Carolina, for seven months, I *am* Michael Martin. Jonathan Bovaro is nothing more than a memory of an old friend, a loved one who died and was buried long ago. Michael Martin does not smoke, loves to cook, knows a lot about Italian culture for a guy with an English heritage, does not travel north of Richmond, south of Jacksonville. Michael Martin measures time in semesters, not months. Michael Martin is Felicia's husband, the one linked to her fabled wedding band, the guy no one had seen for three years at two different universities, the one always absent from Felicia's side at the department dinners and holiday parties and picnics, the guy no one thought existed. How wrong they were.

As I wipe my face dry and look at myself in the mirror, Felicia slowly walks up behind me, closes her eyes as she slips her arms around my body, slides her hands under my T-shirt and rubs my stomach, kisses my back. I reach behind me and put my hands to her lower back and pull her in a little, close my eyes as well, assure myself it is all real. *Forget the past*, I think. *Ignore the future*, I think.

Though Sean obviously knows where we are, he's remained absent from our lives in any real sense. Whatever it is he thought I might "owe" him, whatever future use he imagined I could possibly have, seems to have been shelved, at least for now. I confided and confessed everything to Felicia, told her how Sean and I battled it out in Baltimore, how he cared enough about her to bring me to her door, how he promised to leave us in seclusion, to never give our location to anyone else, to never admit we were even alive. That our secret was "three people deep." That I had no choice but to let him take care of making me officially disappear.

Even though Sean is a link to our current and former lives—the final one—we never considered running again. The words never passed our lips, the thoughts never materialized. Clemson is our home, the place where Felicia works on her doctoral dissertation and I work as a sous-chef at a local bistro via a social security number that belonged to a Michael Martin who died twenty-seven years ago. We are determined to be the people we say we are, to stay and live and grow here, to become a part of the community. Nothing has shaken us, nothing has scared or disturbed us, even when we strolled out from Memorial Stadium—*Death Valley*—embedded in a sea of orange after Clemson went into overtime against Georgia Tech, and walked right past Sean as he ate a hot dog at the end of our exitway, passing us a wink and a nod as he noshed. We slowed, but nothing more. Not a smile, not a lingering glance, not a word.

Forget the past, we think. *Ignore the future*, we think.

Perhaps the greatest vanishing act of all was the way the Bovaros disappeared from the newscape. I've been hard pressed to find any new information over the last half year. I've tried repeatedly, and as far as I can tell Justice has grown to ignore the entire organization, focused increasingly on the families we once battled; those crews now appear with regularity. I can only imagine how Randall told Justice time and again that he never gave me any list, that producing one would have been risky in and of itself, that he was above that kind of behavior. I do not doubt, despite the proof that Randall gave me information of one particular witness, he eventually swayed them all into thinking I was the liar I claimed not to be.

But over time, as key figures in the other crews drop and go missing, become popular news items for no more than a week or two, I do not for one second believe that Justice is truly incapable of gaining evidence against all things Bovaro, would be like living in Miami and assuming a hurricane will never hit. I hope that Pop and Peter and my brothers understand what I know from this far distance: Justice is saving the best for last.

One bitter cold day between the fall and spring semesters, South Carolina's Department of Motor Vehicles contacted Florida's to get a digital copy of my lost driver's license—in order to issue me a new one by way of the Palmetto State. With that new license, the plastic still warm as I plunged it into my pocket, Felicia and I traveled to Kentucky, where the only requirement for marriage is one proof of identification; you don't even need to be a resident of the state. Though so much of what we are was fabricated, right down to calling each other husband and wife to those around us, this was the one component we wanted to be original, to be real.

This winter she became—legally—Felicia Martin.

Felicia and I are slowly becoming who we claim to be. We speak of things that've occurred in our short history, recall events from our new life together. Lives built on truths. We have made a collective transformation that could only occur through the reflection of another human being, another person who can step up and say, "That's not how I remember it." We are real because we are loved—by each other; the false personas are given life through this love. We are perfectly cast for the roles we have to play, two people with experience in lying and manipulation, in convincing those around us we are something other than what everyone sees—something else, if not something greater.

We were magicians performing vanishing acts upon ourselves. Now we're here to stay.

We appear so happy, so enamored. There is something different about us, something unusual that can't be identified. Whatever rules are applied to relationships, however couples are assembled and fueled through life's inspirations and survive through its trials, we're doing it in ways that could hardly be understood. Those around us say, "All the couples we know have gone through this type of thing"—then the pause—"except maybe Felicia and Michael." Compare us to the multitude and know this: We are the exceptions.

You might wonder about your own neighbors, the ones with the incongruous backstory to their lives. You might wonder, "He doesn't seem like the accountant type," or "I would never guess she grew up in Georgia." You might wonder what has them moving into your neighborhood in the middle of the night, has them staying out of view. You might wonder.

At your next block party, church gathering, company social event: *Look closer.*

And so here we are, Felicia and I, walking and living around you South Carolinians, the nice married couple down the street. We accidentally bump your cart in the grocery store. You wait behind us in line at the coffee shop. You wave our car in front of you as we exit the ramp. We blend in, then wash out and fade away. We're the couple walking hand in hand down the shoreline until completely out of view. Could you ever be sure we're even here? Indeed, we are. We're right behind you. We're all breathing the same air. Ghosts among the real, my friend. Ghosts among the real.

ACKNOWLEDGMENTS

This book was written in the dark—or during it, at least. The entire manuscript was composed between 3 and 6 a.m. in the basement of my home, seven days a week, for a full year, the only way I could balance writing and working a full-time job with the federal government. And it would not have been possible without the support of my wife, Jana, whose endurance of my crankiness, exhaustion, and lack of availability was far greater than any burden I had to bear. She is a true partner in every sense of the word, and this book could never have been completed without her. From her daily encouragement to her editing skills, this story would not be what it is were she not in my life.

That said, I should also thank the Mayorga Coffee Company of Rockville, Maryland. I drank over sixty-six gallons of their Colombia Supremo while writing this book. It was 3 a.m., after all.

And thanks to God, for perseverance on the days I wasn't sure that I could do it anymore. Indeed, all things are possible.

Special thanks to my editor, Michele Bidelspach, for possessing the remarkable skill of being able to refine the big picture and the pixels simultaneously, and for knowing exactly what needs to be modified and why. She is a pleasure to work with, and this book is all the better because of her. Thanks also to my copy editor,

Roland Ottewell, for his astounding attention to detail, and to Claire Brown for designing a beautiful cover. And to everyone at Grand Central, especially Mari Okuda and Bob Castillo for putting it all together.

Much appreciation must be given to my agent, Pamela Harty, who has guided me through an industry I still struggle to understand, and for being a genuine advocate and perpetually available for guidance and direction. She has been with me since day one. Thanks also to Deidre Knight, Elaine Spencer, and all the wonderful folks at the Knight Agency. You guys are awesome.

And thanks always to Jacob and Megan for being the best, and for cracking me up when I needed it most. To my family and friends who have been so enthusiastic and supportive throughout this journey, and to all the booksellers and librarians who tirelessly help bring my books to a greater audience. And to every reader and for all the wonderful emails. You are what make this possible.

ABOUT THE AUTHOR

David Cristofano has worked for different branches of the federal government for over fifteen years, serving such agencies as the Department of Justice and the Department of Defense. His debut novel, *The Girl She Used to Be*, was nominated for an Edgar Award for Best First Novel by an American Author. He currently works in the Washington, DC, area, where he lives with his wife, son, and daughter.